MW01364236

The Fifth Dimension

The Fifth Dimension

A STORY OF COURAGE
THROUGH FAITH

Ramma Kher

Library of Congress Control Number:		2017908251
ISBN:	Hardcover	978-1-5434-2542-0
	Softcover	978-1-5434-2541-3
	eBook	978-1-5434-2630-4

Print information available on the last page.

Rev. date: 06/08/2017

To order additional copies of this book, contact:
Xlibris
1-888-795-4274
www.Xlibris.com
Orders@Xlibris.com
758130

To Papaji
whose infinite love and
boundless wisdom
lighted up the dark paths of my life.

Contents

Preface

Asato ma Sadgamaya
Tamaso ma Jyotirgamaya
Mrtyor ma Amrityogamaya
Brihadaranyak Upanishad

O God, From the Unreal, Lead me to the Real
From darkness, lead me to the light
From death, lead me to Immortality

Who dares to name Him
Who to say of Him, I believe?
Who is there ever with a heart to dare
to utter "I believe Him not"?

- Goethe's Faust

Index of Characters

Meera	Protagonist
Mohit	Meera's husband
Sunil	Mohit's friend
Bela	Sunil's wife
Anita and Rohit	Sunil and Bela's daughter and son
Anil	Mohit's friend
Asha	Anil's wife
Chachaji	Anil's father
Satish	Mohit's friend
Kanchan	Satish's wife
Rohini	Satish and Kanchan's daughter
Prashant	Mohit's friend
Ahmed	Mohit's friend
Nazma	Ahmed's wife
Arun	Mohit's friend
Maalti	Arun's wife
Veena and Vivek	Arun and Maalti's daughter and son
Jane	Meera's friend

Rishi	Jane's son, Meera's adopted son
Helena	Jane's mother
Mrs. Henderson	Jane's mother
Balwant	Lawyer
Atul	Meera's brother
Asha	Atul's wife
Neeti and Nishant	Atul and Asha's daughter and son
Rakesh	Meera's brother
Nalini	Rakesh's wife
Keshav and Krishan	Rakesh and Nalini's sons
Shoba	Meera's sister
Tayaji	Meera's father's older brother
Prabodh	Tayaji's student
Yadav	Mohit's brother
Kanta	Yadav's wife
Ravi, Bhavani and Kanti	Prashant's brothers
Neeta	Prashant's sister
Rai Saheb Tayaji	Owner of the house Meeera's family lived in when she was young
Vineet	Rai Saheb Tayaji's son

Index of Relationships

Bhaiya	Brother or friend
Bhai	Brother or friend
Bhabi	Brother's or friend's wife
Di	Sister or friend
Didi	Sister or friend
Dada	Brother
Da	Brother
Beta	Son
Beti	Daughter
Dadaji	Paternal grandfather
Dadi	Paternal grandmother
Nanaji	Maternal grandfather
Nani	Maternal grandmother
Chacha	Father's younger brother
Chachi	Chacha's wife
Tayaji	Father's older brother
Tayiji	Tayaji's wife
Bua	Father's sister

Mama.. Mother's brother
Mami.. Mama's wife
Masi... Mother's sister

Note: The terms Bhai, Bhaiya, Bhabi, Da, Didi, Di, Beta, Beti, Chachiji, Chachaji, Tayaji, Tayiji are also used for friends and friend's parents.

Acknowledgements

I cannot find adequate words to thank my wonderful parents and my dearest brother, for their blessings, infinite love, understanding, generosity and compassion for my difficult life.

I thank my children Eric and Anjana and my dearest grandson Chethan, who are the light of my life.

My gratitude goes to Carol Oczkowska for reading part of my manuscript and her valuable suggestions and to Sandra Burgess for reading part of my manuscript and encouraging me.

I am grateful to Bev Garnet for the original typing, and Drew Smith and Sharon Vanderhilt for typing the final corrections. I thank Anna Ell for doing an excellent job of formatting the 'digital book' for "Kindle Direct Publishing".

My heartfelt gratitude goes to Sharon Vanderhilt for her patience and excellence in preparing the manuscript for publication by X-libris. I could not have done it without her help.

Chapter One

He sat on a flat stone under the cool shade of a large bodhi tree; the long brown branches, shrouded by fluttering leaves, sprawled over an extensive area. On the absinthe grass that stretched to the horizon, resplendent polychromatic posies blossomed as though an invisible hand had strewn specks of radiant color purely out of jest.

Oblivious to the picturesque scenery around, he had his eyes shut in meditation. Birds were quiet, wind was motionless, the pervading stillness was similar to the silence that reigned before anything was when, according to Rig Veda, an ancient Hindu Scripture, there was nothing but only the possibility of being.

Suddenly, at a distance, a woman emerged against the blue horizon; her bent frame was suggestive of her old age. She carried something long but not too large in her frail arms, and as she came closer, it could be construed that the bundle was a small, stiff body, likely a child's, wrapped in a white cloth.

Tears ran down the woman's old cheek;, her wailing became more shrill as she approached the stone. With quavering hands, she placed the dead child at the feet of the meditating man.

"O Budha, please open your eyes and hear my woe! They say you have power over the manifest and unmanifest existence. You can command, and death will bow to you."

There was no motion in the man.

"If you don't help me, O compassionate one, who will?" The woman lamented.

A cloud of movement passed over the man's smooth, noble face. He opened his transparent eyes and looked at the woman; love effused from his gaze.

"Mother, don't cry and vex yourself. Whatever it is, is only a dream."

The woman knelt in front of him, color returned to her pallid cheeks at hearing Budha's sweet voice. There was hope.

She explained earnestly, "No, Budha, my grandson is not a dream! My daughter and son-in-law died when he was a little baby. I raised him. He is dead now, and I cannot live without him." The woman placed her gray head on her dead grandson's corpse and bawled in agony.

Her heart-wrenching ululation touched Budha deeply.

It has been said and written that Budha was Gyani, erudite, the wise one, because he was cognizant of the complex workings of manifest existence that is changeable and unreal. He was equanimous in pain and pleasure.

But no matter what his disciples and others say, Budha had tears in his eyes. He knew, even if he had transcended pain, others had not overcome theirs; and hence, they suffered from it.

A dark cloud passed over his saddened face; his eyes glistened. He raised his hand and placed it on the woman's bent head. With a tender voice full of commiseration, he said, "Mother, what can I do for you? Should I speak words of wisdom to console you? Can I explain the ephemeral nature of life, which is to be borne and die and no one, not even a Budha, can escape the clutches of death?"

"No," the woman insisted. "I don't want wisdom, Budha, I want my grandson!"

Budha sat nonplussed, only for a few minutes. His features became firm with determination; his voice achieved calm assurance. He said softly but resolutely, "Fine, Mother. I can bring your grandson back to life, but I need you to do something."

The woman's bearing was transformed from hopeless to hopeful. Her back straightened; an incredulous expression came over her wrinkled face.

"You can? I knew it. My grandson will come back to me! I am so happy!"

Suddenly, she remembered, "What do you want me to do?"

Budha sat unperturbed now. "You have to get something for me."

"Anything! Whatever! I can lay my life for my grandson." She was eager, impatient.

Budha smiled calmly. "Your life cannot bring your grandson's life back. It does not work that way."

He pointed his finger toward the village that lay beyond the horizon and said, "Please, Mother, go to that village and get some mustard seeds from a house where no one has died. I will put the seeds in your grandson's mouth, and he will become alive."

Life ran through the woman's body like lightning. She got up and ran with animated steps across the grass; her face shone with love and hope.

The sun was setting; the mud huts of the village had an orange hue. Children played outside, bells of the temple rang in the background, and smoke arose from the top of the huts. Women were cooking the evening meal.

She did not notice the landscape around her; all she saw was the first hut and knocked at the wooden door, earnestly.

"Yes?"

"Baba, Father, has anyone died in your house?"

The old man's face became drawn, and tears started to roll down his wrinkled cheeks. "Two months ago, my wife died. Ah, I miss her so . . ."

She did not wait for him to finish but sprang forward and knocked on the door of another hut. A young boy opened the door and looked at her questioningly.

"Son, has anyone died in your house?"

The young boy started to cry loudly. "My mother left me and went to heaven, my Baba says. Is that dying?"

Her feet felt frozen and hesitant, but her heart was still hopeful. She knocked at another door, and another and yet another.

Not a single hut was bereft of tears of death and loss, where wings of sorrow had not settled in the heart of loved ones.

The woman walked back slowly but not dragging her feet, sad but not desolate, in pain but not crushed. Darkness had fallen around Budha, but he glowed with his own aura. She fell on his feet.

Meera saw it all. She is that woman walking barefoot on the hot burning sands of life, carrying the dead body of her husband in her tottering arms.

She installs him at the aureate feet of Budha. She is the one staggering away, her hair flying in the air, gathering dust. The veil is off her head. She is running wildly, knocking at doors, begging, weeping. Her feet have blisters; her lips are parched with thirst. She cannot ask for water but only the nectar of those tiny life-giving mustard seeds that can bring Mohit back to life.

At every door, there are eyes with tears dimming the sight, wet cheeks flushed with painful memories. There are quivering hands and weakening knees at the question, "Has anyone died in this house? Please say no. You can then save my sweet husband, Mohit."

Meera is dead tired. Her feet and heart are aching, and there is no consolation from the knowledge she has just stumbled upon, the truth life has forced upon her, the eternal truth of birth and death and its omnipresence.

With a heart full of anguish of all the humans who have lost, all the humans from the dawn of existence who have gone before her, she feels like asking the Budha, "I know all about death now, but can you still feel my pain?"

But yes, He understands and feels her agony. He is said to have been the "compassionate one." He even felt the pain of birds and ants it has been said and written. He was the embodiment of piety and pity.

Meera cannot find solace though, not yet, but she is trying to hold on to the newly found wisdom and clutch it to her bosom. Truth shall set her free.

Mohit was lying on a white bed, his empty eyes staring at the ceiling. Papa and Tayaji, *father's older brother,* stood holding hands, pain splattered over their drawn, ill faces. They walked away with slow steps without looking at Meera. She yelled, "Don't go! Please!" But the sound died in her throat. Her feet turned into cement, and Meera stood alone, crying in the dark.

She woke up with a start, sat up in the bed, and pressed her chest to quiet her pounding heart that had been transformed into a twisted metal that pierced the innermost depths of her being.

Bela sighed and turned in the bed; deep furrows crossed her forehead, corners of her mouth slanted downward in readiness to cry.

Meera was slumped on the bench outside ward number 201 or 210, doubled over in unbearable pain, weeping out of control, oblivious to the glares of nurses, doctors, visitors. A small-built nurse sat next to Meera and held on to her cold hands.

Bela ran through the hallway and embraced Meera. "Oh God, how did it happen? How could it happen?"

Meera collapsed in Bela's arms and started to bawl loudly. Sunil acknowledged sympathetic glances of people by nodding an apology.

Sunil turned to the nurse. "Thank you so much, we will take care of her now."

He placed his hand on Meera's back and said softly, "Let us go home, Beti, *daughter*."

"I don't want to go!" she protested vehemently. How could she leave Mohit alone in a smelly ward, lying on a hospital bed covered with a white inauspicious sheet?

Bela and Sunil looked at each other. They held Meera by the arms and dragged her to the car that was parked outside the hospital.

Chachaji, *uncle,* walked into the living room with unstable steps and a dazed, lost look. He sat by Meera and placed his wrinkled hand on her bent head; she fell in his lap and broke down.

Mohit had a white bandage on his head soaked with fresh, deep-vermillion blood. But red is auspicious. She wore a scarlet saree laced with gold at her wedding!

Someone sat by her in slow motion and spoke softly, hesitantly, "I am so sorry, Meera."

She stared blankly.

Meera had never experienced such annihilating anguish before. With one merciless blow, the sharp sword of Yama, *the demi-God of death,* had split her smack in her center; her one-half suffering excruciating horror, the other watching desperately in utter disbelief and confusion. Is he really dead?

Where is everyone? She is going through hell, alone, so far away. Do they even know?

Satish informed her in an aggrieved tone, "Yes, Meera, Atul Bhai, *brother,* is coming tomorrow." A slight breeze of hope brought her some coolness even if so diminutive that it was almost unnoticed by her benumbed heart.

In a show of innocent camaraderie, Anita placed her tiny hand in Meera's crumpled lap. Her face became increasingly drawn as she watched everyone's afflicted demeanor. Unable to do much else, she inched closer to Meera, lifted her puny fair face, tears shining in her big, black bewildered eyes. "Aunty, why did my uncle leave us? He was the 'bestest' uncle I had. I am so sad."

Anita's words were forthright, transparent, unfeigned. While people fumbled with emotions, the child faced herself and her innermost sensibilities with veracity, articulating them without hesitation.

With age, humans erect inane impediments between them and their inner selves; feelings lose their way in a maze of confounding rationalization invented to evade facing emotions dauntlessly. "I am not afraid of you. You are there and I know this is life."

Meera looked at Anita with gratitude.

But how could this happen? Only a few months ago, Mohit and she sat on the Vedi, *the decorated space where the marriage rituals are performed,* decorated with roses and carnations, golden flames playing on Meera's shy, bowed beautiful face. Her gold saree and ornaments glittered like aureate mini suns, ethereal dreams glowed in Mohit's eyes behind the sehra, *a decorated head gear a groom wears with strings of flowers falling in front of his face,* of Motia, *jasmine,* strings. The priest added ghee, *heated butter,* and incense to the burning sandalwood pyre, chanting suitable wedding mantras, *verses from Scriptures,* in Sanskrit that only he understood. God of fire, Agnidev, duly gratified, his blessing for a felicitous union for seven consecutive lives was assured for the happy couple.

Now, betrayed, wrapped in an unpropitious pure white saree, she stands barefeet on a blaze of fire like ancient Rajput women who climbed with sure steps onto the crematory pyre to accompany their husbands to the yonder lands of death.

The tall, hungry, many-tongued flames are leaping upward; the tenebrous, thick, senseless smoke is engulfing her.

Meera is concentrating hard to find her God, but He seems to have dissolved in the lurid veil of fumes. Dispossessed, she is wandering in a murky haze of obscurity.

In long-lost past, she rambled like a happy ghost in the cool mists and translucent fog; graceful deodar trees stood tall, covering the Himalayan mountains. (The name *deodar* was derived from *devdaru*, timber of the gods.) The shroud of drifting clouds would gather quite suddenly, and she would run home, take her clothes off in a hurry, leaving a tiny panty wrapped around her puny bum and stand under magical pouring skies. Celestial music descended on the chariot of clear raindrops and drenched her. She danced like a peacock and sang.

The neighbor aunty, who lived next door, would open up her window and shout, "Aré, go in, go in, Meera. Where is your ma? Not home, no? I thought so. She would never let you out in this torrent of rain, silly girl, the best way to catch cold or even pneumonia, who knows."

Meera would jump up and down in the puddles of water that gathered in her front yard and giggle, "Nai, Masiji, *aunt*, I will be fine. I have never got cold before."

At that, Masiji would frown deeply and yell harder, "Tsh-tsh! Never say that, Budhu, *silly*, you are sure to get it if you announce that. Touch wood. Chalo under, *go in*."

Kanta Masiji had a round plump face and a red bindi, *red dot on married women's forehead*, smack in the center of her forehead. She exuded charm and motherly love that has been Indian womens' most consequential identity since time immemorial.

Papa believed that a mother is the fountainhead and pillar of life itself. If you do not honor your very source, you cannot flourish materially, morally, and spiritually. Maybe Hindu civilization has declined over thousands of years because we stopped treating our women with reverence.

Mrs. Mukherji had different ideas. She told Ma and Papa in no uncertain terms that women have run amok, lost their motherhood and their essence. This betrayal of their Dharma, *duty, essence*, is at the root of all worldly ills, wars, famine, earthquakes, etc. Pralay, *doomsday*, according to her, is not far behind.

She had twisted her face to express disgust. "Chee, chee, did you see Neelima at Shekhar's party? The skimpy blouse was only a pretense, the flesh hanging from her thick naked arms was wobbling, her stomach and back was totally exposed, her saree was flying all over except where it belonged—to cover her big front that was bulging out of the low-neck blouse. That too in a party full of men? And men? They want feast for their eyes, don't they? If you place it in front of them conveniently, why wouldn't their eyes pop out and gawk, eh?"

Mr. Mukherjee, a quiet man with dark shiny skin and serene black eyes, blushed at the rather luscious description of Neelima's anatomy and tried to downplay his wife's vociferation. He explained somberly, "You see, in Bengal, all women, even little girls, are called Ma. If a little girl is playing in the yard and a beggar approaches, he will say, 'Ma, give me food.' Such purity and respect."

Mrs. Mukherjee sang Rabinder Sangeet, *lyrics and music composed by the Nobel Laureate Rabinder Nath Thakur,* in Koyal, *songbird,* voice.

In Bengal, as soon as little girls start talking, they are furnished with a harmonium and a female music teacher to teach them Rabinder Sangeet. That is the most significant criterion for a prospective groom seeking the hand of the maiden. The boy's party—that may include the parents, grandparents on both sides, siblings, friends, uncles and aunts, of course the Vichola, *in-between,*—arrives en masse to check on the girl's credentials.

They are seated on the best pieces of furniture while the girl's relatives may have to crowd on the floor for the lack of sufficient chairs. The most expensive mithais, *sweets,* and glasses of boiled milk with green cardamom floating on the foam are served in the best-looking crockery borrowed from a rich neighbor; the hope is to soften them toward any shortcomings the girl may display.

The nervous girl is required to perform three acts. First, she has to walk in front of the gathering to assure that her legs and feet are in good order.

Then she has to let down her coconut-oil-greased shiny hair. The longer the hair, the prettier she is considered, not withstanding a thick nose, drooping lips, or fat hips.

Last but not the least, the jittery lass sits on a mat on the floor, her trembling sweaty fingers on the keys of her harmonium. She sings some song, "Rabinder Babu" might have written and composed in his moments of ecstasy without any idea that his creations would determine the future of Bengali girls.

One wonders what Bengali did before Rabinder Nath came into being.

Now, if the damsel aces all three tests, she can claim the most lucrative, first-class catch, which means a handsome boy with a good salary, a car, a fridge, and a gas stove.

The girl who fails one of the performances can still achieve a groom with average looks, a reasonable salary, a motorbike, and no fridge but with a gas stove in the kitchen.

Two failures mean that prospects are getting meager. The lad could border on ugly, have quite a low job, just a bike, and maybe a gas stove in the kitchenette.

The one who falls short on all exams, only Durga Ma, *demi-Goddess worshipped in Bengal area,* can save her from sure doom. The news of her nonsuccess will spread faster than fire. She and her miserable parents might as well forget another showing or a second chance. If she lands with an ugly groom with a menial job, one small bedroom, no gas stove, just a coal burner in a shared kitchen, which could be located across on the other side of the building, she is considered lucky.

The ill-fated damsel, who is disgracefully rejected by all, is condemned for life—the butt of sharp thorns of cruel words by friends, neighbours, and relatives, including the parents.

The miserable and desperate father is sometimes forced into taking desperate, bizarre measures. He presents the younger, pretty sister, cousin. or friend of the doomed maiden during the critical moment of showing. The boy's party is ecstatic; the marriage ceremony is performed satisfactorily, without a hitch, because in India, brides keep their faces veiled with the brocaded palloo, *edge part of a saree,* of their silk and gold saree. As soon as she leaves with the baraat, *groom's party,* the girl's relatives start praying for the whole groom's family to become blind.

The bride is brought to the groom's lighted house amid much laughter and cheer. Seeing all the guests well fed and their beds arranged, the exhausted mother of the boy goes to her bedroom and collapses instantly. Organizing and executing the son's wedding is no joke! She sighs with great relief that all went well, and letting her aching body sink into the mattress of the bed, she rests her weary head on the pillow.

Not for long though. A shriek pierces the still night! The door of the bride and bridegroom's decorated-with-flowers room opens with a thud, and the shocked, angry boy shouts, "We have been cheated!"

There can be several endings of the saga. All sad.

Unfortunately, even after the girl aces all tests, there is still a huge hurdle to overcome. Dowry! If her father is poor, the deal is off.

With all the demeaning impediments, it is surprising that so many Bengali girls do land up getting married. That may happen because of greed. Can greed result in any positive outcome? Yes. The criteria can be interconvertible. Even if the girl has passed only one test, a substantial dowry can compensate for her failures.

A similar procedure for bride selection may be followed in other states of India, but is nowhere as rigorous, systematic, and absolute as in Bengal.

The situation has changed, especially in cities, but it's likely that village girls are still seen as commodities, their value depending on an age-old degrading system of evaluation.

Bela di's, *sister's*, gloomy voice floated by Meera's unhearing ears, "Tea, beti, *daughter*, it will give you strength."

"Yes," she replied.

She was ashamed; her Mohit is lying alone in a smelly morgue imprisoned in the smothering silence of the coffin, and she is craving tea?

But it is many hours past four o'clock. She always had an uncontrollable urge at that hour ever since she was allowed to drink tea. Before that?

Dadi, *paternal grandmother*, would open her eyes wide and exclaim, "Chai? Young girl drinking tea? Are you suicidal, Choti? You want to become dark like tea and stay spinster all your life? Who will marry you, eh? Chalo, wait until you are married. We were not even allowed tea after we came to our in-law's house. But times have changed!" She let out a deep sigh. "Look at your ma. She has to pump tea into her every hour. She was so fair and pretty when your papa brought her home. Look at her now, so dark!"

Ma, having heard it before, would suppress a smile.

Unbeknownst to Dadi, of course, after her classes were over at around four o'clock, Meera could be seen with religious punctuality, along with a bunch of giggly friends, at the open-air dhaba, *open-air tented food outlet*, famously known as Meshi ka Dhaba. It was located behind the dark moss-covered brick college building, under the cool, damp shade of the clump of tall deodars seemingly touching the skies. Depending on the season, some wet or dry wooden benches would be scattered around.

That is also where clusters of young boys stood scoping the other groups of young lasses for possible romance.

Many a romance blossomed in front of Meshi Ka Dhaba under the unsuspecting deodars, over the mist-laden valley, steam rising from the rust-colored earthen cups.

Those were the days of hot romances in the midst of cool, foggy peaks of Simla, the dangerous hide-and-seek, running away to the movies and restaurant, disappearing behind trees and shrubs in mysterious shadowy valleys.

The previous generation who had immolated their lives at the altar of freedom for India now demanded from their offspring, both boys and girls, to prove their worthiness for a motherland that had suffered the indignity of slavery for centuries.

Schools, colleges, universities proliferated like mushrooms all over India. But the institutions of education not only spewed out graduates but also excited grooms and coy brides.

Especially in Simla—who could blame them? They were encaptured by the dazzling white snow, the moisture-laden clouds shrouding the mountains, the deep-green of the valleys and the tall majesty of the deodar trees, the deep, azure sky of the spring, and the umpteen kaleidoscopic flowers gleaming in the bright sunrays.

With every breath, the puerile youth were intoxicated by the magic of the place. How could they not love the rosy-cheeked maidens and the youthful, excitable lads with a reflection of the sun sparkling in their eyes?

One of Meera's group, Sarita—a fair, sweet girl with dimples—fell in love with Surjit, a tall Sikh boy.

Meera rendered serious contribution to the blossoming of their liaison; she covered for Sarita, who in her pretense of visiting Meera would be sitting under some protecting tree with Surjit by her side in some umbrageous dell, hands clasped in cold hands, submerged in each other's eyes.

A red-faced, growling father locked up a bawling Sarita in her room. "Anyone who lets her out will not be alive tomorrow, understand?"

The whole clan, chachas and mamas, uncles, cousins, and close friends, scrambled to find a boy within one week of discovering the "affair," as it was delicately called. Over threats of suicide by the wailing mother, a numb Sarita sat on the vedi, *the decorated space where the marriage rituals are performed*, like a gilded statue with an unknown groom of their own caste. Her hot tears were impotent to quench the "sacred fire" around which she was literally carried by her brothers during the pheras, *bride and groom walk around the sacred fire.* Knots tied, sindoor, *a red powder the bridegroom places in the parting of bride's hair,* in place, smack in the parting of her silky hair, Sarita was packed away to England for better or worse.

Meera returned from winter holidays at Tayaji's, *father's older brother,* house in Delhi to find Sarita missing and Surjit with a dagger in his heart.

He killed himself.

Still, the dhaba did evoke a lot of good memories that she could still taste in her mouth. The famous sizzling hot samosas, *deep fried snack,* fried in oil darkened from repeated use, in a skillet with a bottom where a thick layer of black soot was deposited from carbon of burning coal, year after year, for God knows how many years. Meshi had been an eternal presence, since how long, no one knew. He was always there since anyone could remember, or it might have been his father before him, but no one knew the difference. The important fact was that he always made his samosas fresh and in accordance with everyone's particular taste, "especial" he called them.

And then, there was his famous karak chai, *strong tea,* deadly, dark, deep-brown stuff that passed for tea. He boiled and brewed it in an aluminum put on a coal stove, all day long, constantly adding tealeaves, milk, water, and brown sugar to the same mixture. By four o'clock, Meera's auspicious teatime, the concoction was a deep dark brown, tasting like rummy or some hard liquor. She had never tasted liquor or rummy or any other alcoholic beverage for that matter but somehow believed that it must taste like Meshi's tea.

White fluffy clouds rose from the fathomless valley, seemingly in defiance against the natural order of things. Dark-gray menacing clouds hung imploringly in the overcast sky, occasionally spewing a drizzle just for fun. The vaporlike mist suspended in the air created a white veil around everything in sight. On rainy days, a powerfully nostalgic odor of wet grass and shrubs, pine needles, wet bark, creepers, flowers drooping with the weight of tearlike clear, fresh raindrops would stubbornly hang in the frigid air around them; gobble-de-gook of loquacious birds formed a lively backdrop.

Meera and her gang would be wrapped in sweaters, shawls, shivering a little with red noses running due to red chilis in samosas and a bitter chill in the breeze, ascending deodars, dark-green shroud covering the mountainous earth below. Who could forget those moments in Sat Janam, *seven births*?

Spread on the heights of the Himalayan range, Simla, a city of indescribable beauty, was built as a haven for the officers of the British Raj, *British colonization of India,* where they escaped from the vengeful torridity of Delhi in the summer.

Such is the grace of Himvan, the eternal king of Himalayan terrain, that even the transgressors are granted refuge.

Himalayas are where the ascetic Lord Shiva abides. He is also called Neelkanth because to save humanity, he drank poison that conferred blue coloration to his neck. Surrounded by the awe-inspiring crests of the rugged mountains, by the banks of stilled, frigid aquamarine lakes, Shiva meditates for thousands of years until an evildoer disrupts his samadhi, *meditation.*

In a flash, he is awake; his feet dance the Tandav, *Lord Shiva's dance,* with energy of lightning. The mountain peaks shake, rocks tumble down with thunderous uproar, the earth moves from its center, leaping fires alight from nowhere; tumultuous waves splash on the shores of lakes and rivers. Shiva aims his scintillating trishul, *a metallic rod with three-pronged sharp edges at one end,* at the demonic miscreant, piercing his heart. His third eye, set in the center of his broad forehead, opens, effusing blazing fire, burning the sinner to ashes.

Self-possessed and serene, Lord Shiva perches on his favorite rock, shuts the three eyes, and merges his consciousness in God consciousness again.

The world around him sinks in pure silence.

It is Lord Shiva's valor that seeps into the masses who inhabit at his feet, the plains below. It is the intrepidity of their spirit that enables millions of poverty-stricken, miserable humans to still look up and laugh against all odds.

Most people left after mumbling their condolence apologetically, incoherently, treading softly on the living room rug.

Meera nodded vaguely without looking up.

Bela Di came twice to ask her to eat. She leaned her back against the wall weakly and made an awful face at the suggestion. "No, Di, I can't."

Di insisted softly, "Beti, *daughter*, you have not eaten anything. It is ten o'clock. It is very late, Meera."

Late? Meera looked up. "Di, how does it matter?"

Morning alighted on aureate wings and tingling laughter, the clatter of pots resounding in the kitchen where she would be making Mohit's favorite alu prantha, *homemade bread stuffed with potatoes*, and spiced omelet for breakfast. In a meek, embarrassed voice, he would call from the bedroom where his tie and socks were.

Evening crept up with elongating shadows, chattering of homesick birds, the dimming multicolor of the setting sun, graying skies of dusk, and shy feelings of expectantly waiting for Mohit's return from the office.

Now, morning and evening had both lost their meaning; Meera's past, present, and future were stripped of any relevance. She was standing, trembling, at the hub of infinite, untamed kal, *infinite time*, a tenebrous nonrhythmic flow of life where day and night merge into an endless, blinding pain that seemed to dissolve her unto itself.

It had been an overcast, depressing day; no rain, just pensive, sorrowful clouds loomed in the sky. The night fell like an opaque, wet heavy blanket, crushing the very prana, *life force*, of this tiny abode where life had once rejoiced at the felicitous eloquence of their ardent love.

Now, an aggrieved aphony filled all the spaces in Meera's home. The living room, where stunned friends sat during the unforgiving evening, now looked deserted.

Bela firmly ordered everyone to eat, since no one had paid any attention to the earlier entreaties.

Meera just shut her eyes to avoid the question. Chachaji, who had been sitting next to Meera silently in the lotus position, nodded an unequivocal no.

The rest had no choice.

Satish bent over Meera and gave her a small white pill. He looked unnecessarily guilty. "Meera, you need sleep."

She looked at the stairs pathetically; they seemed like a precipitous mountain. Meera felt decrepit.

Bela understood. "Come," she said. "I will help you."

After collapsing in the bed, she looked pleadingly at Di. "Will you sleep with me?"

"Tell me where blankets and pillows are. Kanchan and Asha left, but everyone else wants to stay."

Bela Di mumbled incoherently, tossing her restless body in her sleep. Meera placed her hand on Di's arm and moved closer. She did not stir.

Tears trickling down her pallid cheeks, Meera looked up for relief; there was no one.

Ma had turned her calm face upward, her vision penetrated the deodars, past the clouds, and told Meera faithfully, "He lives there."

There had to be a daily investigation of flowering beds to see if the flower buds had opened overnight. Meera was doing just that in the garden, small ponytailed frame bent on each dahlia, pansy, larkspur, and rose plant to note their progress. It was downright annoying at how leisurely the buds unfurled. Why could they not bloom swiftly into polychromatic blossoms that emitted heavenly perfume? Meera would become dizzy as she sniffed them too hard.

Mali Baba, *gardener,* nodded his gray, sagacious head sideways in disapproval, "Oh, Choti, don't take away all the fragrance? You must leave some for the flowers too."

The clatter of collective footsteps hitting against the little stones of the gravel pathway was uncommon in the quiet residential area. Meera, filled with curiosity, picked up Rani, *Meera's doll,* and ran up the steps that led to the road.

The pathway ran a little above the Summer Hill house, winded for a small distance, though at the time it had seemed quite long, then led straight to the diminutive railway station, from where they took a train to go to Simla every day.

Four sturdy men, their heads covered with white scarves, carried something on a wooden platform that was propped on their shoulders. A white sheet covered whatever it was; garlands of yellow and orange marigolds lay on top.

What seemed like a large crowd at that time, maybe twenty or twenty-five adults, followed the four men. Everyone was clad in white or cream apparel, and with their heads covered, they treaded painfully in slow motion.

On and off the mantra, *verse from Hindu Scripture,* "God's name is truth" was uttered solemnly, rising like a wave of sound that died in people's throats. Anguished sobs, occasionally wailing, sounded sinister, piercing Meera's heart. Her eyes filled with tears, and she ran inside into the kitchen, clutching at Ma's palloo, *edge part of a saree,* and crying.

Ma picked up and hugged Meera in her bosom. The memory of the assuaging warmth of Ma's body still soothed her.

Ma installed Meera on a stool and wiped her tears, "Choti, don't cry. The person they were carrying lived well and long. It is time for him to go away."

"Go away where, Mummy?"

"Go to God."

"Where is God?"

That is when Ma had looked up and showed Meera where.

"But I do not see Him."

"When you grow up and learn to use the special eyes of wisdom, you will see Him."

Perhaps Meera had still not acquired the eyes of wisdom?

Meera got out of bed carefully, trying not to disturb Di, and staggered to the adjoining bathroom. Sitting on the toilet seat, she covered her face with her cold hands and wept in unendurable anguish.

Pray, silly, pray! In her desperation Meera had forgotten the Mantra of her childhood.

Barely four or five, Meera was terror stricken of darkness where two-thousand-year-old witches lived. They had two-foot-long nails, seven-foot-long white hair touching their heels, walked half stooped with a wooden pole in their crooked hands that touched the black skies; and they laughed cruelly, showing sharp, gnawing, black teeth on an extensively creased face. When she looked out the window at night, the long-limbed deodars turned into shadowy swaying bhoots, *demons*, their multiple arms ready to grab her.

She ran to Ma's cozy bed and hid in her arms.

Ma said one day, "Choti, if you chant the Bhagwat mantra, *prayer to God*, all the wicked creatures run away. They are evil *na*, frightened of the Good God."

The next time, as soon as Meera climbed into her bed, she squatted, folded her wee hands, and chanted, "Om Namo Bhagwate Vasudev Vai." The witches dissolved in the air, *bhoots* metamorphosed into deodars, smiling and nodding their heads musically. The oblation truly worked to purge all fears, real or imaginary. Of course, she did not know then if the divine words could also scare away the horror of death, so final and brutal.

Meera mustered all her sinew to focus on God's invocation. Only Mohit's silenced face, wrapped in white bloody bandage, surfaced in her tormented consciousness.

- # -

The same face, full of calm curiosity, had looked at Meera across the table. "What do you think of living in a foreign country?"

The dim light of the hanging lamp fell on Mohit's finely chiseled face, reminding her of Michaelanglo's *David*. His black twinkling eyes settled on Meera's face.

He was unassuming, unselfconscious. She liked him.

The bearer, wearing a white stiff starched uniform, moved noiselessly and inquired in a conscious, disciplined voice, "More coffee, sir?"

"Sure." Mohit smiled at the young man. A couple in the next booth chuckled gleefully; the girl had a shrill girly voice in contrast with the man's deep, coming-from-the-lungs intonation. In the background, the Beatles sang in boyish, sweet voices.

Mohit raised his head and caught Meera's glance. Blood rushed to her face in embarrassment. "Girls are supposed to look down coyly.

Boys like submissive girls." Sheela Aunty had sighed with vexation. "Shakuntala, you don't want me to go with them. But I could have handled the delicate situation. They don't even know each other, *na*!"

It is indeed an utterly hopeless goal to figure out a person's reality in a few hours over coffee or tutti-frutti ice cream. Worse still, the so-called interview often incorporates the stringent chaperonage by parents, or more perilously, the aunty, whose shrewd mediation brought the two families together in the first place.

Vichola, *in-between,* Aunty's undisputed status wins her infinite rights that she would claim during the marriage ceremony and much later. With obvious exaltation and reiteration, she would chime to the girl's parents, "Bahenji, *sister,* what a perfect match! That is why I brought this rishta, *proposal,* to you. As soon as I laid eyes on Vinny, my sister-in-law's, brother's, brother-in-law's son, I said to myself, your Sushma will be so lucky to be his wife!" Girls are the more vulnerable party; a good match is more consequential for them than the other way around.

"Vinny immediately fell for your sweet Sushma! The way he looked at her and all. God bless them, all is well. Don't thank me, no, no, no, all daughters are common. You will help me when I look for a boy for my Sujata? Won't you? Of course you will. So it is okay, congratulations to you too, Bhai Saheb, *respected brother.* God is great," and so on.

"Do you believe in God?" Meera posed her question rather abruptly.

Mohit was startled. He looked deep into her light-brown, transparent eyes to ensure she really meant it. He became introspective and stared at the plate of samosas, hoping for some inspiration for an appropriate answer.

After a short pause, he spoke with self-cognizant certitude, "When I am in trouble, I pray to God." Then he laughed.

Meera smiled. "Then you do believe in God." She poured more coffee in Mohit's cup and stirred in a sugar cube.

Mohit became solemn. "Are you very religious?"

"Depends what you mean by that. I do not go to temple often, don't rub my head in front of God's statue all day. But I am in love with God and pray every day. Would it bother you if I don't force it upon you?"

His sense of relief was undisguised. They both laughed.

Hours flew while they both peeled away the layers of each other's lives to grasp the verity at the center of their existence.

They did not notice the demi goddess of night shrouded the manifest world with her black veil. Faithful to itself, January was cold as ever, and a slight drizzle added to the bitterness of the chill.

The glittering neon lights of Cannought Place Shopping Centre in Delhi gleamed on the wet road. A sea of swarming humans confronted Meera and Mohit as they stepped out of Volgas restaurant. Tired, grumbling husbands stooping down with the weight of their wives' shopping spree, couples discussing and more often disagreeing, mothers shouting to keep their excited offspring from running too far. Young girls dressed in flowery "sack" shirts walked with difficult grace, there being no room whatsoever for the legs to maneuver, prompting whistling and snickering remarks by the young boys. They would intentionally bump into pretty lasses then plead sorry with dubious sincerity. Some lads sang the latest "filmy" songs, mostly out of tune, and laughed at the fiery looks from inside-laughing-outside-angry girls. Some elders nodded in disapproval and rebuked the young chokras, *young lads,* without noticeable effect.

Concessions of multifarious goods were installed under the covered areas in front of the big shops of Cannought Place. The stall owners, hoarse from a whole day of yelling to compete with their comrades, were still trying to attract more customers.

"Memsaheb, such a beautiful necklace, only Nargis and Madhubala, *film actresses,* have it, and they have spent *lakhs*! This is more real than real and cheap too. It will look lovely, Sab, give her this precious gift as proof of your love."

"Books, demi Goddess Saraswati lives in every word. Knowledge is shakti, *power.* Read and be wise overnight."

"Leather goods all imported from Egypt, will be gone tomorrow, take it today. Baby, this small purse matches with your frock, only ten ruprees. Your mummy will get it for you, won't you, Bahenji, *sister?*"

"Madrasi silk, khalis, no mixture, straight from Madras. Didi, this saree was spun just for you. Bhai, *brother,* silk kurta, Kashmiri embroidery, you will look chikna, *smooth,* like Raj Kapoor, *actor,* in *Chori Chori film.*"

"Cigarette, wala. Warm your heart, look romantic."

"Pan, *betel leaves,* is a must, Sahib. How will you digest what you ate at Volgas?"

These calls and more formed a backdrop of many-pronged, rumbling voice machines.

For the stall owners, it is a matter of almost life and death. To take home less money than what wife expects is a great peril involving severe consequences. "Aré, only ten rupees? How can I feed my family with this pittance? Aashish's fees are overdue. Do you want me to sell all my jewelry sets? Oh God, why did you give me this chuddu, *useless,* who can't even feed me." A few tears may be prompted.

Denial of dinner will definitely follow since in all likelihood, she will go to the bedroom, slam doors, and weep to God.

At small distances, bundles of rags squatted on the cold, hard, cement floor, leaning against the walls. Their brown, soiled raiments blended with the obscurity of the unlighted area, making them almost invisible. Only scrawny, emaciated faces poked out; suffering eyes shone in search for impossible relief against hunger and cold. "Garib ko paisa, *do give money to the poor,* Saheb. I have not eaten today."

They were beggars, blind, deaf, crippled, sick, young and old, with one metallic begging bowl in common.

A uniformed guard outside a fancy restaurant would try to shoo them away. "Oy, chalo, get lost. Is this your bap's, *father's,* property? Are you going, or should I call the police?" Perhaps the sordid reality of the penniless disrupted the immaculate polish of the ambience for the rich. Treated as the undesirable debris of an unjust world order, there is no place for these innocuous archetypes of humanity.

Meera opened her embroidered purse and distributed some money; the beggars poured out Indians' favorite blessing, "God bless you with many children."

Mohit smiled at Meera mischieviously; she just blushed.

Right next to one of the thick cement pillars that prop the Cannought Place, two shriveled little girls sat, barely six or seven years old, wearing undersized salwar kameez, *Indian style pant and shirt for women,* and worn-out, faded sweaters. On a straw mat in front of them lay a pile of beautiful fragrant venis, *strings of flowers,* of small red and white roses. Jasmine flowers are the first choice for venis all over India, but in the north, jasmine does not bloom in the cold temperature; it is rose season.

Stray raindrops wafted with wind and fell on velvety, delicate petals of roses and glowed like diamonds in the neon lights.

Mohit saw Meera look down at the venis, their comeliness reflected in her light-brown eyes.

The girls' eyes glowed in hope.

"Beti, *daughter*, give me the best one," he asked the older girl.

Both girls perked up immediately, hurriedly sifted through the pile, and found one with large roses; "Here, Sabji. The bestest."

Extending his hand toward the back of Meera's head, Mohit attempted to tie the veni in her shiny hair that were neatly tied in a bun.

She smiled and took it from his hands shyly. Meera bent her long, graceful neck, brought the flowers to her nose, shut her eyes, and sniffed the aroma with obvious pleasure.

Tender feelings brushed against Mohit's heart like a wave of soothing warm breeze. He beheld Meera wistfully and wished he could have her. Forever.

"Now." Meera passed on the veni to him to fasten on her hair.

That night, the sublime aroma ascended from the delicate blooms that lay in a wet plate on her night table and drenched her dreams.

- # -

During the last two weeks, she had sensed something of a lull before the storm; the hushed silence of darkening clouds festered imploringly beyond the horizons of her consciousness. Meera felt restless and weary for no tangible reason. Her intuition kept whispering in her inner ear warning of some dark impending danger waiting treacherously just around the corner. The ancient sages believed that intuition is our unconscious perception of the potential subtle cause that in time consummates into the manifest sequential outcome. We have no conscious cognition of this extrasensory perception, but we are all the same apprehending the subtle elements of the cause-consequence chain.

Meera did book a call to India and spoke to Ma and Papa; everyone was fine. But the cruel chains of foreboding held her heart hostage and crushed it under its avoirdupois burden.

Meera was sitting listlessly in the armchair that she had installed, over Mohit's polite protestation, just in front of the large dining room window, never mind that the dining table and chairs appeared out of place. Her view was perfect.

The deep-green juniper, tall, spruce and triangular cedar growing at the far end of the backyard could take a fair bit of credit for preserving Meera's sanity in the otherwise bleak brown-and-white landscape of the winter.

At the distance, a mountain range endured; snowcaps on the pointed peaks pierced the skies above.

A verdant veil was beginning to enliven the dead landscape. Some perennials poked out their pristine yellow-green heads to ensure safety of emergence. Pockets of flaunting wildflowers dotted the green environ resolutely, refusing to follow any order, thereby justifying their nomenclature as wild.

Meera denied the first knock, ignored the second, at the getting-louder third tap, wondered why someone was so persistent; the fourth pounding left her no choice.

She hoped it was not a Jehovah Witness. They were very polite and civil but found it unbelievable that the Almighty God could have made himself known to Hindus of India some five thousand years ago. Although God is not called Jehovah but Bhagwan in Hindi, God in English and Allah in Arabic, it is more than likely that He is the same God; there can only be one God ruling over the universe.

Meera was surprised though. She had understood, slowly, that in Canada no one just shows up at your door; they phone first. Back home anyone, anytime can lay claim on the lives of unsuspecting hosts. Worst still, you must express delight at the intrusion into your space and time. This can be an unfair calling because you could be having a bad hair day or doing something that needed to be done a year ago; if you are married, you could have just had a fierce confrontation with your hubby; if you have recently blossomed into a young woman, you could be very busy with your newly acquired calling: to lie on the soft bed and daydream about a handsome husband and cute children. Naturally, you hate to be brought down to the hard ground of reality.

However, social drop-ins are a fact of life, and that is that.

Two uniformed men stood at the door; one was young perhaps fresh out of academy with uncertainty in his light blue eyes. The other was older, had a mature confident demeanor.

Both cops were fairly tall and well built and looked quite authoritative in their fashionable navy pants with red stripes and sky-blue starched shirts. A sleek car stood outside to augment their power and prestige.

And then there are bleak looking cops in India called constables; you see them on the streets holding unavailing wooden clubs in their irresolute sweaty hands. The ones in charge of traffic stand on a raised round cement platform smack in the center of the crossings. Their match stick legs barely support their torso; flailing arms waving frantically in the air are ineffective in starting or stopping traffic of vehicles, people, bikes, rickshaws, cows, and dogs. Every one proceeds unimpeded by the feeble presence of frustrated, helpless constables.

The constable's uniform consists of under or oversized cheap cotton knickers and half-sleeve shirts, old-fashioned turban that overflows around their small heads. The uniform is a pathetic khaki brown color, which makes them invisible since they blend perfectly in the hot dusty surroundings. Furthermore, the constable's low status in the hierarchy of Indian socioeconomic order is common knowledge; how can they exude any power?

Thanedar, *police inspector,* the boss remains in thana, *police station,* his feet up on the huge wooden desk that is fully occupied with unorderly piles of dusty files. He sips tea almost continuously, "Oy, chai la, sale, *bring tea,*" does little excepting boss around and scare the hapless victims who blunder and arrive at the thana with high hopes of finding a missing child or catch a thief or ruffian who assaulted them.

They are duly intimidated, made to feel responsible for whatever happened to them, and shown the exit door rather rudely.

Meera asked in a questioning tone, "Yes?"

Unprepared for what stood in front of them, the cops appeared hesitant. The younger cop shifted on his feet uneasily.

Meera understood.

The sudden appearance of her brown color and saree perhaps dislodged the balance of their minds. When she met Mohit's white friends for the first time, they looked flustered. Not belonging to any concrete a priori known category in their cognitive systems, she challenged their complacent psyche. She learned to smile and talk a great deal to substantiate that she was, in fact, much like other women, hence they could start treating her as such.

It worked.

Meera smiled broadly. "Hello, how are you?" They relaxed.

"Fine, ma'am." After an uncomfortable pause, the older cop overcame some hurdle and spoke gravely. "We called you on the phone a few times, no one answered."

Meera smiled. "I must have been taking my late bath."

He did not smile back. "Ma'am, your husband was in a car accident."

"No, he's at the office!" she replied with certainty.

The cop was unflinching, but sad. "Ma'am, he is in the hospital, we would like you to come with us."

Something hit Meera in the heart like an unbeknown bolt. She queried anxiously, "Is he okay?"

The younger cop looked at her sympathetically and said, "Ma'am, don't worry, it will be all right."

The older cop gave him a stern and reproachful stare.

Meera did not notice. "I am sure he is all right," she assured herself.

She grabbed her purse and sweater. Her feet were steady, her heart unperturbed.

Leaning against the leather back of the police car, she shut her eyes, "Please, God, take care of him."

"But how did it happen?" a touch of worry crept in her voice.

"He hit a tree, ma'am."

"What! How could he? He is a careful driver!"

It dawned on her now; maybe Mohit is seriously injured. Why else would the police pick her up?

A sinking sensation squirmed in Meera's gut. Reality cut through the heart of her optimism like a sharp knife. Drums reverberated in her arteries clamorously; her heart quavered.

A film of tears gathered in Meera's eyes; a silent prayer rose in her throat.

The police car stopped at the red light. Meera glanced out. The pristine buds lent a white-and-pink hue to the branches of cherry trees that lined the road on both sides.

"You cannot believe the stunning beauty of the cherry blossoms when they flower in unison in mid-April. Meera, you will lose yourself!" Mohit had told her excitedly.

"I hope, I pray he is okay, God, please." A pungent fear gripped Meera like a slithering poisonous snake that squeezed the life out of her. A million thorns suddenly cropped all over her body.

Stepping out of the car, she staggered; the young cop held her arm. The three of them walked through the entrance, hallway, elevator, more corridors with nurses, doctors, voices, smells, glances, all without Meera's awareness.

Her mouth was dry, and tears choked her throat when a doctor came out of the room 210 or 201. Quietly, he nodded to the cops and took over Meera's slim arm from the younger cop. He towed Meera gently toward a wooden bench that lay nearby.

The doctor had a kind face, pepper-gray hair, black-rimmed glasses, and wore a white gown and tiredness as a given.

Fixing his intelligent eyes on Meera's face, he asked sadly, "Do you have family or friends here?"

Suddenly, Meera's whole world went silent, occluded to her senses. Vision introverted inward, she saw a burning lake engulfing both Mohit and her. In excruciating pain, she got up abruptly and walked into the adjacent ward with unsteady steps.

The doctor followed her, "I am so sorry, there was internal bleeding in the head."

Her Mohit lay still, covered with a pure-white sheet up to his neck, cotton plugs stuffed in his nostrils; fresh blood sparkled against the white bandage on his head.

The room went in circles, and Meera plunged in a bottomless, dark, abyss.

- # -

Atul looked at Bela and asked in a whisper, "Did she eat?" Bela just nodded in the negative.

Atul's square jaw clenched with tension.

Bela encouraged him. "I will take milk with honey, it will give her strength, don't worry, Bhaiya, *brother.*"

Bela got up and walked towards the kitchen.

Atul straightened his stiff back. Asha had told him many times, "Go to the doctor, you are too young to have a back problem."

Sitting in the small seat of the plane for almost twenty hours did not help.

Everyone sat in the living room, their heads lowered, their minds frantically searching for appropriate words to console Atul. They did not realize that there are no words that can take the pain of death away.

Atul broke the silence. "I will take Meera and leave tomorrow morning."

After going through customs at the airport, Atul had hurried toward Meera and held her in his arms tightly as she broke down and cried loudly, prompting curious glances from the people around.

Fighting with his tears, Atul kept repeating, "Oh, my baby, my poor child." Atul, being the oldest, treated his siblings as his children, much to the chagrin of Shoba and Rakesh, who were thoroughly irritated because he also assumed the right to boss around.

Through her blurry vision, Meera looked up and sobbed, "What took you so long, Bhaiya, *brother*?"

The judge, Mr. Mishra, had glared at Atul sitting across his desk and retorted gruffly, "It is a very unusual request, Mr. Yadav. Life has to go on."

Atul looked at the judge with expectation of a more reasonable utterance. He had been warned not to count upon a man well known for his insensitivity toward existential matters, especially if they were someone else's. Mr. Mishra was one of the most erudite occupants of the bench, but law school seemed to have taught him only dry, cold, blind legal jargon, not pulsating life systems.

"My sister is alone in a foreign land. I have to go." Atul was firm. After all, what could the judge do? Send him to jail for contempt? He could appeal and win.

"You can have three days' postponement of your case."

Atul kissed her on her forehead. "I am here now, Choti. Don't worry about a thing."

A large crowd gathered in the semidark hall of the funeral home. Mohit's colleagues and friends paid homage. Hans spoke of his high character and kindness with heavy voice. Satish could not finish; words got stuck in his teary throat.

Meera did not hear or see anything. The excruciating torment of her heart blocked every other reality from reaching her mind. "Is this the ultimate conclusion of life?" was her last thought as she wailed and fainted in Atul's arms. Intense deafening inferno of the crematorium reduced Mohit to dust and ashes.

An aggrieved silence hung in the living room. It had been an obscure cloudy day; another mournful night weighed heavily on everyone's tired spirits. After the cremation, they had all staggered to Meera's house, emotionally exhausted.

Meera dragged herself literally and went up to lie down in her bedroom. The earth under her feet had melted away; she was suspended in a scary vacuum of nothingness. Is it possible to be annihilated and become non-xistent? Budha said, "*Shunya*, in its nothingness, is blissful." But Meera's *shunya* was fiery, dark, and hopeless.

Bela came down the stairs with the untouched cup of milk in her hand. She had half heard Atul and peeked in the living room questioningly. Atul turned to her. "Bela Behen, *sister*, please pack up Meera's essentials. The rest can come later."

Bela planted the cup in a corner table and sat down on the sofa chair pensively. Meaningful glances were exchanged between everyone, and all eyes finally converged on Sunil.

You cannot take India out of Indians no matter where they go. On all serious matters, age achieves a profound significance and determines who gets to carry the torch.

Atul, *brother*, noticed. "What?"

Sunil coughed to clear his throat. "Bhaiya, Mohit's finances have to be dealt with."

Atul interrupted impatiently. "Hell with the money. I can't leave her here alone." Right away he, knew that his words were untrue and ungrateful.

He corrected himself and looked at everyone apologetically. "I know she is not alone. I have never met such a caring bunch of people. But everyone is waiting for her in Simla and Bombay. Can Meera give power of attorney to you or Satish?"

Satish was honest. "It will not work. We will have to consult her on every action we take. It will delay the settlements unnecessarily. I know a good lawyer, Balwant, he will deal with it as quickly as possible."

Atul appeared uneasy, unconvinced. Chachaji, *uncle,* was sitting on the sofa upright and poised. He lifted his eyes, looked at Atul, and concluded the discussion by a few simple words. "Atul, Meera is my daughter. Leave her here and go in peace." There was candor and soothing coolness of love in Chachaji's soft voice. For Atul, there was nothing more to say.

At the airport, Meera clung to Atul.

"Don't go, Bhai," knowing full well the futility of her request.

Atul held her to his chest. "You come soon, we are waiting." His eyes became damp. Chachaji's time-worn hands quavered as he touched the round brass vessel that contained Mohit's ashes to his forehead, kissed it, and passed it on to Atul. He whispered an incoherent blessing as Atul touched his sandaled feet.

Atul passed through customs and waved them good-bye. Meera stood like a phantom and waved her hand weakly. Bela took her arm gently. "Let us go, Beti, *daughter.*"

That night after Atul left, she lay in bed and wept bitterly. She cried for Mohit's absence, truancy of his loving arms, his overarching protection, and the frightening permanence of his void. But her tears were also for the forfeiture of her faith, the lapse of her closeness with God. Fog of woe stood like a thick opaque veil between her and God. She was scared as never before at the thought that maybe she never had a veritable relationship with God. Why else could she not feel his assuaging omnipresence at this critical juncture?

Meera sat lifelessly on the couch, still wearing a nightgown, gazing into space. A gentle touch on the back of her head startled her. She looked up; Chachaji had walked in quietly. He smiled, "The door was unlocked, Beti." He posited himself on the sofa close to Meera and queried cautiously, "Should we sit outside for a while? It is sunny and pleasant."

Weeks had gone by without Meera's awareness. Cherry blossoms fetched the spring on velvety petals and woke up a hibernating city. Air was silky soft, perfumed; silver puffs glided in the infinite sky; daylight stayed longer to enjoy the festival of life; human voices were flushed out of their cubbyholes and became the heartbeat of the ambiance.

Sunil and Anil had come early in the morning to work on the yard. Sunil mowed her lawn, Anil cleaned the weeds and dead brown plants from last year and planted some annuals like pansies, petunias, and marigolds in the flower beds; these plants were easygoing, did not require much care. Meera asked them weakly if they wanted tea. When they declined, she did not insist.

Meera sighed with resignation and nodded sideways, which meant no in Indian body language, without looking at Chachaji.

Chachaji got up, said, "I will talk to Anil," opened the patio door, and walked out.

Atul was gone; there was nothing left. He took Mohit's last relics to deliver to Mohit's family. The male members of his immediate family would then proceed to Haridwar.

Haridwar, "God's door step", is an ancient city that abides at the shores of the sacred river Ganga. As the story goes, Ganga originates from the feet of God in heaven. At first, it descends on the head of Lord Shiva, who bears it on his head to slow down its magnanimous force, hence saving the world from flooding. The river falls slowly on the Himalayas; Gangotori is where it begins its benevolent journey to wash off sins of humans. Haridwar is the sacred land where Ganges serves as the receiving vessel of human remains after death, thereby purifying them by its touch.

Thousands of priests live in Haridwar. Each has a thick book that has been passed on to him for generations. The book contains family names and lists of all the ancestors who came to the holy city to ensure that the spirits of their loved ones were freed from the corporeal body by submerging the ashes and *phul* in the sacred river Ganga. Some ancient sage must have made a wise decision to name the bones of the dead as phul, *flowers*, definitely a more aesthetic nomenclature. It is less heartbreaking to say, "Let us throw *phul* in the Ganges" than "Let us throw the bones."

The soul then moves on wherever the deceased's karma or destiny determines, to yet another birth.

So, the first act upon arriving in Haridwar would be to search for the particular priest who carried out your ancestors' rituals. It is not too hard because every stall or shopkeeper has that knowledge.

"Pandit Sharma? No problem, Ji. Actually, Panditji died last year. Too sad. But his young son has taken over. Just go straight then turn where the sweets shop is, turn khaba, *left*, where ice cream *wala* stands, walk ten steps, not long, but short steps and his kholi, *small windowless room*, is on the sajja, *right*, opposite the Bawra cloth house."

You have to figure out which way you turn because the shop wala is not too sure which side is khaba and which is sajja.

You find the priest eventually with much investigation. The Panditji will open up a humungous book, with records of hundreds of years of ancestry of thousands of people; pages are yellow due to ageing. With a frown on his forehead, he turns the pages to find your family name.

"There, babuji, *sir*, your father had brought your grandfather's remains in the year 1939. And your dadaji, *paternal grandfather*, came in 1910 to fulfill his duty for your great grandfather . . ." He could go on, and you are too misty-eyed to stop him.

You are relieved. The deceased will find his rightful place amongst his long-departed paternal forefathers, and you have done your duty well. Now, if unfortunately you have no male descendent, the family tree is finished for good. The pertinent yellow pages are placed on shelves where multilayers of other humans' past lie, gathering dust. Perhaps on a later date, due to limitations of space, those pages are burnt and ashes thrown in the sacred river Ganga with utmost respect. Hopefully.

The priest then takes you to the white marble steps leading to the river. While he chants appropriate mantras, *verses from Scripture*, gently surrenders the *phul*, ashes, flowers, a lighted deeva, *a small earthen curved cup with oil and a wick of cotton lighted at the end*, into the welcoming embrace of Ganga, you sit on the wet white shiny steps, bury your face in your knees, and weep as never before. You want to jump in the river to be with your loved one, but the memory of grieving faces at home who need you, holds you back.

Chachaji took Meera's damp hand in his strong palms and stroked it gently. She could not even cry anymore, just felt numb, dead like a stone. Chachaji assumed an unusual no-nonsense manner.

"Meera, we humans are like birds. We are endowed with wings, metaphorically speaking, that have the power to lift us upwards away from the peril that constantly confronts us in life. The problem is we have no cognizance of this gift. We despair and cry for help from God who has already provided us with enough pussiance to conquer life. We are impotent to grasp the nature of His mercy. To receive strong light, we must possess strong eyes."

Meera sat like an immovable statue, unmoved by Chachaji's wise words that just flowed over her without penetrating. Chachaji sighed, waited for a minute, then continued, "Beti, *daughter*, there are two kinds of people. The first kind, when they hurt, they try to understand their pain in a larger context that encompasses all humanity: they generalize it and submerge their experience in the totality of consciousness. They realize the universality of pain and constantly spread their arms to embrace all human anguish by extending themselves and reaching outwards. They flow out into streams, joining other streams to make a roaring river that finally culminates its journey by merging in the sea. They lose their pain completely in this magnanimous act of uniting with the whole, absorbing others' pain as well as absolving their own.

"The other kind, the egoist, the ultimate *I* person, is hurt and drowns himself totally in his own pain. He will wallow in self-pity and end it there. To him, there are no connections, extensions, expansions, there is only condensation into his own little self. These people are the most wretched because they experience concentrated pain and have no rationalization mechanism to understand the universality of pain. They stink because they are like tiny ponds, or they reduce themselves to such. Their thinking is static, aware only of the painful moment at hand. They cannot move forwards, backwards, inwards, or outwards. Totally alone, devoid of any continuity with the past and future, their experience is utterly shallow. They cannot derive any wisdom from the past and incorporate it into the present, or a vision of the future to extend the present. Try to be like the former, Beti, and move outwards and forwards."

Chachaji's sagacious words mingled in a chaotic mix of emotions scattered around her like dust particles. Meera still stood on tremulous ground, painstakingly slow to regain her equilibrium.

- # -

"Ah." Kanchan wiped sweat from her face. "It is cool here, thank God."

A pretty young waitress, her blonde hair tied in a flailing ponytail, chirped cheerfully, "Hi, may I get you drinks?"

Kanchan and Satish responded simultaneously, "Root beer." They all laughed.

Meera had refused to try it. Dadi, *paternal grandmother*, had crinkled her nose in disgust. "In Vilayat, England people lose their minds and do bad things when they drink sharab, *liquor*. Swear to God, you will not touch it!"

How could she?

When told there was no alcohol, the question arose: why is it called *beer* then?

Prashant ordered 7-Up, and Meera looked up and smiled at the waitress. "Coke, of course."

During the summer holidays that were mostly spent at Tayaji's, *father's older brother*, house in Delhi, Meera and her siblings gravitated toward, cool air-conditioned, thickly draped semi-darkness of volgas or quality restaurant to escape the tortuous inferno during shopping at Cannaught Place. There was a greater attraction, the latest fad imported from the Western Hemisphere, namely Coca-Cola. Especial trips, in cold or heat, hail or storm, pedaling the bikes or walking strenuously for miles for a tall glass of Coke, were not uncommon.

Meera poked the straw in one of the floating ice cubes; it drowned in Coke but bounced right back. "I am with Mohit's friends, and he is not here."

Meera's creative excuses were dismissed as lame by Prashant. "Be ready at twelve-thirty." That was that.

Meera had been up quite early in the morning and had already performed the ritual of walking on the grass in the backyard.

Meera's nani, *maternal grandmother,* had indoctrinated the grandchildren to wake up at dawn and tread on the grass barefeet. The sparkling dew poised at the tips of the grass blades is a gift of the demiGoddess of night, who is the sister of the demi Goddess of knowledge. The celestial blessings seep into the soles of the feet, ascend to the brain, and immediately augment the "intelligence quotient."

Atul was born brilliant hence did not seek supplementary succor. But the rest of Meera's siblings and cousins were lagging behind in school, much to the chagrin of parents. The children had the insight that the low marks had nothing to do with lack of intelligence; it was the deficiency in toil. Yet it was worth trying.

Not finding the desired results within a week, all the kids quit, excepting Meera. Mesmerized by the awakening of nature, sheen of the pink sky of early dawn, the touch of dewy grass effused through her tiny body and made her ecstatic if not intelligent.

Sun was bright; Meera sought out shade to work under. Spade in hand, palloo tugged in front of her belly, she squatted on the grass, rooting out the weeds from the flower beds.

Anil and Sunil had kept Meera's garden in shape. Only now, after two months, she had taken over. It still hurt like hell. She buried her face in her knees and wept.

A bird chirped in the background, startling her. She looked up. The emerald leaves of trees and bushes flickered in the summer zephyr. Rose blossoms smiled at her. A coil of tension lifted from her heart.

Man is a queer creature. He would rather tromp around the globe in quest of joy rather than enjoy what is free and obvious, right in front of his eyes.

Wasn't the immaculately grand pulchritude of creation God-given potion to save man from life itself? For hope and restoration, He ensures eternal existence of nature; flowers in particular may perish, but blossoms in general are forever—with demise of one, many more take its place with ardor.

An impeccably aligned row of ducks flew against the summer aquamarine sky; their quacks resounded in its vast expanse. Through the cracks in the white wooden fence, Irene, the neighbor, who was lying on a garden chair half naked, shining with suntan lotion, said loudly, "Hi, Meera, what a lovely day for tanning."

"Of course," Meera assented amicably, though she had never figured out the why of this enigmatic rubric.

Blessed with a readymade tan, women in India never bare themselves on beaches or backyard to bathe in the fervid scintillation of the sun god. In fact, anyone caught performing this ritual would be immediately sacked away to an asylum for brain inspection.

Furthermore, in India, the complexion card can achieve great significance in girls' lives; not playing it right could lead to a serious condition called spinsterhood. Most prospective grooms prefer fair brides, perhaps a complex vengefully bequeathed by the departing British. A dark-complexioned girl, even if she is in possession of perfect facial features and curves at the right places, is doomed right from birth, mother taking the lead in deprecating her in public. "Bahenji, *sister*, you are so lucky. Your Mala is so fair, she will catch a rich groom! I ask God, What sin did I do? Who will marry this kali kaluti, *black*?" A deep sigh would follow.

Who is going to tell the mother that it is not God who should be blamed but the genetic pool of ancestors toward which she made serious contribution?

Meera raised her right arm towards her forehead and wiped the sweat off with her blouse sleeve. She thought of Mohit, then Jane.

"Where are you? Jane, call me."

At that very instant, the phone rang; her heart beat faster. Maybe it is her.

It was Prashant.

Meera could not believe that such torridity was possible in a place that resembled a deep freeze just a few months ago.

An elderly lady dressed in a halter top and a short skirt, her sagging wrinkled flesh wobbling joyfully, stopped and smiled at Meera condescendingly. "What a beautiful saree. Silk from India? I thought so. My sister and brother-in-law lived in India for many years."

Meera feigned interest. "Really?"

The lady's face clouded, "Of course they had to go back to England when India became independent. They did not want to go, you know. My brother-in-law was born in India."

"Yes, I understand." She had heard a similar saga from Paul.

Meera had strolled by the river for barely fifteen minutes when she felt tired and slumped on a wooden bench to catch her breath.

People walked by, cheery at the arrival of much awaited spring. Some smiled, said, "How are you?" and walked on.

The melodious murmur of the flowing river soothed her weary spirit; sunrays excursed through the pristine, translucent pale-green leaves of trees, splitting into shifting beams; birds exchanged cordialities much like their more evolved brethren, the *Homo sapiens.*

"Namaste, Bahenji," *Greetings, sister.* A jogger had stopped right in front of Meera. "Kya hal hai apka, *how are you*?"

Meera was startled at pure Hindi words pouring out of a unquestionably white mouth; she almost fell off the bench. He also brought his hands together in a typical Indian gesture of greeting. Speechless for a few moments, Meera laughed happily, "Namaste, *greetings,* wow, very good Hindi! Where did you learn it?"

Oddly enough, she spoke in English. He responded in Hindi, "Bharat me seekhi thi, *Learnt it in India.* Mai Missouri me rehta tha, *I lived in Missouri.* Mere Pitaji ek Padri they Girija me, *my father was a priest in a church.*"

It felt awesome. He employed some Hindi words that even Indians do not use anymore. They would say *church* not *girija* and *priest* instead of *padri.*

Paul, that was his name, sat by her and reminisced. His father had stuck to his guns if that expression could be applied for a God's man and tarried in India after Independence.

Paul spoke ruefully, "It was horrid to leave my country. My ma died of malaria when I was four years old. When Pitaji was away, my friends' mothers took care of me like their own. I was just ten when we left, I cried a lot. Pitaji stroked my hair and said, 'Son, we have to go. We will go to a brand-new place. That would be fun, eh?' I did not want fun. I wanted my friends and auntys."

Paul overcame his emotion. "When our ship landed at London, I thought we were on a different planet—only white faces! For a long time, I searched for some brownness in the crowds. Pitaji was very lonely, I realized when I grew up. I was a young boy and adapted, but he never felt at home in a land that was so foreign to his heart. For him, England remained a foreign country till the end."

David uncle had told Papa, "Mr. Yadav, my father, his paternal family, my siblings and cousins were all born and raised in India! We want to be buried in our motherland beside our ancestors. We had nothing to do with British Empire! We supported the cause of freedom because it was just. Can we not live here as Indians, as part of this ancient civilization that we love? Gandhi's India will have some room for us, wouldn't it?"

Gandhi was dead, and ordinary people were not Gandhi. They glanced angrily at the British. "What are you still doing here? We threw you out, remember?"

Slowly, the collective virulence broke David uncle's will. They left for a foreign country, England, that was supposed to be their homeland.

David uncle and Rachel Aunty belonged to the landscape of Meera's early childhood. David was heavy built, tall, always dressed in suit and a felt hat. His free open laughter was much like Dadaji, *paternal grandfather*, Papa said.

They lived on the first floor of the same house where Meera's family lived. Rachel Aunty was very fair, her blue eyes sparkled; actually, Meera had a crush on her. She baked cakes and puddings and sent them to Meera's family.

When Ma apologized for the racket kids made, Rachel Aunty smiled, dimples appearing on her pink cheeks, "Oh no, Mrs. Yadav, I love your children. Mine are grown-up and gone, let them be."

After moving to Rai Saheb's house in Summer Hill, Meera's family went to visit David and Rachel. A brown face poked out of the door, "Yes?"

David and Rachel had left for England in a hurry. Their son was ill.

The brown man laughed ungraciously. "What a deal I got for this house!"

"Well, well, that is life. But are you not hot in the saree, dear?" the old lady asked curiously.

Meera smiled. "Thank you, but I am so used to it."

She agreed readily. "Of course, of course. Bye for now," and rambled slowly, painfully, indicating arthritis. At that point, Meera noticed that everyone around her was scantily dressed; their glances revealed amusement. Kanchan laughed. "Really, Meera, even I am not used to saree anymore, I would boil." Meera actually started to feel uncomfortable and hot.

Prashant assured her casually, "Don't listen to them. You look lovely in the pink saree."

Meera blushed and blurted thanks in a confused, rusted voice that confounded Prashant who, unable to do much else, just whistled and looked away.

A couple of little boys hopped around and ran in front of Meera, looking back to stare at her.

Their mom shouted, "Watch where you go, stupid."

To compensate for the jarring crudeness, Meera looked condescendingly at the boys, who grinned and ran away.

At a distance, native women and children strolled with a slow gait. Meera was not conversant with Native American history. In the English school she went to, the teachers taught English and European history along with Indian history even after the British left. It took Meera years to wipe off British version of Indian history from her psyche and replace it with the real stuff.

It was through Marco's political ramblings at one of Mohit's office parties that Meera learned, much to her surprise, that the only authentic Canadians in Canada were the First Nations. The rest arrived as a consequence of a tired blundering Columbus, who set out to find spices, fine muslin, and gold in India but stumbled on the land later called America. He opened the gateway for later immigrants escaping their varied destinies.

Meera was thoroughly amused at the discovery that she was, in fact, East Indian, a nonexistent nomenclature in India. She was struck by the similarity in appearance between North Himalayan locals of India and the Red Indians of Canada. The histories of the two distantly located peoples run parallel; both civilizations are ancient, realized the spiritual dimension of existence early in their development. The Red Indians retained their spiritualism to the present day. India lost it for the most part with the various invasions, Tamur lane, Turks, Mughals, and British. Modern Indian himself dealt the final death blow, in the name of Westernization or progress after India gained freedom from foreign powers finishing the job for them.

Both nations were conquered by the colonials' golden policy of divide and rule. Both have been called uncivilized savages.

Few distortions of history have been as gross as the popular nineteenth-century British conception of civilized Englishman introducing law and erudition to barbaric India.

Much before Athens became the hubbub of learning and wisdom, gurus, *spiritual teachers,* and shishyas, *students,* in India renounced the world of craving and glitter and lived in gurukuls, *teacher's abode,* in straw huts tucked away in the bosom of remote jungles. Squatted on the green grass under shady mango or pippal tree, they meditated on the dazzling display of Divine creativity that surrounded them. They gazed at the twinkling stars at night and the aureate sun in the daytime and unraveled the mystery of existence as well as the Divine behind the creation.

Reality surrendered itself and revealed the truth to their chaste consciousness that had achieved unity with the Absolute God. During those ecstatic moments of revelation, the principles of ethics, morality, the nature of Reality of existence, God and spirit, as well as astronomy, astrology, grammar, mathematics, metaphysics, and psychology were penned for posterity.

Prashant waved to someone.

"Prashant, can't you go anywhere without bumping into someone waving at you? Now do not start heavy socializing, we have to go to Bela Bhabi's, *friend's wife,* after," Satish cautioned him.

Apparently, the guy was mighty gregarious himself; he sauntered toward their table. After introducing him to Satish and Kanchan, Prashant turned to Meera, "She is my late friend Mohit's wife, Meera."

Paul's green eyes softened. "I am so very sorry, Meera. Prashant raves about how wonderful Mohit was. It is a great loss."

Meera nodded politely, looked down at the ice cubes, much diminished by now but still floating exuberantly in the glass of Coke.

Paul looked at Meera intently, his voice was low. "It is strange, I saw Mohit that day in a bar."

Everyone was startled in unison. "No, man! Mohit did not drink!" Prashant blurted out.

"Maybe he was with a client?" Satish asked.

"No, he was alone. I was with a client. It was late afternoon, it was not too crowded."

They sat in stunned silence.

Paul's vision inverted inward to confirm the facts etched in his memory.

"He did look distraught," he continued. "The next day I found out about his accident."

Satish looked at Meera questioningly.

She fought with her tears, fumbling to find words to contradict him. Mohit hated drinks, why is Paul lying? Her heart pounded against her chest fiercely, but Meera held herself back.

Prashant was agitated. "Paul, are you sure it was him? You have met him only once? He did not touch drinks, man."

"It was him all right," Paul was apologetic but resolute.

Turning toward Meera, Paul said, "I am sorry again. Please take care. Bye, Prashant, nice meeting you all." He smiled at Kanchan and Satish.

Satish asked Meera softly, "Did anything happen that day to upset him? A call from India?"

She nodded negatively without looking up. The ice cubes had dissolved, annihilated, like Mohit.

"Now listen." Satish was older, he could advise. "Don't think about it, it will not change anything."

Kanchan echoed, "Meera, he is right."

Prashant just looked down.

Meera was devastated. Paul had dealt a death blow to her adamant repudiation of the hospital report that there was alcohol in Mohit's blood. Denial had certainty, comfort, and closure.

She raised her head, "Satish Bhai, *brother*, tell me the truth, was he diagnosed with some serious illness?"

"Of course not!"

Meera groped in the darkness of confusion, "Maybe he was fired?"

Prashant said gently, "Please do not get caught in this conundrum. It is insolvable, leave it."

She did not go to Bela's.

Meera phoned Hans the next day. "Please tell me the truth, was Mohit fired?"

"Are you crazy?" he almost shouted. "He was the best man in our team!"

- # -

Meera pulled the car out of the garage. Irene waved hi and disappeared behind the lush golden alder bush in the corner of her front yard.

In India, it is not so easy to get out of the house. The neighbor aunty is curious. "Where are you going? Don't be too late, come before dark. Beti, you have to protect yourself being a girl and all! Can't Atul go with you? Bhai, I couldn't let Sheela go alone. Where is your ma? Does she know?"

Aunty's little chubby pink-cheeked daughter, wearing a short frock and ponytails, jumps in circles around you. "Didi, can I come with you, can I, can I? I will be good. Can I, Mommy, please?"

At this juncture, Grandpa, who is reading the newspaper for the tenth time, emerges from the far end of the veranda, hoping for some thrill in his otherwise prosaic existence. He implores you with a toothless sucked-in-cheeks, anxious face, "It is cold tonight, Meera. Take a shawl with you. Do not catch cold," simultaneously wrapping a gray shawl tightly around his drooping shoulders, to ward off that eventuality for himself. He nods his gray head vigorously for emphasis, or does he always shake due to Parkinson's? She could not figure it out.

The uncle is returning from the office, looking jaded but stops. "How is your papa? I heard he came home early? Is he okay? I could take him to the doctor if he needs?"

Aunty pounces on him with great satisfaction. "Look at you? You come home so late and then try to be goody-goody? If Bhai sahib, *respected brother*, needed help, you should have come home early? Every day late, every day late," she grumbles on.

If you are already late for wherever you are heading, it could be annoying. But now, she missed the intruding conviviality of the chatty neighbors.

Meera could not sleep with anguish and doubt. Why would Paul lie? What if he was speaking the truth? On their wedding night, Mohit had embraced Meera in his arms and promised to love her and speak the truth, always.

Before Meera could ring the doorbell, Chachaji opened the door and whispered, "Just come in, I will not be long." They both tiptoed upstairs to his room. Asha was sleeping in; disturbing her was like putting your hand in a beehive.

Meera held a belief that all human actions are guided by an uncomplex, logical, cosmic ordinance; goodness giveth, goodness receiveth. Chachaji was a caring father to Asha; she responded with disdainful hauteur that was obvious to everyone. Meera was initiated into the real world where human nature is infinitely more intricate to fit into any elementary precept of equivalence.

Chachaji remained unruffled.

According to J. C. Campbell, twentieth-century philosopher, Absolute is a full circle—no beginning, no end. But it has a center. Humans are miniature replicas of the Absolute macrocosm. Chachaji said he had found his center; he could plunge in the depths of his being and attain unchallenged peace.

The very first time Meera met Chachaji at Bela's party, he sat back comfortably in a corner and closed his eyes, often his lips moved. She knew he was silently chanting Gayatri mantra, *an important verse from Hindu scriptures.*

Rishi Vishwamitra was a king before he became a sage. His cows, hundreds of them, grazed on the land around the ashram, *abode of gurus,* of Rishi Vashishth. The pupils seized the opportunity to escape from the rigors of exploring the esoteric truths of existence hidden in the labyrinthine pages of scriptures; abandoning the books, they repeatedly chased the cows out of the grounds with obvious enthusiasm. Rishi Vashishta sent a disciple to Raja Vishwamitra's court with a request that the cow herders be stopped from bringing the cows to his ashram.

Vishwamitra not only refused but arrogantly challenged Vashishta, "If you are such a great sage, don't you have power over mere cows?"

Vashistha was a godly man of high order; showing off his prepotency to others was not his favored activity. But challenged thus, he did.

The cows decided to stay around the ashram. Vishwamitra's armies could not budge them. The excited pupils had a heyday with ample milk and butter with their otherwise austere meals.

Humiliated by his impotence, Vishwamitra relinquished his kingdom, went to a jungle, and started to meditate on the demiGoddess Gayatari.

She was pleased and appeared in due course. "I am pleased by your devotion, my son. Ask for any *boon*."

He fell at her feet. "I want power over the whole universe."

Gayatri smiled. "Son, only God possesses that kind of infinite omnipotence." However, she did give him something. "You will be Sidh, *fulfilled spritualist*—such a man rules over his own 'Self,' hence, no one can subdue him."

Meera was mesmerized by the calm glow on Chachaji's still features. He opened his eyes and laughed gently in embarrassment. "Beti, I like to take hold of my inner chaos and smooth it on a constant basis. When I die, I don't want to leave any wrinkles on my soul."

After settling Chachaji on the garden chair on the patio, Meera proposed, "A cup of tea could make our world perfect."

Chachaji smiled. "Amen."

It was a relatively calm day in a valley where winds often got trapped and swirled at uncomfortable speeds, making walking difficult for the weight-challenged humans; they had to hold on to the normal people for fear of being blown away. Hendersonville was the only place where you could find newspapers flying around in the air and plastic bags hanging by the trees.

White flower clusters of small wild roses, maroon dahlias, mauve delphiniums, white and red petunias sparkled against the deep-green background of sunbathed leaves. Gentle wind brushed against the flamboyant blooms, dispersing their redolence in celebration of life. A few birds, with round orange bellies, hopped at a safe distance in the grass, their wee heads jerked and eyes blinked rapidly in search of manna.

The mauve roses set in a vase on the dining table had wilted. Vaultra and Hans had dropped by last week and brought exquisitely unique-colored roses for her. Meera's face shone with glee. "Vaultra, thanks so much. How did you know I love roses?"

Vaultra smiled sadly. "Mohit had once mentioned your craze for roses."

Mohit's office friends had been calling her on regular basis, to check on her. Marco Giovanni and voluptuous Sally had come a month ago. Before he could start up his usual political musings, Sally warned him sternly, "Don't you start anything. We have to go soon." He understood.

Meera made pakoras, *deep fried snack*, for Hans and Vaultra, unspiced because she was not sure about their tolerance level. Hans bit into the first pakora and exclaimed, "Nice, but where is the tang?"

Vaultra laughed. "Hans lived in Vancouver for several years. He knew a Sikh family. He invited himself to their house often."

"How about you?" Meera inquired.

"I had to learn. He makes me use cumin, turmeric, ginger, garlic, and the rest in everything I cook. He loves Indian food to the point that when we were invited to a potluck and asked to bring our ethnic food, guess what he took?"

"What?"

"Curried chicken!"

About flowers, an unknown sage had written, "Sun radiates its light. Wind breathes prana, *life force*. Flowers shower their ambrosia to sinner and pious alike. O man, give your love to one and all without judging." Indeed one's self is the foremost beneficiary of one's own fragrance; others acquire what they are capable of.

Chachaji is waiting for a cup of tea Meera promised, but a spurious thorn has impeded the flow of her own redolence to herself.

Doorbell rang in an impatient succession; the gang of Meera's friends stood on the doorstep. Excepting Prashant, who had his hands tucked in his pockets, as always, everyone else carried a pot in their hands.

Meera grinned widely at the much-needed company but protested, "This is not fair! You don't even let me cook for you!" Prashant shrugged his shoulders. "Actually, we want to eat good food, just couldn't take a chance with your—" Before he could finish, Bela feigned annoyance. "Aré, how dare you insult your host, she cooks well. Chalo apologize!"

Much gratified by the rise from Bela, Prashant pretended to look punished, bowed down, and held his ears. Meera laughed, "Okay, okay, I forgive you. But next time, consequences could be severe!" Kanchan added, "No food for the evening!" Anil protested, "Don't kill him, yar, *friend*, that would be cruel!"

Meera could not figure Prashant out. He was the joker, easygoing, his lips always stretched wide in readiness to laugh. And yet every time he looked at her, she sensed a raging storm approaching her; he seemed to hold it back to protect her.

Bela Di, *sister*, had dropped comments like, "You should have seen him before, he was mast, *carefree*. His contentedness seeped into others . . . he is only a shadow now. Bhai, what can we do?" Meera did not know why she was afraid to probe into detail. She was awestruck by his mettle and ashamed of her own decrepitude.

Bela was condescending. "Meera, we women find nothing wrong with accepting pain and crying over it. Prashant bottled his agony and had a major breakdown."

Mohit and Di both had an inner intuitive quality of knowing what to say at the right time.

Chachaji called from outside, "What happened to my tea, Ji?" The whole gang was surprised. "Chachaji is here?" And they immediately trodded toward the backyard with hasty steps.

Meera put a pot on the stove to make halwa, *a dessert*. It was an easy dessert; Mohit liked it.

Bela walked in the kitchen. "Meera, we are moving inside. These men, especially Prashant, are so loud, your neighbor may call the police. Let me take the bowl." She sniffed it and looked happy. "Smells tasty, Meera. What did you put in it, cardamom and pistachio? You have to give me the recipe."

Meera laughed. "Don't put me on, Di. This is your recipe."

Kanchan appeared. "Can I take something, anything?"

Meera asked, "Di, where is Anita?" Then turned to Kanchan, "And Rohini?"

Bela Di shrugged her shoulders. "Aré, it is Vimmy's birthday, Anita and Rohini had to be dropped off. Actually, Anita loves to come to your place. But you know Neelima, *toba*, such sharp tongue. She would slice me with it if Anita did not go."

Di took the bowl of halwa to the living room then came back with the vase of purple roses in her hand. She wrinkled her nose in disgust. "Meera, these look so ugly—all dried up and discolored. Why didn't you throw them?"

Meera found it cruel to pluck flowers from their mother branch. And it was even more cold-blooded to discard them after they had lavished their all for human pleasure. How could she tell Di?

"Throw them, Di."

"Kanchan, you can take plates and cutlery, please."

Meera installed teapot, mugs, sugar, and milk in a large silver tray and followed Di and Kanchan

Chachaji was sitting in lotus position on the couch and speaking softly, "The trouble is, Satish, that skeptic's starting point is a total denial of God's existence. By not wanting to know the Truth, he has already closed the door to the light of God's knowledge. Thus, he confines himself to only half of world of possible existence: the facts of soul, ideal, and God are lost to him. And yet we are aware of spiritual facts just as directly and indubitably as we are aware of physical facts. In fact, there are more spiritual than bodily experiences.

"The believers' faith is founded on their personal experiences and intuition, that is a higher faculty of perception, the sixth sense. Satish, you base your repudiation on inadequate tools like senses and science. Actually, the believers have subjective evidence of God's existence, but skeptics have no proof of His nonexistence.

"There is only one way to find the truth: you have to educate yourself. As you go deep into the formulations and conceptualization of God in the Upanishads, *the essence of Hindu philosophy*, you find that the development of thought is logical and rational. The idea of 'God' is not as far-fetched as you think. Try treading the same path that has been trodden by sages, Rishis saints, mystics, and the religious believers who have experienced God directly. If at the end of your journey you do not find Him, then you can fairly claim that God does not exist. But you have to seek him at the right place. If you look for Him as you look at this table and chair, you will be disappointed. Ask the right questions to arrive at the right answers. Start with reading the scriptures."

Satish became contemplative; his tone was more profound, less challenging, "Chachaji, once I did try to read an Upanishad, a thick one."

"Must be Brihadaranyaka."

"I ran into problems because it did not make any sense. It seemed unreal, insubstantial."

Sunil agreed. "I had the same difficulty. Rishis who wrote them obviously ran amok with their flight of imagination."

Prashant quipped, "That is why I don't even bother, why waste time? More halwa, Meeraji!" Everyone ignored him; Meera smiled and put some halwa in his plate. Prashant was gratified. "That is better, now, what do you say to that, Chachaji?"

Chachaji laughed softly. "I know exactly what you are saying. In early writings of Vedas, *ancient Hindu scriptures*, and later Upanishads, *the essence of Hindu philosophy*, there is a profuse usage of mythology that is interwoven in the fabric of the main narrative. Inspired by God's glory, a fountainhead of incisive, trenchant poetry sprang forth from the Rishis' spirits and Hindu scriptures were created. Poetry is nothing but a flight of fancy that carries the truth adorned in the garb of metaphors and similes. Mythological story forms were used to illustrate the essence of the poems.

"But in those ancient times, children spent their early years exclusively to learn the meaning behind ancient texts. Erudite gurus in gurukuls had ample chance to expound the complex conceptualizations regarding the nature of Reality. Presently, we are left with written musings full of penetrating brilliance but shrouded in dust of ignorance. There are no gurus competent enough to wipe the dirt and let the truth shine."

"Chachaji, shouldn't Reality and Truth be more visible, more straightforward for us to grasp?"

"It is simple. But we overlook it because we have no idea what we are looking for. At harvesttime, you have a pile of straw and some seeds, all intermixed. The knowledgeable farmer culls the precious seeds and discards the rest. Mythology is a mixed bag of seed of truth and chaffe of mythology. The wise knows what the seed looks like and gathers it. The skeptic does not recognize the seed, gets embroiled in the mound of hay, bent on proving it useless.

"It is all about finding the essence, the hub of the wheel of truth. The usage of mythology was an integral component in the early development of thought in all older civilizations. The concretization of our thought processes, much due to stress on the exclusivity of empiricism, has clipped the wings of our minds. Our intellect is trapped in the cage of science. It cannot fly beyond it into the realm of infinity.

"Mythology is important because it does not contradict but accentuates Reality unless we mistake mythology for Reality. We have missed the point then.

"*Katha Upanishad* describes five ashwas, *horses*, pulling a carriage with a driver and a person sitting in the carriage. The five ashwas are our five senses carrying our 'body,' the carriage. The driver is man's mind, and the person sitting in the carriage is our 'Soul.' The message is for the soul to make decisions, for the mind to hold the reign tight, direct the senses, for a smooth ride in life.

"Malcolm Muggeridge, Christianity's acclaimed champion of this century, reflected that he did not know if there was a virgin birth and did not care. He did not know if the rock moved from the tomb, it was not important. To him the truth was 'nailed at the crossroads of eternity—in living we die and in dying we live.' He had separated the chaffe from the seed."

Meera was dazzled by the depth of Chachaji's erudition and extent of his humility the first time she met him.

- # -

Mohit sat by Meera on the bed and gently stroked her thick black, shining-with-coconut-oil hair and broke it to her with a familiar twinkle in his eyes, "There is no getting out of it, so better wear a lovely saree and look elegant for the occasion."

Meera looked at him incredulously, dropped on the bed like a truncated tree, buried her face in the soft white pillow and moaned, "No, no!"

She was weepy, drained, jet-lagged, and beleagured by an exotic mix of emotions that pulled her in two opposite directions. The very thought of facing a crowd of Mohit's friends before she could extricate herself out of the precarious tenor of spirit scared her out of her wits.

Contrary to everyone's cautionary forewarnings, Meera procured her visa within two weeks after her marriage. Mohit had an uncle whose son-in-law's cousin's brother-in-law's uncle's son worked in the Canadian embassy. The influential relatives of relatives are absolutely indispensible for the precarious workings of the wheel of life in India.

The chaos in the guest room of Tayaji's house in Delhi was akin to a disaster area; clothes, gifts, sandals, packs of bhujia, *snack*, were scattered all over the place. An open, half-filled suitcase lay on the bed; Meera was folding the blouses that she bought to match with the silk sarees she received as gifts at the wedding.

Asha lifted the curtain and walked briskly, "Choti, I don't think you have quite enough sweaters."

Mohit was folding his shirt. "Bhabi, she will be fine, plenty of sweaters in Canada."

Atul knocked. Asha laughed. "Mohitji, this courtesy is for you, normally he just barges in."

Atul feigned disapprobation, "Aré, what are you telling Mohit against me? Mohit you know these women should never be trusted. What do they say, you know, triya chritra, *women's pretensions*?"

Meera took a cushion and threw it at him. "Bhai, don't you fill innocent Mohitji with this garbage."

Asha pushed Ahul out of the room and followed him, "Choti, you better finish the packing. In the evening, relatives are coming, and we have to be at the airport at 8:00 p.m. to check in."

Meera turned her face sideways to hide her tears and picked up a saree to put in the suitcase.

Mohit came from behind, placed his hands tenderly on her shoulders, and said, "Meera, it is quite normal to feel this way, we all do. But you will be fine."

Meera was touched by his sensitivity; if he continues to behave this well, life should be okay. She smiled at the thought.

The plane had taken off from New Delhi airport at 10:00 p.m. in the pitch of darkness of the skies; lights of Delhi twinkled like stars.

Soon the plane was flying over Pakistan airspace. The captain's voice quivered as he made the announcement; it was likely that he was born in Pakistan before partition, *at the time of India's freedom from the British Raj, India was partitioned into secular India and religious Pakistan.* Meera looked down. Lahore is at the border fifteen miles away from Amritsar. Meera peeped down and wondered which of the flickering lights belonged to the house where she was born.

Meera leaned her head against the back of the seat and shut her weary eyes.

Mohit and Meera were hopelessly fagged even before embarking on their journey. The never-ending shopping, a steady flow of relatives and friends, lack of sleep due to incessant talking and occasional weeping through the hot nights. No one paid any attention to the dazed and sleepy Papa and Tayaji, who would straggle slowly into the bedroom where everyone was huddled on two beds and order everyone in a meager voice to go to sleep.

Mohit got up from his seat to stretch his legs. "Excuse me," he smiled apologetically as he squeezed in front of a white-haired lady to get to the aisle. The old lady raised her white shriveled head sleepily, her annoyance indubitably manifested on her wrinkled visage.

"Sorry, my husband disturbed you," Meera said humbly; the lady was instantly mollified. She turned her head and scanned Meera with her slit narrow blue eyes, her vision settled on her dazzling jewelry.

Dadi, *paternal grandmother*, knowing full well how much Meera disliked gold, commanded her right after the wedding. "Nai dulhan, *new bride*, has to look beautiful for her husband. Otherwise, his eyes wander. Understand?"

Meera endeavored to secure some sleep without any inkling that it was an illogical goal. How can you slumber when every fifteen minutes you are subjected to the agonizing "Chinese" torture by some trivial announcement by a gruff-sounding, though sincere, captain? None of the passengers are remotely concerned about the speed of the plane, the weather, temperature, direction and velocity of the wind, etc. They are busy twisting and turning, bending and folding in diverse positions in the futile attempt to get comfortable in the paltry seat and catch a nap if not sleep. By the time they figure out the most appropriate configuration of their bodies for a siesta and sigh with relief at the sheer possibility, there is a warning of food; the cranking of carts offering scotch and vodka at some Godforsaken hour. Just because it happens to be dinnertime in Iran when you fly over it, why should you be punished to eat while your stomach is in a relaxed mode at midnight India time?

The food distribution over, you immediately adjust your puny cushion, get under a thorny rough blanket, adjust your body curves, and hope against all odds for an undisturbed small snooze. But no, at that very moment, turbulence chooses to rock the plane, startling you. "Fasten seat belts" blink in front of your sleepy eyes. You grip the sides of your seat, too afraid to yawn or even sweat profusely if this is your first time flying. Thankfully, after an hour or two of mental anguish, turbulence happily moves on to more meaningful parts of the atmosphere.

You are tough and optimistic and still hang on to hope for a short quiet time to gather yourself. You may get a few minutes before the person sitting beside you decides to go to the bathroom. He crosses over your knees while you fold them unto yourself from an illogical fear of foreign legs touching yours in spite of the barrier of two sets of pants.

Another turbulence comes and passes on quietly, but do not get too felicitous. It is time to fill the customs card for disembarking at an airport of the country where you are changing planes. That done with utmost difficulty, using slumbering hands, the light from above shining too brightly on your folding table, vision is unfocused because your handbag containing your glasses is tucked away far under the seat, the captain's victorious voice resonates, "We are now landing."

Changing planes, enduring what felt like an eternal wait at London, Toronto, and Vancouver airports, the muffled incoherent announcements by seemingly-suffering-from-a-bad throat announcer, mixed phonetic babble of different languages and tortuous lineups had finished Meera off.

Bela Di, *sister*, opened the door and her arms, in that order, and hugged Meera warmly. She was plump and short; a wide grin adorned her round, fair face. A big red bindi, *red dot on married women's forehead*, shone smack in the center of her forehead, reminding Meera of kanta masi, *aunt*.

"Come on in, we are all waiting for the nai dulhan. Did you have problems walking on the snow? It is so cold. You must have brought cold from Simla! I have never been there, but I hear it is beautiful. So snow is not new for you, eh? Oh, you look so lovely. You got this saree from Delhi only?"

Sunil appeared from behind and scolded Bela. "Aré, are you going to let them stand in the doorway and freeze? Come in please." He shivered, making his point more poignant.

The foyer was spacious. A closet for coats was situated on the right side; on the left a mat lay on the floor where winter boots of different brands, colors, sizes, and styles were scattered around. A painting of a peacock gleefully displaying his multicolored fan, the myriad eyes scanning the world, hung on the wall above. The peacock danced in a picturesque garden that was full of vivid lush trees covered with glowing deep-green leaves, ornamental bushes, and plants with vibrant kaleidoscope flowers.

The foyer led into a small corridor ending in a door, which opened into the kitchen; on the left, stairs went upstairs and on the right, cheerful chatter floated indicating a living room.

"Come, come, don't be shy Beti. Sunilji, hang this scarf also."

Mellifluous, subdued music greeted them at the entrance of the living room. Meera focused and instantly recognized Ravi Shankar playing on sitar, *a string instrument,* "Raga Darbari." This raga, *musical composition,* is a composition that rang often in the darbars, *courts,* of rajas and Mughal badshahs *emperors.* A spirited evening Raga, it can conjure up images of gleaming, soft, silk apparels, dazzling jewelry, and the glittering brilliance of bejeweled crowns; the intoxicating scent of exotic, extravagant perfumes imported from Persia; the lush green lawns illuminated by gold painted lamps while gaudy flamboyant flowers transported from Turkish mountains effuse their exalting aroma in the luxurious environ around. Small, noiseless fountains spew clear pearls into the seductive night air; cool rays of the full moon shine in the eyes of fair maidens, whose tinkling laughter can bring crowns at their fair feet. The aureate waves of celestial music embrace and drench you in the sweet nectar of life.

What else is ecstasy?

Listening to the Indian classical music could take you by your hand and walk you through the past centuries. You can hear the clatter of horseshoes on the narrow, stone-paved alleys, small red brick houses and straw huts, a mosque on the right then a temple on the left, prattle of youngsters playing and yelling on the street. You ignore the mundane and go toward the fort that soars against the horizon. It appears hazy because the dust roused by horseshoes when they strike the dirt pathway blocks your vision. A wave of breeze moves across the lush fields air touches your hot, excited cheeks. Soon your carriage is at the gigantic, metallic gates guarded by two, or more during wartime, formidable, awe-inspiring musclemen decked with shining spears and swords. Your carriage goes in unimpeded if you are wealthy and currently on good terms with the badshah.

At the gate of the palace, two milder guards, their swords much smaller, help you alight. You pretend not to notice them and walk straight through marble corridors, lined by bright-red Persian carpet, marble pillars, gold statues, satiny curtains hanging everywhere, and arrive at the heart of the Mughal empire, the darbar. That is where the best musicians from the whole country converge for the pleasure of the Badshah. Music was the second most revered item of those times, the emperor himself topping the list.

In one such darbar, the last emperor of the Mughal empire, Bahadur Shah Jaffar, a renowned poet and musician, was captured by the British and exiled to Rangoon, Burma—a sad demise of Mughal rule and a sadder commencement of the British Raj.

It is more than ironic that the music created by ancient Hindu sages, in their state of transcendence and union with God found such understanding and appreciation by Muslim, Mughal badshahs. Before Mughals' arrival on the Indian soil, classical music and dancing were exclusively associated with worship in temples.

Being tempermentally aesthetic, beauty in any form enthralled the badshahs; they brought classical Indian music from the circumscription of temples in the open—at least available to the elite who gathered in the darbars. The music was sung unchanged from its original form as compiled in the ancient Hindu scripture called Samved, *a Hindu scripture with all musical compositions.* The lyrics are devotional, not addressing Allah but glorifying Bhagwan, *Hindu name for God.* The erudite badshahs understood that Bhagwan and Allah are the same, just addressed differently in the two languages. Many of the badshahs belonged to a sect of Islam called Suffi. The tenents of Suffism are akin to Vaishnav sect of Hinduism; both the believers are devotional and seek union with God in the present existence by surrending their own egos to the Absolute God.

Meera stepped into the living room amidst loud greetings and teasing laughter; women immediately started to comment on her lovely turquoise silk saree with a gold border and sapphire-studded gold necklace and earings. Everyone stood and folded their hands.

A reintroduction followed. They all understood. As soon as Mohit and Meera had emerged from customs, a bunch of excited friends literally swamped them, hugs and all, started to tease the couple rather loudly without delay, overwhelming Meera.

She was mortified. "Your friends must be feeling sorry for you, having brought such a cold wife all the way from India. I couldn't even respond to their warmth!"

Holding Di's hand, with modest steps and a bashful demeanor, Meera walked around the spacious well-lighted living room. Arun and Maalti, Vijeyta and Rahul, Anil and Asha, Satish and Kanchan, Nazma and Ahmed were couples. Prashant was the only lone one.

Meera greeted Nazma and Ahmed with a smile, "As-Salaam-alaikum," a Muslim greeting; quite surprised, they grinned refreshingly. "Wa-alaikum-salaam!"

Suddenly she found herself standing in front of an elderly but well-built man who was sitting on a sofa in a quiet corner, dressed simply in a traditional cotton dhoti and kurta, *a cloth wrapped from waist falling around ankles and a loose shirt.* She half heard Bela Di, "This is our Jagat Chachaji, *universal uncle,* Anil's dad." She laughed amicably.

Meera spontaneously stepped forward and touched his feet. He smiled gratefully, placed his aged but firm hand on her bent head, and gave her beautiful blessings that elderly people in India carry at the tip of their tongues to be dished out generously at short notice to appropriate recipients.

Chachaji's, laughter was unusually soft for a man of his stature. "Beti, *daughter,* it feels rather good to be revered. Not because I am worthy but because it is heartening to know that the art of reverence is still alive." Of course, this practice, like many other venerable traditions, is the victim of the cynicism of modern times. Young people of today grumble, "Why show respect to old people, they don't always deserve it!"

In ancient times, the one who received feet touching made sure that he did deserve the esteem.

A young man was returning home after twelve long years of education at the gurukul, *teacher's abode.* His father saw the beloved son from a window as he approached the house with animated steps. The young man knocked at the door, impatiently. His mother opened the door, tears flowing on her cheeks, she hugged him tight. He bent and touched her feet and received the appropriate blessings.

The father was nowhere to be found.

There was no trace of him for twelve long years. One day, he reappeared suddenly. The son asked in puzzlement, "Baba, *father,* where did you go? I have been waiting!"

A contented smile playing on the father's face, he replied, "Son, when I saw you from the window twelve years ago, the glow of Brahmvidya, *knowledge of the Absolute God,* shone on your forehead. I asked myself if I was worthy to have a God's man touch my feet. I knew I was not. To be on par with you, I went away to a guru to Realize Enlightenment. Now you can touch my feet, and I will bless you."

The ancient custom of feet touching is considered highly spiritual and holds a great significance. It bestows humility to the one who touches feet and humanity to the other whose feet are touched because the latter has to rise above himself and confer blessings.

Ahmed couldn't wait for Meera to settle down. "Meeraji, Mohit tells me you were born in Lahore?"

"Yes, Bhai." She looked at him curiously; unfeigned delight flashed in his black eyes.

"You are truly my sister then! I was also born in Lahore!" Everyone looked felicitous at the unlikely coincidence.

"What about you, Nazmaji?" Mohit looked at Ahmed's wife. Stunningly attractive, as most Muslim girls are reputed to be, her voice matched her beauty.

"I was born in Gujerat," she said sweetly.

Meera threw her modesty in the winds and gasped with disbelief. "Goodness, that's where my Dadaji, *paternal grandfather,* and papa are from."

"Really?" both Ahmed and Nazma said spontaneously.

"Small world, I'd say." Prashant had been quiet too long. He made an attempt to enter into the conversation.

"Nazma Didi, tell me the name of your Dadaji and Abba, *father.* I will ask Papa. Maybe they were friends!"

"Very likely," Ahmed chuckled.

Nazma was cool. "My Dadaji's name was Muhamed Baksh and Baba's Hashim Baksh!"

Meera turned to Ahmed with lively expectancy. "Where did your Valid Saheb, *father,* settle in India after partition?"

An estranged silence fell over the bright room that suddenly seemed dark. A brush of incertitude wiped the thrill off Ahmed's face. He looked at Mohit; he smiled reassuringly.

Ahmed overcame his conundrum. "Meeraji, we live in Pakistan. My Valid Saheb decided to stay in Lahore. All our relatives are there." Meera's smile all but disappeared.

The issue of Kashmir had been an acicular thorn between India and Pakistan ever since partition. India's government blamed Pakistan for constant border violations and skirmishes. Also the massacre of partition still had crushing grip on the Indian's psyche.

At that point, Indians were not too pleased with Pakistan. Dark shadow clouded Meera's face. She looked searchingly at Ahmed's eyes; they were unapologetic, candid, and transparent.

"Meeraji, to this day, my family and I mourn the anguish experienced by millions of Hindus and Muslims during partition. My Abba, *father,* helped all his Hindu and Sikh friends escape to the border to Armistrar. I feel deeply apologetic for what Muslims did."

Meera knew he meant it.

All reservations melted, a calm descended in her voice, "Ahmed Bhai, Hindus and Sikhs were equally guilty."

A sharp voice shattered the air of conciliation, "God is a curse on humanity!"

All necks turned in that direction. Bela was shocked, "Aré, don't talk like that, Satish!"

He threw up his hands in the air. "What did I say wrong, Bhabi? Can you deny history? So much violence has taken place due to religion!"

"If people are stupid and do not understand the true meaning of religion, how is that God's fault, oy?" Sunil raised his voice.

Chachaji smiled. "Thousands of years ago, Hindu rishis declared that God is one. Paths leading to Him are many. Conflicts occur when all religious adherents claim that they are the chosen people and their faith is superior to 'others.' Man's ego severs him from all 'others' because ego is an impediment between man and man. He falters in his understanding of unity amongst living beings and God."

Chachaji looked at Satish. "Fundamentalism and violence are a direct consequence of nescience regarding the essence of religion. True religion is a personal pursuit for union of our soul with God that leads to ecstasy of everlasting bliss. If understood correctly, how can it ever result in war? There is no possibility of negativity in God. How can He be the inspiration for hatred or violence? These are creations of man, Beta, *son.* God has given man the tools of transcendence to rise above his ego and dissolve the hatred in nothingness where it came from. Hatred has no absolute existence."

Normally patient, Satish had already lost his patience. "But, Chachaji, religion also traps man in impotency. He surrenders his will to some dubious deity he hasn't even seen! The priests have a heyday entangling people in all kinds of rituals and fill their big round bellies."

Sunil admitted, "It's true that organised religion has ceased to be a path unto God. It has metamorphed into an aggregate of superficial, cultural, social practices and dogmas that have actually become a barrier to man's spiritual growth. People have lost sight of the core essence of religion, which is love—God's love for His creation and man's love for God and humanity."

Chachaji agreed. "A single human who has severed the bondage of ignorance and ego and comprehended the truth of God's existence as well the unity with mankind wields such compelling power that it dazzles the mind. His every act resonates with immeasurable puissance that can move mountains. It is such because he has not circumscribed himself by the decrepitude of the material body and ego. His transcendence crystallizes as infinite love for all. His righteous actions do not originate in the mind that is muddled with paraphernalias of egocentricity, desires, anger, etc., but spring forth from his untainted 'Soul,' hence are full of love and truth.

"Jesus was son of God, and he knew it. His words had such immense power that two thousand years later, humans are still mesmerized by Him.

"Budha, established in his 'Real Self,' spoke words that still echo in the corridors of history. If followed honestly, these could lead to total peace in this warring world.

"Gandhi Ji asked millions of Indians to stop working as a measure of nonviolent protests against the British Raj. That day in 1922, India was shut down—not a single Indian went to work. Such was the ascendancy of his spiritual personality. Look at the selflessness and altruism reflected in the lives of Mother Teresa and saints, They live true religiosity."

Prashant had moved to the rug, a cushion behind his back, and leaned against the sofa with his legs stretched. He concluded happily, "Let us hope one day Meeraji can go back to her birthplace and have kebabs, *beef dish,* with Ahmed's parents!"

"Why not." Mohit looked pleased.

Ahmed's open face beamed with obvious relief, "Insha Allah, *God's will,* that will be a great day. Amin, *amen.* Allah, is great."

- # -

"Guess what, I found mangoes in the supermarket today at a killing price of five dollars each. But so what?"

As Bela sliced the mangoes on the kitchen counter, Meera was overcome by nostalgia; she could taste the delectable, luscious sweet-sour pulp of mango melting in her mouth as she sucked it from one end while pressing the other; the musical sounds of Glen Falls resonated in the background.

Masis, *mother's sisters,* threw a woven colorful spread on the ground and unpacked the lunch within five minutes, the famished kids urging them on with vociferous persistence. Samosas and Pakoras, potato fingers, eggs, sandwiches, hot tea for adults, hot milk for children, Ovaltine and Horlicks for the finicky ones, jugs of lemon juice, and tons of locally grown fruit, apples, peaches, apricots, plums—and the king of all fruit, juicy large mangoes.

Ma and Masis had installed themselves where the land was relatively flat, without the overgrowth of shrubs; only green grass covered the earth. Scattered plastic cups, dried peels, and cigarette butts at a distance were evidence that this was a favored spot for picnics. Glen creek glided lazily along the side emitting friendly murmur of KalKal. Sunrays passing through the playful waves created a succession of patterns on the pebbles that lay at the bottom of the brook. To clean and chill simultaneously, Ma dumped all the different kinds of mangoes—Dussehra, Langra, Chaunsa, and last but not least, the king of all mangoes, Alphonso—in the brook where water was shallow.

Choti Masi, *youngest sister,* announced in a nasal sharp voice, "Children, have lunch first, then mangoes!"

Naturally, all the youngsters rushed toward the stream to seize the biggest, most ripe mangoes. The older ones grabbed the best; the Lilliputian cousins whined vigorously to attract the attention of some just or wise adult to arbiterate a fairer distribution of the loot. Their trivial, puny voices were drowned by the much more vocally potent shouts of glee of the older youth. By the time Chote Mamaji, *mother's youngest brother,* appeared on the scene to settle the matter, there was nothing to settle. All the mangoes had disappeared.

Meera must be five or six years old; it was her first lucid memory of the trek to Glen Falls.

"Bahenji, *sister,* we will not come to Simla this year. It is so much work for you, *na*!" Every spring Ma's siblings declared such with much concern.

Come summer, the month of May, wrath of sun god in the plains would become unbearable; they would pack up in a hurry and head for Simla, apologetically though.

Picnics at the Glen Falls became an annual pilgrimage of sorts. Chadwick Falls were grander; capacious amounts of pure water flowed over huge rocks and fell from high elevation, looking like thick fluid pillars, making much pandemonium. But the hike was too precipitous; women's fashionable, multicolored sandals, matching the color of the saree of course, failed to provide stability on unpaved paths laid with many small stones. During those years, running shoes were worn only by schoolchildren for physical education class and sports.

Glen just streamed along, falling gently on small slopes. You could touch the frigid waters anytime.

That year, all of Ma's brothers and sister, all seven of them, with their respective spouses and offsprings, Meera's cousins ranging from two to eighteen years of age, converged on her house. Recipients of favouritism—much to the chagrin of male kids, there were only three girls, Meera, Shoba and Rekha, the older two being about the same age—left Meera at the mercy of boys. Whenever she won in any game, the boys ganged up on her, threw her out cruelly, and told her indignantly, "You don't even know how to play boys' games! Go play with your dolls."

The aunty downstairs complained sonorously with a deep frown, "Aré, it is impossible to take any rest!" The stuffy, hoarse-voiced Masi warned them sternly, "Kids, stop running and jumping around like monkeys!"

The children were quite busy planning mischief, "Did you hear me? Stop now or else . . ."

The youngsters did not pay any attention to the meaningless "Or else . . ." that would never eventuate in Badi Masis's, *oldest sister's*, house.

En route to Glen from Meera's house in Simla, you walk on a stony uphill pathway that merges with the main thoroughfare. At a distance of approximately a mile on the winding road, a gravel path descends steeply on the right and peters down into a narrow trail. Thin long pristine green fern fronds, darker broad-leafed bushes, weedy grasses, their narrow tips pointed toward the sky, and some other low-lying wild plants encroached on both sides of the lane. Dainty white, purple, blue, yellow, and red wildflowers form clusters that shine as bright spots of color in a sea of variegated green. While you concentrate on where to plant your next step on the narrow lane, you fail to notice the transition in the flora around you. Suddenly, you are swallowed by a huge shadow; looking up anxiously, you find yourself in the fortress of woodlands. Your ears become aware of the resounding bird melodies in the green forest.

A natural garden of umpteen shades and tones, dark-brown bark encrusted by flourishing colonies of light-bronze mosses and jade-green lichens floor enriched with diverse species of emerald plants, meets the eye wherever you look. Overbearing deodars look down upon inhabitants that grow closer to the ground; they consider the land as their personal domain. Poplars, birch, willows, pines, juniper, and other trees find elbow room. Wide-leaved, deep-green creepers valiantly twine around the unwilling trunks of their oppressor and reach the top to welcome sunlight, victoriously sapping the light energy, prompting photosynthesis leading to production of food and sending it down to the roots effectively through their efficient transport system.

"Walk carefully!" dictates Dictator Masi because of thick slippery carpet of pine needles, shed from the evergreens, overlays the floor of the timberland in some areas. The wet forest is deep and mysterious, an alien realm that is quite apart from the world outside. Only some splashes of light sneak through the intimidating canopy of the trees creating a chiaroscuro by a gloomy artist in his dark moments, yet peaceful.

About half-an-hour walk in the forest, the crystal clear stream of glen joins you in your journey.

What started as a wave of whimpering "Are we there already?", "I am hungry Mommy!", "My feet hurt, pick me up." evolved into a roaring chorus, "We want food, we want food!" Atul being the conductor.

"Okay, okay, we heard you, have patience, children," said the impatient Masi.

Meera's cousins and siblings gobbled up the food in a hurry since more consequential tasks were waiting for them: playing hide and seek, jungle being the perfect place; playing ludo; jumping up and down the stream splashing water on the lesser smaller kids. The most exciting stint was to run down the stream and see how far it went.

The formidable Masi forbade them sternly, "Don't you go looking for the end of Glen Falls. It is very far. Atul!"

Atul was the only one not intimidated by her; she was constantly irked by his regular noncompliance. "Listen, you look after them!" Atul, the oldest, was assigned a herculean task to keep an eye, simultaneously, on twelve impetuous, thrill-seeking youngsters running in different directions. Masi smiled cruelly; she'd cornered him this time.

Meera had a vague recollection of chasing an animated, butterfly with multicolor-pattern wings, the background chattering slowly, fading in the thin mountain air. The uninterrupted melodies of music of the creek remained. The green shiny leaves of the trees stirred with the touch of the soft breeze, the birds talked incessantly, delicate velvet-petaled wildflowers looked up and smiled at her. Meera started to pluck some blossoms for puja, *worship*. God must be oh so bored having to wear marigold garlands every day in the summer!

Meera stretched on the wet lush grass to rest. Attempting to catch a butterfly could be so strenuous!

The golden sunrays filtered through the vacillating leaves of the poplar tree, under which she lay, and danced on her face. Meera felt at home. She let herself sink into the grass, looking up at the tree branches, blinking when the sunrays fell on her innocent brown eyes.

Suddenly, she felt another presence. She looked around, still relaxing on the grass, but did not see anyone. Soon a shadow fell on her face; she tilted her head to look backwards.

A young girl around Meera's age was standing a couple of feet away behind her. She was gazing at Meera in curiosity. Meera sat up and smiled courteously. The girl wore a loose long shirt and pajama bottoms, both brown in color. The girl appeared anxious; she pressed her lips tight together. It was obvious to Meera that she was not going to initiate any dialogue.

Meera tried to think what to say. Why not ask the girl what people always ask her?

"What is your name?"

The girl hesitated. "Name, name!"

"Paro."

"Nice name."

Silence. Meera searched painstakingly for a follow-up.

"How old are you?"

Paro looked at Meera innocently, bewildered by the strange-sounding question.

"How old?" Paro stared blankly.

It was apparent that she did not know the answer because she did not understand the question. Now what?

"What is your father's name?"

"Harilal."

"Mother?"

"Gomti."

Meera struggled to expand the scope of her one-side conversation.

School! That is what people always ask her.

"Which school do you go to?"

Paro blinked. Meera understood by now what the blink meant. What do you say to someone who does not know what a school is?

"Where do you live?"

Paro smiled. Now, she not only understood the question, she could show Meera the answer.

"Come," she said, turning around and beginning to walk quickly. Of course, she expected Meera to follow. "Why not." Meera was also a little thirsty.

The hut stood like a toy in the midst of the dense forest; mud walls supported a tin roof. Some broad leaf creepers clung to the sides of the hut, reaching the roof. There were no windows.

Meera could not see anything as she followed Paro through the low door into the hut. The strange semidarkness slowly cleared after a few seconds. Meera's shoes were sticking to the floor. She looked down to find the floor was made of mud and still wet due to the rain from a few days ago. Why don't they have a rug?

A cloud of anxiety passed over Paro's mother's smooth, gentle face at their entry into the hut. Paro spoke to her mother in a language that was not familiar to Meera. Paro's ma spoke softly, much like Ma. She smiled reassuringly at Meera and pointed to a charpoy, *a woven bed,* that lay on one side of the hut, covered with crumpled brown sheet and a brown blanket with gaping holes.

Paro was excited. "This is a dog I made and a lion." She looked at Meera expectantly for praise.

"Nice, very nice."

"They like mud," Meera concluded; the toys were also made of mud.

Both Paro and her mother were extremely beautiful; their pure fair oval faces, with big blue eyes full of innocence, struck Meera, even at that young age.

But Meera was increasingly puzzled. There was no kitchen.

In front of a coal angeethi, *mud stove,* in the right-hand corner of the hut, Paro's ma sat on the mud floor to make tea for them. The stove was black, the pot was black, and everything else Meera could see in terms of utensils was all black.

Paro's ma handed clay cups to Paro and Meera. Thin tea, not much milk, but Meera liked it. She smiled at Meera. "I will make something to eat. You are hungry?" Her Hindi was decipherable.

Meera nodded, "Yes."

Paro's ma placed a black skillet on the coal stove and made roti amidst much smoke and coughing.

Paro informed Meera with gestures that it was dinner. She was incredulous; how could you not eat other delicious stuff and why not?

Lines of worry deepened the wrinkles on Paro's father's haggard face when he saw the well-dressed little girl in his hut. He looked sternly at Paro's ma and queried in their language. She looked at Meera and tried to explain. Paro added more relevant information, but she was clearly scared.

He was not impressed, nodded his head disapprovingly and vigorously. Then he turned to Meera, "Baby, your papa must be worried. Let us go!" his Hindi was perfect.

Paro hesitated for a moment then stepped forward to hug Meera. Paro's ma got up and ran her fingers through her hair. Meera did not know what that gesture meant, but her heart understood.

Meera remembered everyone hugging her, Ma crying for no reason. Some of Meera's cousins and uncles were still out looking for her.

"Ma, why are you crying?"

"Meera, you were lost!"

"No, I was not lost, I was with Paro."

A sweet friend had led her into an entirely different universe that was in utter dissonance with Meera's reality. That fleeting encounter opened up Meera's spirit to Paro's world, creating a new all-encompassing, larger-than-life paradigm that helped mold her idealism.

Paro's father refused to accept reward money, patting Meera's head paternally. "My beti, *daughter*, Saheb, my beti."

He was not tall, wore a colorful woolen pahari, *mountain people,* cap on his slender face that flowed on the sides of his sunken cheeks, highlighting his cheekbones. Eyes were light brown, tired but fluid with gentleness.

He looked frail and hungry; his long shirt hung on narrow stooped shoulders. Yet he had dignity and self-respect, the qualities that would soon disappear in a country that was to become ravaged by an age of unscrupulous plunder in Papa's lifetime.

Asha was waving her gold-ringed hand in front of Meera's eyes, "Where are you? Come back."

Meera was lost in the woods of long shadows, singing streams, dreamland of warm sunshine, little flowers, and great souls.

Asha was a prime model of superiority complex. Many psychoanalysts reject the notion of a superiority complex, treating it as an unconscious attempt to camouflage an inferiority complex. Who was going to tell her that?

Meera looked at Asha, adorned with heavy jewelry and Madras silk saree with gold border, much makeup, and high hairdo. She was a striking contrast to Jane's angelic simplicity and the nonchalant lack of interest in her appearance. Yet Jane was the most elegant and comely person Meera had ever come across. The calm pain in her blue eyes she carried like one carries a beloved child in one's arms, fondly, intimately, with ownership.

Meera felt awkward, uncertain, and self-conscious in her peach silk brocaded saree and all. Mohit had insisted, "Meera, wear the peach saree and heavy gold set that Ma gave you. You look stunning."

Despite loud protestation, she wore it to please him. To her, any jewelry is an extravagance of the exterior, the material body. The harm lies in the fact that it obscures, with its blinding glitter, the true inner resplendence of a person.

Soon after Mohit and Meera's arrival in Canada, his office gang threw a party in honor of the newlyweds. Meera was still dazed and could not keep faces and names in the right order.

A tall slim girl, with long, down-to-the waist, curly blond hair approached Meera shyly and hugged her. "I am Jane, Mohit's secretary."

She had finely chiseled features and an amiable smiling face. But the façade of cheerfulness was divulged by vulnerability of her soft sea-green eyes.

In that gathering, Jane was the only one Meera could bond with, maybe because Jane was also disconnected from everyone else.

"Control," Arun declared and banged his fist on the center table for greater effect; the glasses of various drinks rattled, some spilt.

Arun was an obstreperous, iterative human with indomitable vocal cords, who often got away with unveracious enunciations with heavy-handed gestures and stentorian grandiloquence accentuated by his huge size. He exuded arrogance, but Meera believed it to be feigned; inside lived an insecure child.

Arun was ebullient about Existentialism. Sartre was his current hero; he changed heroes often, depending on his mind-set on a given month.

Meera sneaked into the living room quietly to not disrupt the process of noise making. In a high-pitched, irritated voice, Asha shouted from the kitchen, "Calm down you. We know about control. Men like to control women."

"No, no, control over our lives. We are the authors of our own destiny, we shape it. I believe it man, pure Existentialism."

Anil looked at Arun amusingly. "I am your friend, but you stole my girlfriend, and I am very angry. I take this fire scrapper"—he picked it up from the fireplace—"and hit you over your head. You are in hospital in coma. Where is your control, my friend? You develop genetic disease or have car accident, you become disabled, end of your career. You toil hard for promotion, but the chairman's son come from Oxford and seizes it from under your nose. We only have limited control, man, the rest lies in destiny."

What did Jane do to deserve her life?

Sunil spoke sadly, "Would Meera have lost Mohit if she had any control?"

Everyone looked at Meera in unison, uncomfortably, apologetically. Meera sat, immobilized by the stunning truth, looked at the rug that floated in her vision.

Prashant's penetrating eyes felt her quivering perturbation. He broke the uneasy taciturnity with a whiny, "What Bela Bhabi? What sin did I do? Can't I even get some halwa, *a dessert,* around here?"

Bela got up, spoke to Meera tenderly. "Come, Beti, let us make halwa for this impossible bhukhar, *greedy.*"

Chachaji coughed to draw attention. "Arun, we believe that we have made our kismet, *destiny,* when life flows in the same direction as our will. But more often than not, in spite of our intelligence, volition, judicious choices, we fail. It is such because we live in a complex, interdependent, interrelated world. Our existence is irrevocably enmeshed with other people's thoughts and actions. Whether extraneous circumstances are favorable to fruition of our will or impose impediments that block our path, it's fate. Malcolm Muggeridge pours the essence of his wisdom in these few lines, 'In all the larger shaping of a life, there is a plan already into which we have no choice but to fit.' However, we are not helpless. We can shatter the humiliating slavery of 'destiny.' Many times, the outcome of our life events may be out of our hands, but we have full command over our reactions. Do we accept events gracefully, learn and evolve, or drown in self-centered misery is our own choice. As Budha said, 'Pain is inevitable, but suffering is not.'"

Anil smiled sadly. "Bapu, it is very hard to do."

Chachaji agreed, "It is difficult but doable. You have to cultivate the mind-set like any other skill. God has given us the gift of intellect for this purpose. Humans can face their existence on earth only by transcending it."

Arun immediately waved his hairy hand in the air. "Chachaji, *uncle*, pardon me, but Chairman Mao was right when he told Dalai Lama, *Tibet's Buddhist spiritual leader*, that religion is the opium of the masses. There is no God *shod*."

A thousand years of utterly futile evenings could not resolve the eternally irresolvable enigma of God's existence. People do not realize that there is no answer because there is no question. That is the beginning and the end of the truth.

Skeptics believe that all life, including us, evolved from a primordial soup of basic atoms like oxygen, hydrogen, nitrogen, and carbon. This is the highest leap of faith that lands them nowhere because life is not RNA, DNA, and proteins. These molecules may have evolved from basic elements, but what separates living from nonliving is pure Consciousness. Even in far-fetched imagination, matter cannot create Consciousness.

Only Consciousness can conceive thought. Thought is the predecessor of any action. Nothing can be brought into existence without preplanning. Philosopher and Saint Aquinas's argument that *watch* necessitates a *watchmaker* is simple but impeccable. Hence, the whole of Reality owes its existence to an Absolute Consciousness called God, personal consciousness being our individual Soul.

To escape the useless to and fro argumentation, Meera slipped outside the patio door of the kitchen.

The seemingly endless days of June amazed her. In India, during summer or winter, advent of night is audacious with certitude; day and night cannot cheat each other of their right to be. Dinner, not supper, is served with the backdrop of deep, unbreachable darkness when moon is not there. In the summer, recalcitrant creatures wake up when the sun retires and shrill loquacious discussions can be heard in the bushes.

Clouds were dark, started to spit, and suddenly, a downpour of rain caught Meera by surprise. She ran inside hurriedly; lightning fell somewhere, illuminating Di's backyard where flowering plants grew. Momentarily, the blossoms shone then plunged in darkness again. Meera looked out, her vision penetrated through her own reflection in the glass patio door and scanned the garden. Through the hazy veil of the rainshower, she thought she saw Mohit, at the far end of the yard, close to the white-clustered flowering bush. He was drenched. Meera wanted to tell him to run in. He stood immobile; she opened the patio door breathlessly and stepped out in the pouring rain. Her eyes were filled with tears, her heart hurt with anguish; how could it be real? She stood there as he faded away. "I miss you, Mohit, let it be a dream, come back. What am I going to do?"

Bela opened the door and said in a shocked and admonishing voice, "Aré, are you crazy, Meera? Come in, gosh you are drenched. Come in right away! Chalo, buddu, *silly*. Go upstairs, I will get you a change of clothes."

As Meera turned, Bela was hit in the heart. Meera looked like a pale, marble statue who had lost the flame of life and could crumble into dust with just a soft touch.

Di pulled her in and folded Meera in her arms without a word. Di knew that sometimes, many times, words stand between intuitive channels of understanding in humans.

- # -

"How is your friend, that sad pretty girl?" Prashant asked out of the blue.

Momentarily puzzled, Meera asked, "Who?" Then understood. "Oh, you mean Jane?"

"Yes."

Instant furrows appeared on Meera's smooth forehead; Prashant was surprised at her reaction. He had asked just out of jest, to follow up with some comical droll. He found Jane strange, unfathomable, which annoyed him. He was enigmatic himself, but from others, he demanded out-in-the-open lucidity.

Two months had passed since Meera had seen Jane in her apartment.

A month after Mohit's death, Meera heard a quivering voice on the phone. "Can I see you, Meera?"

Mohit had described Jane as a figure right out of Shakespeare's tragedies. In parties, she would choose an inconspicuous corner and attempt to be invisible; even Zorba the Greek could not budge the barrier of her self-imposed exile. Jane was the only one who refused to succumb to his strategic advances for a dance.

His real name was Georgeo Gestapolis, renamed by his friends Zorba the Greek. Dancing was his passion; no one could deter him. Much to the hostess's objections, he would move furniture in the largest room in the house to make commodious space for animated Greek steps. To strip the hostess of any excuse, he carried his own long-playing records in a leather bag. "Music and dance free the spirit of man from the bondage of life," he claimed.

During the first office party, a reluctant and shy saree-clad Meera had to yield to Zorba's polite but "You cannot escape" power of persuasion. He placed his right hand around her waist at the bare back between the blouse and the saree. His touch on her flesh gave her goose bumps. She looked at Mohit for relief, who was talking to Marco. Mohit said, "Excuse me", happy to wiggle out of Marco's complex but impassioned enunciations, pretended to push George aside and take over, "Zorba, you have lost the charming woman's affection. She is impressed no more," and quite gallantly took Meera away.

Never discouraged, George picked up Sally, the gorgeous Italian with thick black curly hair and ample bosom. He swirled her around; she shrieked with feigned distress. Marco Giovanni, Sally's bearded, bespectacled, studious husband, ambushed someone—anyone—to entrap him or her into discussion of some world injustice. He was enraged. "After destroying democracy in Guatemala and invading Cuba, you will see more violent, covert operations by CIA planned by the American government."

He would throw his long arms in the air out of frustration. "The successive US administrations decimate Democracy in helpless third world countries, install brutal right-wing military dictators who use "death squads," trained by CIA, to strangle any voice for social justice and Democracy. Yet the White House has the audacity to claim that they are protecting the Democracy in those countries. Gosh! And the world buys it?"

Marco had all the dark secrets of the CIA covert operations up his sleeve, dug from some dusty archive, untouched by human hands for decades. No one could win an argument with him; he had overdone his homework. Everyone knew that he spoke the truth; if nothing else, he shook a lot of consciences.

The only way to shake off Marco was to turn to Hans. "How about a song? We want song!" Everyone in the room would join in.

Hans, Mohit's boss, was a German. His parents had moved to Ireland in the 1930s because they could not face the changed brutal face of their beloved fatherland. He was chubby and cheery fellow who sang "Kiss of Fire" in a deep resonating voice that emerged from somewhere beyond his throat, much to tumultuous applause. His wife, Vaultra, was also German with pale skin and apologetic gray eyes, perhaps still atoning for Hitler's murderous fanaticism.

Nina, Georgeo's wife, seldom joined the office parties. She suffered from arthritis at a young age. George would announce pathetically, "Nina did not want to come today again? All this story to avoid dancing with her husband, eh?" He had a legitimate excuse to excite pity and drag other women to the dance floor moaning and groaning all the way until they agreed.

Jane's elegant face had lost its flesh—cheeks looked hollow, eyes bigger, and lips drooped at a downward angle. The swan-like neck was thinner; she was a mere shadow of her older self. When Meera hugged her, she felt the trepidation of Jane's frail body.

Jane's hands were ice-cold in spite of the balmy spring temperature outside. Meera rubbed them with her warm palms. They sat quietly on the sofa on the living room for a few moments.

"I am so sorry, Meera. He was such a good man."

Meera nodded, tears welled in her eyes. Jane continued, "I have never seen any man love his wife as much as he did."

Meera fixed her moist eyes on Jane's face in expectation. Encouraged, Jane recounted every word she could remember that Mohit had proudly uttered about Meera.

Meera sobbed uncontrollably. Gone forever, her very soul was burnt to death in the crematorium along with his dead body. That is how it had felt.

But isn't the soul immortal?

On the dark, tormented night of the day Mohit died, Meera lay on the bed with her hand on Bela Di's arm. Nightmares haunted her tortured consciousness; the pain in her heart was unbearable.

She got out of bed slowly to not wake up Bela Di and walked limply to the washroom. She bent down to the washroom sink and splashed cold water on her face where layers of salt from her tears had deposited during the tortuous evening. A gaunt, anguished face looked back at her when she glanced in the mirror while settling her hair with her fingers. Meera sat on the toilet seat and wept bitterly. Why couldn't it be a dream, why couldn't Mohit open the bathroom door and say, "Aré, what are you doing sitting on the toilet seat and crying?"

Meera got up, wiped her tears, and walked out.

Di's blanket had slipped off her torso. Meera draped it on her body gently; she did not move. As Meera dawdled down the stairs in semidarkness, the aroma of mogra, *jasmine,* incense floated toward her.

Meera had purchased the incense sticks from an old wrinkled drab woman, who perched on the side walk of Janpath shopping center in New Delhi; unable to compete with younger louder vocal cords, she just looked at passerbys with suffering eyes.

Blessings poured out of her toothless mouth when Meera bought ten, forty stick packs of incense at once, carefully selecting mogra and kewra, *rose.*

Asha Bhabi laughed. "Choti, I am worried about you, where will you get jasmine flowers in Canada? Roses, yes. But jasmine?"

On top of a small end table, Anil and Sunil had hastily set up a small temple in the right-hand corner of the living room. The table was covered with cream-colored table cloth that Dadi, *paternal grandmother,* had embroidered for Meera's dowry. An ivory-colored marble statue of Shri Krisha—flute on his smiling lips, crown of peacock feather over his curly locks—stood on the table. The other sculpture of Shri Rama was made of red marble from Rajasthan.

The two woeful, pale flames of the candles that were burning on the temple table fell on the silent forms of the two incarnations of God. Shri Ram lived a quintessential Godly life in order to edify mankind to the attainability after God's image. To Shri Krishna, even perfection can be transcended to merge the Soul with God and achieve blissful, eternal life.

Lying lifelessly at the feet of the statues, wilted flowers seemed to have surrendered to the inevitable. The incense fumes rose in rings and dissolved in the thick air that shrouded the room, creating a mysterious aura.

Someone sleeping on the carpeted floor, wrapped in beige printed quilt that Meera and Mohit had bought just recently from Sears, groaned in a low voice and turned. Meera could not make out who it was and lacked the energy for curiosity.

With blurry vision, unsteady feet, aching heart, Meera straggled toward Chachaji's upright, though vague figure, sitting in front of the temple. He did not move until she slumped next to him. He turned his head, looked at Meera sadly, raised his right arm, and wrapped it around her drooping shoulders. Leaning her throbbing head on Chachaji's arm, she started to weep; her body heaved with emotion.

Chachaji closed his weary eyes in prayer; they both sat motionless and mute like statues. Time stood still, an impotent witness to the eternal woe of man.

Chachaji took a deep breath, his voice resounded from the depth of his spirit, "Na Hanyate Hanyamane Shrire, *soul does not die when body perishes.* The wind of kal, *infinite time,* blows on the infinite sea of Consciousness, that is the Absolute God, and a wave, a sentient being is born. Just as sea imbues the waves, God pervades us living beings. Since beginningless time, waves are created and reabsorbed back in the sea.

"Mohit's true identity is his Soul, which is immortal, imperishable, never to be obliterated out of existence. The body, a mere vehicle of Soul for its journey of one life, is panch bhautik, *made of five elements,* and dies. But even the material body does not vanish, it is transformed into ashes. Who can stop the ceaseless cycle of change, Beti?

"According to Shri Krishna, the Supreme Teacher, Soul changes body like we change clothes. I read somewhere '*Death* nay but as when one layeth his worn-out robes away. And taking new ones sayeth, "These will I wear today," so puteth by the spirit lightly, its garb of fresh and passeth to inherit a residence afresh.'

"Meera," Chachaji continued, "do not grieve. Mohit is alive, always one with our spirits as well as God."

Meera had heard these words of wisdom hundreds of time in her short life, but they just flowed over her mind like a stream glides over pebbles without leaving a mark.

But unawares, Chachaji's words did leave a miniscule residue in Meera's consciousness.

Meera wiped Jane's tears with the palloo of her saree. "Don't cry, Jane, Mohit has not died, he is within you, within me, one with our Soul." Her voice broke.

Jane's eyes widened in bewilderment; pallor came over her face, and she passed out.

Mohit had described her as emotionally fragile.

Meera was uneasy. "I don't know, Prashantji, Jane has not called me for two months, and her phone was disconnected."

"Did you try the office?"

"Yes, Mona, Hans's secretary, sounded very worried. Jane resigned, and no one knows her whereabouts."

"Doesn't she have any relatives you could contact?"

"Oh yes, a so-called mother. When I called her, I will quote, 'There is no reason to fuss and fret, Jane has ridiculously childish habit of disappearing, an attention-getting gimmick. And who the hell are you?'"

Prashant said thoughtfully, “Meera, tell the police.”

“I did, I did! A constable, Mr. Smith or whoever, scoffed and informed me sarcastically that Miss Jane Hawthorne had a history of running away, and they have a file on her. I pointed out that she had not done that ever since she came of age and left her mother. She could be a victim of some violent crime.”

“Then?”

Meera said hopelessly, “Well, he was too focused on intimidating me. When I refused to oblige, he waved me away dismissively with the words, ‘If Jane’s mother requested police assistance, we could launch a search. We have no idea who you are and why you are so keen to find her.’ When I said that I am Jane’s best friend, he had disbelief in his corny eyes and asked for proof!”

Prashant’s face hardened with annoyance.

Meera didn’t notice. She looked at the weeping willow tree that grew outside Prashant’s living room. Light from the large bay window shone on Meera’s tranquil face. The swaying green branches of the weeping willow reflected in her lucid eyes, creating shifting images. She always sat across windows; walls imprisoned, suffocated, and severed her from the continuum of space outside. She wished to fly into the infinite, aquamarine sky, atop tall trees and touch the glossy leaves, while soft breeze brushed against her cheeks.

Meera looked up and spoke vaguely to no one in particular, “I don’t know if my skin color and salwar kameez had prompted his delinquent conduct. It has happened before.”

Patients trickled in and out; the nurse at the front desk tossed a cheerful “Hi” and “Bye” to all but Meera. When she approached her, the nurse’s upper lip stiffened noticeably, and her voice turned hoarse as she uttered a reluctant, dry, “Have a seat.”

Meera sat down next to the side table that had health magazines scattered without any order. She picked up a health journal for stimulation.

A white young couple came in, the woman held a small bald baby. She looked around and chose to sit where three chairs were empty, settling the baby on her lap. The white man placed a bag, perhaps full of baby stuff, on one chair and sauntered toward the front desk. The nurse grinned widely and said with jovial cordiality, "Ah, my favourite family. How is Natasha?"

The young man made concerted effort to retrieve appropriate words out of his brain and took a few moments before stuttering, "Fine, thank you," indicating his recent arrival in the land of opportunity. Canada and America are considered "much desired" domains around the world where happiness is as simple as shiny hair, lean figure, and gleaming teeth; excellent health is achieved by cornflakes fortified with iron as well as rich Campbell soup; brides can be easily obtained by driving in a brand-new Chrysler; shaving with the newly invented electric shaver could bring down a dozen pretty girls at your feet.

The man raised his voice a few notches and asked, "How long we wait?"

"Oh no," the nurse said encouragingly. "Only a few persons, then you."

He walked back to his wife rather sluggishly, suggestive of a night job in addition to the day's toil that new immigrants take up to fill the chasm between dreams and reality.

Meera smiled at them; they pretended not to notice and made themselves very busy with "cuddling" the infant.

The wife had a complaining voice'; her sentences always ended with a question mark. Meera was certain that they were not speaking German. Tayaji, *father's older brother,* had a German scholar stay with him once. His words bore deep consequential ballast, quite similar to the Punjabi language, which is spoken with intimidating cacophony.

Meera wanted to ask them all about their homeland, to take her by the hand and walk through the rolling hills, emerald vineyards, thicket of evergreens; ancient small brick houses, exquisite roses blooming in their small gardens; hundred years old ivy covering the outside walls, velvety mosses filling the crevices and winding narrow stone paved lanes. Cotton puffs with silver lining play "merge and part" games in a lucid cerulean sky not to be found anywhere else in the world.

The nurse looked in Meera's general direction; it was her turn next. Before she could get up, she realized that the name did not sound anything like hers. Meera looked at the nurse questioningly, whose gaze pierced right through, rendering her invisible, and stopped at the couple. In confusion, they looked at Meera and hesitated momentarily but got up and walked toward the doctor's office.

Meera looked straight at the nurse, who looked back defiantly. There was no point making a scene, knowing full well that the nurse would undoubtedly present some creative but absurd excuse. Besides, Meera had no inclination to spoil her mood at someone else's pettiness.

Meera leaned back in her uncomfortable chair and wondered at the prevalence of the phenomenon of differently colored people being subject to every day biases, subtle or gross, in a land they now call their own.

The situation is all the more complicated because you can never prove it! And yet you are irrevocably damaged, suffering a constant dissonance in the territory of your psyche that, under extreme situations, entertains such aberrations as paranoia. Whenever someone stares at you in a mall or restaurant, passes you illegitimately in a legitimate queue, or is not polite at doctor's office, plane, police station, you can't help but wonder if your moccasin skin color has prompted such gratuitous conduct. You try to rise above this disturbing notion and make a sincere attempt to examine alternative, mitigating options; maybe the person is having a bad hair day, had a fight with the spouse. Perhaps the arrogance is handed down from ancestors, or the parents were too busy to teach their offspring stuff about civility.

The issue is irresolvable. You can never pose the question, "Excuse me, are you rude to me because I am brown?"

Ironically, you are subject to double whammy. Every time you experience such negative thoughts, you feel ashamed of the possibility that you have turned into an oversensitive pathological paranoid. Now imagine if your observation of others' bigotry is correct, you are blaming yourself of victim mentality while you cannot openly accuse the "other" of misdemeanour.

Prashant spoke in his usual glib style. "Don't worry, I know Robin in the police department. I will call him. Jane is a grown-up woman, intelligent enough to get away from it all. We all should, if you ask me."

Meera sat self-absorbed.

"Just stay here." He got up from the chair. "I have something interesting to show you."

Rare as it was Prashant had invited Bela, Sunil, Satish, Kanchan, and Meera for afternoon tea. It was indeed an act of courage since he was clueless how to be a host; being single, he was the perpetual guest at friends' places.

Last minute, an uninvited virus decided to visit Kanchan's inviting body; Bela's sister's sister-in-law's mother's sister decided to drive a distance of two hundred miles from Vancouver to surprise them. Which they did.

Being descendants of an ancient civilization, time-honed traditions nested in their collective unconscious; Meera and Prashant sensed a certain awkwardness at the unprecedented predicament of being with each other alone. Meera dismissed the thought. *We are just friends,* and sat more comfortably on the sofa.

Prashant went inside, smiling enigmatically; he returned with a framed painting approximately three feet by two feet, thrust it in front of Meera, and said challengingly, "Look!"

It was a painting, black chains crisscrossing all over the canvass; quite unremarkable design. Did he make it himself and sought compliments? That was tricky because lying was an arduous act for her. Quite unperturbed by Meera's lack of enthusiasm, he quipped, "Keep it at least a couple of feet away from your long nose." He grinned. "And look at your reflection in the transparent glass over the picture. Focus on your lovely eyes"—an obvious attempt to whitewash the earlier teasing remark about her perfectly normal nose—"and ignore the rest which will look blurry anyway."

Meera blushed.

"Okay." Still mystified, Meera had no choice but to take the venture to its final outcome.

The simple light-green silk saree augmented the transparency of her fair skin. She had tied her jet-black lustrous hair in a bun that partly reached the upper area of her nape. Meera looked freshly bathed and unpretentiously comely. The innocent unawareness of her own beauty lended a refined grace to her visage.

Prashant looked away at the space outside, embarrassed by the bent of his musings.

A pair of light-brown tranquil eyes reflected in the glass and looked back at Meera; unwittingly, her glance scanned the painting, but she brought it back.

Then it happened.

Slowly, miraculously, the chains started to soar upward in a pattern of hearts and loops. The painting turned into a vividly three-dimensional, vibrant abstraction of bracing, intertwined yet disconnected fetters.

"Wow!" she exclaimed.

Prashant was astonished. "You got it already? Many people cannot see its reality at all, no matter how much time they spend looking. Do you meditate?"

"Yes." So there it was, an enigmatic design with obvious depth that now refused to go away. She looked away then gazed at it again, but the multidimensionality endured. Much like Nirvana, *ultimate bliss*, or Moksha, *ultimate freedom*; once you attain it, it is irrevocable.

Meera looked at Prashant quizzically. "How can it change in a minute?"

Prashant was sitting on a sofa chair across from Meera. He bent forward a little as though he was going to share a secret. "Meeraji, it did not change. Your perception changed. People think that humans are flat, plain, and unidimensional because our perceptions are superficial, unable to cut deep into the hub of truth. Reality is multidimensional, but no one bothers to go deep into its labyrinths. Then we wonder why relationships do not work. We live in a world of shadows without any idea whom they are shadows of. If we make a genuine effort, we can know others' realities and develop true spiritual bonds with them."

Behind the serenity of his eyes lay his reality, but Meera was afraid to plunge in. She made a concerted effort to deny that her trepidation was not caused by Prashant's eyes but the effect they had on her.

That night, lying in her warm bed, Meera's right hand extended on the right side and groped in the cold vacuum where once there was fullness of Mohit's ardent body. Longing brought tears to her eyes. Meera flew over the seven seas and hovered over the frigid, obdurate peaks of the Himalayas, wandering around the abode of her childhood, her past sanctuary that still kept her heart warm when life was cold.

Atul had called repeatedly, "Aré, what is holding you back, Meera?"

Meera called Balwant the next day. "Bhai, how is everything proceeding? Everyone in India is waiting."

Meera met Balwant and Surinder at Satish's party soon after her arrival in Canada.

Every time she looked at Surinder, she saw a field of lush green crop where the body parts of her father were scattered. Meera shuddered every time at the cruelty of man.

Moni squatted on the dirty floor of the cell; he looked up calmly through the iron bars when Amarjit and Charan Das arrived in the police station. Charan Das spoke hurriedly, "Moni, do not confess. No one will squeal, you know that."

"How can I lie under oath, Uncleji?"

The lean debilitated cow blinked her dismal eyes and let her heavy head droop forward. The Hakim, *naturopath,* told Jeet, "Her liver is too damaged. She will not live." Satinder controlled her tears and looked away.

Suddenly she noticed a man emerge from the fully ripe golden fields of wheat and run towards her. His face was red, sweat trailed on his dark, rugged face.

"Madhav, come sit. I will get lassi, *buttermilk,* for you."

"Nai Biji, *no mother*", he was panting heavily, his black eyes were filled with dread. "Where is Masterji, *teacher*?"

"He has gone to market."

Madhav turned around and sped towards the fields again.

"Aré, what happened?"

"Biji, pray."

Satinder's legs trembled; she slumped on a pile of hay and watched the receding figure of Madhav.

Moni came running out of the house whining, "Biji, Bahen, *sister,* is not giving me my car." Surinder followed and explained, "Biji, I told him that he has to eat first."

Satinder's eyes filled with tears, she got up, folded them in her arms and kissed their heads passionately. Both of them looked at her face questioningly. Surinder whispered in panic, "Kee hoya eh, Biji, *what happened, mother*?"

Jeet was the only educated human in those parts; the villagers of Manpur as well as neighbouring localities, poured into his small brick house for resolution of their life enigmas that were not necessarily created by life, per se, but other scary living beings called Homo sapiens. Satinder, quite unwittingly, became a significant contributor to her husband's altruism. Preparing cold lassi, *buttermilk,* in the hot summers and hot tea in the cold winters and lunch and dinner for all complainants whose arrival was unpredictable because it depended on their own convenience.

If Jeet was away at school attending to his supposedly primary profession, that was teaching, the rugged farm labourers convened in the shaded verandah, *a covered area in front of a house,* sharing alimants and anguish with other oppressed brethren while Satinder ensured a constant flow of goodies.

Jeet was up late at night after his wife, children, and mother were deep in sleep, bent over his small table in the dim yellow light of kerosene lamp and wrote strong worded, fearless complaints against the affluent landowners who considered it their genetically endowed right to stomp on the workers; they squeezed maximum blood out of them for minimum restitution.

Although he had fought shoulder to shoulder with the Congress Party during the freedom struggle, Jeet was disgusted by the ruling Congress Government's meager advancement in uprooting the structural paradigms that underpinned the unabated perpetuation of political-economic-social injustice. Consequently, overall progression in the quality of life of the poor, suffering masses of newly freed India was nil.

Nehruji, the first Prime Minister of free India, a true son of Mahatama Gandhi, pushed many just and equitable legislations through the Parliament to protect the rights of the downtrodden but the vacuum was at the level of local implementation of those policies. The directives outlining the necessary changes were stored by the local authorities in steel filing cabinets, never to be seen again.

Jeet joined the Communist Party that had become the voice of the voiceless. He thundered at rallies to awaken the indomitable

Demi-Goddess of Shakti, *power,* who had been slumbering in the obscure, unconscious recesses of the hopeless masses for millenniums. She had waited for the potent voice of a Jeet to awaken her.

Mahatama Gandhi had said, "The moment the slave resolves that he will no longer be a slave, his fetters fall."

Shakti opened eyes, the fetters fell apart; the electrifying wave of unrestrained, collective cry of the poor, shattered the walls of complacency of the wealthy landowners.

Madhav stood dauntlessly and told Jaggu, the landlord, in a strong voice, "You pay me to work. You have no right to hit me. I am leaving." Of course, Madhav was duly punched and kicked to bring home to him that Jaggu's clan did not require a right to beat him, they could do it anyway. Some other rebellious activities of the labour class prompted a conference of the affluent citizenry of the locality.

A variety of imported booze, Kebab, *a beef dish,* Tandoori chicken and much other paraphernalia of luscious dishes was laid out on a huge table that was set outside on the absinthe grass. Over nourished, hence, overweight men, wearing fine starched apparel, perched uncomfortably on garden chairs that were meant for normal size humans.

Of course, women were never invited to such gatherings where crucial decision-making occurred. Firstly, they were not considered sufficiently intelligent; secondly they suffered from weak bellies that could not hold a secret. Thirdly, their place had always been within the four walls of the home to breed children and gossip, in that order. They were content as long as new shiny, fashionable clothes and glittery, gold jewellery was supplied frequently, what did they care?

One of the landlords swore.

"Haramzada, *bastard,* he thinks he is 'Gandhi'! Doesn't he remember what happened to him?"

"Situation is grave; it demands serious measures, Yar, *friend.*"

"We have to protect our families, Na."

"Give me another peg of scotch!"

This year the wheat crop was bountiful, taller than ever before; long, golden spikes pointed proudly towards the heavens.

Jeet was a farmer at heart; a glow of satisfaction sparkled in his eyes, his feet were steady, heart at peace as he walked through the swaying crop. July was tepid and humid. Jeet quickened his steps. He looked back intuitively, there was no one. The wind stopped abruptly, wheat plants became still, a cloud appeared from nowhere and floated between earth and the sun; portent darkness fell on the expanse. Jeet started to run, he did not know why. Within minutes many footsteps pounded on the ground behind him; he looked back, four shining daggers held in four crude hands met his eyes. Jeet's physique was the envy of every young man in the region, he sprung forward and dashed at the speed of a race horse.

The shoppers in the bazaar halted, the merchants looked out of their stores, why was Masterji, *teacher,* running like a leopard chasing a kill?

Jeet ignored all queries and scurried into Jagat's shop, he was out of breath.

"What?" Jagat asked Jeet without looking up; he was packing groceries for a woman.

"Jagat, hide me, yar, *friend;* Preet and his Gundas, *hooligans,* are after me."

Within a few seconds, Jagat handed the bag to the customer and rushed into the back of his store, "Come, come." Large canisters of wheat, rice, corn, lentils, sugar, etc. were piled in a small space. "Hide between these!" He covered everything with a dirty sheet that was lying around.

Harmeet, Preet, Bobla and Kalia entered the market with a familiar nasty demeanor. Everyone scattered immediately; the foursome were bad news.

Harmeet twisted his black, lush moustache and yelled, "Oy coward, come out and face us or we will kill everyone in the bazaar."

The shoppers sprinted and vanished in surrounding fields. Most merchants lowered the metal door of their store with shaky hands. However, some defiant stalwarts stayed where they were.

"Oy Kalia", Preet addressed one of his personal mercenaries, "beat the hell out of them," pointing towards the store keepers.

Elated at the golden opportunity to utilize their much-honed-mean-muscle-machine Kalia and Bobla stepped into the nearest store, pulled Gurdas out, threw him on the ground and started to kick him with their giant, filthy sandals.

Gurdas spit on Kalia with obvious abhorrence, "Fear God, He is watching you, Harami, *a swear word.* You think you can scare us?"

Harmeet stomped on his legs while Kalia hit his bruised face with fists.

Gurdas's ten year old son was hiding in the shop. "Don't move from here, stay behind the counter," Gurdas had instructed him, firmly. But he could not bear the sight of his bleeding and humiliated father. He ran out of the store and cried, "Don't hurt my Bapu, I will tell you where Masterji, *teacher,* is."

Gurdas wiped the blood from his nose with his sleeves and yelled, "Befkoof, *stupid,* don't tell, I am fine."

But the young lad was scared as never before; what if they kill 'Bapu'? What will Mataji, *mother,* do? He pointed his little forefinger towards Jagat's shop, "He went there."

A cold bloodied smirk lit Preet's distorted face. They entered the shop and pushed Jagat aside who fell against the shelves of pickle bottles that toppled on him. Shattered glass pieces flew everywhere cutting Jagat all over his body and face; he yelled curses while attempting to get on his feet. Some glass cut the foursome, who responded with some obscenities with greater zeal.

Bobla held Jeet by his neck and dragged him to the centre of the bazaar. The foursome fell on him immediately and started to pierce his body with the shiny daggers.

Jeet did not holler or cry.

The shopkeepers went out of their minds; their screams shook the skies as they raced towards the gruesome scene looking for stones on their way.

Unaffected by the befuddlement, the sanguinary killers continued slashing Jeet's wounded, defenseless body, every strike dealt with vengeance and rancor. Stones hit them from all directions, the foursome roared and sped towards the wild crowd that galloped and disappeared, some into shops and others in the protection of lush crops.

Jeet's black eyes stared at the heavens, seeking answers. His bloodied body had fallen under the ancient Pippal tree of unknown age that had stood at the centre of the market, a reluctant witness to the history of perpetual brutality of humans towards one another, but never as grotesque and ferocious as this one.

The four butchers picked up Jeet's blood soaked limp body, threw it at the back of the jeep like discarded garbage and drove off laughing and whistling triumphantly.

Men poured out of their hiding. Benumbed by the unimaginable savagery and devastated by their own cowardice, they walked like robots towards the bloody, bright red, patch of ground where they had seen Jeet alive for the last time. They stood around and stared, tears flowed on their rough faces but tongues lost their voices. An eerie silence gripped the air.

Madhav saw the crowd from far and knew. He fell on his knees and bawled in such agony that the pent up emotions of all the men were unleashed. They slumped down and let out a stentorian cry for God to burn the merciless killers in hell without mercy.

"Leena, I will be late. Don't wait for me." Amarjit stepped out on the porch to get into his jeep, when he saw Madhav open the wooden gate and run towards him. Before he could query, Madhav collapsed face down right in front of him.

In the woeful, dark haze, Amarjit could barely make out white forms of women huddled together in the living room floor of Jeet's house. He looked around searchingly. In one corner of the room, the white head of Balbir Kaur, Jeet's mother, and young teary faces of Moni and Surinder stood out. Where was his sister?

He treaded carefully between the sitting woman and walked towards them. Amarjit sat down on the floor, pulled Balbir Kaur towards his chest and stroked her white hair. She bellowed, "My womb is bleeding, son".

Moni and Surinder's anguished ululation merged in hers, the other women raised the pitch of their cries, the men who were accustomed to suppress their sufferance, let it flow. The whole world condensed into a black hole of, pandemonium filled, hell in Jeet's house.

Only one voice was missing. Satinder's legs had caved in when a bawling Madhav staggered into her home and fell on her feet. He was incoherent but Satinder saw the black cloud that followed him, the portent umbra of her future; her world collapsed and buried her in the debris. She was lying on the floor, her wounded, bewildered, black, fluid eyes were fixated on the roof and beyond.

Amarjit lifted his sister's lifeless head and placed it gently on his lap. He bent over her, "Satti, look at me, please?"

Satinder brought her blank vision down as she heard the grief stricken voice of the love of her childhood. Amarjit bent down and kissed her forehead, "I am here, na, don't worry." The stricken face of her brother touched upon the strings of her deadened heart and awoke the song of pathos. Satinder wept bitterly while Amarjit held her against his throbbing heart.

Surinder and Moni cried aloud, "Mamaji, *mother's brother,* what will we do?"

Amarjit let Satinder go, hugged both the children and spoke tenderly, "I am here, na," with full knowledge that his words meant very little to the bereaved children who had lost the assuaging shelter of their father at such a young age.

He wiped Satinder's tears, took her moist face in his firm hands and swore, "I will see those Haramzadas, *bastards,* hang."

He stood up tall and walked outside. He was told by many men, who spoke simultaneously, that Jeet's body was missing.

With determined jaw and angry brow Amarjit entered the police station. "Jeet has been murdered, find his body."

Amarjit was a powerful man. He had fought in the World War II; his medals and guns hung in a glass cabinet as trophies. The Thanedar, *Police Inspector,* was afraid of none other than Amarjit. He held the belief in his tremulous heart that Amarjit, with his high connections in the military, could summon them anytime to shoot him, if he so desired.

"Bhaji, *brother,* very sad, very sad. Jeet was such a good man", although at the order of Jaggu, the land owner, he had threatened him constantly.

Amarjit took the weak kneed Thanedar and two constables in his jeep that stopped at Jaggu's mansion where his sons and alter egos were celebrating their victory.

"Ao, *come,* Amarjit Saheb, *gentleman,* Dhan Bhag Sade, *we are blessed.* Come and sit, oy Lalu get drinks for the guests."

Amarjit stood like a rock in front of him and spoke harshly, "Jaggu, make no mistake, I will make sure that you and your criminal sons are hung."

Jaggu instantly wore an innocent and sheepish aspect on his visage that did nothing to hide his mean reality. "What are you talking about? Thanedar, did we do anything wrong? Wahe Guru, *Sikh's name for God,* knows we are innocent", and wiped a couple of invisible, crocodile tears. Unaffected by the theatricals, Amarjit gestured to Thanedar, "Please go over every inch of the house and find the body."

Thanedar was in a serious quandary; he was dammed if he did and more dammed if he did not. He became pale and nervous.

Suddenly it occurred to Amarjit that the killers would never keep their kill in their own house.

He said, "No, wait" and turned to Harmeet and Preet, "where is the body?"

"What body, Uncleji?"

Amarjit thundered, "Don't play games with me!"

"How would we know anything, we have been home all day with Darji, *father.* Ask him."

Amarjit understood the futility of his line of action. He said gravely, "I will see you in court", and turned to Thanedar, "Get your constables; we will search all areas around."

Police and a vengeful and earnest army of volunteers scattered in different directions to scan every inch of the territory. They did not have to go too far. Parts of Jeet's body were strewn all over his own field.

Moni was too young. Amarjit lit the pyre with a wooden bar burning at one end; the body that could fight elephants lay dismembered and mute on a pile of wood. Amarjit wept aloud, looked at the leaping flames and swore, "With the whole village as my witness, 'Wahe Guru', *God,* I will not rest until I see the dead faces of the devils who murdered a saint." A few wild dogs howled in the dark background in approval.

Amarjit and a mob of witnesses barged into the Thana, *police station,* and laid charges against Preet, Harmeet, Bobla and Kalia for the murder of his brother-in-law.

Based on the accounts of vociferous and inflamed witnesses, a trembling Thanedar had no choice but to arrest Preet, Harmeet, Kalia, and Bobla at Jaggu's mansion. Amarjit and the mob had accompanied him and he understood that the exigency of the moment demanded that he save his life rather than please Jaggu.

Thanedar made a feeble attempt to deflect the acicular glare of Jaggu's eyes as well as the inflamed twitching of his long moustache that almost reached his ears.

"Sardarji, *a respectful address,* I am forced to do this, na; of course I will make sure that they are freed soon!"

The murderers were released on a small bail the next day, in spite of Amarjit's lawyer, Charan Das's impassioned remonstrance.

"They are not a flight risk", the young Magistrate expounded unhesitatingly.

"Sir, they are murderers! They may kill the witnesses!"

But the Magistrate Saheb, who had wined and dined at Jaggu's mansion just the night before, could not afford to spoil his mutually beneficial camaraderie with Jaggu whose uncle was a rich influential contractor in Chandigarh. The latter's real talent lay in contraband and surreptitious activities including selling, illegally imported, hard liquor, underground. The high-up authorities, including the various Ministers of the Panjab Government, received free boxes of whiskey, made in the United States, to overlook his transgressions.

In other words, Jaggu owned the power structures of the Panjab Government. The murderers roamed around freely terrorizing everyone especially the witnesses of their evil actions.

The frightened populace of Manpur decided to take a holiday from their respective careers and stay in the safety of their own homes. Schools, shops, offices were all locked away. For essential supplies, men knocked at the back door of the stores, bought the stuff and ran home at full speed. The village became a shadow town.

Two months later the Court hearing took place in the High Court, Chandigarh. Charan Das presented a strong case supported by enough signatures of the witnesses. The Judge made a decision to proceed with the charge of first degree murder against the four brutes and set the date of trial six months later. Charan Das requested that the assassins should be barred from entering the village because they were a threat to the witnesses. The Judge placed the foursome under house arrest in Chandigarh.

They stayed at Jaggu's uncle's lavish home in sector nine; the term 'house arrest' was a farce. The policemen assigned to guard the house arrestees, were bribed handsomely, invited to all the parties and picnics that Harmeet and Preet organized. As a result, the grateful policemen escorted the four criminals to Jagat cinema themselves where they pushed or pinched a lass or two, or tossed crude, cheap remarks in their direction. Harmeet and Preet went to twenty two sector bazaar where they looted shops by walking out without paying a paisa, *penny*. No one dared mess with hooligans who had two policemen protecting them.

In the nifty evenings of Chandigarh, at the brand new exclusive club, that reflected in the pure, blue waters of the artificial 'Sukhna' lake, Preet and Harmeet mingled with the so-called cream of society and shared drinks and laughter with, amongst others, the very Judge who was presiding over the case against them.

During the next five years, truth was sullied, dragged in the mud of mendacity, false witnesses were bought, real witnesses disappeared, to be found dead in ditches later. Justice was sold to the highest bidder, Jaggu, injustice was served to the victim's family. The killers were acquitted due to lack of evidence. The decision was arrived at by the Judge alone; there was no jury.

Under the same Pippal tree where Jeet had laid helplessly in a pool of his own blood, Harmeet, Preet, Bobla and Kalia squatted and drank homemade brew, snickering and jeering at the shoppers and merchants alike. "Take a lesson, you lowly dogs! You have seen what happens to those who cross us?"

From the shadows of the thicket of trees that circumscribed the market, a young turbaned man emerged, aimed a small pistol with a steady hand and shot the four in their heads with perfect precision. They fell in a heap.

Moni stepped forward and threw the gun with disgust as though it was a snake. He walked upright towards a wooden bench that lay on one side of the main market and sat with perfect poise.

Within seconds the bazaar was filled with people clapping in jubilation. Jagat ran towards him, "Moni, run away. We will tell the police that a masked man killed them and drove off in a jeep." Many others who had grasped the consequence of Moni's actions joined their voices.

Moni smiled sadly, "Chachaji, *uncle*, I have taken lives, that is a moral sin in God's eyes."

An uproar of protest overwhelmed him. “They killed your saintly father!” “The sinful Haramzadas, *bastards,* deserved it.” “They should have been hung.” “You have done justice.” “You have given us a new lease on life.”

Close family friends fell on his feet. “Think of Biji and Surinder. How can they bear to lose you?”

Moni was unshaken, “My Bapu, *father,* taught me that truth is the hub of our lives. If I lie, how will I live without my soul?”

Men of all ages and statures sat around him on the ground, many of them wept bitterly. No one noticed, dusk crept in and turned into a gloomy night. The mournful crowd dissolved in the murky, moonless, pitch darkness.

They ignored the dead bodies that became irrelevant demons of the past conquered by the chivalrous son of the village.

A servant came looking for Jaggu’s sons. He saw the crowd from far and started to run in anticipation. He came closer recognized the stack of bodies; he hopped around the bodies with joy and clapped his hands, “God is there for us.”

Soon Jaggu’s Manager arrived on the ghastly scene. He shook with anger, “Who did this? Who is the murderer?”

Jagat stood up defiantly, “Stupid, these are the murderers who deserved to die”, and pointed towards the mound of bloody, dead bodies. The Manager looked around; he could sense that the mob would lynch him unhesitatingly unless he removed himself from the possibility. He drove to the police station.

One hour later four constables and the Thanedar showed up. The constables refused to handcuff Moni. “He has surrendered; he is not going anywhere, Thanedar Saheb.”

Once more injustice was served, Moni’s confession was admitted, and he was sentenced to death by hanging.

Balwant Kaur, Moni’s grandmother died of shock the same day.

Amarjit and Charan Das met with Panjab Justice Minister and Chief Minister without achieving any ground. They sent an appeal to the Supreme Court in New Delhi for a stay of Moni’s execution on humanitarian grounds.

One of the Judges happened to be Amarjit’s wife’s niece’s brother-in-law’s sister’s father-in-law. Execution was stayed. Amarjit and Charan Das took the earliest train to Delhi the same day. They approached the High Command of the Congress Party. Congress leaders had not forgotten the zealful idealist, Jeet, who had spent many years with them in jails. A strong-worded letter was submitted to the Supreme Court. "The young man acted under duress" and recounted Jeet's murder as well as acquittal of the murderers.

"Furthermore, he is too young to be tried as an adult. His father fought courageously for freedom of our Mother India. That should be taken into account. Mohinder Singh has no previous criminal record hence should not be treated as one."

The death sentence was reduced to life in prison.

After Jeet was killed, at the tender age of thirteen, Surinder had become a nurse to her mother and grandmother, a mother to her brother and custodian of the farm. Satinder's failing health, Moni's innocent clouded face and the culls from the cows for their feed, forced her to shake the dust off her body and spirit to face life.

After the Judge ruled to hang Moni, Satinder gave up on life. The only thread that kept her hanging in the cruel world was Surinder.

"Suri, I cannot even die, you will be all alone?" she cried in anguish.

Surinder sat on the cool grass near her fields, folded her supple body in fetus position and wailed to mourn her own life.

Surinder was supporting Satinder and encouraging her to sit up to drink milk. Satinder's eyes had no tears and body no life. She just looked up despairingly when Amarjit came in and stroked her white hair.

"Get up, Satti. Moni will live." He turned to Surinder who hugged him and wept on his shoulder without control. "Beti, prepare for Puja, *worship,* in the Gurdwara, *Sikh temple.*"

Satinder slipped out of her bed in a daze, bent down, laid her wee white head on her brother's feet and passed out.

He sat uncomfortably on the charpoy, *a woven bed,* held Satinder's trembling hand and swore, "Biji, I will bring your son to you."

Five years after Moni's incarceration, a brilliant student, who had just earned his bachelor degree from Law College, Chandigarh, happened to read about Jeet and Moni's cases.

Balwant retrieved the proceedings of Jeet and Moni's trials, from the dusty shelves of the archives of the High Court in Chandigarh. He also compiled all the newspaper clippings related to the cases. For the next year, he could be seen bent over piles of documents, in one booth of the High Court library, to ascertain the truth behind each and every line of the proceedings. He studied thick books of law of the centuries seeking some precedents that could enable him to prepare grounds for his fight for justice.

Balwant went back and forth from Manpur to Chandigarh to tape the testimonies of the witnesses of Jeet's murder. Many had been killed by Jaggu during Preet and Harmeet's trial. The rest had not forgotten a single detail of the searing memories of that day.

Balwant prepared a well thought out and articulately written appeal and sent it to the Supreme Court in New Delhi.

With a small suitcase in his hand, he stood at the front door of his uncle's house.

"Chachaji, Pairi Pauna, *I touch your feet.* Can I stay here for a while?"

Chachiji was coming down the stairs and heard him. "First, close the door Ballu, it is only November but the wind is so cold. Now, come here. I can beat you up for asking permission to stay in your own home."

She kissed his forehead and spoke tenderly, "I know you have become Bada Vakil, *big lawyer,* but you have to give me justice, too. Is it lawful not to see your 'Chachi' for so many years?"

Veer emerged from his room and a grin spread on his bearded face, "Oy, Bhra, *brother,* you cannot beat our 'Biji', *mother,* in any Court of Law."

"I admit defeat!"

Balwant bent his head in surrender.

It was unfortunate that the Judge, who was Amarjit's wife's niece's brother-in-law's sister's father-in-law and was instrumental in reducing Moni's death sentence to life imprisonment, had retired. The other Judges deemed it unnecessary to open solved cases that were uncomplicated and lucid; Balwant was unable to present any new facts.

Balwant travelled on dusty bumpy roads of New Delhi and commuted on packed buses. He charmed the young secretaries and managed to get his name on the filled-to-the-brim pages of the appointment books of the Congress leaders, Justice Minister, Judges, Home Secretary.

"But Son, Mohinder Singh did commit the crime."

"But it is important to take into account the circumstances that prompted a decent young man to pick up the gun that he abhorred, Sir."

"Well, because of these considerations he was not hung. Isn't that enough?"

"No, that is not justice, Sir."

Hopelessly exhausted and discouraged, Balwant tossed and turned in his bed. In his restless sleep he saw 'Raj Bhavan', the Prime Minister's house; the green, white and orange flag of India with King Ashok's chakra, *wheel,* in the centre, flew proudly with the slight breeze on the roof of the ancient, expansive mansion.

Balwant woke up refreshed, whistled while shaving, came down the stairs with animated steps.

Chachiji was happy. "Ballu, I have not seen you smile ever since you came."

He touched her feet and asked for blessings for the success of his mission. With much gratification she blessed him without asking what the mission was.

Balwant perched himself on the lush, well maintained lawn outside the tall gates of 'Raj Bhavan'. He carried a bag with a thermos full of water, Pranthas, *fried bread,* and yogurt in a small tiffin carrier, as well as two ripe Simla apples. Of course, Chachiji had not forgotten the cutlery.

When Nehruji's, *the first Prime Minister of Free India,* car approached the gate, he stood on one side with folded hands. Nehruji waved absentmindedly.

One week went by; slowly some curious perhaps retired pedestrians noticed his daily, punctual presence and approached him. Balwant narrated the heart wrenching saga of Jeet's murder and Moni's incarceration.

With heavy hearts, they went home. Many of them came back in the early morning next day and brought their respective lunches perhaps made by the wrinkled but loving hands of their wives, or by young soft hands of grumbling daughters-in-law. The food carried them during a whole day, nevertheless.

Slowly the crowd grew. One law college student brought fifteen of his fellow college mates. Differently shaped and coloured banners went up, "We want justice."

The gathering metamorphosed into a picnic of sorts. A vast variety of groups were formed who busied themselves with appropriate activities. Young college and university students played cards, 'Rummy' most of the time, sometimes indulging in spontaneous singing competitions and joke telling causing joyful ripples in the crisp March air.

The older men brought newspapers; grave discussions took place while they squatted on the jade, dewed grass. The very next day many of them brought folding chairs; at their age serious repercussions could result if the rights of their spines were not honored.

Even housewives joined the cause. They sat with other women and knitted sweaters of different colors and sizes for their progeny while gossiping with the usual "Did you know…?" Once the gentle-women affiliated with the mob, plenty of food became available. What kind of picnic would it be without tea, cold-shakanjvi, *lemon water,* since it was already getting warm in mid-March, fruit, homemade biscuits, salty snacks, etc.? One altruistic and dynamic woman brought forty paranthas, *homemade fried bread,* with mango pickle. Everyone, including the ones with weak spines stood up, clapped and cheered, profusely.

Of course, the press noticed, news cameras began to roll and the photograph of the 'picnic' made the front page of New Delhi Times.

Nehruji drove by in the evening and thoroughly enjoyed the sight that he believed was some celebration. He passingly noticed the placards but in the cheery atmosphere, somehow missed the significance.

Nehruji, the first Prime Minister of Independent India, was leading a brand new democracy of 300 million people of diverse religions, cultures, traditions and languages with hundreds of dialects; it was an all consuming commission. However, in spite of the diversity, each and every citizen of New India held a single purpose, goal and dream, to bring back the long lost glory to their Motherland.

The Congress leaders of newly elected Government of Independent India were proficient in sacrificing their lives and rotting in jails to free India, but did not have a clue how to run a nation. Before Independence, an absolute unity of purpose prevailed in the Congress. Now, conflicting ideas, aims, and ambitions surfaced, as these should, in a democracy with freedom of thought and speech as a given. However, perpetual infighting in the Congress fell in Nehruji's lap for resolution.

There was drought in Bihar again, flooding in Uttar Pradesh, South Indians were up in arms against the imposition of 'Hindi' as the National Language.

"Why not Tamil, Telugu, Malyalam, Nehruji?"

In the North-East of India, Bengali Marxists, Naxalites, were demanding an end to feudalism that strangled the dreams of 'kisans', *laborers in farms,* and shattered their hope that promises of Independence would be inclusive and uplift their lives. A peaceful non-violent struggle evolved into a violent movement, out of frustration.

Army was sent to subdue the Naxalites.

Panjab was one of the most consequential States because it was the 'food basket' of India; good soil, rivers, rains and hardworking Panjabis fed the whole nation. The Chief Minister of Panjab, Kairon was an able man. However, his progeny, their cousins and friends, indulged in felonious activities like kidnapping and raping girls before returning them to the agonized parents. They followed their own kind of wisdom; only lasses of poor men were targeted because what could they do? No money, no clout!

Also, Kairon's better or worse-half became a headache for him; she was dubbed 'Queen Noorjahan' by the masses of Panjab.

Stunningly beautiful and cunningly intelligent, 'Noor Jahan' was married to an Army General in Mogul Badshah Jahangir's reign. Soon after Emperor Jahangir laid his eyes on the resplendent, seductive Noor Jahan, her husband was conveniently killed in a war in the south. Jahangir was easily conquered by Noor Jahan and she became the empress of the most powerful Mogul Empire. It is said that she possessed more ascendancy than the Emperor, to the extent that she held her own court. The subjects brought their grievances to her; whether she dealt justice of injustice, history is vague on that.

Mrs. Kairon likewise set up her court in Chandigarh on the roof of her mansion in the summer and living room in the winter. Without a clue of the intricacies of the laws of the land, she hijacked justice on a daily basis. Chief Minister Kairon had no idea of the parallel reign of his wife that many times cancelled the effectiveness of his own.

Slowly the reports of nefarious activities of Kairon clan arrived at Nahruji's desk. He rested his elbows on the sturdy desk, looked up at Mr. Das, hopelessly, "Tell me who else is as capable as Kairon?"

Internationally the Western democracies, especially the United States of America held their breath waiting for dice to fall; to befriend an enormous democracy like India could pay heavy dividends in future conflicts of the world.

During their freedom struggle, Congress' vision for future India was to be a secular and just society. After Independence, groups of planners, administrators and lawmakers went to Russia to learn the many aspects of building an equitable nation from scratch.

The concepts of free health care, education and subsidized food were borrowed from the Russian system. For production of wealth, the western capitalistic model of free enterprise was adopted. However, businesses, banks, monetary institutions were tightly regulated by the Government, measures that would stomp on the tendency of greedy accumulation of wealth by individuals.

Russia also helped India in its goal to become an industrialized progressive country; collaborations occurred in construction of dams, steel plants, mining, etc.

India's relations with China also grew, perhaps, due to common destiny. Both the nations stood at the crossroads, their chosen path could make or break the future of millions of lives.

Nehruji and Congress leaders made a unique decision in a conflicting world. They declared India as a 'non-aligned' nation that would maintain friendly relations with all countries. The policy befitted a civilization that had followed the tradition of non-violence and tolerance for thousands of years.

The American government was not pleased. When Krishna Menon, a Marxist and Defense Minister of New India visited Washington, he was given a cold shoulder. A schism developed within the governing Congress party. Moraiji Desai, a veteran leader of great intelligence was pro-west and coerced many MPs to support him in the Parliament.

To keep a balance and harmony in the government took a toll on Nehruji's health.

Within a few days, Nehruji became serious about the writing on the placards and the perpetual presence of Balwant standing close to the main gate of his abode.

Nehruji bent forward and asked the driver, "Gopal Chacha, *uncle*, what is going on?" Gopal was Nehruji's constant companion since 1942.

Nehruji and some other prominent congress leaders were quarantined in an army camp of unknown location in 1942.

That year, a highly successful 'Quit India' movement shook the roots of British Raj, *British occupation of India.*

England was now embroiled in a deadly war against Hitler. Prime Minister Churchill knew that to fight on two fronts meant defeat in both. In a surprise move, Congress leaders and thousands of supporters, all over India, were captured and imprisoned.

The Congress leaders in the camp were given full freedom of movement within the fence; they could confer with one another. In small barracks, sitting on hard wooden chairs or squatting on a Dari, *woven carpet,* on the cracked cement floor, or half laying on the single bed, wrapped in thorny army blankets or woolen shawls in the winter, the most astute and perspicacious minds converged to fashion the future of India, nurturing their dreams with determination to create a moral and humane society.

Access to newspapers, telephone calls, visitors, or letters was strictly prohibited, obviously to keep the leaders in the dark regarding the fate of their countrymen.

The prisoners read profusely; they were provided with all the books they wanted. Brilliant literary works about the freedom struggle were penned in the simplicity of their confinement.

Gopal was an elderly man assigned to the job of a cook in the camp. Painstakingly, he prepared everyone's favourite dishes with meager rations allocated for the captives. But he was creative; he requested the authorities for seeds of different vegetables and he planted a lush vegetable garden.

Nehruji was a nature lover. Gopal and he planted, weeded, and harvested the fruit of their labour together before anyone else woke in the morning. The soil and climate was favourable in the region wherever it was, for no one, not even the caretakers and the guards knew the exact location. As a result, the prisoners enjoyed culinary treats even in their captivity.

In 1945, after the World War II, the detainees and prisoners all over India were freed. Nehruji held Gopal's hand and said, "Gopal Chacha, you have looked after us like your own children. I will never forget your kindness."

Gopal clutched Nehruji's soft, artistic hand in his crude one, "But I cannot leave you. Please take me with you."

He became Nehruji's driver

Gopal was firm, "Nehruji, I am not going to stop. You have not eaten, you are exhausted. Send Das Saheb to talk to them."

That sounded like a reasonable proposition. But as soon as Nehruji walked into Raj Bhavan, Das was waiting anxiously, "Nehruji, General Monikshaw is here." All else was wiped off his mind.

Monikshaw was tense, "Secret Service have confirmed the buildup of arms and tanks at the Northwest Indochina border!"

Nehruji's heart just refused to believe it. Maybe Chinese were just doing military exercises?

The following evening, Nehruji ordered Gopal to stop the car at the gate. He lowered his window, "Come inside, Son, and tell me your grievance."

Gopal opened the car door reluctantly and let Balwant in; the crowd cheered, "Nehruji ki jai," *Nehruji is great.*

Outside the open window of Nehruji's study, the dark night was breached by nocturnal creatures speaking indecipherable words to one another. The curtain fluttered with the soft April breeze.

It was one o'clock at night. Das looked at his watch, peeped in Nehruji's study and phoned his wife. "Rajshree, sleep. I don't know how long it will take", and let out a wide yawn.

At one-thirty he went into the kitchen. There was no point waking up the servant. Das filled a glass of milk, peeled and sliced an apple, put Nehruji's favourite glucose biscuits on a plate and arranged everything on a Kashmiri, *wooden carved tray.* In an indefatigable commitment to build his India, Nehruji worked eighteen straight hours a day, without awareness of time or his own body. When friends told him not to work so hard, he is said to have quoted Robert Frost: "Woods are lovely, dark and deep, but I have promises to keep. I have to walk miles before I sleep. I have to walk miles before I sleep."

The responsibility of nourishing and keeping him healthy and alive fell on everyone else around him. Without disturbing Nehruji, Das quietly placed the plates and glass of milk on the study desk on which Nehruji was bent gravely studying the documents that Balwant had left for him.

Nehruji raised his graying head, took off his glasses and wiped them with a white handkerchief; tears shone in his longing eyes. "Das, how could this happen in my India?"

Moni staggered out of the central jail in New Delhi, seven years after he was incarcerated.

Balwant and Surinder got married the same year.

Balwant explained apologetically, "I am sorry. The market is in a slump. Would you like to reduce the price of the house? I will advise you against it, but it is up to you."

"I will think about it Bhai. And how about Chris?"

Chris made it clear, "I cannot afford to buy out Mohit's portion of the property. Prices are too low to sell. I couldn't take that much loss, Balwant."

To further complicate matters, the Canadian government was slow to release Mohit's pension. The quandary was legitimate in a way; Meera did not have a marriage certificate. Of course, how would Canadian government know that Indian marriages are not founded on a signature of a government official you've met for the first time? When the priest has the needful connection with the Demi God of Fire, the indisputed attestor to such consequential occasions, along with throngs of rapturous relatives and friends to authenticate their union, who cares about a piece of paper?

Apparently, the Canadian government did.

Meera phoned Atul. "Bhaiya, please send the marriage certificate with signatures of the priest and witnesses and stamped by some judge. Maybe Grover uncle could do that."

"No problem, Choti, consider it done."

Atul had grossly underestimated the task. He had not realized yet that in India to trace people could be as arduous as tracking Gods. The priest's mother fell ill, and he disappeared into some remote village without a word to anyone. Grover uncle had been transferred to the high court in Trivandrum, the southern tip of India, while Simla was close to the north side of the country.

Finally, after much detective work, Atul found the priest. Some three hundred people, every single one who attended the auspicious occasion, were not only available but eager to sign a document that was to be used across the seven seas in a "foreign country office" as well bring Meera home soon. Another judge was contacted to stamp the certificate.

- # -

In spite of curious glances of mostly a white, Western crowd, Prabodh looked poised in his simple beige, knee-long Khadi kurta, *handwoven cotton long shirt,* and white dhoti that reached his ankles. He stood tall and upright at the baggage area, his deep-black piercing eyes looked around searchingly. In a moving crowd, he gave a sense of stillness.

Tayaji had asserted that Prabodh's exceptionally expansive forehead, furrowed by deep horizontal lines, was a sure sign of spiritual wisdom.

Meera wiped her hands with the kitchen towel and picked up the phone.

"Tayaji?" She almost jumped with joy.

"Yes, I am fine . . . how are you? . . . I said how are you . . . and your health? . . . I can't hear you, speak loudly . . . how are Mama and Papa . . . What? . . . I said how is everyone . . . say it again?"

From the elevated pitch and the excitement in Meera's tone, it was obvious that the call was from India. Hushed excitement, curiosity, worry, apprehension swept across everyone's faces in a curious amalgamation. Calls from India were a rarity, not only due to exorbitant charges but also because voices were obscured by intensive background conversations in multilanguages of India picked up by your phone line, crackling circuits, the shshing sound of the oceans.

Only someone with strong lung power could overcome the hurdles and be heard.

"I will come soon, Tayaji . . . I miss you too . . . I know it has been six months . . ." Meera's voice broke.

"Yes? Can't hear you . . . what? Prabodh Da, *brother*? What happened to him? Really." Thrill reappeared in her teary voice.

"I would love to . . . I will wait for his call . . . who . . . Mr. . . . Malik? No, I don't know anyone by that name . . . Rampur? Did you say Rampur . . . oh gosh . . . I can't believe it . . . what . . . yes . . . I know him . . . speak loudly please?" She strained to hear.

"I can't hear a word," Meera mumbled to herself, then made another daring attempt to continue. "Tayaji, give my love to everyone . . . I am fine . . . don't worry."

Meera deposited the phone on the receiver; she was utterly fagged from the emotion, shouting match, and exertion of communicating through the ripples of the seven seas.

"I don't know if he heard me. He sounds worried . . ." Meera walked from the kitchen to the living room.

Quietened, uplifted faces of everyone were marked by a distinct question mark. "Oh, it was Tayaji. Everyone is fine," Meera assured them.

With a mysterious glint in her eyes, she turned to Chachaji playfully. "Chachaji, here is a test for your memory."

Chachaji raised his wrinkled hands in the air, lowered his gray head in a gesture of surrender. "I concede defeat. Memory is my friend no more ever since I set foot in decrepit domain of oldness."

Sunil laughed and took Chachaji's side. "Meera, this is not fair to strain him thus . . ."

"That too without the cup of tea we are all waiting for!" quipped Prashant. "Bela Bhabi, can you kindly make tea while Meeraji unfolds the masala, *spice,* of intrigue that I smell?"

Meera was intractable. "No, no, Chachaji, you must. You were a teacher in Rampur, yes?" Chachaji nodded a perplexed yes.

"Did you have a Bengali student named Prabodh?" Chachaji leaned back on the sofa, shut his eyes, and strolled in the sometimes green, sometimes barren maze of memory lane.

Everyone looked at him keenly.

Befitting a doctor, Satish laughed. "I can see Chachaji's neurons firing desperately."

All of a sudden, Chachaji opened his eyes, his face broke into a brilliant smile. "Ah, his father was in civil service stationed in our district, eh." He turned to Anil. "Anu, you remember? He was younger than you and you both fought for copies and pencils. A tall, dark boy."

Meera clapped in childlike glee. "Yes, yes." Anil crinkled his brow in concentration then laughed. "Oh, I think I do remember. His servant propped him in front of the bicycle and brought him to school. We used to chase the bike and annoy the servant who would then swear profanities in Bengali."

"Oh, he was a naughty boy. But I could not bring myself to punish him because he absorbed knowledge like a sponge. Even at a tender age, he showed great interest in Sanskrit and scriptures. He could recite verses of Vedas, *ancient Hindu scriptures*, Upanishads, *the essence of Hindu philosophy*, from memory and explain the meaning to other students. What happened?" Chachaji gave Meera a quizzical glance.

"Such a small world, Chachaji. Prabodh Da is Tayaji's PhD student at the Department of Religious Studies in Delhi University."

Suddenly, gloom clouded her face. She sat down on the nearest chair and fought her tears. "Atul Bhai and Papa were from Simla, Rakesh Bhai from Chandigarh. They had no idea where to begin. Prabodh Da had been living in Delhi for years and had the necessary contacts. He put aside this thesis and plunged himself wholeheartedly to arrange our wedding in such a short time."

It seemed like yesterday when Meera wore expensive red Banarasi saree laced with gold embroidery, aureate ornaments adoring every part of her fair body; her head was covered with a deep-red chiffon veil with gold border. The willful tikka, *jewelry piece hung on forehead*, hung from the parting of her jet-black hair and glittered on her forehead just above the red bindi, *red dot on married women's forehead.*

Mohit looked very tall in knee-long cream brocade achkan, *long coat*, and silk pajama of the same soft color. Strands of tender, pure, pearl-like white motia, *jasmine*, posies hung from the red-and-gold sehra, *a decorated head gear a groom wears with strings of flowers falling in front of his face*, and partially covered his handsome face. From behind the blossoms, his twinkling eyes and flickering smile captured the hearts of every young girl. Meera could not look up; it was considered immodest. Later, friends informed her in detailed frenzy what Meera missed when Mohit walked toward her to place a rose and carnation jaimala, *garland*, around her delicate goldened neck.

"Ah, ooh", they sighed. "God, please send us such a handsome husband, too . . ."

It was a sunny fall day with some silvery clouds floating listlessly in the skies. Meera kept all windows open to let light and breeze enter the house at will, without having to knock. Just then, gray clouds passed over the beaming sun; a dark shadow fell from the skies and gripped everyone.

Meera tried to smile. "Well, Prabodh Da is on a tour at the various American universities. He will stop here to see me." Her voice softened with affection. "He is like a real brother. When I was living with Tayaji for my music degree at the Delhi University, Prabodh Da was often at his house, both working way into the night, paying no heed to Gangu's threats to quit if they didn't stop.

"And listen to this." Life returned to Meera's voice. "Prabodh Da told Tayaji that his favorite teacher lives in this town, who inspired him to fathom reality and find God."

She looked at Chachaji. "I did not associate Malik with you, but when he said Rampur, it hit me that you are from Rampur."

Chachaji grinned from ear to ear. "I have often thought of where his father was posted after Independence. I have to punish Prabodh for his final prank of disappearing without a word. But then"—he smiled—"I could never punish him . . ."

Prabodh spotted Chachaji in the crowd. He ran toward him, bumping into some people in the process, ignored everyone else, and bent down to touch Chachaji's feet. Chachaji's smiling lips quivered; he lifted Prabodh from his feet and hugged him, showering the ultimate blessing of 'God Realization'.

Prabodh was speechless with incredulity, almost like a child who had unexpectedly found his favorite toy.

Prabodh noticed Meera standing quietly, tearfully. She came forward and touched his feet. Prabodh was much older to her, but her reverence for him was not rooted in his age; it was his spiritual stature that dwarfed everyone else.

He rested his firm hand on her head. “May God bless you with gyan, *wisdom*, and shakti, *power*.” How did he know that her heart had lost direction? She craved Gyan to find her way. Her feet were faltering; she needed shakti to walk the inescapable thorny paths of life.

Meera’s wedding flashed in both minds; she buried her face in Prabodh’s chest. He embraced her with his long arms protectively, silently; in spite of his profound wisdom, he could not find adequate words to express his understanding of her grief.

Meera smiled feebly, “I am okay, Prabodh Da. It is so good to see you.” She turned to others who were standing still, witnessing the reunion. “Meet my dear brother, Prabodh Da.”

Prabodh hugged Sunil, Anil, Satish, Prashant, and rendered a warm pranam, *greeting*, with humbly folded hands to Kanchan and Bela Di.

He looked intensely at Anil and chuckled, “Anil Da?” and gave him a bear hug. “I would never have dreamt that life will ever bring me close to you and respected Guruji.”

Anil laughed, “I hope you are staying for a few months. There is all the catching up to do.”

Prabodh became serious. “We are indebted to you all forever. I cannot say any more.”

Sunil interrupted. “Please don’t, there is no debt. Meera is our sister. too.”

Chachaji reminded them with his usual sagacity that they should leave some words unsaid for later and to pick up the luggage before it lands up in lost and found.

India mourned the loss of Pandit Jawahar Lal Nehru, the second father and custodian of newly freed India. Gandhiji, the first father had expressed, “‘Jawahar’ is a true gem!” Radios aired the sad melodies played on sitar, *a string instrument*, and deeply resonant sarod, *a string instrument*, for a week. People walked in dazed silence, apprehensive about the future of their young nation. In Canada, Meera and her friends slipped into denial. Nehruji died almost a month and a half after Mohit’s accident.

Prabodh arrived carrying the fresh scars of the aftermath.

He spoke sadly. "Nehruji never forgave himself for betraying his mother India, for whom he had sacrificed his whole life, first by freeing her from the shackles of slavery and then dedicating himself to heal her wounds."

Nehruji died on May 27, 1964; immediate cause was a rupture of an artery, but everyone knew it was heartbreak that finished him for good. He died of shock and disbelief.

It was widely believed that Chinese invasion of India in 1962 was in retaliation of the welcoming refuge that Dalai Lama, *Tibet's Buddhist spiritual leader*, received in India. How could Nehruji refuse shelter to an incarnation of Budha in the birthplace of Budha? Why could the Chinese not understand?

They had trekked the towering, intractable, barren rocky Himalayas for weeks, months. Starting with one followed by thousands of famished, frostbitten, exhausted, and ill Tibetan refugees staggered and collapsed at the Indian border post, situated at eleven-thousand-feet elevation in the northern Himalayas.

The Chinese left them no choice. Committed in his own words, "I am but a reflection of Budha," the Dalai Lama refused to betray the vow of absolute nonviolence.

In his most revered sermon, Shrimad Bhagavad Gita, *Song of God*, appropriately delivered in the midst of the most ferocious war between good and evil, Shri Krishna, *an incarnation of God*, allowed humans to pick up the sword for dharmic, *righteous purpose*, to vanquish evil.

But Budha? He arrived on the scene smack in the thick of Kaliyug, an adharmic, *unrighteous epoch,* when ethics and moral principles had become hollow words, priests were anything but holy and looted the illiterate masses, scriptures were distorted to suit egotistical ends. Instead of guiding people onto the path of knowledge of God, they started to charge ignorant masses to perform rituals that the yajman, *client*, was told, would give him happiness on earth and a seat in heaven.

Shri Krishna had faith in man's sense of discretion to identify evil correctly. Budha understood that humans had fallen to the extent that their minds were blurred completely by a fog of ignorance; they could not be trusted to discern the thin line between good and evil. The sword, hence, that was meant to slay the sinful, could be raised against the innocent.

Buddha declared absolute nonviolence as one of the most significant pillars of a Buddhist "Dharmic life," taking away the possibility of harm to the virtuous.

Yet how do you fight soldiers with guns slung on their shoulders with nonviolence and compassion, kindness and love, even forgiveness? They were not taught the pure language of the spirit at their military academy.

Seated on a large chair, surrounded by worried, desperate monks, with his head in his hands, Dalai Lama asserted, "They will soon realize their folly. Our goodness shall win their hearts."

"But," a frequent query was, "they are killing our babies, women, how about self-defense, my Buddha?"

Tears trickling down his young cheeks, Dalai Lama doubled over in pain and wept.

The frustrated head monk pleaded, "Kundun, you must escape! Chinese government has decided to kill you!"

He looked up firmly. "What good am I if I betray my people?"

"What good are you dead?" The monk had a point.

Realizing the scale and immensity of the exodus, Indian Prime Minister Nehru sent personnels, doctors, food, blankets, jeeps to the point of entry of the refugees. The military post was normally manned by a couple of shivering, bored soldiers with nothing to do but peep into the binoculars occasionally.

A crop of bald heads on saffron torsos grew within weeks in the ancient narrow, stone-paved streets of Dharamsala.

In the birth country of Buddha, Buddhist monks were welcomed, fed, clothed, sheltered by the simple mountain people who felt honoured that Dalai Lama, an incarnation of Buddha, who is in turn considered to be an incarnation of Lord Vishu, had set his sacred feet on their evergreen forested land, in person.

"Something is brewing on the northern heights of the Himalayas that has a foul smell," the military generals reported to the foreign minister Krishna Menon. He was from the south of India where elected Marxist governments ruled a couple of states. He was a staunch Marxist hence felt a certain camaraderie with the Chinese. He did not believe they intended harm.

"How could Nehruji trust them?" most Indians lamented hopelessly. "After the unprovoked invasion of Tibet and threats to kill Dalai Lama, how could we be friends with the Chinese? Why wasn't Nehruji cautious, prepared, or aware when Chinese were building up military presence at the Himalayan peaks?"

"How can they attack us, Chinese and Indian are bhai bhai, *brothers*? We have treaties of cooperation and friendship. How can they break those?" Nehruji lamented.

The masses were too ordinary to understand that Nehruji belonged to that rare category of magnanimous humans who abide in a higher sphere of existence, guided by the loftiest moral principles of truth and honesty. He could not even imagine deceit and treachery in others.

Nehruji was not the same man after the Chinese invasion in 1962. He was shattered, disillusioned, lost interest in life. He never recovered.

Even Prashant was serious. "Dada, *brother*, do you think Pandit Lal Bahadur Shastri can fill Nehruji's shoes?"

"No one can. He worked for eighteen hours a day to build a sovereign republic from ruinous past. People loved him, even his critics had to agree that he served his nation like a true son."

Prabodh continued, "As to Pt. Lal Bahadur Shastri, he is a saintly human like Gandhiji, but he is not a politician. You need a different mettle and worldly wisdom to deal diplomatically with educated as well as uneducated elected members of Parliament, who lack the insight into democratic political institutions. Luckily, masses do like and respect him. In a gargantuan civilization, it can be of great significance to hold credibility and sway amongst those you rule."

Sunil queried, "How about Morarji Desai? He is a seasoned politician, quite brilliant and strong minded, takes a stand. Lal Bahadur Shastri is too polite and gentle to assert his mind and draw support for unpopular but good decisions."

Prabodh agreed, "Yes, there was a strong support for Morarji at the Congress meeting after Nehruji died. But not everyone likes his rightist leanings. There is definite schism in the Congress party. Actually, factionalism has always been there. Maybe disjunction is a norm in Democratic systems where people are allowed to think differently. But Nehruji was the binding force. All members of the Parliament had trust and awe for him even if there was disagreement. He could still sway votes for the measures he stood for."

Chacha, *uncle,* Nehru, that is what he was called by all the children of India, because he had a very soft corner for them. He came to Simla several times. Schoolchildren in the hundreds lined up at the "Upper Mall" road and "Ridge" and showered petals of carnations, marigolds, and roses on him as he strolled by, touching some rosy cheeks with his famous hands, hugging some tiny tots, patting older kids on their oily, shiny heads, and shaking hands with still older boys.

Nehruji was garlanded by all the big, big personalities of Simla with bright marigold flowers, the most auspicious of Indian blooms, as he stepped down from the helicopter. He unloaded some by throwing them at the children as new garlands were dotingly placed around his handsome neck. Every child would shout with innocent glee, "Chacha Nehru ki Jai."

Meera's classmate, Nalini, was considered the most fortunate girl of her school because she happened to catch one perfumed garland. But she committed a grave blunder for which the children of the whole school united to ostracize her. She showed it to every classroom and continued to do it even after the marigolds had dried up. She was not forgiven until she cried and promised not to ever bring the garland to school or brag about it.

Meera heard Nehruji's inspirational speeches time and again as she grew older, at mass rallies or lectures in universities.

But Chacha Nehru of her childhood, fair and strikingly handsome with a typical Kashmiri long nose that he inherited from his ancestors and delicate nonmuscular long-fingered hands, was etched in her consciousness forever. Even at a young age, Meera had noticed that his eyes looked sad with unspoken dark longings lingering behind his eyelids. She could sense his loneliness in the midst of crowds.

Anil was dismayed. "That cohesion is going to disappear, vested interests will take precedence over national unity. The trend was fettered by Nehruji's winsome personality. Now, I don't know. I hope the India of Gandhiji's dream survives this blow."

Not impressed by the doomsday scenario, Chachaji resisted, "Nai nai, *no no,* pessimism robs man of hope and sinew. Have faith.

Throughout history, India has fostered great souls. I see no reason why the future should change that."

Anil laughed. "Bauji, *father*, I know you are a chronic optimist, but we have to be realistic too."

Chachaji feigned resignation. "Well, I am getting old. But our generation had to keep the 'light at the end of the tunnel' in our hearts and minds. Otherwise, we could not have sustained and won the struggle for independence."

Prabodh smiled. "Guruji, you are always wise, I agree with you."

He called out, "Meera, how come no music-shusic?"

It was common knowledge that as soon as Meera opened her eyes in the morning, she extended her hand to turn the radio on, which lay conveniently close to her night table. Right after returning from school or college, she would turn the needle of the radio to all the radio stations until she found classical music. If not, ghazals would do. If even that failed, she would sing herself.

Meera's throat was clogged with pent-up music that rippled within her heart, unable to find release. Seven long months, but she could not sing. "Da, can you understand?" Bela looked at Prabodh meaningfully; Prasant got up from the sofa chair. "Why am I always the victim, Bela Bhabi, tell me that?"

Bela looked at him amusingl., "What?"

"I did not even have lunch! Where is the food, man, so many announcements, no action. Like Indian politicians, all slogans no performance . . . Meera!"

He started walking toward the kitchen. "I am very disappointed. I thought once you leave India, there is some hope of corrective measures."

Meera wiped sweat off her forehead with the palloo. "Prashantji, calm down! It is absolutely ready. Just announce it!"

Bela came to the kitchen and started taking dongas, *casseroles*, to the dining room. Everyone filled their plates without delay.

"Meera, food is so . . . good," Anil exclaimed, licking chicken curry from his spoon.

"Anilda, where is Ashaji? I was hoping to meet her," Prabodh asked. Anil smiled. "She is Doctor Sahiba, on call today."

"Great, what a noble profession to heal the sick."

Prashant appeared content, reclined on the comfortable love seat, spread his legs in front. He looked at Meera and Bela, who had finally sat down to feed themselves after feeding everyone else.

"No, paan-shan, *betel leaves*, what kind of establishment are you running anyway, eh?"

Bela looked at him with feigned annoyance. "Aré you, bhukhar, *greedy!* Eat good food, no thanks-shakns, now demanding *paan*? Why don't you go out and get it yourself from the corner of Rivolli cinema *paanwalla*?"

Prashant was, as usual, gratified by the effect. "Bhabi, unfortunately that *paanwalla* has been sent to jail. He was putting bhang, *opium,* in the pans, and the cinema goers were hallucinating and fighting amongst themselves." Everyone rolled in loud laughter.

Satish had been attempting to get Prabodh's attention, but the latter was completely humoured and charmed by Prashant's lightheartedness.

Finally, he raised his voice a few pitches. "Prabodh Da, don't listen to this joker, he will get encouraged and never stop. Please listen. A professor at the philosophy department, John Walker, specializes in Eastern religions especially Hinduism. He asks me, an atheist, all kinds of questions. I know nothing. He came to my office the other day, and I told him about your visit. Apparently, he is familiar with Meera's Tayaji's writings. He wants you to give a lecture at the college tomorrow. What do you say?"

Prabodh delved into his memory bank and went over the itinerary.

"I am sorry, Satish, I have to leave tomorrow."

"So soon?" Meera was cleaning the dining table; she looked disappointed.

"Yes, Choti, I have commitments I cannot cancel. But in India, we are all waiting for you? What is keeping you?"

Meera said encouragingly, "Some things have to be sorted out, Da. But I should be there soon."

"Actually, Guruji wanted me to bring you back. You better hurry up."

Satish asked abruptly, "Prabodh Da, answer a question for me that you are most qualified to know."

"What?"

"Why can't I see God?"

Prabodh smiled. Wasn't it the most sought-after enigma that was as easy to understand as breathing, once you acquire a deeper insight into Reality.

"Yes, I can explain it. But first find the answer to this riddle. Why can't you see your own face?"

Satish protested, "But you cannot answer a question with another question. That is not allowed. But I can see my face in the mirror!"

"No, that is not your face, that is reflection of your face."

"Oh."

"Just think about it. When I come next time, we will discuss it."

"Da, if you want to convert me, you will have to do better than that. Anyway, I will wait."

Prabodh became thoughtful for a few moments.

"You know, I think I can stop on my way back. I don't have too many commitments when I get back to Delhi."

Meera clapped jubilantly like a little child.

Satish was happy. "Well, let me know the detail. I will tell John to arrange your lecture."

- # -

"The topic of my lecture is 'God in the age of science.'"

Prabodh thanked the hosts and an audience that consisted of a blend of bright-eyed, keen, bored, complacent, male, female, young, old students, for showing up to hear his blabber.

He opened with, "Einstein, one of the greatest scientists of our century proclaimed, 'Science without religion is lame, religion without science is blind.' He was a true scientist but did not find any contradiction between his belief in God and his work in science. Seventy to eighty percent of all scientists around the world echo his sentiment. Early scientists from Copernicus to Newton were men of deep faith for whom scientific study of heavens was a glimpse into the majesty of God's handiwork.

"It is interesting that a vast majority of skeptics are not scientists but invoke science in their denial of the verity of God.

Prabodh had called from Berkeley University, "Choti, one of my meetings is cancelled. I can come for a day and a half before leaving for India. Tell Satish to arrange the lecture."

It was a Friday. Posters appeared all over in the different departments, informing students that they had a chance to hear about the great religion of India, Hinduism, by a well-known scholar from Delhi.

"First, let me define a few words that I shall be using profusely during my lecture. I will explain those in detail later during the discourse. These terms have been derived from the *Vedanta,* philosophy of ancient India. *Vedanta* literally means culmination of knowledge.

"The principles of Hinduism were expounded in the scriptures called Upanishads, *the essence of Hindu philosophy,* that were penned thousands of years ago by highly spiritual rishis. Upanishads constitute the backbone of Hinduism and are the fountainhead from which most Hindu philosophical thoughts spring forth.

"According to Upanishads the ultimate Reality of existence is 'Brahm,' that is also known as Absolute, the Supreme Reality, the Universal Self or God. The spark of Brahm or God confined within the bounds of all living beings is *Soul* or *Spirit, Atma* or *Self.* Brahm and *Atma* are essentially the same, existing in a state of inviolated unity.

"With the age of faith behind us, the question that has plagued the modern, thinking man is, 'If God exists why we can't we perceive Him with our senses?'

"The argument that God is not because we cannot perceive Him with our senses is not even logical because we know the limitation, fallibility and imperfection of our sense organs. Our eyes cannot detect short (UV) and long (far-red) wavelengths of light. We can only discern the intermediate range of wavelengths. In the dark, of course, we are as good as blind while owls have no difficulty. We believe with deadly certainty that our eyes are viewing water, an oasis in a desert. Sand blowing in our faces proves it to be a mirage instead. We are unable to descry very fine particles of matter such as molecules, atoms, protons, etc. Our capacity to see far objects is pathetically short-sighted. It is obvious that our eyes are an imprecise, restricted sense of optics.

"Our auditory apparatus presents us with the same story of limitedness. Ears can only pick up certain radio waves of specific frequency. Many times, we hear ringing out of silence. Distant sounds are not audible to us. Even dogs, horses, and many other animals possess a more acutely sensitive acoustic organ. It is a well-known observation that immediately prior to earthquakes or other impending disasters, these animals react with anxious hyperactive restlessness. Humans sleep until disaster knocks at their doorsteps.

"Our sense of touch is easily confused. After exposure to really hot water, our skin feels hot touch as lukewarm and lukewarm as cold. Following a dip in cold water, even lukewarm feels hot.

"We are unable to see, hear, touch, or grasp the air we breathe, yet we know it to be existent.

"Admittedly imperfect, if our senses do not detect 'something,' it does not necessarily mean that 'something' is nonexistent.

"The Vedanta has declared thousands of years ago, 'Where eye goes not, speech goes not . . . beyond the reaches of the senses . . . is the realm of Brahm.'

"Western philosophers of the last centuries—Immanuel Kant, George Berkeley, Arthur Schopenhauer, and many others—have admitted that human senses are inadequate to perceive God.

"The most fashionably contemporary claim disputing the existence of God is that His Reality has not been substantiated by science, hence He is not. There are several obvious fallacies inherent in this supposition. Firstly, skeptics believe that science has already reached the summit of perfection, and it is an impeccable instrument of knowledge to reveal 100 percent of Reality. Hence, if science does not prove the existence of 'something,' that something does not exist.

"The fact is that science is constantly progressing, adding to our pool of knowledge, every day. If we know more today, it is obvious that we did not know everything yesterday or yesteryear. Hence, at any given moment in time, science cannot claim to know all the truths of Reality, including that of the existence of God.

"Since the advent of the scientific age, science has been regarded as the greater God, infallible and absolute. If it looks unfavourably even upon God, well, who is God to argue?

"Let us reverse our stand and examine our blind faith in science and ask ourselves what is that we have given so much power to? What really is science?

Science, by definition, is knowledge covering general truths or the operations of general laws, as obtained and tested through scientific method.

"And what is scientific method? It is a tool, a systematic procedure and logical methodology for attaining knowledge.

"However, the scope of science has serious limitations that are intrinsic to its very nature. You see, scientific method is founded on 'empirical' knowledge, which is the insight we achieve through observation using our 'senses' and scientific instruments that merely augment the perception of a particular sense. For example, binoculars are a scientific instrument that intensify and broaden the range of our otherwise limited eye sight. But that vision is not unlimited or absolute. We cannot see everything in the sky with binoculars. Even with wonderfully complicated telescopes we can barely see a fraction of the universe that lies beyond us.

"By far the greatest limitation of science is that its activity is restricted within the bounds of empirical, material Reality—every other Reality is beyond its reach.

"For instance, senses and scientific tools have not been able to detect or elucidate the 'Mind' stuff that the 'Vedanta' considers as subtler than 'gross matter.' And only the mindless do not know for sure that mind exists. The philosopher Descarte, went as far to say, "I am because I think," thereby underlying the importance of mind that science is inadequate to prove the existence of. Of course, scientific instruments have been invented to detect brain activity, but brain and mind are different though closely related.

"We cannot empirically measure or demonstrate the existence of feelings, emotions, pain, pleasure, thought and other 'subjective' experiences that are confined to the domain of 'Mental Reality.' And yet their legitimacy and truth is never in doubt.

"It implies that we can arrive at 'Truth' of pain, pleasure, love, feelings, thoughts, etc., through purely 'subjective experience' without any empirical proof of the senses or objective evidence of science. Hence, 'subjective' experiences can hold valid ground and are able to form the underpinnings of knowledge.

"It follows that the 'subjective' experiences of thousands of saints, devotees of God, sages, spiritual mystics, who have encountered and realized their inner 'Spirit' and God, should be considered sound, logical, well-grounded proof of existence of God without the necessity of invoking science.

"The realms of 'Mental' and 'Spiritual' Reality are transcendent and far above the phenomenal aspirations of science; the operations of science belong to a different realm altogether, that of 'gross matter.' God is unmanifest to our senses and empirical tools because he is not constituted of 'gross matter.' Science is not qualified to prove or disprove the verity of God.

"Dr. Radhakrishnan, a brilliant philosopher and scholar of Vedanta, the second president of free India, wrote, 'Real insight into science reveals that it is useful in dispelling the darkness oppressing the mind. It also reveals its own limitations and prepares the mind for something beyond itself. If we mistake the partial truths of science for the whole truth of the "Spirit," we are stuck with inferior knowledge . . .'

"Science is a small vessel that cannot contain the vast sea of Transcendental Reality in its infinitesimal space. There is no doubt that the dawn of scientific age has advanced our search for material knowledge, but it has rejected every other path that promises a glimpse of the metaphysical. Hence started the age of doubt and skepticism. Science has become a constraining cage of empiricism. Beyond lies a larger Reality, but it is beyond our reach. What is gained in material is lost in 'spirit.'

"Next obvious question is if senses and science are inadequate to reach and reveal God, how else is man to seek and attain Him?

"One of the most important devices that man has used for thousands of years to grope into the intricacies of nature and Reality is the power of mind, logic, or reason. In Hindu scriptures Buddhi, *mind,* is considered one of the perceptive senses that use philosophical thought and inner reflection for perceiving 'Reality.'

"Most of what we construe and presume as scientific has also been derived through reason and indirect inference. Have you seen atoms, protons, electrons, neutrons? Of course you have not. Neither have the scientists who claim unequivocally that these particles exist. We have not seen electromagnetic waves, gravity, or earth moving around the sun using our senses. Yet we find it credible to conclude that these are important phenomenon of nature and hold the conviction of their certainty as fact.

"These so-called scientific truths or beliefs have been 'deduced' from assumptions and observations of effects, attributes, and properties using logic and reason to associate 'invisible cause' with 'visible effect.' Most of the principles underlying the sciences of chemistry, physics, astronomy, even biology (have you seen a DNA molecule?) are founded on reason and logic. Reason and logic are the most important endowments of human existence.

"Having established mind and reason as one of the most important instruments of knowledge, the question faces us, can we prove God through reason?

"The answer is no, we cannot elucidate God through reason. Here is why.

"Reason stands on the foundation of some premises, 'a priori knowledge' acquired through prior 'empirical experience.' According to David Hume, a brilliant eighteenth-century Western philosopher, 'Reasoning as well as ideas originate from experience.' And experience essentially springs from sense-based perceptions. He emphasized, 'All our ideas are derived from our impressions, emotions and images of the external world through senses.'

"Immanuel Kant, one of the greatest philosophers of the eighteenth century, concluded, 'All our knowledge begins with experiences.'

"Arthur Schaopenhauer, a nineteenth century religious thinker, mused, 'Reflection—the abstract discursive concepts of reason obtain their whole context from knowledge of perception and in relation to it.'

"We already know that the depth and range of sense-based knowledge is finite, senses are known to reach only as far as material Reality. Hence 'a priori' knowledge can only encompass the 'material' realm. Sadly, all the handicaps, follies, and limitations of senses are visited upon reason. Hume understood the limitations of thought. 'Though thought seems to possess unbounded liberty . . . it is really confined within very narrow limits . . . all the creative power of mind amounts to no more than the faculty of compounding, transposing, augmenting or diminishing the materials afforded us by the sense experience.'

"George Berkeley, an eighteenth-century 'idealist' reflected, 'The mind of man being finite, when it treats of things which partake of infinity, it is not be wondered at, if it runs into absurdities and contradictions, out of which it is impossible it should even extricate itself, it being of the nature of infinite not to be comprehended by that which is finite.'

"Säntidev, an ancient Indian philosopher believed that mind or thought cannot perceive God because, 'Absolute Reality' does not fall within the domain of intellect that is confined to the realm of 'relativity.' And whole empirical existence is relative no matter how you look at it. The only 'Absolute' is Brahm, God, where there is no dualism or 'relative' existence. Thought is limited 'self.' God is unlimited and so thought cannot grasp the unlimited.

"An ancient Hindu sage wrote, 'My own limitations, not only of senses but also of intellect are so apparent and obvious, that I am not capable of understanding all of Reality. Limited can never grasp unlimited. Therefore, the truth of the existence of God, that I cannot grasp in its fullness, is never in doubt, definitely not because I cannot grasp it hence, it is not . . .'

"Dr. Radhakrishnan went on to say, 'There is a "Real," but we cannot know it, and what we know is not "Real." Thought is structurally incapacitated because it deals with parts and not the whole. It is self-contradictory and inadequate because thought works with the opposition of subject and object. "Absolute Real" is something in which these antithesis are annulled. If we want to grasp the Real, we will have to give up thought.'

"Immanuel Kant whose influence on the way 'reason' is viewed in philosophical realm, is still felt today, realized the limitations of the faculty of reason. 'God, Immortality, freedom, and metaphysical concepts cannot be understood by pure reason . . . I have, therefore, found it necessary to deny knowledge in order to make room for faith.' He reasoned that human understanding can only know appearances, phenomena, it can never penetrate Reality . . . can never answer questions about God and Soul, beginnings and ends. God, Immortality, freedom are supersensible realities—cannot be proved by theoretical reason.'

"William James, the nineteenth-century founder of the pragmatic school of thought in America, called Religion 'a fact of experience. Abstract reasoning cannot provide it with support . . . feeling is a deeper source of religion . . . attempt to demonstrate by purely intellectual processes, the truth of the deliverance of direct religious experience is absolutely hopeless.'

"Vedanta admits and warns against applying the categories of the phenomenal world to God. The world of experience does not reveal God within its limits. The seer of the Vedanta, when called upon to describe the nature of Brahm, kept silent and, when the question persisted ultimately, declared, 'Brahm is silence. Where eye goes not, speech goes not, nor the mind, we know not, we understand not, how one would teach it? It is other than the known and above the unknown.'

"Berkeley believed that, 'the reason we do not have an idea of Soul or Spirit is not because our senses are defective, but this "substance" that supports and perceives ideas cannot be an idea like other ideas.' He further stated, 'Spirit is one simple, undivided active being . . . no idea can be formed of a Soul or Spirit . . . such is the nature of Spirit, that it cannot be itself perceived . . . so Spirit is different from the ideas it supports . . . being an agent, cannot be represented by any idea at all . . .'

"God or Soul, by their very nature, are neither an 'object' of empirical scientific observation nor a matter of reason. If we adhere dogmatically to reason, it can become an impossible impediment that we are unable to transcend in order to grasp the higher Realities of the Absolute God and Spirit.

"Hence, God is beyond the sphere of reason.

"The question still remains: how is God known or experienced? According to Dr. Radhakrishnam, 'If we mistake partial truth of science for the whole of the Spirit, we are stuck with inferior knowledge. It has to be supplemented with another power, power of intuition for higher knowledge.'

"Blaise Pascal, a seventeenth-century philosopher, proclaimed, 'We know the truth not only by reason but also by heart (intuition) . . . the heart has its own order, the intellect has its own. The heart has his reasons that reason does not know . . . it is the heart that experiences God and not the reason.'

"Intuition is one of the important but unacknowledged faculties of knowing whatever cannot be discerned by the five senses, scientific inquiry, and reason. This perceptive quality is so evolved in some individuals that it is given a legitimate name, 'the sixth sense.' Every individual perhaps possesses this supersensory ability but has no awareness of its power. Even science relies heavily on intuition when it extends itself beyond the known and delves into the unknown. Scholars have speculated that it was Einstein's unshakable 'intuitive belief' in the unity of the universe that led him to his breakthrough discovery of the 'special theory of relativity,' which postulates that matter and energy are interconvertible hence fundamentally identical.

"According to Vedanta, Reality of Absolute God has been 'intuited' by the 'Seers,' the Mukt, *free*, and others have to accept their authority. The knowledge of the ancient rishis was intuitive hence untainted by the biases of human mind. Rishi Pätanjali, a spiritualist who lived 3,500 years ago, elaborated in his treatise on Yoga-Sutra, *the way to unite with God*, that 'man has mystic power and divine insight by which he can transcend the limitations and distinctions of intellect and discern the Brahm.' He called it Intuitive Realization or Direct Knowledge.

"Rishi Pätanjali expounded a systematic path, a step-by-step logical process of inner meditation for 'Direct Realization' or experience of God. We humans can experience our 'Soul' directly as 'subject' when awareness of body and mind is effaced from the mind consciousness by calming all external sense experiences as well as internal thoughts. Having transcended the subject/object duality, the 'Soul' shines forth in such a Samadhi of the East and mysticism of the West, as pure untainted 'Self-illumining Consciousness.' That is our true 'Self,' *I*.

"The moment our Soul experiences 'itself by itself,' the 'Soul' realizes that it is one with the Absolute God Himself.

"Vedanta declares, '*Atma* illumines itself and illumines Brahm at the same moment. This Soul, *Atma* is not to be known by study, not by more developed understanding, not by listening or hearing more about it. It is to be known, experienced, attained by the person who devoutly covets only Atma, procures Atma by Atma. Face-to-face with the ardent seeker, Atma throws away all its veils and illumines its Reality to such a person.'

"Therefore, our instrument for experiencing God is our own 'Self,', Soul, Atma or Spirit, that experiences God by reflecting upon itself since it is essentially one with the Absolute God.

"Hence, the 'Direct Knowledge' or direct experience of God or 'Soul' is possible, but can only occur through a 'subjective' experience. The seventh-century philosopher Shankracharya, explained, 'The witness "Self" illumines consciousness (mind) but is never itself in consciousness (mind). It is not a "datum" of experience, it is "who" experiences all the objects. It never becomes object. It is the perfect subject with no trace of objectivity.'

"Arthur Schopenhauer arrived at a similar conclusion, 'That which knows all things and is known by none, is the subject. Subject is always the "knower" never the "known" . . . we never "know" it, but it is always the "knower" wherever there is knowledge.'

"According to Vedanta, the reason why mind or thought cannot perceive God is because 'thought' cannot make 'Him' its object. On the contrary, thought and mind are a scene, Drishya, or object for the subject, 'Soul' and God. Therefore, God is never an object of our experience, we cannot know Him as 'it,' as we know this table, this room, and other material or living objects. But God is behind this phenomenal world *Who* knows all these objects. He is the 'Collective Universal Consciousness,' the 'knower' of this whole phenomenal existence. 'Soul,' 'Self-consciousness,' is the knower of the body.

"In their philosophical pursuit, Western philosophers of the last centuries arrived at a similar conceptualization of 'Universal Consciousness.' Immanuel Kant had approached the idea of a 'Universal Consciousness' and called it 'Transcendental Ego of Apperception.' But for him, the 'Transcendental Ego' had no theological implications.

"Kant's successors converted 'Abstract Consciousness' into an infinite 'Concrete Self-Consciousness' which is the 'Soul' of the universe (Brahm, God) and in which our sundry personal self-consciousness (Souls) have their being.

"Principal Caird, a Scottish transcendentalist of the nineteenth century, mused, 'The "Reality" in which all intelligence rests . . . is an "Absolute Spirit" and only in communion with this "Absolute Spirit" our "Finite Spirit," "Soul" can realize itself. It is Absolute . . . in its independence . . . an Absolute thought or "Self-Consciousness."' Principal Caird made the transition that Kant did not. He converted the omnipresence of 'Consciousness' in general as a condition of

'Truth being anywhere possible,' into an 'Omnipresent Universal Consciousness,' which he identified with God in His concreteness.

"The most profound tragedy of our times is that we have lost touch with our inner Reality, our Selfhood, our moorings. Hence, our inner experience is void. We identify with our ego self that is forever battered by the brutal winds of sense experience and the dualities of pain and pleasure. We are not even aware of the 'Experiencee,' that is our true 'Self,' 'Soul,' the witness who stands unmoved, calm, and unaffected by this drama called life. Hence, 'Self' is implicit in all experiences as the ultimate 'Subject' of experience, 'I,' never as 'it,' the object.

"When a human, through true knowledge and wisdom, is able to live established in his true 'Self' or Soul, he is called Jeevan Mukt, *free while alive*. He has attained moksha, *ultimate freedom*, total freedom, bliss, and peace that we all crave for.

"Swami Vivekananda, the late nineteenth-century philosopher and saint proclaimed in his moments of ecstasy, 'If I can experience God, so can all humans.'

"But if humans are looking outside of themselves to find God, they will be disappointed. He is not a person like us, he is all pervading hence formless since form limits us in space and time. We must delve within ourselves, reach our 'Real Self,' the 'Soul,' God will show Himself to us."

Chapter Two

Thousands of years ago, 'Uddhalak,' a rich and famous Brahmin was performing a 'Yajna,' a ritual using fire. He offered the participating Brahmins appropriate money and cows. His young son, Nachiketa, observed that his father was giving away ill, old useless cows to them. He pondered and came to the conclusion that his father would not get the desired reward for his yajna. To rectify his stingy father's imprudence, he suggested to him, "Father, I am your property, who are you going to give me to?"

Uddhalak misunderstood his son's intentions and spoke in anger, "I give you to Death."

To fulfil his father's words, Nachiketa went to the Lord of Death, Yama's residence.

Yama was not at home. Nachiketa waited at the gate for three days and nights, without food and water.

Upon Yama's return, his wife admonished him. "A Brahmin guest is akin to Lord Agni, the demi god of fire. You better appease him."

Yama addressed Nachiketa humbly, "O Brahmin, I am sorry that I neglected you for three days and nights. Please ask me for three boons, one for every day you suffered."

Nachiketa folded his hands and said, "Lord Yama, please ensure that my father would forgive and love me upon my return to earth."

Yama was pleased at Nachiketa's devotion to his father.

"Your father will love you all his life. Now, the second boom?"

"I understand that 'heaven' is a wonderful place. There is no fear of old age, death, hunger, thirst, pain or sorrow; people are always happy. But to go there, we humans need to know 'Agnividya,' a special Yajna. Please teach it to me."

Yama expounded, "Agnividya, for attainment of Heaven, the procedure is to build the 'Havan-kund,' a hollow structure made with bricks where the fire is lit, light the fire, add ghee, concentrated butter and other specific stuff to the fire as well as mantras, verses from Scripture, to be chanted for the Yajna."

"Now, the third boon, son?"

"Lord, there are different speculations about whether soul perishes or lives after a person's death. O wise one, I want to know the truth."

Yama wondered if Nachiketa, a young boy, was urged by idle curiosity to ask such an abstruse question. 'AtmaVidya', knowledge of the Soul Self, the greatest of all knowledge was meant to be revealed only to highly deserving, pure, genuine and pertinacious pursuant. So, Yama tested Nachiketa.

"Son, this question is too subtle and profound. Even devtas (demi gods) tried but could not resolve it, so, ask me another boon."

"No, Lord, I just want to know the truth about this complex enigma."

"I will make you the king of the whole universe, give you palaces, thousands of horses, cows, elephants, gold, and treasures. You can live as long as you wish."

"No, thank you, Lord."

"I can give you the most beautiful women with all their musical instruments from heaven to please you."

"O Lord Yama, whatever you have offered me, is transient, the happiness these may grant me is temporary. Also, fulfilling my worldly desires will make me weak and thirsty for more. You can keep all these materials, pleasures to yourself. You are the most erudite teacher, and the knowledge of the 'Soul' is of great significance. Please, teach me."

Yama was gratified by Nachiketa's wisdom, determination, as well as detachment from the world of illusory material gratification.

"Oh, son, I have tested you, you are indeed a true seeker of 'Atmavidya'.

"'Soul' is unborn, eternal, unchangeable, unpolluted, pure consciousness. It cannot be cut with a sword, burnt in fire, drowned in water or dried by air. It is indestructible and does not perish when body dies.

"'Soul' resides within all living sentient beings. Man cannot see it because of a veil of maya, illusion. When someone pure and sagacious with unsatiable desire for truth lifts the veil, he experiences his 'Atma', Soul. When he achieves self-enlightenment, simultaneously he unites with blissful Absolute Soul, God, Brahm."

Nachiketa touched Lord Yama's feet, thanked him, and returned to earth. In due time, he did achieve 'Atmavidya', union with blissful God, and eternal life.

Kathopnishad, an important Scripture of Hinduism

Meera stroked her dishevelled hair and leaned forward, "Oh, Bhabi, *sister-in-law*, you must be so tired with Rishi in your lap. Let me lay him in his carriage at the back. Bhai, *brother,* we will have to stop, I have to make formula for him."

Rishi was up and whined at the strange lap he found himself in as well as pangs of hunger.

Atul yawned, "Good idea. I need tea to wake me up, Meera. There is a clean dhaba, *tented food outlet,* just half a mile away."

Meera laughed, "Dhaba and clean? You are kidding!"

Soon, a *dhaba* appeared out of nowhere.

"Bhai, it was not here before? And it does look tidy!"

"Thankfully, there are fewer flies to compete for goodies."

Atul parked the car on one side of the dhaba. It was surrounded by a clump of mango and pippal trees on the both sides and emerald farmland in the background. He picked up Rishi from Asha's lap, who straightened her saree and stretched her still legs.

"Hello, Mansingh ji, how are you?" Atul walked toward the wooden stools that lay scattered in front of the dhaba.

The dhaba owner was a short and skinny fellow, with unusually fair complexion; wore khaki pants, blue shirt and a tight red turban. He was strikingly better dressed than the worn-out-brown-with-dirt pajama-and-kameez-clad dhabawallas.

"Sat Sri Akal, *Sikh greeting,* Bhaji, *brother.*"

Mansingh folded his hands in greeting. "Where are you coming from this early in the morning?" His jet-black eyes twinkled with youthful zeal.

"We went to Delhi to pick up my sister. She's come from Canada."

"Oho, Canna-da." Mansingh was visibly impressed. "Verry faraway Behenji, *sister.* Sat Sri Akal. Your bawa, *child*?" He pointed toward Rishi.

Meera nodded with a smile.

"Wah, wah, bilkul Angrez lagda eh, *looks English*!"

In India, everyone who has fair complexion is Angrez, *British.* Call it revenge; the departing British dumped avoirdupois of negative complexes on the collective psyche of Indian masses; it may take many generations to get rid of their lingering hold and be truly free.

"Te Jijaji kithe ne, *where is your husband*?"

Meera was hit across her chest. She had prepared herself for such discomforting querries, but it was obvious that no amount of readiness was enough to face such painful questions head-on.

Atul glanced at Meera anxiously then spoke to Mansingh in a hushed voice, "Unfortunately, he died in an accident last year."

Mansingh's deep eyes mellowed, his voice took a sharp dive, "Wahe Guru, *God in Punjabi language*, we don't know why God does these things. So young, so young." He sighed sincerely.

Before he could proceed any further with his pain-rendering condolence, Atul said, "We are in a hurry. We have to catch the train from Kalka to Simla. So please, a quick omelet for three and boiled water for the baby's milk."

Mansingh dropped his delicate demeanor on the dusty ground and sprung into swift action, "Loji, loji phata phat. *It will be done quickly.* Oy Surjit . . .," he yelled loudly to some invisible helper. "Get up you bum. Cut onions ekdum, *immediately*. Chalo, *go*."

A puny face with hair tied up in a small bun on the top of his head popped up from the hazy semidarkness inside the dhaba. He made a brave attempt to sound enthusiastic in spite of his sleepy voice "Ekdum, Chachaji, hune lo, *right away*."

Mansingh straightened the stools and wiped them with a duster.

"Come, come, Behenji, you sit here with bawa, *child*," he dished out especial cordiality to the Canada-returned Meera. He wiped the table with wet clean cloth and disappeared inside the mysterious space in the dhaba.

Meera grinned in satisfaction. "Wow! Not bad I'd say, he does know about hygiene."

A truck rolled by, creating harsh pandemonium; it stopped at a distance.

"Ooh," Atul frowned and grumbled in a low voice.

Two blue turbaned Sikhs descended from the truck. The older, middle-aged, heavyset man had a bulging belly; the younger fellow looked smart but subdued and intimidated by the older, who was perhaps his father, uncle, or more likely father-in-law.

"Do Karak, *too strong teacups,* oy, Man," the older one shouted authoritatively as he sat on a stool and stretched his legs.

Mansingh responded with equal vociferation.

A scrawny brown dog emerged from behind the dhaba and lethargically sniffed around, searching for lunch. He barked weakly for attention.

Surjit came running outside and threw a few bread crumbs toward the dog, imploring him to shut up or else, using crude, swear words.

"Oy, oy, Bache, *child.*" Atul was not pleased. "Don't talk bad words."

The young lad grinned sheepishly and explained in defence, "Sabji, Chacha, *uncle*, says them all the time."

Mansingh bellowed from inside, "I am listening, I am listening. Blaming me for your bad deeds, oy? Come here, I will tell you with my chithar, *slipper*, when did I teach you?"

Atul chuckled. "Man, I know where he learnt it. Teach him good things, Yar, *friend.*"

The boy appeared nine or ten years old; he wore clean blue shirt that hung from his narrow shoulders and reached his knees, effectively hiding the navy knickers.

Mansingh appeared with a large wooden tray and placed plates, sizzling omelets, three toasts, mugs of steaming tea, and cutlery on the wooden table. He went in again and brought tomato sauce and a big mug full of boiled water for Rishi's milk.

He looked content with his lot in life.

Meera said softly, "Bhai, send Surjit to school. He seems intelligent."

Mansingh's face became clouded, his jaw stiffened.

"Bahenji, you come for Cannada-shanada, you don't know anything. Even if he goes to school, then what? No jobs unless your chacha, *uncle*, is a minister or a rich businessman who can buy ministers. I am a dhabawalla. I will give this readymade business to him. At least he can feed his family. You don't know India. Rich people got azadi, *freedom*, but poor people are still slaves. Before, they were servants of white Sahibs, now they serve brown Sahibs!"

He was intense.

Atul said, "It could not be that bad! At least let him get a BA."

"BA? BA?" His face turned red with anger. "BA graduates are crawling like ants. I am one of them. My father Sahib said, 'Man, I want you to be someone, with high job, not laborer like me.' He toiled in fields, took the abuse and insults of the haramzada, *a swear word*, jamindar, *landlord*. My mother washed dishes of other kameena, *low*, people. A reward for their sweat and blood, what did I get? No jobs, no jobs. The employers offered me to become a chaprasi, *peon*!" he said incredulously. "I spit on them and opened my own dhaba. At least I have my own money, no one can abuse me. I am happy. I will make sure Surjit learns this trade."

He turned to Meera, much subdued, "My brother Sahib, Surjit's father, died in an accident like your Sahib, Behenji." His eyes moistened.

"Let me not hold you with my stories. Life is very difficult."

How could Meera disagree with him?

Quite contented, Rishi lay peacefully in the hand carriage; he was wide awake, looking at Meera with his innocent blue eyes. She was filled with radiant warmth and played with his toys for him. The motion of the car lulled him to sleep again.

Asha leaned her head against the headrest. Atul pleaded, "Yar, *friend,* if you sleep, I will definitely doze off on the wheel."

Asha smiled weakly. "Nai ji, *no please.* I am up. I hope Rakesh will be able to come to Simla. Mummy and Papa are waiting. Otherwise we would have stopped in Chandigarh to see them." Atul was irritated. "What is his problem? Meera is tired and should go straight to Simla and relax. Traveling from Canada is no joke. It kills you." Meera mumbled, "Tell me about it!" in her half sleep.

A saree-clad young Indian woman, who was sitting across Meera and glancing in her direction frequently, walked toward her and queried in an innocuous, puzzled voice, "Yeh, apka bacha hai? *Is he your child*?" She pointed toward the baby carriage.

At the New York airport, Meera had noticed people gawking at her, their multicoloured eyes filled with undisguised curiosity. Is it her salwar kameez, *pants and shirt*? Or is her slip showing? She moved in her seat, smoothed the wrinkles of her shirt while tucking her slip slyly under her.

Soon enough, the origin of the staring was revealed.

The woman obviously descended from some small city. The large-city populace has loftier preoccupations engrossing their minds; they become indifferent, or pretend to and wear a mask of frozen, smileless, unconcerned expression on their physiognomy.

The woman was plain, unaffected, without the modern-day sophistication and skill of hiding her ardor.

"Yes," Meera looked up and answered evenly. *So this is it.*

The gentle woman's black shiny eyes twinkled with fascinating thoughts of multifarious scenarios that Meera's reply unleashed.

A benign smile spread on her smooth, plump, and guileless face, "Oh, so sweet."

She continued unabatedly with a secretive and whispering tone. "The father must be chitta, *white*, yah?"

Meera was lost for words. This was the first time she was confronted with this question. Who *is* his father? What a quagmire. If she answers no, the betraying fair visage of Rishi will raise horrifying assumption of his illegitimacy and her infidelity.

Meera recovered quickly and replied in a hushed voice, "He is adopted," and wondered why it took her so long to come up with a perfectly simple answer.

"Oh yes! Yes!" A tremendous, unfeigned sigh of relief emerged from the lady's bright-red-lipsticked lips as though a grave and ponderous weight had been lifted from her heart.

She grinned broadly, showing her evenly distributed teeth, "I was afraid maybe . . ." Then giggled uncontrollably. Maybe Meera was married to a white man! Must be quite an opprobrious abstraction, almost a sin in her round, snoopy, and prying eyes.

Decked with plenty of extravagant, glittering, gold jewelry, the damsel wore a bright peacock silk saree; she appeared happy in her limitedness. Meera marvelled if she would ever be moved by an urge to analyze life, events, and the world beyond her. Maybe, maybe not.

Meera realized quickly she was being judgemental and harsh. Maybe the woman is quite learned and has reasons other than witless nescience for delving into Meera's life. She might have reflected extensively upon the state of Western nuptial affairs and inferred that mixing races is not a good idea after all. Meera herself wasn't sure at times. Some couples exuded relative harmony, but most appeared out of tune with each other.

But then, many Indian couples seem incompatible and discordant. Maybe the institution of marriage itself is to be blamed with its various complexities, expectations, demands, different mind-sets, clash of the egos, etc. Is it not a miracle when a union succeeds, all aspects considered?

The blonde, fair wife asked the tall albino husband anxiously, while holding the arm of the fair young boy who wanted to run away, "Was this for us? Is our plane leaving? What did she say?"

The husband was irritated as much at the whining wife as the noisy universe at large. He snapped, "How do I know? I cannot hear that damn announcement any more than you do." He mellowed down when he noticed that Meera was looking in his general direction.

"I will find out," he grumbled and got up abruptly.

Rishi slept indifferently in the hand carriage, oblivious to the pandemonium around him. After checking in the luggage and tucking away the boarding pass safely in the back pocket of her purse, where it was easy to retrieve, Meera settled on a comfortable sofa chair in the waiting area of the airport.

The New York airport is a consequential crossroads for global voyageurs—a central point of entry converging into America and exit route diverging to everywhere in the world. It offers a rare feast to the mind's eye, a smorgasbord of infinitely varied skin colors, voices, languages, accents, statures, garbs belonging to the most immediate and the most distant cultures. It could almost be declared a United Nations territory.

Tired humans were standing in lineups with anxious brows, counting luggage and children—sometimes in that order, repeatedly, just in case—or rushing to board the plane literally dragging their unwilling trailing offspring, who rightly consider being cooped up in the confines of a small and stuffy plane a direct assault on their freedom. Sometimes travelers bumped into other hurried masses and mumbled an unmeaning sorry since there was no time for reflection or repentance. The collective solemnity in everyone's faces gave the impression that they were performing a grave assignment that could make or break the world. While the whole crowd was involved in the making of a purposeful chaos, the ensuing disorder made it impossible to decipher what the announcer was announcing in incoherent English, with a sore-due-to-flu voice.

Though Meera loved the window seat from where she could enjoy the thrill of gliding through the cottony fluffy clouds, the aisle seat was more practical to deal with the multiple tasks that little babies demand.

The air hostess supplanted the carriage with Rishi lying in it wide-eyed, in the large open area in front of the first row. The jet was truly jumbo, with an infinite array of seats as far as the eye could reach.

The passengers, even the fussy ones, mollified and tied into place in their respective seats, the door closed ostentatiously and engine hummed to warm up. A cute blond, pleasant, green-eyed air host stood close to the front end of the cabin, near Meera, and waved his hands in the air to draw attention. He smiled gregariously. "Please listen to the safety features. Since you all look so bored, I will give instructions in poetry."

And there he went with a musically humorous poem about how to wear seat belts, when to use the oxygen mask, what to sing to attract the air hostess, when to crawl or race in the aisle, and last but not the least, when to jump off the plane. He finished and bowed dramatically to much laughter and applause.

Meera had not laughed that vigorously in a long time. Her sense of humor had been badly rusted from disuse. Since childhood, she was in the habit of perceiving hilarity in most situations. Sometimes it got her in deep trouble with her friends.

It was a pleasant, warm, and breezy September day; the scorching heat of the summer and pouring monsoons were behind them, excepting a few clouds that glided smoothly in the sky. Meera and her friends planned a picnic at Kutb Minar, a tall fourteen-storey tower built by the Mughal emperor Kutub.

Of late, the government had placed a prohibition on climbing higher than the second storey of Kutub Meenar. Many lovelorn, impassioned young lads found a fatal way to prove their devotion once for all, by the ultimate act of jumping down the fourteenth storey and landing just in front of their beloved's beautiful but incredulous eyes.

The road was straight and uncrowded; the fields were lush and rich with a full crop of wheat. The taxiwalla Sardarji, *Sikh,* whistled happily; he was quite overwhelmed by the unusual treat of his taxi brimming with beautiful, young chatty girls. Sardarji was paying too much attention to the young lasses, to the extent that he failed to notice a herd of cows that seemed to appear from nowhere and walked directly toward the taxi. A screeching was heard as the brakes were mercilessly pressed, the car turned around a full 360 degrees, and landed in a dry ditch on the left side of the road. The swift acrobatics performed by the car were ludicrous even for the cows; the whole flock halted and gazed at the car keenly, with their enormous, black, unblinking eyes. Meera convulsed with laughter at the empathetic expression the cows were wearing on their massive faces.

Meera was ostracised the rest of the day, and for many more days, for her inappropriate nonseriousness at such a grave predicament.

The car had tilted sideways, effectively jamming the doors on the left side. To be toppled in a heap, attempting to disentangle themselves in order to spring from the position—squeeze out of the right door that happened to be slanted in an uncomfortable angle against gravity, wearing "sac" shirts that were tight, particularly around the hips, thighs, and just about everywhere else—was a hopeless assignment. No one was hurt physically, but it was downright mortifying to be escorted out by young college boys who happened to be passing by on their motorbikes. Condescendingly tight-lipped to suppress their laughter, which was showing at the corners of their lips, they literally extracted each girl from the car and stood her up by the side.

Meera said a polite, "No, thank you," and proudly got out herself, thanks to her old-fashioned loose shirt. To further exacerbate the girls' quandary, a horde of people promptly congregated, materializing mysteriously out of thin air since the traffic was mediocre and pedestrians practically nonexistent before the accident occurred.

To add salt to the injury, some stray dogs also joined the throng, donning a visage of innocent curiosity on their open-mouth, tongue-hanging faces. A few dogs even jumped up and down and barked sonorously, excitement gleaming in their doggy, droopy eyes from the pantomime performing unexpectedly in their otherwise dull lives.

Behind the wall of glass that was erected between Customs and the viewers' gallery, obviously to prevent stampede of excited relatives, Atul and Asha stood, scanning the Customs area. Frantically waving to catch their kins' attention, kids and adults alike were clamoring with joy.

"Look, Mummy, there are Uncle and Auntie."

"Where is Neetu?"

"I can see Bhaiya. Mummy, is he going to marry all the photos of girls you sent to him?"

"Darling look, Mataji, *mother*, and Pitaji, *father*. Pitaji looks a little weak, doesn't he?"

A man standing next to them overheard and vigorously nodded his head in agreement. "Yes, yes. You are right, Bhaijan, *brother in Urdu*. Amrika is no place for our parents. My father, Saheb, died there! My brother and sister-in-law both worked! Who could look after him?"

Meera's heart leapt. Through blurry vision, she saw Atul and Asha and waved at them. They grinned widely and waved back.

How can a heart carry two directly opposite emotions simultaneously? She would soar with joy at the thought of finally being with her loved ones. The next moment, like a cloud floating over a bright sun, panic overwhelmed her. To exhume and face the scathing memories of Mohit's death that she had buried without dealing with them and to feel their sharp poignancy was an unbearable scenario. She also understood that when she would mourn with her loving family, her healing would finally, truly begin.

The air hostess, carrying Rishi in the hand carriage, rushed Meera through Customs, perhaps to get rid of a cranky baby who was getting on everybody's nerves as much as everyone was getting on his.

Atul spread his arms wide, took Meera in his fold, and kissed her forehead, repeatedly. She struggled with her tears. Bhai's embrace was like a repository, a tepid cave where the cruel and chilly winds of life dared not enter.

"Thank you so much for your help." Atul took the hand carriage from the pleasant, pretty air hostess. Rishi peeped up at him; his soft lips quivered and curved downwards in preparation for a whine.

Meera ignored him and hugged Asha tight. "Bhabi, *sister-in-law*, I am so sorry about Nitin."

Asha broke down instantly. "Choti, why did this happen, he was so young!" she cried.

In Chandigarh, during the torrid afternoons of summer holidays, Nitin and Meera played Ludo, cards, Snakes and Ladders—even dolls—the fan humming in the background, the rooms darkened with thick curtains to curtail the blinding-white heat. Chachiji, *aunty,* would call from downstairs, "Come down right away, budhu, *silly,* kahin ke! Don't you feel hot?"

No one in their right mind would be found on the second floor of the house, where the sun beat its blazing heat mercilessly on the cemented roof.

Nitin was Asha's younger brother, the same age as Meera.

Asha's family visited Simla often. They picnicked at the Glen Falls, Chadwick falls, and Anendale—the large, oval, flat field in the deep valley where all the cricket matches were held. Cool, soft summer breeze touched their red chubby cheeks; they played hide and seek in the dense forest, slipping on the ground overlaid by pine needles, and giggled. A lot.

Nitin indulged in all the naughty pranks that brothers pull on little sisters: he teased, shoved, tugged her long braids, and last but not the least, cheated in the games they played together. Being of mild temperament, Meera did not let anything wreck their innocent world of fun and frolic; they quarrelled and made up on a regular basis.

Asha had raised the idea of their marriage when they grew up. Meera was scandalized. "Bhabi! He is my brother, how can you even think that?"

Anyway, he was in love with Sneh, a comely, tall, fair girl.

Nitin and Sneh were married a few months before Meera's nuptials, but she had to miss the occasion because of exams. He flew to Bangalore with his bride. His air force commanding officer refused to allow him another holiday; he could not attend Meera's wedding.

"We lost Nitin," Atul had written briefly.

Early spring, 1965, teasing skirmishes between young hot-blooded soldiers entrenched on the opposite sides of Indo-Pak border turned into serious hostilities and finally full-blown war, a short war with a lifelong purgatory for the loved ones left behind by fallen soldiers.

Shanti Chachiji, *aunty,* had a heart attack at the sight of a pale, devastated, empty-eyed Sneh, clad in a plain white saree, her fair arms hanging bare without the lively clinking red bangles, the barren parting of her silky dark-brown hair without the auspicious red sindoor, *red powder,* the pride of suhag, *state of being married.*

Overnight, the curse of widowhood descended on Sneh from the war-weary heavens.

In the face of blazing air guns, many Indian Air Force pilots daringly flew deep into Pakistan airspace to bomb military targets. Many planes were shot down by enemy gunfire. The sky lit momentarily, in glory of the pilots' brave deaths, before the burning plane fell on Pak territory.

Nitin was one of them.

Asha composed herself, stroked Meera's dishevelled hair fondly, and smiled sadly, "Life is like that, Choti. I am sorry about Mohit." They both stood on the shared ground of bereavement with perfect understanding of each other's grief.

Asha took Rishi in her arms. "How cute, Meera! He is adorable." Rishi started to cry. "He looks so tired, poor thing."

The plane had landed at Delhi airport at some Godforsaken hour at night, smack in the middle of the sleep cycle, if any endogenous rhythm had survived the timeless journey.

The pilot's gruff announcement, "We are now landing," brought tears to Meera's eyes. The air hostess passing by, checking the seat belts, did not look surprised. She just smiled condescendingly.

Meera requested her sleepy neighbour to exchange seats. The lady was a fair Westerner and, in all likelihood, possessed no feelings of nostalgia for India.

"Of course, dear." She smiled, got up with difficulty, and let Meera move to the window seat. Rishi slept in the hand carriage, oblivious to the transformation his life was about to undergo once the plane touched the land called India.

There it was, her sweet Motherland beckoning to her. An expansive carpet of flickering lights against the pitch darkness of moonless night looked like a Diwali, *festival of lights,* of Ayodhya. Thousands of years ago, Shri Ram, the incarnation of God, returned from his exile of fourteen years, that was orchestrated by his stepmother who wanted her own son to inherit the throne. His subjects, who had counted agonising days and nights, were intoxicated with such joy that they lighted up the whole city with oil lamps, danced, and sang in the streets.

Short in comparison, Meera's exile had seemed just as long. It was over; she too was home.

Meera almost collapsed at the rear seat of the car and let her throbbing head rest against the back; she closed her weary eyes. Rishi had taken to Asha and slept off in her lap.

The warm humid breeze of monsoons brushed wildly against her cheeks as the car sped. Meera's hair played on her languid but hopeful face.

Meera looked outside at the racing trees, big houses, small houses, huts whizzing past in quick succession, in the stillness of the umbrageous night. They were almost outside Delhi.

Asha turned her drowsy head toward Atul and implored, "I know the streets are empty ji, but don't overspeed. The roads have huge potholes. Rishi will wake up with the bumps."

Atul just nodded in agreement.

Soon, the scorched, patched-up territory arose from the somnolent body of the earth like a grotesque blister. Rows upon rows of murky, dilapidated shacks, sheets of rusted tin roofs kept in place by stones, or bundles of hay serving as the roof that is supported by crumbing mud walls hide the hideous face of penury within their windowless confines. In the hopeless darkness, illness and death stalk with soundless, stealthy footsteps, sneaking heartlessly through the many fissures and cracks of the worn-out doors while the unknowing inhabitants sleep snuggled together for warmth and security.

This is where the conscience of India sleeps beyond the reaches of the awakening calls of the gods.

Dim, pink light of dawn slowly spread its wings and settled on the languid huts; life stirred and emerged out of the creaking doors. Forlorn men in unclean pajama shirts staggered around in the golden, soft hue of the rising sun. In front of the huts, haggard women with many-holed sarees covering their heads were trying to light their mud stoves with cheap coal that produced more smoke than fire; they coughed vigorously from inhaling the dense fumes.

A few scantily clad, groggy-eyed children, their torn shirts and bodies wearing the same discoloration of dirt, stood on either side of the thoroughfare. The miniature archetypes of man stood frozen in time, like Lilliputian statues watching cars, bullock carts, buses, cycles, trucks, people go by—watching life go by. Ostracised to tarry behind a shatter-proof transparent glass of indifference, faces and noses pressed against it, they gawk with wide-eyed innocence. At a young age, life has already divulged the reality that they are doomed to be spectators, exiled in their own land, relinquished on the purlieu of the land of haves.

Tears dimmed Meera's eyes.

Atul looked at the rearview mirror and spoke lovingly, "Meera, everything is going to be fine, we are all there for you, na? Don't worry."

"No, Bhai, I am not worried." She did not elaborate.

It turned out to be a bright sunny day. Sun shone with its full irradiance, on humid-with-monsoon land. The traffic picked up. Small streams of dirty water ran on both sides of the highway, as well as on the road. Big splashes of water rose as the car sped by, unintentionally splattering muddy water on the pedestrians. They glanced at the car with resentment, eyes glared and mouths moved in obscenities; fortunately, the people inside the car could not hear anything.

"Slow ji, please," Asha mumbled, looking apologetically at the indignant walkers who were trying to shake the muddy water off their clothing while still continuing teeth grinding and swearing. Atul was irritated. "Do we want to catch the train or not?"

The whole vista looked fresh and virgin, recently bathed with a generous outpour of monsoons; transparent waterdrops slid from glazed leaves of trees, tips of grass blades, or colorful petals of wildflowers and glimmered in the aureate sunlight.

The well-nurtured broad-leaved foliage of trees that lined the highway almost created a shining green shield, obscuring the expanse of deep lush fields of wheat, corn, and barley that extended far away, embracing the horizon. The emerald surface of the crops trembled in waves with the silky morning breeze. Overhead, in the clear aquamarine sky, formations of chirping birds flew over, searching for a seedier pasture. Farmers were already out in the fields looking like brown specks against the bottle-green backdrop.

Rishi slept tranquilly after having a sumptuous meal of milk and pablum at Mansingh's dhaba.

Atul slowed down the car and spoke hesitantly, "Meera, should we stop at Pinjore Gardens?"

Meera heard him vaguely; she was shaken out of her half sleep and her heart leapt. "Yah!"

The most enduring, undeniably magnificent legacy of the Mughal reign in India is the artistically laid Mughal gardens.

Descendants of Genghis Khan and Temurlanq, the term *Mughal* was derived from Mongols; they ruled Kabul during their exile. Fighters for generations they invaded India on horses and easily overcame the foot soldiers defending the northwest kingdoms.

The first Mughal conqueror, who became emperor of India, Babur's first act upon reaching Agra, the city that became the capital of Mughal empire, was to lay out a garden; the last act of the last emperor was to do the same.

During Meera's family's regular trips to Chandigarh to visit Asha's family, picnics at the Pinjore Gardens were unquestionable, an imperative.

Nitin would scare Meera, "Do not touch the flowers. The police will put you in jail! There are mice running all over, and you get no food or water."

In spite of the scary portent, Meera would daringly bend down to smell a vividly colored carnation or a hard-to-resist, soft-petaled rose.

The gardeners, there were many, would implore from a distance.

"Aré baby, plucking flowers is not allowed."

Meera would say, ever so politely, "But . . . but . . . Mali baba, I am only smelling. See? My hands are behind my back? I will never hurt these cute flowers."

Quite impressed by her graciousness, the gardener would pluck a small flower and present it with a loving pat on her puny head. For someone who subsists at the bottom echelon of a hierarchical system and is accustomed to crude, uncivil conduct from a supposedly civilised citizenry of higher classes, to be treated as a regular human is a rare treat.

A spring of shimmering water flows in the center of the Pinjore Gardens from upper level to the lowest, lined with four-hundred-year-old red bricks, at least that is what they were told.

In the torrid summer weather, it was a huge temptation to jump in the spring water and wet your burning body. But it was banned. Meera, Shobha, and Asha sat at the brick ledge and dipped their feet in the soothing water; no one could object to that.

Water fountains are set at regular distances in the stream and spew crystal clear diamonds high up in the air. Sunrays passing through each globule are refracted and split into innumerable, tiny, polychromatic rainbows.

The mist riding on the wings of the hot wind would drench the three of them. They were not drenched for too long though; heat and the sun quickly vaporized the clamminess out of their clothes.

Under the variegated shadow of mango or pippal trees, Ma and Chachiji, *aunty*, lay on the bed cover that was spread on the damp, cool grass and gossiped, something they never admitted.

"Aré, Budhu, *silly*, we do not gossip! We just talk about people. Don't you know the difference?"

Shoba teased, "Yes, I know, but you are gossiping."

At a distance, Dayal Chachaji and Papa, perched on folding lawn chairs that were placed under the shade of some tree, tackled all the perplexing enigmas facing a confused world. As a little girl, Meera could not understand why Papa could not be the governor of the world and fix everything with his wisdom. Why governor? Because it was easier to say rather than president or prime minister; they were the same anyway, coming on the radio and talking about stuff she never understood.

Of course, boys could not sit still. They ran, barefeet, on green carpeted grounds that were interspersed by bushes of chandni with moonlight-color flowers, kaner, with pink and white blooms, and hisbiscus flaunted huge orange blossoms. Green cedars carved into a giraffe, camel, horse, or some other animal, grew at distances.

The boys climbed on the colossal ancient trees that grew at the periphery of the Pinjore Gardens or raced to the two-foot thick and sixteen-foot tall wall that circumscribed the garden and served as a feeble defence against the onslaught of invaders and looters. The winner of the race was supposed to be carried on the back of the laggard until the latter whined or, more likely, dropped the hero on the grass and made a run for it.

Within a split second, the nostalgia was replaced by a sharp ache in Meera's heart.

The flower buds were still hiding in the sepals for protection against the January cold. Chilly fog had descended from the

Himalayas that were only a few miles away from Pinjore Gardens and prompted many a runny nose amongst the scanty crowd of visitors to the gardens. Mohit, Papa, Ma, Asha, Atul, and Meera, wrapped in shawls or winter coats, stood outside the high main entrance that was guarded by dark, thick, and heavy carved wooden gates and ate bhutta, *cob of corn,* roasted directly on a small flat coal stove. The sparsely dressed, shivering thin boy, the cook, squatted on the cold ground; he sprinkled salt, black pepper, and lemon juice on the roasted cob and presented it. "Loji, garam, garam, *take hot roasted corn.*"

He smiled shyly and asked Meera, "Aunty, you just got married?"

Meera was startled. "Aré, bache, *child,* how did you know?"

He just pointed to her arm that was adorned with at least ten red bangles and giggled at his cleverness.

Meera blushed, pulled out a hundred rupee note from her embroidered purse, and extended her hand toward the kid. "Take it and buy a sweater. If you get ill, who will make bhutta for us?"

Suspicion darkened his sad black eyes. Is it a trap? Is she going to call him a thief afterward and get him beaten by the crowd? He just looked at her in confusion. Mohit encouraged him, "Give it to your Mai, *mother,* not Baba. He will drink it away."

With shaky, hesitant hands, he took it and stuffed it in the pocket of his pants that were too short on him.

After spending two weeks in Simla after the wedding, Meera and Mohit were to leave for Canada. Meera was ready to embark on a new life with a perfect stranger who, within the twenty days' span had transcended that notion completely and niched a sense of belonging in Meera's palpitating heart.

Meera suppressed a sigh and leaned back on her seat. "No, Bhai, some other time."

Asha said sadly, "It is so hard, na, I am so sorry, Choti."

Meera was the youngest in a large extended family; at emotional moments, everyone called her Choti.

While Ma's time and energy was fairly distributed between other kids, Papa and Dadi, *paternal grandmother,* Meera had Asha to herself. Getting a reluctant child ready for school, helping with homework, do shopping, Asha had practically raised Meera, who was a bare ten-year-old when Asha and Atul got married.

Dayal Chachaji and Papa were old friends from Lahore. Both the mothers had long ago made a decision, unilaterally, on Atul and Asha's union, while they were still little children.

Ma announced to all friends and relatives excitedly, "Isn't she so pretty?"

Papa was cautious, "Don't tell everyone yet, Shakuntala, who has seen the future?"

Ma dismissed him hastily. "Why are you always such a prude? The future is bright for our children!"

As Atul and Asha grew older, Papa was firm. "Dayal, let Atul prove himself worthy. I will then ask you for your daughter's hand."

Atul was still in the final year of law school when Dayal Chachaji had a heart attack and absconded the world without notice.

Once the rituals of death were behind the families, Ma spoke to Shanti Chachiji, *aunty*, "Behan, *sister*, I want to take Asha home."

Dadi was horrified, "Aré, are you crazy, Shakuntala? We have to wait for a year! Otherwise, it is inauspicious, anything can happen. Na, Bhai, wait."

The ancient sages, who took upon themselves to ensure that the Manu's Vidhan, *guide of conduct written by rishi Manu*, was followed by Hindus, were not into festivities anyway. Living in jungles, their full-time occupation was to strive to be with God; it did not matter to them if there was a waiting period of one year to have fun! They spoilt it for everyone else.

Thirteen months after Dayal Chachaji's demise, Asha was brought home as a bride. Secure in Asha's love, Ma and Papa escaped horrifying torture by modern-day daughters-in-law who were hell-bent on turning tables on the in-laws. For unknown centuries, they had claimed a monopoly on oppression of their sons' brides. In this cleverly contrived situation, tyranny was unlikely on either side.

Meera opened the glass window and peeped out through the metallic bars of the train cabin; the hubbub from the railway platform wafted in eagerly. Dressed in uniforms that consisted of deep-red shirts, beige pajamas, and deep-red turbans, kulis, *baggage handlers*, squatted in small groups on the platform, catching breath, wiping sweaty foreheads and smoking bidis, *cheap cigarette.* The chaotic and exhausting prelude to the egression of the demanding Howrah Mail was behind them. A black, monstrous smoke-issuing, pandemonium-creating engine led and transported many miles long, thumping, earth-shaking-clamorous train with endless array of compartments, overflowing with passengers, all the way from Kalka in the northwest, down the Ganges plain to Howrah, eastern port of Bengal, hence the name.

The railway platform was relieved of its tension. People waiting for the next, less pompous train, sat on holdalls or stood around with stooped shoulders, limp hanging arms, gazing at the tracks hoping to create an electromagnetic pull to suck forth the train in a hurry. Others loitered purposelessly, lashing piqued glances at everyone as though it was all their fault whatever was bothering them. Creative children remodelled the railway platform into a regular playground. Mothers shouted, children did not listen, husbands scurried toward the newspaper-walla, chaiwalla, tikkiwalla, soft drink-walla, paan-walla, etc., to escape the misdirected wrath of their wives.

A skinny and dark-complexioned cleaner, in all likelihood a jobseeker from the southern or eastern parts of India, broomed the platform to clean the debris of crumpled papers, broken cups that were tossed thoughtlessly after the last drop of tea was consumed, banana peels, cigarette butts, apple rinds, and bread crumbs scattered by the uncivic passengers of Howrah Mail. A black-suited man shouted obscene abuses at the janitor for stirring dust in the air and spoiling his meticulously dry-cleaned apparel.

A fashionable young woman dressed in heavily embroidered yellow saree and much glittering gold jewelry perched delicately on a metallic trunk. Her puny, pouting child stared sulkily down on the much-spitted-upon-platform floor after receiving a sound thrashing from her for running around on the platform. The lady retrieved a small mirror out of an ostensibly expensive leather handbag and started to inspect her much-made-up face and patted her rebellious hair to conform. Did she know that you can never see your real face in a mirror? You can only see the reflection. A deeper analysis of the above fact reveals philosophical and spiritual ramifications, the understanding of which could lead to a glimpse into your real self.

An incoherent announcement resonated in the upper stratum of the stratosphere; unable to penetrate the thick slab of racket at the lower, human-populated zone, it dissipated in the skies above.

"I am so hungry. Mansingh's omelet was delicious but disappeared pretty fast," Atul grumbled.

Asha turned to him. "Ji, can you tell the dining car bearers to bring our food here?"

Meera, Atul, Asha, and Rishi had arrived in Kalka around ten o'clock on the bright upbeat morning. Meera was thrilled at the familiarity of Kalka, a small town at the feet of the Himalayan range. The rented car duly returned at the car stand that was located next to the railway station, they checked in at the crowded, jostling platform. Their train was to leave in an hour after Howrah Mail's departure.

After settling inside the train compartment, Meera sighed with relief. Rishi sat up in his hand carriage confidently now that the menace of so many different faces was gone. He played with his plastic rattle and giggled at the sound. Meera looked at him lovingly and shuddered, "If I ever lose him, I'll die."

"You see, they went to the river for a swim, three of them . . . I knew something was wrong even before that boy—I forget his name—came running and told me."

The elderly lady's pure-white hair was set like a substantial halo; Meera wondered how she slept. Maybe it was a wig! Her ancient age did not deter the lady from talking incessantly from New York to London, her destination. Meera was relieved; she could not have survived another twelve hours of cranky Rishi with the lady filling in the gaps when he slept.

When the woman became tearful, Meera was forced to pay full attention to her story.

"He was just seventeen! Only my Jay drowned. He was going to be a priest, you know."

Meera was jilted out her sleepy state of mind at the tragic utterance.

"Oh my God, I am so sorry to hear that, so sad."

Meera's empathetic eyes prompted the lady to elaborate the event in details; she sighed often, leaned back on her seat occasionally to retrieve some half-forgotten detail while delving in a past of some sixty,

sixty-five years ago. Her narrative was exceptionally vivid considering that she could not remember if she had already eaten her lunch; the air hostess had to convince her when she kept asking, "When are we having lunch?" It hit Meera that the traumatic memory of losing her child did not fade even with overlying layers of miscellaneous events during a span of around six decades.

Meera shut the windows to prevent getting coated in black soot. The train started on time; Rishi slept, Asha read, Atul spread his legs, occupying a full berth, and shut his tired eyes. Meera looked out wistfully as people, electric poles, trees, houses ran past.

The Kalka Mail to Simla is rather puny, toylike train. It creeps lazily up the winding small hills, gradually taking on the higher loftier mountains, the plunging cliffs on the one side, and rising slopes on the other; the train crawls perilously. The vegetation changes with altitude; deodar, cedar, pines take over with some scattered birches and poplars braving out the snowy-cold of the winter. At this point, the chill is carried by lighter, purer, more lucent mountainous air that brushes against your warm cheeks; you do not mind because of the realization that you are close to Simla.

Meera opened the window and took in a deep whiff. They were now ascending the Himalayan heights into the welcoming embrace of the white rugged peeks.

Meera was home, to her world of tall deodars, where radiant sun and floating clouds play hide and seek around the crests that pierce the cerulean skies, friendly fog flows into your home unannounced and the pure mountainous zephyr smoothes away all the wrinkles from your brow.

- # -

Manu's song irritated all of Meera's siblings. It was an unwelcome toxin at a crucial juncture in their sleep cycle when dreams were most vivid!

"Oh, Papa please."

Shobha was irritated.

Whether it was a holiday or working day, Papa was up early, took his bath, dressed, and headed for the temple that was installed in a small, neatly kept room facing the east. Through the large window, the pastel peach rays of dawn entered about the same time Papa walked in the room.

He sat on a silky small rug that lay in front of the Temple, placed fresh flowers, that Mali, *gardener,* would bring in quite early in the morning, on the feet of Shri Ram and Shri Krishna. The light of the candles and the incense fumes diffused in the room, shrouding him with mystery. Papa prayed quietly for the most part, but ended his puja, *prayers,* with 'Manu's song' which he sang with his musical voice. It was Papa's futile hope that repetitive exposition of the sacred mantra, *verse from Scripture,* at dawn, may awaken not only his descendants' minds but also their spirits, without which the integrality between God and man can never be achieved.

"I am the creator of the moon; sun and stars originate from me . . ." sage Manu's poem resonated in the dewed morning air.

It was too profound for Meera to grasp the latent drift, but it hardly mattered. Papa's gentle, melodious tonality rendered a meaning of significance without words. She felt it in her heart.

Clad in her night suit, Meera climbed the apple tree that grew smack in the centre of the front yard. Puja room was on the second floor of the house at the same level as the middle branches of the apple tree, where Meera perched with her wee soft legs flailing in the air. She could hear the "song" lucidly. Dadi, *paternal grandmother,* sitting on a cot under the very same tree chanted, "Om Namo Bhagvate vasudevai", *a verse from scriptures.*

"Dadi, sing low! I cannot hear Manu's song!"

Dadi was irritated by the daring of the little girl to give her orders; she lashed back, "Befkoof, *stupid,* come down, come down! Why do you want to hurt yourself in God's hour?"

Ma's voice resounded from the kitchen, "Beji, *mother,* leave her, she will just have to learn when she gets hurt."

That was Ma, soft and tough at the same time, if that is possible. Did Meera ever fall down? Of course not! The kind spirit of the sage Manu, who lived thousands of years ago, protected her. She was listening carefully and also chanting his verse. Wasn't she?

Manu was the son of Brahma, the creator of the universe. Vishnu sustains the existence, and Shiva takes charge of the death aspect, which is essential if the cycle of birth is to continue. The three deities represent the Trinity, the three aspects of the "one" Absolute God.

Manu was given the wisdom and insight by his great father Brahma to lay down the rules of conduct for the praja, *humanity*. The fat scripture is known as Manu's Vidhan, *a scripture and guide of conduct*! However, Manu's song might not have been written by Manu. Since the poet was unknown, Papa decided to give it a name for reference purposes. In reality the rishis who penned the great scriptures, Vedas and Upanishads believed that the true inspirer and author was God Himself; they never claimed it as their own creation! They indeed had no ego issues because the imperative of the first step towards true spirituality is to abandon your 'ego.'

Papa explained the essence conveyed in the song. "In moments of meditative bliss the Rishi experienced his oneness with God. Hence, whatever God created, the Rishi could claim to be a part of the creative process, hence 'I am the Creator.' The most important premise for the true cogitation of the verse is that, 'I' does not denote the 'ego Self' but the 'Soul Self,' our true Self and identity.

"Take a gold ornament. If it regards itself as an earring or necklace, it has a distinct, disparate identity from other jewellery. But if it conceives itself as 'gold' the fundamental tattwa, *raw material,* of all adornments, it will experience the underlying unity amongst all ornaments."

"Accomplishment of this transcendental state of unity with God and other sentients, is the pinnacle of spirituality; rishis of ancient India called it Advait, *unity amongst existence,* "not two," implying the reality of one and only Existence, God. Altruism is a child of Advait; only an altruistic human can transcend his 'ego,' renounce his own good for others' happiness because for him 'you' and 'I' are one," Papa had explained.

During early childhood, Meera's favourite activity was to scramble up the propitious apple tree. Ensconced by emerald-leaved boughs, Rani in her lap, she beheld the heavens above and scanned the world at her feet. The sun shining brilliantly through the fluttering leaves created umpteen twinkling stars that sparkled in her light brown eyes. Deodars stood at the helm of the garden to protect Meera's home from evil spirits.

In fact, it was Vineet who initiated her into tree climbing. Built at an elevation, Rai Saheb Tayaji's, *owner of the house Meera's family lived in,* mansion in Summer Hill faced a stunning picturesque view of the valley below and lofty mountains across.

To buy his loyalty, British Raj bestowed him with the title Rai Saheb that he threw on their faces in disgust after the Avinash-Clarke incidence. People still called him by his title.

Rai Saheb was an intellectual aristocrat. His huge library was lined with countless books; no one was allowed to trespass—not even Meera, who was his special baby. He sat comfortably on a huge beige and velvet-lined sofa chair, a pole lamp illuminated the pages that were imbued with human reflections; he had no awareness of the world around him at such moments.

A frustrated Tayiji, *Tayaji's wife,* often told the servant Bansi, "Go and bang on his door before the food got cold. If he complains tell him I asked you to."

An aesthetic man, flowers were his other passion that he did not pass on even to his own children, but to Meera. A full-time gardener tended the colorific garden where all the hues of the spectrum found home. Strangers often dropped by to enjoy the immaculate richness and tranquillity of the sanctuary.

Pittering-pattering with her tiny feet on the damp grass, that is where Meera discovered and fell in love with the dazzling beauty of God's creation.

In the summer, after the last light of the huge mansion was turned off and the night creatures found their voices, little feet and big feet alike treaded softly on the wet-with-dew slumbering grass, furtively scurrying and shivering sometimes. Who would risk opening the almirah to get sweaters and wake up the respective mummy? The inexplicably runny noses the next day took mummys by surprise, "Aré, where did you get the cold from? You kick the quilt off all night. I have to put it back on you!"

All feet converged onto the apple orchard that thrived on one side of the mansion. The whispering silhouettes sometimes bumped into one another in the dark. "Ouch, watch where you are going, yar, *friend*!" Like ghosts, they climbed on the trees, plucked and dropped ripe as well as unripe apples; suppressed shrieks of Meera and Vineet could be heard when the hard fruit landed on their wee heads intentionally or unintentionally—who could tell—followed by, "Shh, shh, silly you want to wake up the Mali and get dandas, *long wooden sticks,* on your head?"

"Shut up you sissy!"

Not that the kids were deprived of the delicious red-yellowish, homegrown apples. But served on plates by mothers was too boring and unadventurous. It was far more fun to watch a dishevelled Mali the next day complaining to Tayaji about the broken branches, half eaten apples scattered on the ground. Kids nodded their multisized heads vigorously. "But, but, Mali baba, I was sleeping! Must be some thief. Would you like us to help catch the bad man?"

The commander in chief of the operation was Vineet's older brother Shiv. Tayaji knew that his own children were equal participants in the exploit; he dismissed the affair with a smile, much to the chagrin of Mali. "Sab does not know anything. What if there will be no apples left in the orchard to sell?" He would proceed back to the scene of the crime, desperately trying to find some evidence to nail the kids because he was one hundred percent sure they were the pilferers.

Those early years of Meera's childhood were times of great exhilaration. She was much too young to fully grapple with what all the commotion was about. But even at the tender age, she was imbued with an abstract sense of a transformation consummating around her. The sensibility was all pervasive and irrefutable; it captured your awareness even if your consciousness was five or six years young.

After a century of tyrannical oppression and rapacious plundering that constituted British rule, the height of which was that Indians were taxed to maintain the army that kept them in slavery, India was unshackled to tread untrammelled toward her destiny. Human struggle and sacrifice finally bore the fruit of freedom and dignity.

People talked and laughed loudly after painful years of whispering, fearful of the undefined mistrust and suspicion. They regained their real voice; eyes gleamed, faces looked up—there was cheer, gaiety, exuberance overflowing in Indians' demeanor.

But there was fallout, like little particles of dust after a meteor strikes earth. Words like *partition, riots, Jinnah, Sohra Vardi, Gandhji, Nehruji,* and *Patel* floated in the air like crackling sparks. One word that ignited the whole room like a forest fire was *Jinnah.* Everyone especially Chote Chacha, *father's younger brother*, and Atul became red-faced and bloody-eyed. At least there was consensus on that one.

The name *Gandhiji* evoked extreme-polarized emotions from utmost reverence to downright rage, though a large majority of people expressed the former sentiment.

"Gandhiji freed us from slavery without shedding a single drop of blood! Future generations will be awed."

"His moral stature shook the British empire!"

But.

"We would have won our independence in nineteen twenty-two when noncooperative movement halted the machinery of the British rule in India. But no! Only, one fire in a police station and one death, he called off the crusade! He said, 'Ours is a nonviolent struggle.'"

"He favoured the Muslims, damn it! He told Hindus not to hurt them. But how about them killing and raping our women?"

"It is a good thing Nathoo Naido killed him. Many of us were ready to do it."

And so on.

Nehruji was unanimously respected as Mahatama Gandhi's true son. His full name was Jawaharlal Nehru.

Meera was told he was the first prime minister of free India. How was she to know what a prime minister was? There were other words too complex for her.

"Mummy, what is *tependence*?"

Ma tried to explain, "We Indians had been slaves for a century. We fought and gained independence."

It was not easy for her to exactly understand what it meant because she had never been nonindependent!

"And what is *'tition*?"

"Partition?"

"Yes."

Ma's voice quivered, "When we got our independence, our Mother India was cut into two pieces. Musalmans got Pakistan. Hindus, Sikhs, Parsis, Christians, Budhists, and some Musalmans who wanted to stay got India."

Ma had to explain what the hell Pakistan was.

"And Fuji?"

Now Ma cried. Meera felt awful, though she could not figure out what she said wrong. Ma wiped her tears with her paloo, *edge part of a saree.*

"People who have to leave homes where they had lived for generations and move to another place are refugees."

"Why did they have to move?"

"Partition, Beti, they had to."

"And riot?"

Ma could not go on. How was she to explain to an innocent five-year-old, the horror, violence, and inhumanity of those dark times? The humans who had lived the torturous days and nights had scorching memories etched with fire on their conscious and unconscious minds, forever tainting and burning whatever came after. Their present, no matter how glorious, could not rid itself of the tenebrous shadows that stalked them, irrevocably defiling their perceptions for good. The brightest sunlight or the coolest moonlight could not efface the dark umbra from their lives.

And yet people learnt to live and laugh again. Birthdays, engagements, and marriages were celebrated; life did get back on its tracks—at least on the surface. But unshed tears lurked underneath all the festivities. At weddings, there was always someone important missing, lost in the madness of partition, and remembered with a heartache. People became inured to crying and laughing at the same time.

In Meera's immediate family, Dadaji, *paternal grandfather,* was the only one who died during the riots. Dadi, *paternal grandmother,* would not let anyone forget.

With her toothless mouth twisted in scorn, Dadi looked up with dimming vision and cursed Dadaji daily. She was sure that Dadaji and Gandhiji were chatting in heaven; at least, she acknowledged that they deserved the celestial bliss. Gandhiji was equally unforgiven because, according to her, he had led Dadaji astray to bloody death and conferred much cursed, untimely widowhood on her.

Dadaji's unworldly and unusual conduct always irked Dadi, to no end.

- # -

The Sadhu, *ascetic,* walked upright with certain steps, his gaze fixed on the infinite sunny-blue sky. He proclaimed in a lucid, nonchalant intonation, "Can anyone give me what I want?"

It was early morning, and Dadaji was engrossed in his favourite calling of expounding the nature of Reality to his wide-eyed students. He conducted the classes in the spacious living room of his haveli, *mansion.*

Although he was a wealthy landowner, Dadaji's favored preoccupation was to educate himself as well as others, especially children. He taught everything under the sun, but his major emphasis was on principles of ethics, morality, philosophy and religion. It was quite surprising that his students did not rebel against the dreary subjects; Dadaji cleverly weaved the yarn of his narrative with colourful fables and mythological tales.

It was that very moment of discovery, a tall, lean Sadhu, quite ordinary-looking excepting his piercing eyes and resplendent face, not so ordinary at closer scrutiny then, was entering the village. Gray ash smeared on his wide forehead, ash being a symbol of perishability of existence, he was clad in usual ascetic clothing, a cotton dhoti and a rough cotton shawl that was wrapped tightly around his broad shoulders and chest.

Ordinarily, the housewives would rush to retrieve a cup of wheat or rice from their stock to fill the anchorite's Jhola, *cloth bag to receive alms.* Many a good woman would request politely, "Baba, it is lunch time. I will get some bhat, *cooked rice and lentil,* for you." She would spread a clean cloth on the cool veranda floor for him to sit on and bring a copper plate, for copper is considered pure, loaded with rice, lentils, vegetables and rotis, *homemade bread,* and offer it humbly. The Sadhu would gulp the food hurriedly because he had not eaten since yesterday. The housewife in the meantime would bring a hot glass of milk, boiled with cardamom seeds for flavour and some mithai, *sweets,* for dessert.

Contented, the ascetic would get up, let out a large burp and bless the woman profusely with many children or grandchildren depending on her age. The woman would fold her hands, bow her covered-with-saree head and touch his dusty, crude feet with her clean hands in gratitude for his kindness in accepting food from her abode which is considered a punya, *good deed,* that may qualify her an entry in heaven.

Those were guileless times; hermits were pious hence revered. Presently, most Sadhus are not chaste and excessive love for money makes it distressing for humans to part with it. It is not that Puritanism has completely disappeared from the land, but discretion between true and false, that was already arduous in Satya, Dwapar, and Treta Yugs is further blurred in the present Yug of Kali, *according to Hinduism these are four ages that go cyclically.* Faced with a reign of deception and dissimulation, common man has rescinded his faith even from the true.

However, this Sadhu? He sounded portentous and terrifying, who knows what he may demand? And if you could not deliver he would most certainly dole out a curse or two.

In panic, women shut the doors and windows tight. Mothers commanded the children "Do not even peep. What if he sees you and knocks at the door? We will have to open the door, then who knows . . ."

Of course, the children climbed on the chairs, beds, frantically seeking a crack in the windows.

The merchants swiftly lowered the metallic doors and closed shops.

Undaunted, the anchorite sauntered stoically through the whole village.

No one dared to open the door.

Dadaji was elucidating the story of Yama and Nachiketa to the children when he heard the call; the vibrant voice of Sadhu rang again, "Can anyone give me what I want?"

Dadaji stopped his narrative. "Bacho, *children,* go on and read what Lord Yama is telling Nachiketa about death. I will be back. Gopal, watch over them."

Dadaji walked to the main wooden carved door. As soon as he tried to push it, the doorkeeper, who was standing outside the door, said, "Malik, *master,* I will open it."

The Sadhu stopped and looked in Dadaji's direction. Dadaji walked down the stairs through the front yard to the gate and opened it wide. The Sadhu was formidable. "I will get what I want."

Dadaji stepped forward, touched the Sadhu's feet, folded his long-fingered hands, and bowed his turbaned head. "I will do my best Prabhu, *Reverend,* please grace my humble home."

The mendicant looked straight through Dadaji's eyes and followed him. Dadaji led him to the study and shut the door behind him. Dadi, Badi Bua, *father's older sister,* all the children poured out of their rooms. Servants dropped their tasks; the students peeked out, hesitated, "Gopal Bhaiya, can we see what is going on?" Emboldened by the crowd gathered outside the study, they joined them. Excitement showed on everyone's faces as they exchanged curious glances. "What?"

Dadi was filled with terror as never before. What if he asks for all their possessions? Dadaji would give, she knew that for sure. Where will they go with the children? She was already leery of Dada's reckless generosity; today, he had committed his ultimate act of irresponsibility. Why couldn't he act normal, like other people for once and let the Pakhandi, *pretender,* Sadhu go his way?

Much whispering, speculation, impatient nodding and eye-rolling occurred outside the study. Two hours later Dadaji opened the door. He stood more upright than before, the furrows of wisdom lines deepened on his shiny forehead, his black eyes were piercing like arrows in the search for their target, the Truth.

A knowing angelic smile played on his lips.

Calmly and firmly, he ordered everyone to go about their respective business. There was no sign of the Sadhu, so they say.

No one knows what eventuated behind the heavy dark wooden door. But after that incident, Dadaji flourished. There were many conjectures; most people believed that the ascetic bequeathed him with a pot full of gold coins.

"Was it true, Papa?" she asked when she was an inquisitive little girl.

Papa laughed affably. "I have not seen it, so I cannot tell you for sure."

But Papa disclosed another narrative.

Due to Dadaji's brilliance and scholarship, all the rich people from far-off villages sent their children to him for education. He was not only learned but also pious. No beggar or Sadhu, *sscetic,* was ever turned away from his doorstep empty-handed. People knew the children would not only study the bookish knowledge but also the highest principles of ethics of true living.

The word of Dadaji's erudition circulated in ever widening circles and landed at the doorstep of a Mahal, *palace.*

One hot summer morning, Kaku the servant came running in and breathlessly told Dadaji with a tremor in his voice, "There is a Sepahi, *sepoy,* on a horse outside the haveli, *mansion.* What will happen to us, Malik? We did not do anything?"

Dadaji smiled reassuringly, "Never fear Kaku. Ask him in."

Then he turned to Dadi. "Send some lassi, *buttermilk,* for the man. It is a hot day, and we don't know how far he has traveled."

Kaku brought a tall, hefty, dark, uniformed, menacing-faced man in the living room and ran for his life to the security of the kitchen.

Dadaji got up from his velvet armed chair and folded his hands humbly. "Namaste. Please sit down," and pointed to a rather luxurious-looking dewan, *a seating place with many cushions,* with green velvet cushions for back support. The man hesitated, "Sire, I have . . ." Dadaji interrupted politely, "Please, relax and have a cool glass of lassi, *buttermilk.*"

Kaku came in, his hands were more steady now and gave the sepoy a glass full of the foamy lassi. He placed a plate of mithais, *sweets,* on a side table and walked back; pride at his own fearlessness showed on his greasy face.

Obviously, the man was thirsty. He gulped down not one but three glasses of the cool, white drink and ate a whole plate of sweets.

All the nourishment brought life and charm to his bearded, stubbled face.

He bent his head and said courteously, "What we had heard about you is true, sire. The prince of Shahepur would like to see you. Here is the letter."

A gray-bearded, bespectacled, short-statured prime minister received Dadaji at the much-guarded main gate of the palace. He was disdainfully respectful, scared out of his mind at the apprehension of losing his prime ministership to this dignified tall man.

Dadaji was led through marble corridors. Huge paintings of grand-looking, gold-red turbaned [rinces with long, velvet achkans, *coats,* encased swords attached to the much-engraved golden waistbands, filled all the spaces on the walls; a proud display of the prince's ancestors.

On the way, the prime minister informed Dadaji in a dark tone that "common people" are never allowed into His Highness's private quarters, a cue that Dadaji should feel honored and show it. He did not know that Dadaji's honour did not rest on the prince's inner quarters but on his intrinsically righteous conduct in life.

The passage led to an expansive chamber fully illuminated with crystalline chandeliers hanging from the high ceiling. The room was extravagantly furnished with ample use of beige and red colors in velvet; all the statues and decorations were either marble or gold. The splintered light from the chandeliers brought lively texture to all the contents of the place.

On a satiny beige sofa chair sat a strikingly handsome young prince. The most conspicuous aspect of the prince's personality was his large, black, confident eyes that pierced and challenged, appropriately because he belonged to the warrior class well trained to employ every kind of weapon to win wars. A square jaw was also a part of the prince's physiognomy indicative of an obstinate and determined mindset.

The prince got up and welcomed Dadaji, further aggravating the prime minister's anguish. The prince was reverent only to the elders of his family; no one else so far had been subject of his benevolence. And now? Drops of sweat emerged on the prime minister's forehead, his impending retirement becoming more real by the minute.

"Please, sit down on the sofa," the prince pointed to a sofa close by. He turned to the prime minister and said, "Dewanji, *Prime Minister,* please arrange for food for guruji," scaring the hell out of him.

"Maybe I am the next peon." He bowed steeply to please the prince as a last-ditch effort to retain his position, threw a resentful glance at Dadaji, and left.

Without mincing his words, the prince spoke, "According to our scriptures, Gyan, *knowledge,* is the key to Shakti, *puissance,* that we need to gain freedom from our oppressors. I know that you understand that. I have heard of your scholarship."

Dadaji was humbled, "Rumours are often exaggerated."

The prince was pleased with Dadaji's humility and smiled. "Some rumors I believe to be true."

A grave shadow passed over the prince's well-carved features. "In appearance, I show cordiality to the Raj, *British Raj,* otherwise, they will find some excuse to throw me behind bars. My subjects, whom I love dearly, will fall prey to oppression and indignity. I want to awaken the children of my kingdom and empower them with erudition and potency in readiness to fight for the freedom of our Mother India from painful shackles of slavery. Can you do it?"

Much to the relief of Dewanji, Dadaji was given charge of the Education Ministry. New schools proliferated like mushrooms in all the villages of the prince's state; Dadaji's pupils became instant teachers overnight. The prince rewarded Dadaji profusely with gifts of land, property, and gold.

Papa leaned back and patted Meera on the head, "I believe this story makes more sense than the pot of gold, but we never know for sure, do we?"

- # -

Mali, *gardener,* gathered up his tools and ran in the house as the rain became thicker. It was a cold October evening shrouded by insipid, dense, gray clouds. Mist floated everywhere concealing the manifest existence.

Suddenly, bulky raindrops hit the glass pane of the large window of the living room. Meera emerged out of her reverie with a start and looked out at the yard. Deep, cold emerald had taken over where the flush of color had dominated until recently. Mali had been cleaning the beds, pruning roses, and raking the leaves. Soon he would head for Chandigarh to tend to Rakesh's garden, there being nothing to do on the frozen landscape of the Himalayas in the winter.

Mali and Meera shared an especial camaraderie ever since she was a little girl. He was one of Rai Saheb Tayaji's, *uncle,* Mali but moved with Meera's family when they left Summer Hill and took up residence in Simla. Many a morning they could be seen together, bent over the flower beds. Meera dug the soil with a little spade Ma got for her birthday, damaged the roots or tore a leaf or two. She would turn her ponytailed head toward Mali and apologize softly, "Oops, sorry, Bhaiya!"

A little while later, she would get bored, tired, or both. "Mali, Bhaiya, I think I need some rest, now," and lay down on the dewed grass, amidst splashed color and feel the sedating warmth of the sunrays on her pink baby cheeks.

While she was sucking on a delicious mango one day, Ma exclaimed, "Meera, do you know that this big hard core is the mango seed?"

"Really?"

"Yes, a mango tree grows out of it!"

Immediately, Meera went to work; Mali and she dug up a hole in the corner of the yard, placed the huge mango seed in the cavity, ever so gently, covered with soil and watered the area profusely.

It was tortuous to wait for the dawn. Meera was up before anyone else, ran to the garden in her night suit, and stared at the spot where she had buried the seed.

Couple of weeks passed. Nothing. She whined to Mali, "Bhaiya, maybe we are not giving it enough water?" Since she was already overflooding the soil, Mali immediately put a stop to this course of action. "Baby, you also have to pray. God gives life, na!"

Meera knelt in front of the temple where Shri Krishna stood crosslegged with a flute on his lips, peacock feather in the crown, and a naughty glint in his pure dark eyes. She prayed three or four times daily.

One early morning, a wee, pristine, lime green needle, so strong and alive, broke out of the ground and smiled at her.

She jumped, clapped, shot upstairs to inform everyone.

Normally, all her siblings would have been highly irritated by an untimely interruption of their sleep. But they had been touched by her anguish during the two preceding weeks. They joined the jubilation. "How nice, Choti!" Atul patted her head. "I am so happy," Shoba mumbled and went back to sleep. Rakesh went farther. "Let me have the first five mangoes, the very first ones when the tree bears fruit, okay?" His act of approbation established her credibility solidly and once for all. Mango seed can indeed become a tree, as she had told them.

Creation and the immensity of its manifestation awed Meera even as a child. On warm summer nights, up on the roof of Tayaji's large house in Delhi, where they spent the summer holidays, Meera lay on pure white sheets on her cot and stared at millions of twinkling stars. The moon moved across the endless sky leisurely like a soft white ball of homemade butter, a benevolent zephyr cooled the night and lulled everyone to quiescent slumber but Meera. Her tiny heart palpitated at the unknowable enigma, where did the stars and moon come from? Where does the sky end? The puzzle presented no immediate solution because, she figured, how can there be no end? But if there is, what is beyond it and where is an end to that?

And where is God and when or where was he born?

The mental exercise was tiring and confounding; her eyelids would finally give in, and she would drift gently into the obliging oblivion of sleep.

Neeti and Nishant came running into the living room after hurriedly getting past their homework. Darkness had obliterated the landscape outside the living room window.

"I will play with him first," Nishant was bossy as usual. "You always play with him first," Neeti whined bitterly and turned to Meera for support, "Bua, *father's sister*, tell him!"

Meera smiled at their unfeigned innocence. "Well, you can both do it together."

Neeti was appeased. She picked up a small soft foam ball and threw it lightly at Rishi. He was startled; his big blue eyes widened at the interruption of his activity. He was chewing on a rubber duck that made a squeaky sound when he pressed it. He giggled at such times. Neeti and Nishant were both enthralled by the cute, fair, aqua-eyed cousin; they did not tire of showing him off to their friends.

Five-year-old Neeti climbed on Meera's silky lap, her chaste, expectant face looking up. "Bua, you are going to stay with us always, na?"

Meera felt cozy and warm; she hugged Neeti. "Would you like us to?"

Neeti tightened her soft young arms around Meera's neck, kissed her on the cheek, and shouted jubilantly, "Yah! Yah! Yah! Nishant, we will never let Bua and Rishi leave, na?"

Meera wrapped her blue woolen shawl that Mohit had bought for her in Simla from Dayal Chachaji's shop. She shifted her gaze to the fireplace. Jane's melancholy eyes rose in the fire like two aquamarine lakes. Meera suppressed a sigh.

Atul was back from the office, changed into his casual kurta pajama and came straight to the living room. "How is my sweet li'l boy? Was everyone nice to you today?" Then noticing Neeti and Nishant, his face became drawn, "Aré. Homework?"

"We've done it," they both said with pride. "Good!"

He turned to Meera. "No music-shusik?" Before she could reply, he placed a long-playing record on the gramophone. "Talat, your favorite."

Talat Mehmood, a Muslim singer, sung in a deep, sorrowful voice, mostly *gazals* that are Urdu, *language of Muslims in India,* poems of longing and love. Before Mohit departed, Meera would join Talat and sing along; Mohit's eyes sparkled with pride.

Now, the soulful lyrics stirred raw memories and ripped apart the seams of her heart. She wanted to tell Bhai to change the record. But change to what? She could not bear to hear classical music either. It was unbelievable that the captivating, creative juxtapositions of the seven notes could fashion such a colorful silky backdrop that had lent pulchritude to their days together; not a single moment was deprived of the richness of music.

Meera looked at Atul on his fours with Rishi on his back, Neeti supporting him, and Nishant tugging the horse, "Tut, tut, chalo, *go,* faster." The irascible Atul, who was a bit of a terror for the siblings excepting Meera, was on his fours, humbly playing with his nephew.

Atul was the only short-tempered one in Meera's family. His belligerence was regarded as a genetic hand-me-down from Vikram Mamaji, *mother's brother,* a fiery lawyer who hated losing his battles. Atul had changed slowly over the years after the Ramu episode.

Mr. Maini was a tough professor; latecomers were banished from the class for a week. Atul was already late, and his shoes were not polished! "Ramu, Ramu!" he shouted so loudly that Papa, who was fixing his tie while getting ready to go to the office, came out of his room the same time Ramu ran up the stairs.

Dharma was their servant, but Papa had insisted that kids call him Kaka, *uncle,* out of respect because he was older. Ramu, Dharma Kaka's nephew, was barely thirteen years old. Dharma Kaka had brought him from the village to help out in the house. Atul glared at Ramu, who stepped back in fear, showed him the shoes, and hit him hard on his young face, "Why did you not polish these?"

Papa's face became red; he ordered a tearful Ramu to go downstairs and turned to Atul. "Wear some other shoes, we will talk this evening."

There was tension in the house all day. Atul knew he had crossed the line. Many speculations floated in the house regarding the punishment Atul was to receive in the evening. Shoba and Rakesh cancelled their usual plans: Rakesh's badminton match at the club, Shoba's fashion parade with her friends at the mall. Nothing was worth missing the drama of retributory justice that was to unfold in the evening. As far as they were concerned, revenge was in order. All those years of bossiness? There is a God after all!

"Maybe he will be jailed in the house for a month," said Rakesh with definite pleasure.

"Maybe . . . maybe . . ." Shoba searched for more severe penalty. "No food for a week . . ." and relished the thought immensely.

Meera started to cry; she was the only one sympathetic to Atul Bhaiya. She whined, "Mummy, but . . . but he did not mean it? And . . . Ramu Bhaiya should have polished his shoes, na?" Ma turned to Meera sternly. "No matter what, Choti, you do not hit anyone, ever!"

Papa and Atul sat in the living room. Shoba, Rakesh, and Meera hung around in the dining room in their attempt to catch every word and action that precipitated on the other side of the curtain. Papa called out, "Kids, go do your stuff." Needless to say, Rakesh and Shoba were crushed, having sacrificed their evening for nothing.

"Akku, I am not only disappointed, I am hurt. It is immoral to be violent towards anyone."

Atul was prepared, nonreticent, "Papa, I got angry. Don't you get irritated, ever?"

"Sometimes, but I do not beat people."

"Papa, you are an exception, we know that. But generally speaking, isn't anger an integral part of human nature?"

"Yes, it is. But it is also one of the most ferocious enemies of man. Man is meant to conquer, not succumb to it. Akku, we must transcend our base weaknesses if we wish to evolve into better, more civilized human beings."

Atul did understand it. He lowered his head. But being a potential lawyer, he could not go down without a decent fight. "Papa tell me, is anger never justified?"

Papa became thoughtful, inner. "Faced with injustice and cruelty, we should be enraged. Otherwise, how can we overthrow evil and protect the innocent? If a landlord is beating a laborer, one should be furious and do everything to put a stop to it. But when your shoes are not polished in time, rage is not acceptable. Most humans' anger is blind, irrational, and devoid of any sense of discretion. It is an egotistical irritation at not having your way, rightly or wrongly. If unheeded, self-centered fury can become a way of life. Man becomes a slave of his enemy and as a consequence turns into a true enemy of himself. We have to tame our negative emotions and use those for human good. Then we are the masters, the outcome can only be utilitarian." Atul apologized to Ramu. He did.

For Rakesh and Shoba, the scenario was disappointingly short of their expectations. But Akku was humbled. It was not too bad then. Meera gave him a loving puppy, *kiss*, for support.

There was clanking of pots and pans in the kitchen. "Hari Kaka, set up the dining table. Kids should sleep early, no one wants to get up in the morning, getting late every day," Asha's voice rang in the kitchen.

Meera looked through the window glass but found only herself staring back.

"Bhabi, *sister-in-law*," she called out in an attempt to be useful. "Should I call everyone for dinner?" Without any response, she still got up.

Meera's room was the large guest room in one corner of the house overlooking the expansive panorama of the valley below. Asha had made sure that Meera and Rishi were relatively remote from the dining area and the main door. They were, hence, spared the early morning hubbub of kids and Bhai getting ready to go to the school, office, eating noisily with much high-pitched protestation from everyone.

"Mummy, I don't want egg."

"My toast is too dark, I like it fair."

"Why I have to drink boring milk every day, Mummy, please?"

"Where is mango jam, Asha, I only like one thing in the morning, and that is missing! A man cannot even start his day with what he likes!"

Papa went later; the government offices opened at ten o'clock; Ma made his breakfast after the early morning hurricane was behind them.

The next room was Papa and Ma's. Before he left for the office, he sat on an armchair across the window and read the newspaper. Of late, newspaper in hand, he was caught staring into space. Meera knew his temporary oblivion was for her. She wanted to hold his hand and tell him, "But, Papa, I am fine, I am happy." How could she lie blatantly when she could not even convince herself?

Meera prayed to God to fulfil Prabodhda's blessing by giving her the wisdom to seek the unrefuted verity behind existence and intuition to believe it. Only the truth of Mohit's oneness with her soul could set her free since there is no separation in reality, only the illusion.

The room next to Papa's was Dadi's. She was older, needed to be watched. At night, Ma got up several times to place the quilt over her that Dadi constantly kicked away. Of course, she was not the spunky spy anymore. Morning surveillance in the front yard all but halted, divesting her most consequential entertainment and pastime; she had become depressed and stubborn.

Dadi would manipulate Dharma. "Beta, my knees are not moving today. Give my breakfast here in the garden." To ensure that she did not miss anything of importance, she conducted a most reluctant swift bath followed by summarily wrapped-up puja, *prayers,* her mind wondering beyond the Gods.

Meera remembered Dadi as the vigil of the neighbourhood. Dharma Kaka's first act in the morning of summer months was to install Dadi's cot outside on the lawn under the apple tree, directly in the sun, since Simla is cool at the wee hour even in summer. It was not Dadi's love for the pink, heartwarming dawn or the mighty mountains as one might assume. Kitchen was close to the apple tree, she could oversee the preparation of breakfast. "Dharma, you are still cutting onions? No wonder everyone gets late. Make bhurji, *scrambled eggs*, it is easier, forget the omelets today! Did you make dalia, *porridge*, for Atul?"

That spot offered a perfect view of on goings of not only her house but also the neighbourhood. Dadi used her vigilante talent for the inhabitants of the closest vicinity. She could see, hear and smell whatever transpired on the other side of the meticulously pruned hedge that cordoned off the bungalows.

It was of utmost importance to spy which Saheb, *gentleman*, sneaked out of office to have lunch with his biwi, *wife*! "Aré, Gupta Saheb every day comes home at twelve! Doesn't he have any work to do? Sarkari Afsar, *government official*, ekdum nikamma, *absolutely useless*. No one to ask him anything, na? No one works these days."

Then a heart-wrenching sigh. "Shiva ke Bapu just worked and worked! He never ate lunch, forgot it? I had to ask him ten times! But what was the use? What did he get? A bullet? Toba, toba."

Her licentious, unlawful activities were not deemed altogether objectionable by the neighbours, especially the women. Not only did Dadi provided masala, *spice*, to spice up the otherwise dull neighbourhood, they procured the daily news firsthand from someone they believed for a long time to be a reliable source. Hence, 50 percent exaggeration passed undetected because of the ardor of the listeners who happily swallowed every bit of the gossip because it was much fun and frolic to believe it. "Oh really, Dadi? You saw that? Neela said that? She said something quite different to me! What is this world coming to! I am going to ask her, eh! What is this? I thought only snakes have two tongues! I am so happy you told me, tell me more? Acha, *really*?"

Papa expressed great displeasure. "Biji, *mother*, why don't you spend your precious time to sudharo, *improve*, your parlok, *life after death*? Remember God, aim your vritti, *attention*, on Him. Leave the world alone."

How could sagacious Dadi repudiate the certitude of present tantalizing life for some unseen, unknown, unreliable future?

The most consequential task for Dadi, whereby she felt most useful and indispensable, was to keep a stern eye on Atul, who studied, pretended to, on the balcony of his room on the second floor. With her much-honed sixth sense, Dadi smelled that something far more interesting than learning was cooking. At frequent intervals, Atul got up from his chair, straightened himself, feigned to look at the mountains across while slyly scoping for the lively, giggly ubiquitous presence of three comely girls, Shalini, Mona, Deepa.

Sunday presented an especially lucrative vista; it was hair-washing day! The girls would sit on their garden chairs or walk on the lawn to dry their long lush hair in the generous warmth of the sun. Atul developed a chikna, *smooth,* gleam on his face on such days. He would shout from the balcony, "Hi, Shalini, hi, Mona, and hi, Deepa" and have an extended balcony to garden chat.

At those precise moments Dadi's otherwise limited hearing would suddenly, inexplicably amplify to unlimited range; she could hear every word to be quoted later at appropriate juncture. She reported to Papa on a regular basis how Atul's tone and inflection was when he spoke with Shalini, and before the situation got out of hand, Papa should meet Mr. Gupta and settle the matter once for all. And Atul? He was a bundle of confusion; the loving young man was enchanted by all three!

Feverish excitement was fermenting in the gossip circle. Allegiances were carved, the loyal partisans of each faction clashed on a regular basis; the once-peaceful neighborhood became a battle zone.

Much jealousy raised its ugly head amongst the contestants. Handsome, fair, tall young man, a bright student of law college, presenting the certainty of opulent future, Atul was unanimously crowned as the most profitable match in those circles.

Frequent plates of samosas, burfi, and halwa poured in Meera's house from the surrounding bungalows. The respective mother of the prospective bride became the commander of the crusade on behalf of her lovely daughter.

Meera became the lucky recipient of hugs, puppies, lollypops, and chocolate bars from the leading competitors who even started to call her Choti, in a precocious display of intimacy meant to find a trail to Atul's heart.

The study sessions at the balcony became more frequent. Atul settled on the film actor Dilip Kumar's hairstyle after trying Dev Anand's and Raj Kapoor's, started whistling the love tunes of latest movies, *Anarkali*, *Barsaat*, *Awara*, etc. The lasses modeled after Nargis, Madhubala, the Bombay movies' beauty queen, and Meena

Kumari whose anguished sweet voice could draw tears even from the hardened hearts. They started to swing their hips while walking, smiling with half-pressed lips.

The commotion ended with a strategic, expediently orchestrated declaration by Ma that Atul was not ready to tie the knot until he finishes his law degree, after which he may leave for the USA for higher studies.

The prudently contrived proclamation immediately halted the flow of plates of goodies to Meera's house. The disappointed girls disappeared from the garden; Atul was forced to retreat into the confines of his much safe study for his scholarly pursuits. The predicament was irresolvable anyway; Dadi loved Shalini, Shoba preferred Deepa, Atul was bewildered. Ma knew all along who Atul was going to marry.

Meera did not particularly like the frivolous talking-funny, too-much-made-up girls. All three were cross with Meera for a short while. She regained their confidence by divulging that Atul was bossy and short-tempered. That inside information made them feel much relieved. Also, because no one got him, it was an even score, and all friendship was duly restored in no time.

When Asha, Atul, and Meera, holding Rishi in her arms, had walked in the living room, Dadi looked vexed. Papa and Ma had hugged Meera and Rishi affectionately as they got out of the taxi. Neeti and Nishant were thrilled and started to fuss over him immediately. "He is so cute. Bua, such big blue eyes, oh, I love him so much already. Can I pick him up?" Neeti was the emotional one. Nishant said with self-importance and authority, "No, Bua, she will drop him. Let me hold him."

Meera feigned hurt. "No hug or kiss for Bua, eh?"

They were both embarrassed, came forward, and hugged her fondly. "Nai, nai, Bua, of course."

"I will let Dadi bless him first, and then you can play with him!"

Rishi was proffered to Dadi for a hug, kiss, and customary blessing or two.

Dadi shrank back, waved her arms in a rejecting gesture, and twisted her face, "Pare, pare, maletch ko mere se door rakho, *keep me away from the low caste.* We threw angrez, *British,* out of Bharat, *India,* and this pagal ladki, *mad girl,* has brought one home."

Meera was shaken by abhorrence in Dadi's toothless voice. Ever since Dadaji died, acridity had incorporated in her breath. She was always irritable but never so bilious. Rishi belonged to the race responsible for making Pakistan on her territory resulting in the bouleversement of her sumptuous life. It was no secret that she never forgave them. Meera cringed with fear. What if others feel the same way? Where will she go?

Intense pain shadowed Papa's calm features. He sat by Dadi on the couch, took her soft shriveled hands in his palm, "Beji, Rishi is Meera's son. He belongs to us now. No one is *maletch.* You have not even hugged her, and last year you gave me headache every day about when she was coming back?"

Dadi burst into tears of anguish, "I am just tired of living, Deva, do you think I enjoy this gibberish I speak all day? Life is worthless without your Bauji, *father.*"

Dadi had broken down when Ma held her on their arrival in Amritsar. "He tried to save everyone but us, Shakuntla. We should have left when we could!"

The neighbor Hashim had knocked at the door of Dadaji's, *paternal grandfather,* haveli, *mansion,* at two o'clock at night. "Bhaijan, *brother,* they burnt my house!" He choked. Behind him stood his wife and two young boys trembling with terror.

Speechless, Dadaji hugged him and brought them into the living room. Dadi came down when she heard the commotion. Silently, tearfully, she embraced Salma and took Mehmood and Zen's hands. "Let us go upstairs Beta, and try to sleep."

Gandhiji and Congress had unwillingly relented to Jinnah's demand for Pakistan. Within two weeks, a British official drew the boundaries on the map. In his hurry to wrap up British Raj in a colony that had become a nuisance rather than asset, the Britisher had no idea that the lines he drew to separate India from Pakistan, at places ran through villages, sometimes houses; brothers, sisters, and parents living in the same home became Indians and Pakistanis. No one knew yet where the borders were. Rumors spread faster than the fires that followed them. Lines of communication had died long ago.

The next day, all the Hindus and Musalmans of the village gathered in Dadaji's living room. Dadaji spoke tenderly, "Let us vow to protect all our brothers, Hindus and Musalmans."

Every day, more and more Musalman friends came to Dadaji's haveli for protection. Mattresses spread all over the house, kitchen steamed all day long until there was no food left on the shelves. Dadi begged the milkman to continue the supply of milk for children at exorbitant prices of course; he risked his life hence it was a fair deal.

There was still some wheat flour left in one canister. For days, everyone ate dry rotis and water. Only youngsters were given milk.

Hindu gundas, *rogues*, came from surrounding villages where Musalmans had burnt Hindus' houses, raped women, killed everyone in sight. They were blind with fury of revenge and instigated enough young Hindu boys in the village. They all roamed the streets like blood hounds with loaded guns and shining knives.

Reports filtered through that Vikram pur, named after Dadaji's grandfather, was to be a part of Pakistan although there was a majority of Hindus living there. Hindu hordes departed for India on trains, jeeps, if they could rent them, bullock carts or on foot. Musalmans gladly took ownership of the vacated houses by entering and not leaving.

Dadaji's haveli was plundered by many Musalmans; everyone knew there was a Tehkhana, *basement,* filled with gold, silver jewelry, and silk, satiny quilts and beddings, big utensils, etc. The mansion was expropriated by the milkman who believed he had earned it by supplying milk to them during the crisis.

Dadaji had finally agreed to leave. Everything was packed. Hashim was assigned the job of taking care of the Musalman friends who had sought shelter in his abode.

It was late at night; children slept innocently, women sat on the cots and talked incredulously about the inhumanity of humans who only a little while ago were normal smiling neighbours. They held hands and cried at their losses, repeatedly expressed gratitude and love to Dadi, "Appa, *sister,* may Allah protect you, without you we were all dead!"

"Our children would have left this world at their tender age!"

Men sat on the dewans in the living room. The pale dim light of the lantern deepened the palor of their anguished faces. Even good memories could bring forth only hollow laughs, tears filled black, brown eyes at the idea of Dadaji leaving them; they hugged him again and again.

Dadi came down and reminded Dadaji that he still had to pack his books. He could not take the whole library but he simply could not part with the Scriptures. Hashim assured him, "Bhaijan, as soon as peace comes, Inshallah, *God willing*, I will send you the whole library! Every single book."

Dadaji said, "Shabakhair, *good night*, we will see you in the morning," and went to the library to sort out the books.

Dadi went to the kitchen and asked Kaku to check with everyone in the living room if they needed anything. That 'anything' had been reduced to water or light tea, there was nothing more left in the kitchen to offer.

In the stark darkness of the night, a repeated loud knock at the main door, heightened the anxiety on all faces; muscles and the bodies achieved sudden tension. Kaku ran in panic to open the door, who knows the person may be running from death!

Gopal stood at the door like a white, bloodless ghost.

Kaku was speechless; he could not move. Dadi shouted from the back of the corridor, "Budhu, *silly*, lock the door right away!"

Dadi walked briskly torward Gopal, her cheeks wet with tears, and wrapped him in her motherly embrace. "So sorry, Beta, may God rest their souls in peace." He stood still and looked at her with unseeing eyes.

Dadaji heard his voice, "Gopal, come in the study."

Gopal dragged his lifeless body into the pious domain of Sarasvati, *the demi goddess of knowledge*, where, sitting on the floor crosslegged, he had learnt the principles of morality, nonviolence and compassion from Dadaji.

He touched Dadaji's feet and collapsed. Dadaji called out, "Kaku, get some water!" and helped Gopal sit up. Dadaji placed his hand on Gopal's head and took a deep sigh. "I pray for peace and strength for you and Naren."

The whole world drowned in Gopal's blurry vision. "Guruji, *teacher*, they cut pieces of my Mataji, *mother*, and Pitaji, *father*, in front of my eyes! I have lost my mind. What should I do?" Gopal broke down like a shattered glass.

Abruptly, Gopal staggered to his feet, such venom poured from his speech that the room turned dark. "Guruji, why, why are you doing it?"

Dadaji understood. "Gopal, we should not be blinded with fury to forget the difference between guilty and innocent. I am helping my friends, whom I love dearly: they have not harmed anyone, and they are victims like you. Gopal, hatred will destroy you."

"But, Guruji, the gyan, *wisdom*, you gave me, I have burnt in the pyre where I cremated my Mataji and Pitaji."

A flood of tears wetted his stubby tortured face. He bowled loudly, his body shaking with unbearable agony, Gopal pulled a small gun from his pocket. "Guruji forgive me, I hate you, I hate you," and pumped three bullets in Dadaji's heart.

Dadaji slumped backwards on his sofa chair; there was no sign of shock or surprise in his kind eyes. Such were the blind times, anything could happen; the pervasive cimmerian darkness of hatred had obscured all paths by obliterating all lights of sanity and goodwill.

Gopal threw the pistol away, wailed loudly as he bent over bleeding Dadaji. "I don't know why I did it, how could I hurt you? You are my God! Guruji!" He quickly took his shirt off, gathered it and pressed it against Dadaji's bleeding heart and pleaded, "Don't go, don't go, Guruji. Who will show me the light to guide me in this darkness?"

Dadaji, smiled sadly, focused his waning life force before he took his last breath, "Forgive, don't lose your Soul." Gopal fell on Dadaji's dead bloody body and howled with such anguish that the whole haveli shook on its foundation.

Communications were nonexistent. Papa was still in Lahore, waiting anxiously for them to arrive safely in the perilous circumstances.

Dadaji's body was cremated quietly by his Hindu and Musalman friends. A copper pot, with Dadaji's still-warm ashes was packed in a shell-shocked, benumbed Dadi's trunk. Bua, Nalini, and Dadi disguised as Musalman women, little Nitin dressed in Muslim garb, and two servants were taken to Lahore in a jeep driven by Hashim's brother and handed over to Papa.

Papa could hear Dadaji's gentle voice full of dismay and regret. "Deva, it is not his fault. I failed to teach my pupils."

"No, Bauji," Papa wept. "You did not fail anyone. Humanity failed itself."

A pungent fear hung in the air, a gloomy tamas, *darkness*, ugly and hopeless had possessed the territory. Deadly gunshots, shrieks of tormented children, men and women, young and old, pierced the heart of the night. The fury of kal, *infinite time*, with its many tongued flames, lapped up the defenceless homes that had stood innocuously for centuries oblivious of the fiery future that was to exterminate them unceremoniously.

One such moonless night, that was all the more blackened by a shroud of pervasive smoke of gun fires as well as burning homes, Ma, Papa, Dadi, Bua, Nalini, Nitin, Meera and her siblings were loaded on a truck furtively, using the back door of the house. Accompanied by two influential Musalman friends of Papa, stopped at various checkpoints but let go unharmed; they covered the mere twenty miles from Lahore to Amritsar in what felt like a throbbing, excruciating eternity.

- # -

"Were you able to sell the property, Meera?"

"Yes, Bhai."

"How much money did you get?"

It was awkward. No one had asked her that question before, but she had to reply.

"Twenty thousand dollars."

"Oh! That is a lot of rupees!"

Yadav looked at Kanta for affirmation. She kept her vision fixed on the oncoming traffic.

"Mohit must have had a reasonable insurance policy."

"Yes, Bhai."

"How much?"

When Meera had touched his feet after the wedding, Yadav had remarked with much fondness. "No, Meera, don't touch my feet, you are like my daughter. I am much older than Mohit."

Is that all he had to say to his grieving daughter?

"Thirty thousand dollars."

"Wow, you raked a lot of money!"

Meera was stunned by his crude materialistic curiosity at a time like this.

Meera's first visit to Bombay, right after the wedding, had a dreamy texture, an unreal quality. All she remembered was happy and loud laughter and grinning-ear-to-ear relatives, women decked up in gold, congratulating them. A shy newlywed, Meera had not looked up closely at anyone. Meera felt concerned; how will she recognize Yadav?

A gust of heavy humid air brushed against her face as she alighted from the plane at the Bombay airport. The sky was overcast with nimbus, like her heart.

An unmistakable shadow of Mohit stood across a sea of humanity at the airport searching for her.

Yadav and Kanta spotted Meera; two blurry images waved at her. She was filled with hope, wiped her tears, squeezed through the impatient crowd, and approached them, hesitantly. As she bent down to touch his feet, Meera felt Yadav's cold unfeeling hand rest on her head momentarily, in silence. Kanta hugged her warmly and asked if the flight was comfortable.

How could Yadav bless her? But how could she not feel hurt? Meera suppressed a sigh and leaned back against the black leather of the car seat; her sweaty blouse stuck to it.

The car moved painfully, deliberately, through the dirty, slushy streets of Bombay, swarming with anxious faces, unnecessarily honking cars, squeezing anywhere and everywhere, scooter rickshaws, scooters with the whole family of five clinging to one another for their lives, double decker buses, over spilling with people hanging by the door handle, most of their torso perilously available for slicing by other buses and trucks. The rattling trucks had fair-sized signs at the back: Allahu Akbar, *Allah is great*; Wahe guru, *God in Punjabi language,* protect us; Ganeshai Namah, *salutations to demi god Ganesh.* Some signboards had declaration of the wisdom of the ages, "Life is fleeting," "Do good to beget good," "Gareebee hatao", *remove poverty,* "Revenge is for cowards," "Soul is eternal," "Death is inevitable." The writing on the wooden plaque that hung on front of the truck right above the windshield carried important information regarding the nomenclature of the truckwalla's family. The trucks are generally named after truckwalla's beloved children: Ravi, Prakash, Gokul, Sukdeep, Paminder, and Gajinder, etc. Girls' names are not honoured because they belong to the husband's clan, even before the nuptials happen.

Through all the chaos, the pedestrians barely escape the brutality of the blind traffic that may also include couple of cows, squatting smack in the middle of the road, or a dog or two as they bravely run across the impossible streets.

Soon Dharvi, *a huge slum in Bombay,* arose at the horizon, a little distance from the main road. Lingering at the cusp of civilization, miles of patched up slums shelter thousands of humans who eke a meagre existence in its shadows. Meera looked away in anguish struggling to fight the centrifugal force that compelled her toward the innermost, murky labyrinths of the penurious unworldly world, toward the very hub of Dante's inferno. It is she who is ablaze in the suffocating torridity of the hut converted into furnace by the undeserved fury of the broiling summer sun. Her lips are parched, but water is as tenuous as mercy. It is she who is drenched to her core by the slashing rain during monsoons; the mud on which the slums stand precariously is sticking to her body and face. She is the one shivering as the frigid arrows of chilly wind pass unimpeded through the straw huts and her much-holed, much-frayed saree. In sickness, she looks up at the skies for God's attention, who has abandoned her for what sins? she asked.

Bauji, *Father,* straggled, dragging his slippers as he came down the stairs to receive Meera. His step was weary, back stooped, cadaverous face appeared drawn and harassed. His hair was snow white.

A little more than a year and a half ago, he looked younger than he was; his face beamed with joy and pride. Between then and now lay a desert of dolor, his soul scorched by the relentless sun of death. He had aged with every painful step that took him nowhere in the infinite vastness of sand and dust around him.

Meera felt the violent trepidation of his hand on her bent head when she touched his feet; like Yadav, he was faced with the quandary—what blessing could he give to the widow of his departed son? He muttered an incoherent, meaningless "Be happy" with full knowledge of its impotency.

Maji, *Mother*, lay wrinkled and emaciated; her wee body looked all the more trivial on the large bed. Her eyes seemed crushed under the unflagging avoirdupois of bereavement, soliloquizing an eloquent why that you could not escape.

Maji tried to get up when Meera entered the room but burst into tears and fell back. Meera walked briskly toward her and held her frail throbbing body in her arms. Quite abruptly, Maji recoiled and fell back on the bed, heaving with emotion.

Meera understood. Maji was Mohit's mother, she was his wife, but the link had forsaken them, leaving a harrowing chasm gaping them in the face. Maji looked away to evade the reality of the loss of connection with Meera.

Mohit's family lived in a sprawling old ancestral house still steadfast on its foundations. An expansive garden with ancient, huge trees surrounded the moss-covered house on all sides and cushioned the inhabitants from the onslaught of street noises.

After their wedding, Meera, the new shy bride was led in the house by Maji, Lalita, Kanta, female cousins, and aunts who sang out-of-tune songs of bridal welcome. Oil was poured on both sides of the door, Meera kicked a small heap of rice that was piled on the floor with her henna-decorated fair feet, stepped over, and entered the house. The demi god of subsistence thus appeased would ensure a plentiful life for the couple.

This particular ritual was completely unknown to Meera. She cringed at the idea of kicking food with her foot while a vast humanity out there was starving. And how stomping on food could please any sensible demi god? But a new bride could not start disputing with her in-laws even before officially stepping into the house. There could be drastic consequences such as taking her to the railway station and dishonourably dispatching her back to her unworthy parents who failed to teach her refined stuff like "arguing with your mother-in-law is a sin."

All corners of the residence was lit with blue, green, red, and purple lights; echoes of jubilation and laughter reverberated everywhere like the waves of celestial music.

Now, the abode stood gaunt, haunted by the ghosts of the past, marks of injury stamped on every face. An eerie silence shadowed spoken words; Bauji and Biji whispered in suffering whines.

A large photo of Mohit hung on the wall across Maji's bed; a garland of artificial red and white roses decorated it.

In India, if you are visiting someone and see a photo frame of someone on the wall with garland around it, you know that the person has departed. Meera made a painful effort to avoid looking at it. Her heartache splashed into her eyes, covering them with tears. On the dresser, wedding pictures of Mohit and Meera, Yadav and Kanta, Lalita and Mahen, and another one of single Yash, stood silently.

Kanta peeped in. "Meera come and have tea. Maji, Bansi will bring yours here." The latter part was spoken loudly, indicating Maji's hearing limitations.

The dining room was fairly large; a good-sized dining table lay in the center; the six chairs had high, beige, velvety backs. Bansi entered with a tray in his hand, a kitchen towel thrown on his shoulder; he looked young, almost Mohit's age, and strong. Obviously, he was well treated with availability of sufficient nourishment.

He placed the tray on the dining table, bent down with folded hands, and spoke in a choked voice, "Choti Bibi, namaste. Our Bhaiya left us, what should we do?" Bansi had served the family for twenty years; Mohit called him yar, *friend.*

Meera swallowed her tears and said soothingly, "Bansi Bhaiya, God's will has to be accepted." Bansi lost control and protested loudly, "What God? No God. Look at Bauji and Maji, how can He see them suffering? What kind of a God is he? Main nahi manta, *I don't believe*!"

Meera was shaken by the intensity of his locution. Kanta gave him a harsh look and stern scolding, "Bansi, what's this? Meera has come after such a long journey and you are doing tamasha, *drama*! Chalo, *go,* bring the rest of the stuff."

Kanta's abrasive speech rubbed against Meera's heart like a thorn bush, the needles dug deep, causing pain.

Bansi ran in, tears flowing down his dark cheeks. Meera just stared at her cup of tea that was consumed in uncomfortable silence.

Meera understood Mohit's family was having problem in finding a place for her in their devastated lives. Who was she to them now?

If only they could allow her, not to take Mohit's place but offer them some semblance of the love they had lost forever.

"Meera, I will show you your room if you want to rest before dinner."

"Yes, Bhabi, *sister-in-law*," Meera said softly.

Lying in the same bed where once Mohit and Meera lay in each other's arms, sent a wave of excruciating torment in her spirit. She hugged the pillow and wept.

A sudden down pour of rain startled her at first, followed by a sense of comfort as the sound of rain on the roof somehow filled the void of reticence in the ambience. It was dark, night insects and water loving frogs crackled in the background.

Dinner was ingested amongst short questions and shorter answers interspersed with clanking of spoons on the plates.

Meera excused herself after the last course of mithai, and chai, and stepped out on the dark moisture laden balcony. She felt suffocated. A strong whiff of breeze sprinkled raindrops on her chiffon saree. Asha had said, "It is hot and humid in Bombay. Meera, chiffon is the most comfortable fabric." Of course, it could not be predicted that rain would urge the barometer to drop considerably. Meera wrapped the palloo of her saree around her shoulder; it was cool, soothing, and embalming. Some streetlights twinkled through the fluttering leaves of the trees.

Kanta opened the balcony door and cautioned Meera, "Meera, don't get wet. Bombay weather is very deceptive."

No one asked about Rishi. Maybe Atul was right.

Atul had declared with a tone of finality, "There is no need, why should you go? Have they shown any concern for you?" In spite of his impulsive and impatient mind-set, Atul's judgement was generally sound and based on facts.

Atul raised his voice and said to Papa, "I don't think Meera should go. Why? Her in-laws don't care about her at all. They have never contacted her! Yash went to Canada for training and did not even phone her."

Meera was startled; she did not know.

Papa looked at her questioningly; Meera kept her eyes glued to the carpet. He took a deep breath and looked out of the window.

The mountain peaks dazzled in the bright sunlight. They sat quietly. Finally, Papa said in an even voice, "Meera, I know you will do the right thing. I do think you can give them one more chance. Go and see them, console them for their loss. If they are still unresponsive, you can bid your final good-bye graciously and leave. You would have done your duty."

Atul was totally dismayed; he said disgustingly, "Oh, Papa!"

But he knew Meera; she would choose to do the right thing even if it was inconvenient. He was resigned. "At least rest for a couple of weeks, it is going to be stressful especially for Rishi." Then suddenly added, "But is it a good idea to take him with you? Maybe we will keep him here."

"I will think about it, Bhai."

She rose up abruptly, came to her room, buried her face in the pillow, and wept uncontrollably.

Meera had come to India with high hopes that Mohit's family would fold her aching life in their embrace and fill, even if partially, the gnawing abyss Mohit had left in her heart. She craved closeness to capture his shadow in their personalities, to feel his presence in the many familiarities of their eyes, smile, gait, voices and gestures. Meera knew Lalita was in Delhi and was excited at the thought of meeting her. At the airport, upon her arrival at Delhi airport, Meera had scanned the crowd and was deeply disappointed at her absence.

Meera looked at little Rishi in her lap, cuddly, innocent, and vulnerable. A fountain of love flowed in her heart for him and bathed her in a cool, milky, moonlight. He looked up with his almond shaped blue eyes and babbled, "Ma, Ma."

Jane's face showed up in Meera's vision. Rishi had her eyes, big, gentle, but timorous. An unknown fear gnawed at Meera's heart. Rishi had spent almost ten months with foster parents. He had appeared happy when she visited him; the foster parents were loving. Yet the apprehensive shadows in his eyes vexed her. She pressed his limber, tiny body against her breasts and kissed him on his rosy plump cheeks. He wiggled to get out of her grip; his bright eyes focused on the ball of red yarn that had fallen down on the beige carpet. Ma was knitting a red-colored sweater for him. "Oh, Dadima, red will look so cute on Rishi, na?" Neeti was excited.

Meera let him on the floor; he walked with wobbly uncertain steps toward the red round object that looked lucrative. Meera felt a surge of pride well in her bosom. She looked at Ma and smiled, "He can walk now, does not need support."

Ma smiled weakly without looking up, a sad smile. She had been unusually quiet ever since Meera's arrival.

Before Meera arrived, Ma had agonized. "You will see, Rishi will become the chains around her ankles. How can she tread the paths of life freely?"

Papa implored her, "God has given her a golden opportunity to raise an orphan. We must love him with kindness and compassion." He did not leave any room for Ma to say much.

Papa was endowed with a rare coalescence of pragmatism and compassion in a just balance. He had no difficulty in reconciling the opposites and do the right thing.

Meera was hesitant. "Ma, are you sure Rishi will be okay?"

Ma kept her eyes fixed on her knitting. After a short silence, she sighed and said blankly, "They will not like to have him there, and you have decided to go. So, what is the choice?"

Meera resolved to go to Bombay. The evening before she flew, she phoned Lalita. The maid informed her that, "Mem Sahib is away for two weeks." Then she called Bombay. A cut-and-dry interlocution with Maji and Bauji followed. They apologized unemotionally for not coming to Delhi airport. They did not ask her to come. Meera was shaken but said in a determined voice, "I will come and see you soon, Bauji."

Lalita was in Bombay but left for Banglore one day before Meera's arrival. Kanta did not look at her when she explained in a deliberately casual voice, "Lalita was sorry she missed you, Meera. But her in-laws were not well. She said she will see you in Delhi sometime."

Meera struggled not to make too much of it.

Meera stayed with them for a punishing, interminable one week. Tension permeated the frigid air; people moved around like robots programmed to avoid her eyes. Bansi was the only one who seemed to acknowledge that she was indeed part of Mohit's family. He talked to Meera about Mohit incessantly, thereby legitimizing her presence. She did belong to her husband's family, whether they owned up to that verity or not.

Painfully, Meera witnessed the full impact of Mohit's untimely demise on his parents; they were completely shattered, reduced to mere shadows of themselves. How could she expect anything from them? They had lost everything, or so they believed. But she had not meant to ask for anything, just an opportunity to give. She tried her best to give them warmth and love; it was excruciatingly arduous since they refused to receive it. There was no common link for a verbal communion and no desire on their part to build bridges. The one nexus that bound them together, they dared not approach; no one talked about Mohit.

She sat at Maji's feet, rubbed them gently, and tried to hold her hand; Maji recoiled from Meera's touch. Were they blaming her for Mohit's death? A primitive, causal equation buried in the shadowy, convoluted depths of the Indian psyche would claim, "Meera came into Mohit's life, and he died." In a village, she would be cursed, her head shaven, dressed poorly in white; young ruthless children would chase her around throwing stones at her. At home, she would be condemned as a servant, not to be touched for fear of contagion of misfortune. Now in more modern times, in a supposedly more civilized society, Meera was spared that horror; she was only imprisoned in a stony cage of brutal silence, Bansi's painful voice echoing against its suffocating confines, the only sign of life.

When she touched his feet before leaving, Bauji, *Father,* mumbled in a suffering, afflicted voice, "Beti, there is no tragedy greater than losing a young son. It rips you apart from your seams. Please forgive us."

When she left Bombay, Meera knew that she would never see them again. Meera hid her face in her hands and cried, uncaring of the curious glances of other passengers in the plane. A young air hostess bent forward and patted her on her shoulder, "Are you okay, ma'am?"

"Yes," she lied.

The kind girl brought her a cup of tea and smiled sympathetically, "Take it easy." Meera was grateful for the understanding gesture.

As for taking it easy, it was difficult. Chachaji had written, "Our problem is that we take this dream of a life too seriously. In fact, life is but a drama. It is not even our drama, we just play the roles. God is the writer, the producer, and the director, but his narrative is based on our own past karma, *our deeds.* Willing or volition is our duty but the outcome or turn of events at momentous moments in the act, is not up to us. We should learn to play our assigned characters well, but not get too personally attached to the given role. Let God's intention unfold as it would—be an actor as well as audience. God is playful but just in his design. He provides us with all the dark and light colours and lets us fashion our own life on the canvas of time. We can make it happy or sad, it is up to us. The courage of our heart and the mettle of our spirit can and does help us transcend the world of pain and create our own life sphere that glows with the aura of our inner being. Unfortunately, most of us are not even aware of the resplendence of our spirit. We abide in dark despair, deeper than a moonless night, though we are the very fountainhead of the luminosity of the stars, the moon and the sun."

Meera was striving to attain the state of inner understanding, but the Truth eluded her. She looked out of the wee window of the plane. Shri Krishna, armed with his alluring smile, perched on the white gray puffy clouds and played his bamboo flute. But Meera could not hear the divine music; he disappeared as she stared out. Jane's sad but smiling face emerged through the clouds instead. Did she come to remind Meera that her life was not so bad after all, it could be worse?

- # -

Gary looked up from the form he was filling and asked Meera politely, "Ms. Meera, please give me all the details of the time you spent with Miss Jane."

"Would you like a cup of coffee before we start?"

"Sure." He smiled congenially.

For a cop, he was unexpectedly gentle and soft-spoken.

Jane looked ill, her flawless transparent face had an undertone of pallor like an old marble statue. That night, tears flooded her ashen cheeks; she had undertaken an agonizing journey on the thorny lanes of her past.

"I went from one foster home to another. Some were good and some were nasty, but none as cruel as Mrs. Henderson." Jane refused to call Mrs. Henderson her mother.

Foster home was new to Meera's vocabulary. "But . . . but didn't you have any relatives or extended family?"

"Mrs. Henderson scared them away. My father was from England. He was raised in an orphanage. His parents were killed during the First World War. He came to Canada and got a job in Grandpa's pulp factory. He was an engineer. Kelley told me that Grandpa was charmed by his gentle smile and calm face. He believed that my dad could bring some sanity to her. Instead, he lost his own. She humiliated and tormented him with her noxious and arrogant temperament. He left for England; no one heard from him. Perhaps he joined World War II and died, who knows."

Jane wept. "You know, Mrs. Henderson burnt all his photos! I don't even have one."

"But your uncles or aunts in your mom's family?"

"Grandpa was British. His parents died of tuberculosis three months apart when he was a teenager. His only older sister, Aunt Annie, raised him. He went to India to serve the Raj, *British Raj.* When he grew up, Grandpa married his general's daughter. She died when Helena, Mrs. Henderson was five. He did not go back to the United Kingdom. Kelley told me that something horrid had happened in India. He moved to Canada. After his death, Aunt Annie tried her best to keep contact for my sake, but Mrs. Henderson snubbed her. I have no one in this whole world!"

The dam Jane had held together all her life, with her sheer will, caved in; a pent-up flood burst out and drowned both Jane and Meera.

Meera was horrified and speechless while Jane relived the wilderness of an innocent child who had no idea why she was subject to undeserved pain, a young girl pushed around and abused by foster parents, no one to explain to her that all the blood on her panties was not cancer but menstruation. She was always standing in the shadows whether it was a classroom or party, ashamed for an unknown gnawing guilt. She shrank into herself when a boy asked her out; was he going to humiliate and hit her?

Jane went to church to find answers and some solace, but Jesus stood on the cross, bleeding, with sad eyes. She asked herself, was her betrayal and humiliation greater than His? He was nailed on the cross by rough, cruel hands of ignorant and insane people, in the company of petty thieves, though His crime was that He tried to take a bruised humanity towards the healing bliss of God's presence. Jane could not ask him anything; she shed many tears for his anguish and never went back to church again.

She rested her splitting head against the back of the sofa and stared at the fire blankly. She was spent, having emptied herself. Her teary blue eyes shone with the golden reflection of the aureate fire, like two orange lotuses floating in a clear pond.

The wind had gathered, the branches of the willow tree knocked at the window, raindrops glittered on the glass pane with yellow street light. Fire crackled, amplifying the silence.

Meera got up slowly, walked toward Jane, and knelt beside her. Taking Jane's wilted, wet face in her hands, she kissed her on the forehead and wiped her tears with the edge of her saree.

"Jane, you are not alone anymore. I will be with you always like a true sister. Maybe we were sisters in our last birth." Pure Indian sentimentality had taken over Meera.

Jane's face had brightened for a few seconds. "Really, do you mean it?"

Before Meera could affirm, she fell back on the sofa bawling in anguish.

The last time Meera was with her, Jane was sitting on the beige couch, fidgeting restlessly with the corner of her pink casual dress.

She looked up at Meera, who was perched comfortably on the loveseat with her feet up on the center table, sipping tea.

"What?"

Jane had something on her mind. Quite abruptly she asked, "Meera, if I have a child and die, will you take care of the baby?"

Meera hated her negativity that was a constant in Jane's utterances. "Don't be silly. You will live long with a handsome husband and raise your own six children. Thank you very much."

Jane was emphatic. "I am serious, will you?"

Meera bent forward and took Jane's hand, "Show me your hand, I learned a bit of palmistry. Let me see your lifeline."

Jane pulled it back. "Really, will you please? Say yes!"

"Of course I will, silly, but there is no reason to believe that you are going to die young. You are a healthy, though skinny, girl."

Meera never saw Jane again.

Autumn had arrived abruptly this year following on the heels of a dip in the mercury for a week. The variegated colors of fall ingressed through the clear glass pane of the dining room in Meera's house. Today, their flamboyance felt disharmonious and jarred in Meera's consciousness.

Gary folded the forms, sheets of paper, and placed those in his briefcase. "I need a recent photograph of Ms. Jane."

"I do not have one. But I will give you Mrs. Henderson's phone number. She must have one." Gary was startled, "Oh, I did not know Ms. Jane was Mrs. Henderson's daughter?" Meera looked at him curiously, why was it important?

Mrs. Henderson did not have a single photo of Jane after she was moved to foster homes. Nevertheless, she called Robin in the police department with unfeigned disdain. "You are being foolish in launching a formal search for Jane. She has vanished before on her childish rampages and reappeared unharmed."

Robin was not too fond of her. "Thanks for your advice, ma'am." And before she could go any further, he banged the phone on the receiver.

On Prashant's insistence, Robin had decided to treat Jane's disappearance as a "missing person" case.

A familiar despondency and nightmares that Meera had experienced days before Mohit's death resurfaced

Meera is walking briskly on a mountain trail that is encroached by tall grass and curly ferns. Dusk has gathered light in its bosom and absconded; darkness is deep and silent. The pungent smell of pine needles on wet ground overpowers her senses. Someone has fallen off the cliff.

Mist is shrouding a small group of people at a distance. She walks faster. Silently, people move aside to let her through. She bends over a dead body that is lying on the mud covered with a white sheet from head to toe. Meera steps forward and with trembling hands uncovers the face. Her knees give in; she slumps on the wet ground and bawls in agony.

Meera had woken up with tears streaming on her hot face.

Mohit sat up in a daze, "What happened?" Meera had tried to smile. "Real bad dream. Go to sleep, Mohitji." He had a meeting the next day. She cuddled against Mohit's broad chest; he wrapped her in his arms. She could not sleep and kept the count of Mohit's snores, ammunition to tease him in the morning.

The next day, Mohit had his accident.

Once again Meera was full of portentous premonition. Images descended in her dreams. A small dim room, a lean shadow bent on a table writing something, a black shawl loosely hanging around her bony shoulders, blond hair tied in a clumsy bun. Nothing else was clear. One night she saw an ambulance, two uniformed men looking in and shutting the door noiselessly. Sometimes a cry of a baby came from nowhere. The memory of Mohit's death was still clear in all detail; nothing was lost with the passage of time. The pain of his loss woke up sharply; there was no escape, no miraculous quick fix. Bereavement seemed to have its own life and momentum; restoration had to take its own time.

No matter how hard she tried, prayed, meditated, and read the scriptures, she could not recover her warm sanctuary; a fog of woe stood like a thick opaque veil between her and God.

Quiet tears trickled on her pale cheeks. "Ever since I was a little girl, I have been taught that we are imperishable Atma, *Soul,* and death of the material body is inevitable. I know my 'Self' is Atma, the witness untouched by sorrow and grief, yet I feel so much pain! This knowledge is not giving me any solace. Why, Chachaji?"

On a chilly late fall day, Meera had called up Chachaji in the morning to stay with her for a whole day.

"The Truth of God and Soul is shining forth in all its splendor, but clouds of avidya, *ignorance,* conceal it. There is an infinite chasm between 'knowing and experiencing.' We comprehend the notion of God but fail to experience because we are unable to surrender our 'ego' to Him, which is the only way to bridge the said chasm. We can read, hear, see photographs of Delhi but unless we go there and see it first hand, we have no idea about how it really looks."

Meera nodded like an obedient child, "Yes, Chachaji, that is true."

"Meera, people abide in different strata of existence. To the 'materialist,' the manifest gross 'matter' is the only reality. He is caught up in desire and lust of things. Pain and pleasure are concrete and all consuming for him.

"The 'idealist' dwells in the intellectual domain of 'essence' rather than matter. Perceptions, thoughts, images, feelings, pain and pleasure are all Real. They constitute his world. Berkeley, a Western philosopher, called it 'idealism,' meaning that there is no world outside of us and all Reality is an idea in the mind. Madhyamic, *a branch of Buddhism,* Buddhists also believe that the world is in our minds.

"According to 'spirtualist,' the manifest existence is Unreal, an illusion. What we perceive with our senses has in fact an entirely different reality, the truth of which we can never discern with our sense apparatus.

"This is why. When we want to see a rose, call it *A*, it has to be brought close to the optic center of our brain to be interpreted. Eyes serve that purpose, they perceive; the optic nerves carry the message to the brain.

"So, to see a rose we require a whole line of mechanisms. Let us call that B. What we have seen at the end of the whole process is an image of the rose determined by A + B. We can never see A by itself, the rose's real reality. If the perception mechanism of a cow is C, then the cow will see the image A + C. Whose reality is real, then?

"The only Reality the 'spiritualist' believes in because he can 'directly experience' it, is the Truth of his Consciousness, 'I am' the 'Self' or Atma, *soul.* Atma is merely the witness, 'seer' of the panorama of the illusory existence outside of his own Reality. He stands back even from his thoughts, perceives the intellectual life from a safe distance. He is unaffected by the dualities of life, pain, pleasure, good-bad, because he has apprehended that nothing related to material existence is true or real.

"The 'spiritualist' has understood the contradictions faced by the 'idealist.' He treats the evident empirical existence, the world, his body, mind, and thoughts as illusion, 'Maya.' Illusion does not mean that there is nothing because in that case, he would not see anything. Empirical existence is outside of us, and what we see is not Real. What we perceive is different from what the object's 'Truth by itself' is.

"A famous example given in Hindu Scriptures that illustrates the concept of 'Maya' is that of 'Serpent and Rope.'

"In the dark, we descry a snake in our path and are duly scared. But when we use a lantern, we realize that it is a rope. It was rope all along though we were certain that it was a snake. That is 'Maya,' *illusion*. Mirage is yet another example of illusion.

"The ultimate rishi reigns the highest strata; he has submerged his soul, spirit, and attained unity with the Absolute sea of consciousness, Absolute God. For him there is no scenery, no differentiation, no 'Maya.' Only God is existent and Real. Rishi is and is not and it is all the same.

"Only the ultimate 'rishi' has absolute autonomy and supremacy over life, he is completely Mukt, *free*. It is not that he relinquishes life, he lives like everyone, excepting he is not attached to anything or anybody including his own body and mind. The thoughts and actions of Mukt do not arise from his ego 'Self' or mind but emerge from his untainted 'Consciousness.' He experiences Truth, Consciousness, and Bliss of God at all times. His love flows for all since God is love.

The reason for suffering is the timeless avidya, *ignorance,* of the true nature of Reality. That nescience relinquishes us in a scorching, illusionary desert of life; we live our lives craving the coolness of mirage forever clutching to the belief that it is real and attainable. The bondage of misery can only be severed by the sharp edge of true knowledge and experience of our own 'Reality.' We have to begin with understanding the discretion between true and false, eternal and momentary, God and his creation, 'Self' and 'not Self', and end our sadhana, *persistent endeavor,* with Realization of unity of our Atma, *Soul,* with God.

"Meera, keep reinforcing the practice constantly, detach from the unreal, and meditate on the Real. One day, some day you will experience Absolute Reality, God. The veil that blinds you will dissolve in the Truth, Soul will shine forth and bathe you in its own irradiance; identity with body and mind will cease with 'Self-Realization.'"

Where did she stand, who was she? Before her life was turned upside down with Mohit's departure, Meera might have found her place in the spiritual domain, but now she had lost her way; her own definition and sense of belonging was a blurry construct. She was not here nor there.

But where are you Jane?

- # -

David had spoken coolly on the phone. "Ms. Meera, we have found your friend." Perhaps it was routine for a policeman, just another mishap, people go missing all the time and are found alive or dead. Next case, please.

Meera's heart leapt, "Oh, thank God, thank God. And thank you! Is she all right?"

The long silence did not bode well. Meera's pulse raced while she waited. Maybe Jane is ill. That is alright; Meera would bring her back to health in no time.

"Ma'am, I am so sorry, she is dead."

Meera could not breathe; her knees gave in, she held on to the wooden arm of the chair close by and slumped on it.

"Ma'am, are you all right? Are you there?" It took Meera all her might to speak. "Yes. Have you informed the mother?"

"Mother? No? You had filed the missing person's report. We have to contact you. Please come and identify the body." The word *body* seemed so cruel; her Jane was reduced to a nameless body.

"The motel manager wants us out soon. Please also take her stuff."

"Call Mrs. Henderson. She will identify the body and take her stuff. Give me the address." Meera searched for a pen though it was lying right in front. Her hands refused to cooperate.

"Please, repeat."

A whirlwind of pungent pain rose from her gut, devastating the heart on its way. Meera doubled over her knees and bawled aloud.

Meera wanted the piercing, annoying, and persistent ringing to stop. She looked at the phone in confusion and then extended her trembling hands to pick it up.

"Are you okay?" Prashant's voice was deeply worried.

"No!" She wept uncontrollably into the phone.

"I am coming."

Prashant walked through the unlocked main door. Meera still had the habit of trusting the world. He placed his firm hand on her dark hair affectionately; Meera embraced him but pulled back awkwardly. Prashant was pained. "Meera, we are friends. It is okay."

He drew her close; she caved in his arms and wept like a child.

Soon, Meera and Prashant were driving by a remote part of the city. Small, unpainted, decayed houses and two story apartment buildings, with balconies hanging precariously from the crumbling bricks, stood on both sides of the much potholed street. Junk, shattered bottles, broken furniture, rusted car parts, used cartons, lay scattered in front of the houses. Perhaps the city officials deemed it unnecessary to clean up and improve the quality of life for the indigent population.

Snow fell silently; it was a chilly day. Young children, grossly underdressed for the cold weather played on the street and dispersed as soon as the car approached them. Some other time, Meera would have been shocked at the sight of such poverty existing in a rich nation like Canada.

But right now, her perception mechanism was completely shut off. All Meera could see was Jane's tangled blond hair and melancholy face. She sat benumbed and wiped her tears often. Prashant turned his head toward her and said softly, "Meera, be strong, okay?"

They stopped in front of an old run-down motel. Paint had peeled off the walls, doors were discolored and patchy, litter lying in front of the motel poked out of the layer of fresh snow. A police car was parked in front of one unit. Meera was scared and looked at Prashant; as she staggered out of the car door, Prashant gave her his arm.

"Please, you have to be strong."

Meera remembered Mohit's long arms and their loving hold; she dropped Prashant's arm abruptly and said in a stifled voice, "Prashantji, I am all right."

The door was half open and creaked painfully when Prashant pushed it. It took Meera a few minutes to get accustomed to the lurid room. Slowly shapes and colors conjured out of the diffused light. It was a small room; the wallpaper was faded, rug had many holes, and it was hard to tell whether its brown color was natural or dirt. The bed, with crumpled clothes strewn on it, lay on one side of the room. A smell of uncleanliness overpowered the air. "Jane lived here?" Meera felt nauseated.

In one corner, on an unstable small table, an ancient lamp was making an unsuccessful attempt to chase away the darkness from the dingy room.

The vision flashed in Meera's consciousness, her temples throbbed; she became pallid and held her breath in disbelief. That was the exact table and chair where the woman in her sleepy unconscious was sitting and writing something in the dim light of the broken lamp. She had dreamt this dream many times in the past months. The black shawl was wrapped around her shoulders loosely. Why didn't Meera recognize Jane to be the woman in her dreams? But Jane never wore her hair in a bun. Meera slumped on the lumpy bed with a white dazed face. Prashant noticed and placed his hand on her back to comfort her.

David materialized out of the nebulous shadows and shook Prashant's hand. He hesitated then expressed an empathetic, "I am so sorry, Ms. Meera, I really am." Suddenly, Meera scanned the room anxiously. The terror of having to view Jane's dead body scared her out of her wits.

She looked at David questioningly. He understood. "Mrs. Henderson came and identified the body. It was sent to the hospital for the autopsy." Meera felt guilty, ashamed at the tremendous sense of relief she felt; she took a deep breath to soothe her insides. David was looking at her, "Ma'am don't worry at all, we contacted the Social Service Department right away. Two social workers took the baby."

"What?" she shuddered "A baby? I didn't know that." She looked up at Prashant. He nodded in the affirmative.

Robin had informed Prashant. "I have really bad news for Meera. The police received a phone call from Ms. Jane stating stoically that she was about to take a cyanide pill. 'The baby is sleeping but should be picked up soon for his next feed. I am leaving instructions for his care in his suitcase.' She emphasized that she was leaving an important letter for her sister Meera, only she should get it. She became very agitated at that point and repeated vehemently that Meera should get the custody of the child, no one else. Police were dispatched immediately, but the motel was at the far end of the city. It took them sixteen minutes to get here. It was too late. I am sorry, man."

Prashant did not know how to tell a devastated Meera about the child. She dug her trembling fingers in the lumpy mattress of the bed, "Where is the baby? The poor child? Where is he, she . . ." She was not handling it well.

David said quietly, "A boy."

"Where is he, I must have him." She looked at Prashant for support.

"And the letter?" Prashant asked David.

He was embarrassed, "I am sorry, Ms. Meera. Dale, my partner explained the details to Mrs. Henderson including the letter. She demanded to see it. Of course I refused. If eyes could kill, I would be dead. She started pacing the room angrily. I ignored her and went to the washroom to check the medicine cabinet. Suddenly, I heard an uproar in the room and came out. She was waving the letter in the air vigorously and shouting obscenities at her daughter. 'How dare she?' she kept repeating. I looked at Dale angrily. He just looked sheepish. When she left, Dale defended himself, 'Mrs. Henderson owns the lumber mills where my brother works! I dared not offend her, I still need my job and my brother needs his, man.'"

In a few quavering lines, Jane had asked Meera for pardon. "I have given you much grief and now a heavy burden. I beg you to raise Rishikesh as your own and not let Mrs. Henderson lay her hands on my precious angel." In the final act of her life, Jane had once more disowned her mother.

Meera's vision was blurry, yet she could see with greater clarity than ever before. Jane had, with the generosity of her spirit, filled the wilderness of Meera's womb that destiny had marked to remain barren.

Bela Di's and Meera's pure-white chiffon sarees prompted some stares. Meera wore the same one that she had donned at Mohit's funeral. No Indian parents would give a plain white, inauspicious clothing, even if it is expensive silk, in the dowry of their daughter. Meera had borrowed Bela's. In India, white is the color of mourning; black is too loud. But then white may appear too bright to the Western eye.

A tall, substantial woman in a black suit sat in the front row flanked by equally black-suited, mafialike men. Meera knew that she was Mrs. Henderson. A sense of nausea and revulsion rose in her heart. What did Jane do to deserve her? The back of her head was hidden behind a wide multicolored embroidered black hat; only the blond bun and her white nape was visible. A black silky shawl was draped around her broad shoulders.

Meera held Bela's hand tight in her sweaty fist; her heart trembled. She had no memory of the details of Mohit's funeral. All she remembered was a sharp-edged acicular dagger that had pierced her heart with repeated brutal strikes. The suppressed memory of those excruciating moments raised its head and grated at her insides. She wanted to run away and keep running until she lost consciousness of the inferno of awakened emotions.

The dim diffused light in the church was overpowered by an air of obscure, invisible gloom; the stifled aphony in the hall was queer. In India, death evokes heart-wrenching, raucous crying with copious tears shedding, especially amongst women.

Jesus, Mary, and saints affixed to the multichromatic glazed glass of long windows of the church looked down compassionately at the inevitable, tragic drama they witnessed so often.

Hans took a few minutes to gather himself at the podium before finding his sad voice, "Jane was the daughter I never had—I will never forget the beauty and grace of her spirit." Many of Jane's friends walked to the podium with heavy unstable steps and spoke kind words about Jane's gentleness and generosity.

One young simply dressed girl, wiped her tears often as she remembered Jane. She was a street kid, wanted to commit suicide because she was gang-raped. Jane saw her at the railway platform ready to jump in front of an oncoming train and grabbed her in time. She took the despondent girl home, who lived there for a year and went back to school. Jane found her a job.

"I owe my very existence to Jane. I was not given a chance to repay her," she agonized.

One hippy-style young man with a small beard and unkempt hair wept bitterly. "Jane was the only person in the world who gave me nonjudgmental love. Rest of the society condemned and ostracized me, even my parents. Jane was like a shining star in my dark world. I waited a whole week to have a weekly lunch with her."

Another middle-aged man agonized. "Jane and I sat on a bench in the park, held hands, and cried together at my wretched life. She gave me hope and courage." Meera wondered if he knew that Jane wept as much for her own pain as for his.

Mona and Sheila from Mohit's office spoke of the love Jane exuded that reached out to all around her. They both came to Meera and hugged her. "I am so sorry, Meera. She told me you were a sister to her. It's a huge loss for you."

Oppressed by grievous silence, everyone got up from their seats and straddled slow motion to line up. Meera's heart was in a seesaw mode. She did not have the courage to lay her eyes on Jane's, mute, lifeless face. Yet how could she miss the last chance to behold her beloved sister?

Jane lay in an expensive dark mahogany, carved, wooden casket; her transparent pale face appeared like a creamy-soft rose blooming on a red satiny casket lining. A garland of red and white tea roses was wrapped around the edge of the casket; roses were also strewn in Jane's plush long white dress.

Huge bouquets of roses, arranged in large cream ceramic vases that were engraved with emerald vines and red roses, were placed all over the church. Mrs. Henderson did remember Jane's love for roses. Maybe this gesture was a peace offering to her daughter for a life time of intentional injury.

Jane looked peaceful, finally, after twenty-five agonizing years of fiery purgatory for some unknown sins. God finally purged her, smoothed the sordid wrinkles from her "kismet."

- # -

"Look, it is not that simple." Sheila was brusque and rudely dismissive.

Meera looked across the table; a heavyset, no-nonsense person with sedulous air and punctilious bearing glared at her with big, cold eyes.

Piles of files on the table and shelves explained why the secretary had snapped at Meera. "Are you kidding? You cannot see Ms. Sheila Owens before one month. She is booked solid."

The chain of influence from Prashant to Robin worked; here she was, sitting across a not-too-pleased Sheila the day after Jane's funeral.

Icicles hung from bare branches of shrubs, trees and needles of evergreen trees. A layer of frigid glassy mantle covered the brown grass. Days had shrunk; it was still semidark when Meera arrived at the Social Service Department at 8:30 a.m. She was still in shock.

"There are complications in this case, you cannot have the child."

Meera was scandalized, "What? I have the mother's letter stating unequivocally that she wanted me to raise the child. I am going to adopt him. What is the problem?"

Sheila leaned forward, placed her unusually large and crude hands on the table for obvious intimidation purposes and spoke with a mean streak in her heavy voice, "Mrs. Henderson has also filed for custody. There will be hearings. You better get a *good* lawyer." The emphasis on *good* was vengefully delivered with a glint of satisfaction in her cattish eyes.

Prashant licked his fingers as he took a bite of the paratha, *homemade fried bread,* dipped it in raita, *spiced yogurt,* and placed it deliberately in his mouth. "Wah, Bela Bhabi, *sister-in-law,* I could kiss your hands, no one, no one in this world can cook like you."

"Chal Pakhandi, *pretender,* don't butter me now." Bela feigned displeasure.

Prashant had just returned from nowhere. Bela had sighed disapprovingly. "He vanishes without a word, never tells, we don't ask."

Meera was astonished, "Di, why don't you? You are so close!"

Bela laughed, "In the West, if people don't tell, you don't ask, otherwise, you could be guilty of intruding into their boundaries."

Meera chuckled at the mere concept.

In India, there are no boundaries; the word *boundary* means *boundary* in a cricket match. Everyone's nose is in everyone else's business, but no one objects; it is highly likely that they enjoy the intrusion. There is a sense of underlying caring, intimacy when you meddle in someone else's life. People would feel unloved if you didn't do it.

"Di, he knows you are asking out of concern!"

"You are right. We all worry, and he just pulls his disappearing act and one fine morning comes with his honeyed grin, 'Hi. What's up, Bhabi?' as though nothing is the matter."

Meera knew it was Prashant on the phone when Bela winked at her. Meera's heart jumped.

"You, Narad Muni, *a sage who never stops travelling,*" Bela scolded him. "You get lost then want parathas! No! Not until you clean up your act."

Obviously, plenty of apologies and counterfeit distress was submitted as a peace offering. Bela laughed, "Okay, liar, come. Meera is also here."

After the "nun episode," Bob fired Meera. "Mrs. Maitra, this is a small Christian town. I can't afford to lose my business."

Umesh, Satish's friend from Uganda, of course a Patel, *mostly business people,* owned a grocery shop; he agreed to hire Meera part-time. Meera got into the habit of having lunch with Di, who was delighted at the break from her loneliness.

Just then there was a resounding clang of the doorbell. Bela looked at Meera with obvious annoyance. "Must be the Mormon boys. They look so sweet, dressed in suits, but I wish they would stop converting the whole world."

Balwant greeted her as Bela opened the door.

Balwant was Satish's friend, who had taken up Meera's case for Rishi's custody.

"Aré, what good timing! I do have some parathas left if Prashant has not devoured them already."

"Bhabi, I had lunch with a client. Is Meera here?" He looked ominous.

Balwant delivered the bad news bitterly that the file was missing.

"What do you mean the file is missing?" Balwant had gasped on the phone.

The secretary in the Social Services Department swore, "I have looked everywhere, it is not here!"

"Maybe it has been filed under a different category! What kind of office do you run? How can a personal, confidential case file disappear without a trace?"

The secretary, who was feeling pretty small already, snapped, "Look, this file has not been used for a decade. We will find it. It does not have legs. It cannot walk away."

"I hope not," Balwant retorted and continued harshly, "Elimination of this critical evidence will be quite beneficial to Mrs. Henderson, wouldn't it?"

That was a mistake. The secretary was furious. "How dare you point fingers at anyone?"

Balwant's pragmatism coerced him to soften up. "I did not mean that Mrs. Henderson did it. I was only pointing facts. Anyway, call me as soon as you locate it."

Meera was stunned with the blow. After fierce battle with her conscience, she had relented to use the evidence in the file.

When Balwant took the case, he was unconcerned. "It is quite simple. The court cannot ignore Jane's desires. Secondly, the documented history of Mrs. Henderson's abuse will prove her unfit to care for the child."

Meera thought for a moment and stated firmly, "We do not have to open those files. Bhai, Mrs. Henderson has already lost a daughter, she is an old lady, why humiliate her?"

Balwant opened his mouth, but looking at Meera's gentle face, shut it back.

The very first day of hearing, Mr. Radley, Jr., Mrs. Henderson's lawyer, waved his hands in the air arrogantly and pointed out sarcastically, "Ms. Jane was obviously not in a rational frame of mind when she wrote the letter that Mr. Singh is waving at our faces. She committed suicide, remember? Are you going to validate someone at the brink of insanity? Also, I may remind the courts that she was always, since childhood, flippant, psychologically frail and incompetent to make responsible decisions."

Much to Meera's chagrin, Jane's past records were introduced as evidence without any compunction.

"Furthermore," Radley took a shot at Meera now, "being a recent immigrant, Mrs. Maitra is unfamiliar with the Western culture and values. To entrust a child's life to someone belonging to a kind of archaic culture, if I may say so frankly, will have disastrous consequences."

There was a dull murmur in the audience.

What would induce some humans to actually forsake their daily calling to show up in the court to watch a drama that is none of their business?

Gratified by the desired effect, he continued triumphantly, "Ms. Maitra does not even have a job, does she plan to ask the state for handouts?" He looked disdainfully in Meera's direction.

Meera bought slacks and tops; Bob, a friend of Prashant's, owned an antique store and agreed to hire her.

Being an introvert by nature, to welcome strangers with a wide grin, "Hi, how are you today, may I help you?" was tedious. Soon she figured that a smile was good enough, and punching keys and counting money fast was the more significant task of this occupation.

Before the next court hearing, Balwant suggested, "Meera, Mrs. Henderson had no problem sullying her daughter's name, we should also use her file."

Meera was confident. "Well, I have a job now, Bhai. Surely that means a lot."

Meera sat on a solid bench, looking wearily at the sleeping river. She inhaled a deep breath of chilly air to regain her bearing. She had been feeling insular, disjointed, and severed from her center. Every season in India arrives with its fragrance and ambiance. The certainty of glistening greenery and iridescent colours of India's landscape was absent in this frozen land.

Indoor life suffocated her. Meera had to be under an open sky, with wind swirling around her. She wrapped her woolen scarf around her face to ward off the cold breeze. The brown, barren, dismal vegetation and grass disappointed her; she forced her gaze on the evergreen trees for relief. They stood upright, with acceptance and perseverance, waiting patiently for the awakening of the virginal spring.

Meera moved on the bench to offer space to two women who had stopped close to her, and smiled, "Hello, still quite cold."

"Yes," the heavy lady scoped Meera cautiously as she sat down with much effort. "Are you from India?"

"Yes," Meera admitted.

The younger woman shrunk into herself to ensure that no damage was done to her by the big woman's huge elbow. She only looked at Meera apprehensively. They were both tightly secure in heavy coat, scarves, caps, boots, and gloves. Meera felt imprisoned just by looking at them.

"Oh, my two sisters, God rest their souls, lived in India for many years"—the older lady glanced at Meera meaningfully—"spreading Christ's word, you know. They died there of some God forsaken illness." Her supercilious tone turned choleric. "So many terrible germs fester in those countries. But they did not leave and perished bravely in the name of Jesus, our Saviour."

The lady looked at Meera expectantly; Meera conveyed the much-expected condolence, "I am sorry about your sisters." She went on and commented congenially, "I believe in Christ's teachings. These are very close to Buddha's, especially the message of nonjudgmental love and absolute nonviolence, compassion, and forgiveness. In fact, Hinduism preaches the same values."

The woman was horrified and accordingly agitated.

"But Christ was the son of God!"

Meera assented again, "Oh, of course, I believe that. There have been incarnations of God in India as well. Shri Krishna and Shri Rama. Even Buddha has been considered as such."

The heavy woman shook with such fury that the bench shuddered. "Christ is the only son of God, my dear. Hindus worship many gods, including snakes and monkeys." Her voice achieved a tone of disgust. "Humans have to go through the Son to reach the Father in the Kingdom of Heaven. Other ways lead to hell." Meera knew that it was futile to explain anything to the woman; she remained quiet and looked away.

Mr. Radley called out, "Sister Mary, please come to the witness stand." Her round face twisted in scorn, the heavy lady, turned out she was a nun, testified that "Meera uttered blasphemy against Jesus, made unchristian statements and does not believe in God." A wave of abhorrence and disapproval rose in the audience.

Meera trembled with disbelief at the disingenuousness of the drama obviously directed by Mrs. Henderson. Balwant was bewildered. "Do you know her?"

The trap had been laid. Meera had to muster all her sinew to cut the threads of deception, or she had already lost.

"Yes, Balwantji. I have to take the stand."

The judge was clad in an authentic black robe of justice but wore a facial expression that was anything but. He looked contemptuously at Meera; she was unquestionably guilty. His insolence reflected in an insinuating tone, "Mrs. Maitra, do you believe in God?"

"Yes, I sure do."

"Are you saying," he offered offensively, "that Sister Mary, an avowed nun, is lying when she told the court that you told her that you don't believe in God?"

"No, I never said that. She misunderstood and misconstrued, I am not responsible for people's false interpretations. I love God as well as Jesus. I am offended by the wrongful accusations."

This was unexpected. The judge asked her in a smaller voice, "Do you believe in Christ?"

"Yes, I believe in his Godhood as well as teachings. Incidentally, one of those is never to lie."

The judge ignored the latter part of her reply. "Are you a Christian then?"

"I am a born Hindu. But I believe in unity amongst religions. I believe in Christ but also Krishna, Rama, and Buddha."

The judge smiled; threads of the snare were tightening around her. He leaned back in satisfaction. "This creates a serious problem. How will you raise the child then? He is Christian, and you are Hindu. The home environment will not reflect Christian values."

He was, of course, unaware that this issue was her arena; she was unfrazzled. "The moral and ethical values are the same in Hindu and Christian religious thought. He will learn universal, humanistic, fundamentals of ethics that are the foundation of a good human."

The judge was irked. He flared up and bellowed irascibly, "Young lady, we all know that Jesus is the only way to God. The child will go to hell with no one to redeem his sins. Jesus already paid for our sins in blood. That is the only way eternal life is possible for us humans."

"But in Hinduism too there is redemption of our sins. If you repent sincerely and surrender to God, your sins are washed away."

"Who said that?"

"Shri Krishna said that, and He was an incarnation of God."

"Whose God?"

"There is only one God to whom all humanity bows."

Meera added, "I am going to teach him Christianity, take him to church, read the Bible, and raise him as a Christian. Surely you cannot object to that."

The judge had been challenged and almost defeated by a mere brown, fresh-off-the boat woman, who, not long ago perhaps, lived in a village in India and worshipped rats. He had enough.

"My decision is final. I cannot grant the child's custody to you."

Meera was sure judges were not supposed to act unjustly like this one.

After that incidence, Balwant was explicit. "Meera, if you plan to win the appeal, you will have to use all the weapons at your disposal."

Meera's dilemma was that she only knew how to be good, like Lao Tzu, a Chinese philosopher, who stated, "Recompense injury with kindness. To those who are good, I am good. Those who are not good to me, I am also good."

Papa had grilled in his children, "If you are good to those who are good to you, it is common place business, no virtue is involved in the transaction. You do not deserve any credit for it. But! If you are good to those who hurt you, that is a truly moral act worthy of admiration. That is victory of light over darkness."

How could Meera hurt Mrs. Henderson? She just did not know how to!

Meera gasped with shock when she looked out of the dining room window. All the apple and peach trees in her garden had been chopped off; the small stumps popped out of the earth like square sores. Wilted leaves and blossoms clung hopelessly to the branches that were strewn all over the green grass.

Mrs. Henderson, wearing a blue chiffon dress and flowered black hat, stood in the center of the yard, with an axe in her begloved right hand laughing loudly, cruelly and hoarsely.

Tears rolled down Meera's cheeks. She wanted to grab and shake her. "Why, why?"

Meera woke with clenched fists.

An innocent refreshing smile flitted across Chachaji's face as he sat on the couch with Meera. "You have read the Gita, *Hindu Bible*, many times, I think?"

"Yes." Meera was surprised.

"Then it is simple."

"Shri Krishna commands us humans to do our Dharma, *duty*."

Chachaji continued. "Meera, Dharma is the verity at the center of existence. Every particle in this infinite existence has a Dharma, nucleus of its life force. If it is displaced from its hub, there is chaos and disorder. If every speck operates within its sphere, there is harmony and peace. However, the trickiest part is to determine one's Dharma in any given circumstance. Selfish and egotistical actions that profit us and hurt others are not Dharmic. We are living in kaliyug, *an immoral age.* Personal 'ego' has become the nave of human lives. They have lost their Dharmic bearing and wander aimlessly in a jungle of self-gratifying materials. It has, thus, become more difficult to ascertain one's Dharma. But I know that you know yours. Mrs. Henderson's conduct was immoral, to expose it cannot be 'adharmic.' Use the file. A child's life is at stake."

Prashant continued to eat placidly after throwing a pleasant, "Hi, man," towards Balwant.

Bela was furious. "Aré, such nonsense, it happens in third world countries where even witnesses disappear, but here in Canada?"

Meera was jolted. "Balwant Bhai, this is serious what should we do?"

After everyone had vented, Prashant finished drinking a tall glass of white, foamy lassi, *buttermilk,* wiped the "white creamy moustache" with a napkin, and spoke calmly, "I will call my dear friend Robin, the police will mount a search, the file will be found, what is the problem?"

Contrary to Prashant's confidence that there was no problem, the search of Mrs. Henderson's mansion was futile; there was no file to be found.

Meera knelt in front of her temple and prayed for the little baby whose destiny was being sacrificed at the altar of egotistical motives of Mrs. Henderson. She asked God for tranquility; the agony of the fight for her Dharma had ravished her inner poise. She was not used to having her centre scattered in the winds.

The phone rang. A tense female voice blabbered hurriedly about some letter in the mailbox and hung up.

With a quizzical frown, Meera stepped out of the front door and opened the metallic mailbox. Her hand was shaky as she opened the letter impatiently.

"I watched helplessly as Baby Jane suffered. I cannot stand by and let her son's life get ruined too. The file is in Mrs. Henderson's night table drawer. An insider had informed her before the search by the police. She removed it. It is back there now. She is leaving for Toronto for a week. No one must know about this letter. I will be harmed. Thank you for helping a helpless child. Keep him away from Mrs. Henderson's shadow. God Bless. Kelley."

Meera could not contain herself; she wept with joy. She hesitated at first but could not resist. She dialed Mrs. Henderson's phone.

Kelley picked it up; she was Mrs. Henderson's housekeeper.

"I am Meera speaking."

Kelley sounded scared, "Please don't ever call me and talk to me. If Mrs. Henderson finds out, there will be terrible consequences for me!"

Meera was saddened, "I had to thank you Kelley, you have saved Rishi's life. I also wanted to ask you, what is a good woman like you doing in Mrs. Henderson's house?"

There was cold silence for a minute. "Life does not give us all the answers, Ms. Meera. Call it destiny, my bondage. I cannot leave."

Bela kept wiping her tears. "I am so happy, Meera, but I don't know why an unknown fear is trembling in my heart. I hope you have done the right thing."

Everyone gathered at Bela's house to celebrate the hard-earned victory. Rishi, a little ten-month-old baby did not have the slightest awareness of the conundrum around him excepting that he got so many hugs and kisses that he started to cry in protest. Meera embraced his soft agile body against her breasts where a warm fullness of love welled like a sea; she caressed his blond silky head gently.

Tears filled Meera's eyes. After a long year and a half after Mohit's passing, she was going to her India. Finally, she will be with Papa, Ma, Bhai, Behen, and Tayaji.

At the airport, Prashant's eyes deepened with unfathomable mystery. She avoided looking at him. Meera did not know why. Instinctively, she bent down and touched his feet. He smiled sadly and placed his strong hand on her head.

"Always be happy, Meera. You deserve to." He paused briefly then continued, "If you don't like it there, come back to us." Bela wiped her tears and nodded in agreement. After hugging Satish, Anil, Asha, Kanchan, Sunil, and Bela, Meera stood in front of Chachaji and bent down to touch his feet.

He stopped her. "Daughters are not supposed to touch the feet of father."

"Why?"

"Daughters are Goddesses!" All the women grinned broadly.

Chachaji hugged Meera. "Be established in your 'Real Self.' Then it does not matter where you are."

- # -

Atul gave Meera an "I told you so" look but kept silent with unusual graciousness.

Tayaji spoke calmly with his usual wisdom, "Judging people correctly is an impossible task. We do not possess enough knowledge about their lives, circumstances, problems, and limitations. Like Vinoba Bhave's grandmother, give love or materials unconditionally."

Vinoba Bhave was a zealful young man living in the midst of an age of interwoven paradigms of tyranny under the British Raj and the struggle of Indians to overcome social improbities that evolve unimpeded in oppressed peoples. India was still stuck in the dark ages that had followed thousands of years of enlightened era of highly evolved spiritual, social, and human values. A rich nation with abundance of gold, high-quality cloth, muslin, spices as well as ancient temples adorned with valuable gems, India was a lure for neighbors, even far away nations like Greece, Turkey, Mongolia, and Persia. The invasions came and brought oppressive nescience with them. Hindus were easily conquered because of their spiritual tendencies of nonviolence.

When the British arrived in the nineteenth century, the backbone of India had already crumbled with repeated assaults of foreign rule. The restrictions imposed by oppression, quashed any possibility of intellectual growth that would renew the stagnating civilization; social ills were prevalent.

Vinoba submerged himself, like many young men in early twentieth century, to overthrow the despotism of the British Raj as well as uplift the ignorant masses to make them aware of the social fallacies that chained them.

Vinoba's venerable grandmother was a pious and compassionate woman who dispensed alms to any beggar who would come to her doorstep. Swept away by the newly acquired Western-style education, Vinoba condemned the beggars fervently as a source of many social ills. Of course later, after he became a social activist and an acclaimed saint who distributed all his belongings to the poor and lived in a straw hut, he understood that begging was the consequence of social evils not the cause.

Anyway, hot-blooded, bright-eyed young man, he argued constantly with Granny. "Ma, these creatures are lazy bums, they beg because they do not want to work. They do not deserve your sympathy. You give them food and that perpetrates their habit of dependence and exploitation of good people."

"Vanya," said his old and wrinkled grandma, who was fed up. "Who am I to judge anyone? They ask me and I give. Let God up there"—she turned her dim eyes toward the sky—"do the judging."

An orange sun rolled down lethargically behind the darkening deodars; the skies turned orange, pink, and gray softened clouds hovered above and between the trees. Tayaji sighed. It seemed like yesterday when Meera and Mohit got married. All the relatives and friends squatted on freshly cleaned and ironed white sheets that lay around the mandap, *canopy where wedding ceremony takes place,* exchanged gossip, only sometimes turning their attention to the solemn on goings, whenever the priest motioned them to throw rose petals on the shy bride and smiling groom. They had attended hundreds of such ceremonies, but some of the friends and relatives they had not met for years. Children ran around and played, aware of the fact that whatever was precipitating here had no impact on their lives.

Tayaji had worn a pink turban and pure white silk Kurta, *long shirt,* and pajama to give Meera away at the marriage ceremony. As laid out in the scriptures, a man must perform one kanyadan, *giving daughter away,* to qualify for entry into the divine domain of heaven. In all likelihood, that was not the reason why Papa had asked him to perform the role of a father at the wedding. It was Tayaji's great love for Meera that would have prompted him.

Tayaji's voice was steadfast, yet pain surfaced. "It is a curse for us old people to see our young children suffer."

Unsummoned tears welled in Meera's eyes. She did mean to say consoling words to his oldness but just lost her voice.

A cloud of tribulation passed over Papa's smooth face, momentarily. "Bhaiji, you are gyani, *erudite,* and know that who is born must die but Atma, *soul,* is imperishable. You yourself taught us."

Tayaji smiled at Papa affectionately. "Deva, to be sthitpragya, *equanimous in pain and pleasure,* like the ultimate Yogi, *someone united with God,* described by Shri Krishna in his preaching, is arduous, and I am still at the bottom of the Himalayas. Who knows how many janams, *births,* it will take me to reach the Mount Everest?"

Meera lifted her head from Tayaji's lap and wiped her tears, "Tayaji, I will live with you like before. You are getting old, so is Gangu Kaka."

Tayaji looked at the heavens. "He looks after us all."

Papa looked at Meera and said firmly, "Here in Simla, we are all there to help you with Rishi. There is a job opening for a music teacher at the St. Thomas School. It is close to our house. You can come home for lunch and be with Rishi. I know the principal. See him."

Music was Ma's gift to Meera. Ma belonged to a liberal family, even the girls were sent to school and college, and yet singing was prohibited. Why in a culture where one of the Vedas, Samved, is dedicated to musical renderings of worship, girls or even boys belonging to families of good standing were frowned upon if they were caught in the "cheap" act of humming a song.

In ancient India, singing bhajans, *devotional songs,* in temples was common place, but only for men. Later, in South Indian temples young girls were initiated, with great feasting and chanting of mantras, *verses from Scripture,* into Dev Dasis, *God's female servants.* Only beautiful, young, virgin girls were chosen who lived in the premises of the temple, danced and sang for God, at various celebrations. No one knows when or how the tradition changed over time; slowly Dev Dasis became Purush Dasis, that is, men's servants. It is quite logical to assume that to fulfill their lust, the change was brought about by the rich and powerful men in a male dominated society of the village. They could create any tradition in the name of religion and the poor masses were forced to follow.

The only good that came out of the tragic and utterly demeaning institution was that the art of classical dancing and music was preserved for millenniums as it was passed from aging Devdasi to the younger one.

After the arrival of Mughals, whose sense of aesthetics was highly evolved, beauty in all its expressions was highly appreciated; the darbar, *emperor's court,* was often entertained by high class music and dancing. Even women performed, but they were not considered 'respectable' and were generally prostitutes of the locale. Classical music, dancing and poetry received great respect and admiration in the darbar; often the emperor himself was educated by learned philosophers who were also musicians or poets.

For the women of good families, singing remained an illegal activity to be indulged in the privacy of the four walls of the bathroom. Nanaji, *maternal grandfather,* took note of Ma's constant attempt to sing quietly and started to look for a music teacher without the realization that there would be grave impediments in his search. It was impossible to find a female music teacher! To let a man into the inner quarters of janana, *where women reside in the house,* was a transgression of the highest order. Just the idea prompted loud condemnation from the older female generation; Nanaji was firm but eventually overrun by the majority of women. Ma retired to the bathroom to give voice to the music that bubbled in her spirit on a constant basis.

In the 1930s, "Bombay talkies" came into existence starting with silent movies that evolved into regular films with plenty of film songs for real entertainment. Ma was caught singing songs of the singer actress, Devika Rani, who was the most beautiful and stunning of them all. A famous Russian painter fell hopelessly in love with her, created a world-famous portrait and whisked her away to Russia as his bride.

Ma's Dadi yelled in chagrin, "Aré, look at this befkoof, *stupid,* girl! No shame, who will marry you if people find out you sing these filthy songs, eh?"

Ma made a promise to herself that at least one of her children will have to be a singer. Having tried music lessons on all her preceding offsprings, Meera was Ma's last hope. The huge responsibility of fulfilling Ma's dream fell on Meera's tiny shoulders; she was launched into the world of music at the tender age of three.

Music, the language of her soul, where did she lose it? For a year and a half, she had not touched her taanpura, *stringed instrument.* The eager face, filled with joy and pride, who looked at her when she sang, where is he?

Mohit had said with a fresh smile, his dimples deepening into lines, "I hear you sing very well." Meera smiled and nodded shyly.

"Sing a song for me then."

"Here?" she laughed "No! People will throw stones at me."

"But there are no people here, and trees and monkeys do not throw stones."

After Meera's wedding in Delhi, her whole family converged to Simla for a week. Mohit's idea of a walk in the woods in Himalayan January cold weather was dismissed politely by Ma. "Beta, it is slippery and cold, there has been so much snow this month."

"Mummy, we will dress up well, and I am used to snow," he assured a worried mother-in-law and, to pacify her further, promised to walk on the main road.

"It is so calm and beautiful. Don't feel shy."

"Okay," she agreed readily. Her guruji, *teacher,* had grilled in her students, "Music is an art for sharing joy. Sing a lot." Meera pondered thoughtfully, "What should I sing? I sing only classical music." Her music teacher was inflexible. "Classical music is a divine gift of God to us humans. It is the highest form of music. Why descend from higher to lower?" Meera wanted to contend with her teacher about the sublimity of Urdu, *language of Muslims in India,* romantic poetry sung as Gazals or devotional, mystical, music of the Sufis, *a sect of Islam,* as in Quawallis or Meera Bai's, *a Hindu saint,* Bhajans, *devotional songs.* But you do not argue with your guru if you want to pass your exams. Obediently, she never sang gazals, only heard them on the radio.

"Okay," Mohit did not care, "classical is fine."

"But I need a tabla, *drum,* and taanpura, *stringed instrument,* for classical songs."

He knew she was being difficult. Mohit feigned so much agony that Meera laughed.

It was early afternoon. She picked "Raga Brindavani Sarang."

Brindavan, *garden,* was where Shri Krishna played his flute and everyone danced in ecstasy. It is a raga, *music composition,* of romance and longing. She hummed it at first, then let her sweet voice amplify the mellifluous notes of her song that spread their wings and flew in the four directions, swirling around snow-covered deodars. The azure of the sky deepened with the pure pleasure of aria ascending towards its infinite expanse, sun blinked with the beat, clouds floated weightlessly in glee. Icy breeze, intermingled with the aroma of wet pine needles and the fragrance of her dreams, swept them away.

After Meera was finished, Mohit hugged her and kissed her passionately on the lips. She blushed and said coyly, "Someone will see us, Ji!"

With a musical incipience of their wedded life, music became a delectable ingredient of their moments together. Meera started singing gazals once she was in Canada, notwithstanding the memory of the stern face of her guru. "She will have to live with it." Meera shrugged.

All her ragas were stilled within her heart when death silenced Mohit. She had installed her taanpura painfully in the closet, out of her sight.

Meera decided to pick it up again. A corner of her heart was happy. So far, she had no reason to overcome her emotions and allow her long thin fingers to play the strings she loved. She did yearn to give voice to the seemingly dead notes but a sense of shame tied her tongue. How could she betray Mohit's memories by overcoming the emotions they evoked?

Now she had to do it for the sake of her son. Meera looked at Tayaji and smiled sadly, "I will sing a Bhajan for you today, Tayaji, in the evening at puja, *prayer,* time." News spread like a forest fire; Neeti and Nishant ran out excitedly and gathered an audience of their friends, to show off their Bua who sings with a "pumpkin" thing.

Meera had a good start, considering that she had not used her musical voice in the last one and half years. Meera's moist eyes searched for her beloved's beaming face in the audience; his void was unbearable. Halfway through the Antra, *middle part of a song,* her voice trembled and broke. She placed the taanpura gently in front of the temple, bowed her head, and went to her room without a word to the audience.

Why couldn't she be like Savitri? Meera agonized.

Savitri had followed Yama, the lord of death, when he took Satyavan, her husband, away. Yama looked back and spoke to her politely, "Daughter, it is not your time yet to go to Mrityulok, *world of the dead.* Go home." How could she? Satyavan was her very life. She begged Lord Yama. "Please, give my dear husband back to me." How could he? Kal had already counted all his breaths; he had none left. Finally, quite fed up of her persistence, he made an attempt to appease her. "All right, daughter, I am impressed by your love and determination. Ask me any boon, excepting Satyavan's life."

Clever Savitri did not think long, "Please, give me one hundred children." Yama was relieved; he could make her happy without any clash with Kal, *eternal time,* or Lord Shiva. "Your wish will be fulfilled, daughter. Now go back."

"But," Savitri queried, "how can I have one hundred children if you take my husband away? Tell me, Lord?" Yama shook his head in dismay; he was outwitted by a humble, loving wife. He had no choice but to reverse the complex interplay of stars and grahas, *astrological planets.* Savitri went home, holding her Satyavan's now-alive and warm hand. She did have one hundred children, so they say.

But Yama had already left with Mohit's Soul. She was too late; where was she to look for him?

Gray did not exist for Meera. She was only cognizant of black and white. Dawn and dusk were incorruptible states of light and darkness. Darkness regenerating into light is dawn, and light dissolving into darkness is dusk; they could not be defined in any other form. Her capacity to feel joy in its purity, crystalline clarity Meera had experienced as a child and then as a young woman. Now, she suffered with equal passion and élan, her experience was integral, true to itself. She lived her moments in indissoluble and unviciated awareness, with full cognizance and courage to stand tall, face-to-face with their poignancy. She did not know if it was good or bad. It just was.

- # -

Krishan and Keshav were totally enthralled and immediately took to their blue-eyed, cute cousin. Meera and Rishi arrived in Chandigarh soon after the first snow fall in Simla.

Rakesh called out, “Dharma kaka, they are here. Get the luggage.”

Dharma came out briskly and opened the door for Meera. Rishi sat bewildered in her lap. He smiled broadly. “Choti bibi, namaste. Rishi Baba, come, I will hold you.”

Two pairs of eyes met, apology in one and acceptance in the other.

“Kaise ho kaka. *How are you*?” Meera asked softly. She had been worried about him.

On the brutal night during partition of India, when Meera and her family escaped from Lahore to Amritsar in the stark gunshot-pierced darkness, the bright headlights of the truck fell on someone lying on the roadside. The truck driver refused to stop. “Saheb, *gentleman*, he must be dead. It is too dangerous to stop.” Papa insisted in the name of Allah; driver, a Musalman, could not defy the holy command. Papa, Atul, and the driver scurried and picked up the body. He was a young man; his shoulder was wounded and bleeding profusely by the gunshots. Ma tore a part of her saree to tie on the wound. Atul was told to press hard in order to curb bleeding. Meera slept in Bua’s arms.

Once in Amritsar, Papa took the man straight to a clamorous, grim, chaotic hospital that was overloaded with wounded and overwhelmed by death. Doctors and nurses looked like bewildered, anguished zombies in the midst of piercing cries of pain, a river of blood, and missing limbs—the unbelievable carnage of human hatred.

Papa prepaid for the treatment, stuffed some money in the unconscious man’s pocket and Nawal Chachaji’s address in Amritsar and left.

Within a week, a languid and gaunt man, his arm in a dirty cloth sling, showed up at the doorstep of Tayaji’s house in Delhi. Ma did not recognize him at first.

Dharma, he told his name, was fed and slept like a log in Gangu, the servant’s, room.

The next morning, he got up early, took a shower, and stood in front of Ma, who was in the kitchen helping Gangu prepare the breakfast. With downcast eyes, he asked, “Maji, what do you want me to cook today?”

Ma looked up at him and said kindly "Dharma beta, you do not have to do anything. Just rest, get well. In the meantime, Bhaiji will find a good job for you. How educated are you?"

Dharma wept. "I have forgotten all that. All I know is that I have a debt to pay. Let me take care of all of you, Maji."

This was a serious matter. Dharma did not argue or respond to Tayaji's queries about his qualifications or experience. He just repeated, "I have forgotten all that, Saheb," and stood unmoved like a statue as Papa and Tayaji discussed his future. After they finished their planning, he stepped forward, touched Tayaji's, Papaji's, and Ma's feet and asked again, "What do you want me to cook today, Maji?"

Quite early that morning, the jamadar, *sweeper,* came in the house to sweep and mop the floors and bathrooms. Dharma was appalled. To make matters worse, the mali, *gardener,* walked into the kitchen for a glass of water. That was it.

Tears rolling down his cheeks, he approached Ma. "Maji, how can you let these shudras, *low caste,* in your home?"

Ma was not pleased. "Dharma, they are humans like us! They have to work here. We cannot throw them out. Are you a Brahmin?"

"Yes, Maji." He stood, trembling in consternation.

Ma knew that he had just gone through hell. She tried to spare him any more emotional upheaval at this time.

"Dharma, I will ask them not to come into the kitchen."

"Maji, I can sweep, Gangu can do the rest, please do not pollute your home with the shadow of these Kameena, *low,* people."

Ma was firm. "Dharma, no one will force you to treat them respectfully. But Bhaiji will not be happy if he finds out. So let us leave it at that. Kitchen is yours."

Dharma clung to his antiquated mind-set, shirked from the shadows of Mali and Jamadar. He had a kind heart though; he cooked extra food, but they had to eat in the backyard, in metal plates that they washed at the tap outside in the garden.

When Meera's family moved to Simla, Dharma acquiesced to the Jamadar's and Mali's entry in the small room at the back of the house where old boots, junk, and other useless stuff was abandoned. When it was cold outside in the winter, after the snow fell, Mali left for

Chandigarh and Jamadar squatted on the wooden floor and warmed himself while consuming his meal.

But now was a crisis of faith. Dharma could not live under the same roof with a gora, *white,* whose race was responsible for the annihilation of his whole family.

During the "quit India," movement in 1942, organized by Mahatama Gandhi and the Congress, a quiet disciplined jalsa, *procession,* was asked to disperse by horse-riding British police. Dharma's father, the leader at the front carrying Congress flag, happened to ask innocently, "On what legal grounds?" That innocuous query cost him his life; he was shot point-blank in the head.

Two of Dharma's older brothers went to jail. Two died of diarrhea and malaria although there was suspicion of torture. The bodies did not see the light of the day and were cremated hastily in the prison. Dharma and his brother received the ashes in earthen pots after much pressure on the British officials by top Congress leaders.

Dharma's remaining brother, Raghav, was assassinated by a Muslim neighbor, who accused him of raping his daughter during the rioting that followed partition. The fact that he kept pleading his innocence was irrelevant. During those stark times, *trust* and *innocence* were two words that were disgracefully thrown out of the dictionary. Truth smeared by the blood of humanity was unrecognizable.

Dharma's mother had died of cholera long ago. He was left all alone in this crowded world.

Dharma sulked and cried quietly in the kitchen corner; he avoided looking at Rishi.

Papa called him in the living room, "Dharma, how would you like to stay at Rakesh's in Chandigarh for a while? Hari can come here instead."

Dharma's eyes filled with tears. "I don't want to leave you, Bauji, *father,* you are my Bhagwan, *God,* and I cannot be ungrateful."

Papa patted him on his shoulder. "But Rakesh is also yours. It is a change of house, not of home."

The day Dharma left, Neeti and Nishant hugged him and wept. Asha kept reassuring them, "Beta, he is not going forever. Nalini Chachiji, *aunty,* is not well na, she needs help, and you know how helpful Dharma Kaka is?"

"You will come back soon, real soon, na, Kaka?" Neeti was emotional; she clung to his legs.

Papa had, early in the morning, already consumed two newspapers, *Tribune*, the regular one, and the *Times of India* that he only subscribed for the weekend. He was now tuning into nine o'clock news on the radio. Atul peeped in and quipped, "Papa, it is the same news in the radio, don't you get fed up?"

Papa, when teased, never countered. He just smiled calmly, neutrally, neither assenting nor dissenting. Atul glanced at Meera, who was sitting languidly with a drawn face and red eyes, on a chair looking out of the window. She could not sleep a wink the night after Dharma left for Chandigarh.

It seemed like a good time to raise the issue. She hesitated then spoke softly, "Bhai, I want to talk to you."

"What is the matter, Choti?" Atul came in the room wearing a worried look on his face and sat down in front of her on Papa's bed. Papa stopped tuning his radio and straightened up, looking at Meera questioningly.

"Bhai, I am thinking I should find another place to live. I could find a job in any school and should live close to my work. It will be more convenient."

Papa's eyes deepened.

Atul stood up in front of Meera and placed his hand on her shiny black hair that she had tied in a lose bun at the back of her long fair neck. "Don't ever say that, Choti. This is your home now. You cannot go anywhere else."

Dark shadows lifted from Papa's eyes; contentedly, he turned to the radio, attempting to find news, again.

- # -

Saraswati Bua, *father's sister,* wiped her tears with the edge of her white saree and cried, "Shiva, why all the pain to our family only? Why so much? That is all I ask, God!"

Profuse tear shedding occurred at Delhi at Tayaji's house. Bua had suffered her widowhood, her daughter's, and now her niece's.

Dadi married Saraswati off at a tender age of fifteen. Nalini was two years old when Lord Yama's astro-celestial calculations revealed that it was time for her husband, Ram, to be taken to the never-neverland. Her in-laws blamed Bua for "eating her husband" and called her manhoos, *inauspicious.* She was duly banished into the inner, darker, smaller rooms of the huge haveli, *mansion,* where sunlight was not allowed.

As the nature of gossip goes, the news of Saraswati's abuse floated into Dadaji's haveli in due time. He is said to have rearranged his turban firmly on his head, took his walking stick, climbed onto his covered horse carriage, and said to the saees, *carriage driver,* "Salamat, chalo, *go.*"

They rode for five hours in the summer heat, only stopping for horses to feed, drink water, and cool off their burning skin in the shade of the mango trees that were prevalent in that area.

Dadaji was led respectfully by the darban, *guard,* to the living room of the haveli. He folded his hands in greeting and spoke directly, "I have come to take my daughter."

The father-in-law, a short and plump fellow with an unproportionately colossal moustache covering his upper lip, was perched on the dewan with his hukkah, *smoking pipe,* that effused much smoke. He made a false attempt to get up but slumped back by the pull of gravity, "Please sit, sit, we are lucky to have you come to our humble hut. Oi, Ramu, get some Shakanjavi, *lemon water,* for our guest."

Dadaji remained where he was. "I thank you for your hospitality. But please ask Saraswati to come out right away. It will be dark soon."

Obviously, the news had passed on to the inner quarters with the speed of lightning. Within minutes, an unadorned Bua emerged holding two-year-old Nalini's puny hand, her bowed head covered with white muslin saree. Tears rolled down her fair, pale, and young cheeks.

Dadaji asked her to touch her father-in-law's feet, who was scared out of his wits at that command and shrank back on the dewan. "No, no, it's okay, God bless you."

What if her touch passed on the contagion of bad luck to his life?

Bua lived with Dadaji. Nalini studied up to high school against Bua's wishes.

"Bauji, she is not going to do a job. What is the point?"

It was futile for Dadaji to explain that education was not just for a job, it was also for insight and knowledge to enhance our understanding of the truth of things, thereby granting us a richer inner life.

Nalini was married right after she finished high school. Dadaji's close friend Mohanlal, who lived right in his village, welcomed her as a bride for his youngest son, Pitamber. When Nitin was just one-year-old, Pitamber was swayed by nationalistic ambitions to free India and joined Gandhiji in the struggle. He died of some disease in jail, they were told.

Mohanlal took care of Nalini and Nitin with great love. But suffering from intolerable agony of his young son's loss, he begged Yama to take his life. Whether it was the calculations or compassion of Yama that took him away, who knows?

Nalini was now at the mercy of her oldest brother-in-law, Kewal, and his wife, Rati. Rati threw her chief maid out of the big haveli door, and quite unceremoniously, Nalini replaced her in the scheme of things.

Once again, Dadaji straightened his turban and picked up his walking stick. He was a little stooped this time with the passage of time. "Bhai, chalo, *go*." Dadaji climbed the carriage and said to Salamat.

Being in the same village, they were at late Mohan Lal's haveli in no time. Dadaji walked in and addressed Kewal plainly, "I am here to take my granddaughter."

Nalini walked out, wrapped in crumpled cotton saree, holding little Nitin's hand.

Tayaji disapproved Bua's bawling, "Bahenji, *older sister,* spend your old age meditating on God. Life is made up of pain and pleasure, like day and night. It cannot change its nature for you."

"But all my life I prayed and prayed and God gave me only pain?"

"Even Pandavs, who were the beloved of Lord Shri Krishna, suffered all their lives. Shri Rama, God incarnate himself, had to face human anguish. Jesus, the son of God, had to bear the torment of being nailed to the cross. How can we ordinary humans expect pain free life?"

Bua was not impressed.

Tayaji continued, nevertheless. "Praying morning and evening is not any guarantee against the blows of destiny and forces of Karma, *our deeds.* But yes, if we ask Him, God does carry us through the difficult times; we should thank Him for this Grace."

Bua looked down.

Noticing that his wisdom was ineffectual, Tayaji rearranged his strategy. "But you also have happiness! Nitin has a good job. Nalini's tapasya, *penance,* has been rewarded. Soon he will get married and bring a good wife to look after both of you."

Bua hid her face in her saree palloo and started to cry.

"What, Bua?" Meera was flabbergasted.

"You don't know anything. He has refused to get married."

"Why?" Tayaji and Meera queried in unison.

"Bas, he says no!"

Nitin visited Delhi two weeks later; Bua had left for Simla. She was old and frail, travelling from Banglore that was far in the south of India to north was arduous for her. She decided to kill two birds with one stone, since she was so close to Simla already.

Meera had not seen Nitin for six years. They were never too close. He was Rakesh's age group; she was shoved away rudely from the boys' gang. But he was warm, fun-loving, and talkative. Now, he bore an air of unexplained insolence and defiance. Yet a certain vulnerability and unease shadowed his bearing. He appeared adrift and certainly not at peace with himself.

He was abrupt. "How is Canada? I want to move there."

Meera was taken by surprise and looked searchingly deep in his eyes. He looked down and said, "Don't mention to anyone, not yet."

Meera was worried, "How will Nalini Didi take it, Nitin?"

His voice assumed the sharpness of a razor's edge. "I have to think about my future! Because Mummy raised me doesn't mean that I cannot have my own life. She wants my happiness anyway, what objection could she have?"

Nitin, what do you know? Meera could not say it to him. Of course, he was a boy, how could he see the bruised feet of a woman who walked the thorny paths of widowhood with no one to embalm her feet?

Meera remembered Nalini Didi lying on bed at quite unseeming hours with her dupatta, *scarf,* on her face, often crying or staring into space and not hearing anyone. She would sit on the balcony until after night fall, not heeding Bua's imploring entreaties. "What is wrong with this stupid girl? It is cold, she will get sick! I am getting old, Bhai, I cannot look after anyone anymore."

Meera and her siblings visited Tayaji during winter holiday; after partition, Bua, Nalini, and Nitin lived with him.

Meera was fond of Nalini Didi, although she never played with her and was no fun at all. She had a delicate, almost defenseless countenance; her eyes were constantly apprehensive of unpredicted besiegement much like a young doe wandering directionless in a dense jungle.

Now Meera understood the fears, desolation, and loneliness that lurked behind Nalini's eyelids. In the invisible dark recesses of your mind, you find yourself disconnected, incomplete, without, even in the midst of a crowd. That darkness can seep into your whole self and engulf you. Meera knew. She came close to it many times. She was pulled out by the loving arms of her God, just in time. But Nalini had become increasingly bitter; bitterness is contrary to faith. And God is where faith is.

Naturally, mother's complexities are handed down to their offspring. Although Nalini grew under the dense spiritual shade of Dadaji, then Tayaji, but mother is a mother after all; she molds children's personalities more than anyone else.

Very few childhood memories of Nalini had survived the flow of time in Meera's life. But now, Meera's own experiences touched upon the collective unconscious where Nalini's past lay; intersecting with the shared encounters with widow hood brought those buried memories to life. Maybe that is the meaning behind suffering; it enhances our understanding of other people's pain, reveals the unity of our spirits, and makes us better, more empathetic humans.

Meera held back her tears. "Canada is a good place, good opportunities."

"Are you going back?"

The round face of Bela di, serene countenance of Chachaji, sober Sunil, vocal Satish, and subdued Anil rose in the mist of her mind. And Prashant. A smile flitted across her face at his memory, and she blushed, stirring confusion in her heart.

"No, not really," she just blurted out in bewilderment.

- # -

A gust of cold squall pushed Meera's umbrella on one side, sprinkling a shower of misty rain on her. Simla is seldom windy; where would the wind come from or go? A meek zephyr would bang its head against the towering mountains and die off. But sometimes the gale is powerful; while walking, your body tilts with the mere force. Thin people have to hang on to fat people to avoid being blown away. Everyone rushes home for safety; trees swoon noisily, hitting against houses. The wind howls, scaring little children. "Mummy, Mummy, are the mountains going to fall on our house?" The mighty peaks stand still and let the tempest swirl and dissipate in the gray skies.

A little girl in pink, printed frock passed Meera and sang in a tiny voice, "Good afternoon, madam." She looked familiar, a student perhaps. Meera smiled, "Good afternoon, child."

The girl held on to the hand of a salwar-kameez-clad young woman, who just nodded as she passed forward. She clung to her mother in an ineffective attempt to take refuge under the umbrella. Meera's thoughts drifted to Rishi. The schoolbag slung on his small shoulders; he will not clutch to her hand, being a boy and all, but scurry ahead, his round fair face red with exertion, tiny luminescent drops of sweat hanging on his brow. Meera felt snug. Certitude of motherhood had given meaning to her life; what is wrong with that picture?

The very fact that she asked herself that question, it was obvious that Meera was not convinced herself. The intimacy of love, Mohit's warm breath on her contented face, his long muscular arms folding her unto himself, the loss of the very essence of her life she could never overcome.

The question had been raised more than once; Ma's tight silent lips constantly admonished her. But if it was not Mohit, there could be no one else. Meera took a deep whiff of the refreshing moisture laden air. If God meant her to have a husband, would he have taken Mohit away?

The old office buildings, erected at the peak of British Raj, stood stoically on the right side of the main road. On the left, the mountain sloped steeply upward; ferns, mosses, and grasses crowded together to create a luscious carpet. Fugitive rain drops slid on the fern leaves and perched on the tips indecisively wondering about their plan of action.

Simla is bright and lively in the spring. Sun plays hide-and-seek with the puerile clouds, snow melts filling the streams with gurgling water, nature tosses away the ascetic, virgin shroud of white purity and transforms into a bride. Green variegated henna on her palms, kumkum, *red powder married Indian women put on their foreheads,* of red roses on the chaste forehead, the body is adorned with glowing, multicolored blossoms bathed in ambrosial fragrance. The bride seduces Krishna to dance at the shores of the Yamuna river that flows everywhere, His melodious flute maddening the three worlds.

After a few kilometers, the main road broadens in a flat area and bifurcates. One narrow street plunges steeply downwards on the right side, to become the Lower Mall Road. That is where Nathu Ram Halwai, *sweets maker,* still squatted in his small sugar-smelling, steamy, smoky, noisy confectionary shop, his red sweaty chubby face smiling from behind the piles of different mithais, *sweets.* Ladoo, gulabjamun, burfi, rasgulla—you name it and he had it. But his "special" jalaibi in hot milk was irresistible; Meera's family and many other loyalists would trek a couple of mountainous steep miles to gorge on it with unlimited rapacity.

The other broader half of the bisected road ascends on the left and curves sharply to become the Upper Mall Road, the famous loitering and shopping center. That is where renowned Gaity Theatre stands on the left side, providing celebrated artists from all over India an imposing dark-brown mahogany stage that is flanked by red velvet curtains, a dazzling setup for the display of their artistry.

Meera had watched the performance of *Cinderella* play when she was five years old and demanded glass shoes for herself.

On the right side of the Mall Road, a few new saree shops had recently cropped up. A large ostentatious shop caught Meera's attention. It was impossible to pass by and not notice the tall, skinny mannequins adorned in glistening silky saree and even more sparkling artificial gold jewelry. They stood perfectly erect inside the glass windows, their bosoms projecting outwards rather shamelessly, and blank eyes staring vacantly across the mountain slope on the opposite side of the road.

To Meera, shopping was a frivolous activity, a complete waste of precious time. There was a tough competition between Asha and Shoba to shop for Meera because that offered them a legitimate excuse to make an entry into those lucrative shops that were intentionally well lighted to augment the sheen of the silk sarees on display. Thus softened, the shopper could be easily talked into buying a couple more sarees by some smart, honey-tongued shopkeeper. "Didi, this Bangloree saree would look beautiful on you, with your fair complexion and all. Aré, don't worry about money, it is not running away, it can come later. Just take it, ji. Oy Kaka, pack these two sarees for Bahenji. But you also liked this pink one, didn't you? Oh, don't say no! I know it by the way you looked at it; Kaka this one too."

"Such earnest insistence, the guy has to feed his family, na, how could you refuse?" Shoba would explain. She was one of those people whose claim on life, existentially speaking, rested on their capacity to shop: "I am because I shop!"

Today, Meera decided to buy a lovely saree for Asha Bhabi, *sister-in-law,* in utter gratitude; it was her birthday next week.

She shook her umbrella to get rid of the waterdrops before she entered the shop. A rather fresh-looking man wearing a navy T-shirt and khaki pants sauntered toward her with a supine gait. He gave Meera a casual look, raised his lush eyebrows, and let them drop swiftly, a north Indian, crude, customary gesticulation for "What do you want?"

In India, as soon as you enter a shop, the merchant measures you up with one calculating, expert glance, catalogues you in some definitive rank, which determines whether you receive a welcoming cheek -to-cheek grin. "Aeye Didi, please come, come, don't worry about the mud on your shoe" or mere raised eyebrows that plunge back expediently to dismiss you as a cheapo.

To qualify for the royal reception, you have to belong to the hierarchically eminent citizenry, be wrapped in heavy silk saree, preferably with gold border; embellished with lustrous diamonds and gold in the neck, arms, fingers, ears, and wherever there is space to place them; high-heeled shoes or sandals to match the color of the saree. Also, you must be "made up" with exorbitant imported Avon makeup. Last but not least, you must descend pompously from a rickshaw pulled by four sturdy, muscular, scantily clad men, wet with sweat or rain. Otherwise, you are dubiously rich, and that can result in immediate disapprobation.

There is yet another infallible indicator to affirm the merchant's appraisal. When he greets you with ever-so-polite and humble "Namaste, Behenji, *sister*," if you smile back and respond with a cordial "Namaste, ji," you lose points because it is quite obvious that you are not sufficiently opulent to be snob-sophisticated. If you are wealthy, you would only give a reluctant and pretentious, dismissive rude nod. Once your affluence is established beyond doubt, then faces would light up with enthusiasm and obsequiousness, backs straightened, one guy will rapidly open as many sarees a minute as humanly possible. The other relatively younger and thinner chap will put it on to enhance your imagination as to how the saree would look. The owner, who may be sitting in the far corner on a comfortable dewan, leaning on the gav takia, *round pillow*, wearing fine silk in the winter and malmal, *muslin*, kurta pajama in the summer, may stroll toward you, expressing his heartfelt desire to make your life a happy one.

Wearing an austere cotton saree that was soaking wet at the bottom, no gold, diamonds, or even silver, ordinary sandals—what could Meera expect?

The whole charade can amuse you or disgust you; select the emotion you want for the next two hours. Meera smiled to herself. "It is more than likely that I will not be offered Coca-Cola or chai, *tea*."

By the time she left, the merchant had a wide grin on his visage, his mustache quivered with glee, he shouted at a "trying to please but not succeeding," anxious miniature boy, "Oi, sale, sitting idle again! Go get Coke for Didi, phataphat chalo, *go fast*."

Every half-decent shop owns one of these Lilliputian slaves; poorly dressed, contemptuously treated, these lesser creatures of God scurry around on their bare, thin, measly legs, executing all the petty chores that are beneath everyone else: "Get a Coke or chai," "Dry Didi's shoes," "Get a rickshaw," "Clean the mud off the floor." He also renders service of much greater significance; he serves as a target for everyone else who would take their frustration and anger on the helpless kid who has nowhere to take his.

Exploited heartlessly, stripped of human dignity so early in their lives, what did they do to deserve this condition? And yet, indigent parents of this child are ecstatic. Their son has a job, even if he is not paid. In all likelihood, if he remains tame and obedient to the owner, he would be duly exalted to the position where he can display ten sarees a minute and yell, "Oy, bring coffee for Didi," to another abused, tiny vassal who has replaced him in the scheme of things. He has a future, and that cannot be said about other impecunious children living in his neighborhood in the slums.

Meera smiled at the fearful boy to reassure him, "No, Beta, don't get Coke, I am in a hurry."

The tide had turned in Meera's favor, finally, when she bought two—not one—seven-hundred-rupee sarees. She received a broad smile and an invitation when she left. "Please, come again. Bring your sister-in-law. She could get sarees of her own choice, na."

The Coffee House was a mere three shops away toward the Ridge. It was impossible to breach the sacred tradition of making a pilgrimage to their favorite hangout. She did need a steaming cup of black, strong South Indian coffee and paper-thin masala, *spice,* dosa.

Her stomach growled in approval. The rain had ceased. Although it was early evening, the demiGoddess of night had decided to perch on the umbrageous clouds and cast her spell of darkness on the lands below. The neon lights rose in defence and succeeded, to a certain degree, to counter the talisman.

A gust of bedlam hit Meera as she opened the heavy wooden door and stepped in the Coffee House. It was packed to the brim; there were no empty tables. Just as she was turning away in disappointment, a bearer beckoned her, "Ma'am the couple in the corner is just leaving. If you could wait for a moment."

A tall, dark, South Indian young man and a short, even-darker wife got up and started to walk toward the door rather precariously through the packed restaurant that had barely any room for a foothold. "Please come this way, ma'am."

Coffee House is a constant in all major cities in India, the hub of social life of truants from college, offices, and homes, who would sneak out at odd hours for a quick dosa and the black stuff misnamed as coffee.

Grumbling in-laws well fed, the housewives hurriedly wrap up a saree, throw a shawl on their shoulders, use shopping as an excuse and escape from their gelid scrutiny. They justify the pretense of shopping by actually doing it. Of course, they need a break at the coffee house to rest their aching feet and enjoy a few moments of in-law battering with a friend doing the same.

At the advent of the evening, in the midst of a thin shroud of steam and smoke, the hubbub of heated argumentation between the intellectuals and those who pretend to be—politicians and lobbyists, idealist students with grand visions of the future and the pragmatic ones watering down their lofty ideals—aggrandize the status of the Coffee House.

Meera settled in the corner facing the window. The translucent mist arose from the valley and serenely covered most of the hills; some snowy crests poked out to kiss the overhanging clouds.

"Your order, ma'am?"

"A masala dosa and coffee, with milk and sugar."

Meera leaned back on the leather seat and closed her eyes. Of late, she had been feeling tired. Mishra Chachaji was right; it was time for a thorough checkup. The thought was still half-backed in her head when she heard a voice, not bearer's, speaking to her.

She was shaken out of her health plan, straightened, arranged her saree, and opened her eyes, simultaneously.

A strange, bearded, bespectacled face bent toward her from the right side of the table and asked politely, "Are you Meera?"

Meera looked up searchingly and spoke hesitantly, "Yes . . ." The face was familiar; her glance fell on the broad forehead. "Vineet?" Her face lightened up.

He laughed softly and took Meera's tender hand in his enormous paws and squeezed it. "My God, you have turned into a beautiful lady!"

Meera blushed and laughed back, "And look at you, six-foot-some, big and scholarly." Vineet's gold-rimmed glasses and a short but thick bearded face lavished savant air to his appearance. His black eyes were sad and deep, their vision turned inward. Meera had different memories of those eyes.

The bearer brought another chair for him; they scanned each other, nodded sideways in incredulity, and broke into gleeful laughter. Meera's face flushed at the memories that mushroomed from a forgotten alcove of her mind.

Orchards and round yellow apples, dolls and ludo, hide-and-seek, friendship, and fights. And humiliation that she would not forget.

Vineet's small chubby face was red with arrogance; he precipitated from nowhere and spoke harshly, "Why did you pluck the flowers from my garden without asking me?"

It was the most shocking revelation to Meera. His garden? She had claim on each blade of grass, leaf, bud, and flower, what does he mean? Meera didn't quite know why she had the claim though, she just blurted out.

"It is mine also!"

"No, it is not!"

"Yes, it is, we also live here."

"That is because my Bauji, *father,* lets you. It is my house."

The ground beneath her wee feet was snatched away rudely; tears of humiliation welled in Meera's eyes. She ran inside, crying bitterly.

Meera's only crime was that she brought a classmate home from school. It was a serious infraction because Vineet was excluded, being a boy and all. To add insult to injury, she started to show off the picturesque garden and even plucked a daisy for her friend to ensure continued visitations. It was rather nice to play with a girl for a change!

Meera had pushed her luck too far.

Rai Saheb Tayaji was coming out of the house at that every moment. He lifted her up in his arms and wiped her pink, wet cheeks.

"Tell me what happened."

Between hiccups and pitiful whining, Meera recounted Vineet's impudence, the bruise on her tiny ego vividly transparent.

Tayaji's jaw assumed a stern angularity; he stood her on the floor and held her wee hand. "Where is he?"

Tayaji and Meera walked out to discover that Vineet had lost himself in anticipation, and her friend had left in a hurry in case Vineet's fury fell on her.

Tayaji promised, "I will find and punish him. Now you go and ask your Mummyji to wash your pretty face."

There was panic; no Vineet even after the night fell. Everyone—Papa, Rakesh, Atul, Raghav, Raju, Shyam and Shiv, even Shoba, and Asha—started to look for him. Arrows of guilt pierced Meera's heart; it was all her fault.

Tayiji, Vineet's mother, was always lying in bed. Meera did not know why. She returned to her bed from the attached bathroom, at the same time Tayaji entered the room from the other door. They both noticed a trembling protrusion on the quilt.

Pangs of hunger could be endured though with much difficulty, but fear of huge white furry bears, who roamed around the woods to carry little children away to serve them as dinner for their cubs, Vineet could not overcome.

Much relieved but still angry, Tayaji was not allowed to speak.

"Poor child, he is cold and hungry! He has been punished enough, ji, no more action is needed. Come Beta," Tayiji pulled him from under the quilt and sat him in her warm lap. "Bansi," she called, "bring food for Vineet right here! Don't look so sinister, Raghav ke Bapu, he will not do it again. Will you, Vinni?"

Vineet nodded pathetically and buried his teary face in Tayiji's assuaging bosom. The matter ended.

At the back of the house, land spread below in layers each with its own special landscape where different species of bushes and flowers grew. At the very lowest level there was an expansive, open playground where Atul, Rakesh, Shyam, Raghav, Raju, and Shiv, along with other boys from the neighbourhood, played cricket.

Vineet, the youngest boy, was considered too small to participate in the crafty sport; naturally, he was left out unless he acquiesced to the degrading job of picking up the white balls that fell astray in the valleys around the playground. He only conceded if Meera was not available; that left him no choice but to join the older gang on their terms. That is where, he explained later, the seeds of Marxism were sown in his seditious heart, at the flagrant and unscrupulous exploitation of his honest labor. In the creases of the valleys and the lofty mountains, the hard white cricket ball clenched in his tiny fist, his face red with humiliation, a rebel was born unbeknownst by the clatter of the bigger boys playing the bourgeois game of cricket.

After Meera's family moved from Summer Hill to Simla, for many years, they had kept in touch with Rai Saheb Tayaji and family. Slowly, life took over, and the two families grew apart.

Vineet had a distinct scar on his forehead; Meera had pushed him against a rock during a moment of discord. Today, she might not have recognized a bigger, much sobered, bearded, bespectacled Vineet without that mark.

Bright lights were turned on inside the coffee house, people came and left, loud discussions took place, but Vineet and Meera were drowned in the flood of memories.

"How is Biji, *mother*?" Meera asked tenderly. As a child, she was constantly puzzled how someone could lay in bed all day and not play at all.

"She is fine but gets lonely after Bauji, *father,* died so suddenly."

Meera felt sorrow in her heart. Rai Saheb Tayaji was a grand, dignified man who was not just an aristocrat but a spiritualist one, with a soft heart, especially for Meera.

"How is Biji's health?"

"She took it to heart and fell seriously ill. That is when Raghav Bhaiya, sitting by her faded body, holding a limp hand, promised to become a doctor. He has."

"How is Raju Bhaiya?"

He was the handsome one; as a little girl, she had a crush on him. He was slim, tall, and fair with a sharply defined face. His huge, black eyes were always looking beyond somewhere; no one understood until later.

Vineet continued, "As soon as he was eighteen, he disappeared. For three excruciating days, we went through hell. On the third day, we received a telegram from London, England, 'I am safe. Do not worry. Love, Raju.'

"Of course, everyone was worried and afraid for his life. We knew who he was looking for. In response to Biji's teary letters he wrote, 'I have waited for this day for many years.' What do you say to that?"

"Oh my God, did he?"

"No." Vineet laughed. "God is kind to us. Raju Bhaiya did not find Clarke. There are thousands of them in England! But the woman detective he had hired had beautiful green eyes that swayed him into loveland. He got married there. As much as Biji hated to have Vilayati, *British,* daughter-in-law, she understood that directly or indirectly, the girl saved Raju from a life in prison. It later turned out that she had found the Clarke who was stationed in India during the Second World War and was treated like a hero for killing a native in Simla. But she loved him too much to let him go to jail for life."

Meera's glee was obvious, "Oh God, that was a close call!"

"Shyam Bhai hated studies so did what all the young men like him were doing: join the armed forces. The Indo-Pak War caused us immense anxiety. But he is fine, stationed in Madras. And Shiv Bhaiya followed Atul Bhaiya's path. He is a fiery lawyer."

"Is he married?"

"Oh yes, all of them, children and all."

Meera looked at him questioningly. He understood, "I am the only one left single."

"Biji must be frantically looking for a lovely girl for you."

Vineet just looked deep in her eyes and remained silent.

Meera narrated her family's lives, in quite detail as Vineet wanted to know everything. She did not say a word about her wedding or Mohit's passing.

He did not ask. It was obvious that he already knew.

- # -

Dadi immediately inquired with her toothless curiosity "Is he married?"

Meera retorted defensively, "I don't know! I did not ask him."

Dadi lost no time. Right after blessing Vineet, when he came for lunch the next day, that happened to be a Sunday, he was subject to blatant, undisguised, inquisition.

"Did you get married, Vini?"

Vineet took her small shrunken hand in his paws fondly. "Dadi, how could I, without your permission?" Obviously, he had not lost his touch.

Dadi smiled contentedly; he was the answer to her prayers! Finally, the stars were blinking favorably on Choti. She folded her shaky hands and thanked God.

Vineet was frustrated, "Chachaji, government projects to build roads, transport, electricity, and wells for the villages are going well. But twenty years after India was freed from slavery, the poor are still in the death grip of feudalism. Grants meant for the moneyless, landless laborers are unconconscientiously devoured by the savage hierarchical lions, Sarpanch, *head of the five Panches who are the main administrators of a village*, being the leader of the pack. The Panches, their cronies, friends, and relatives roam around the village fearlessly just helping themselves to the shops without paying a paisa, *penny*. Their houses have evolved into red brick mansions with swimming pools by usurping small farmers' farmsteads, the boundaries of the big landlords' territories are expanding. It is easy since there are no banks. The poor have to knock at the doors of the rich for financial help, dowry for the daughter's marriage, illnesses, or some other curse of the Gods. The Jameendar, *landowner*, would say, 'Aré, no problem, we are all brothers! We have to help each other, na.' Soon the poor farmer finds out that his land has been duly possessed by the 'brotherly' Jameendar, permanently. How can he even pay the huge interest? Every hard-earned rupee goes towards feeding and clothing his family."

"Vineet, hasn't the government supplied small farmers with tractors to share that could bring money in their hands?"

"Chachaji, that is the joke! The tractors are taken over and used by the Sarpanch, the Panches, and their pack. Then it stands as a trophy in the backyard of Sarpanch's mansion. The water from the tube well, that is supposed to be shared, is favorably directly towards the Jameendars' fields. The laborers are still paid one rupee a day. To contravene the 'minimum wage' laws, they falsify papers or get the illiterate farmers' thumbprints on larger figures."

Papa said in a sad voice, "I know, it is too sad."

There was no end to Vineet's fury. "The feudal lords have now taken over the political arena as well. Any poor or justice seeker, compassionate human who stands against them in elections is intimidated, beaten and sometimes killed. So are his supporters. So, the rich landlords now have a free reach in the political structure of the government. Police are in their pockets. Who can touch them?"

Vineet paused and looked out of the window. Clouds had shrouded the sun, and a shadow of darkness passed inside the room.

"Chachaji, I firmly believe that in underdeveloped or developing countries with huge population of poor, Marxism is the only system that can render justice to the suffering masses."

Papa agreed. "In principle, it should but considering that human nature is grossly imperfect, it may not work. Marx was a brilliant philosopher, a political thinker, and an idealist. Ordinary humans are not able to rise to the occasion to make sacrifices that are needed to fulfill the promises of Marxism."

"Chachaji, this is what Western propaganda machines would have us believe, but look at the facts. Marxism is working very well in Russia. During the Second World War, Russia was demolished to the ground. It arose from the ashes like a phoenix and has built a strong nation where people have free education and medical care, subsidized food, security of job, and shelter. It has progressed tremendously in industrialization and scientific research. As a matter of fact, Russia achieved all that success without the injection of millions of dollars of 'Marshall Plan' that the Western European countries received from the USA after the destruction of World War II.

"So, there is no doubt that the socioeconomic political system carved by Karl Marx does work. My fear is that Russia is under siege by the American cold war that will hinder the progress. Russia shall be forced to spend immense resources on military, weapons, nuclear weapons for self-defense. The diversion of funds to the nonproductive military-industrial complex would be a huge economic burden. Russians would have to make sacrifices. Danger from outside would lead to less tolerance for dissidence, that could lead to oppression. Russia is walking precariously on slippery grounds. If the leaders fail to deliver the promises of Marxism, more dissention could occur leading to an inner schism. The west will claim that Marxism does not work, which is not true."

He paused then looked at Papa.

"Chachaji, pray to your God that Russia succeeds and gives the poor, exploited masses of the world some ray of hope for social justice."

Suddenly, he challenged, "Chachaji, if God is really there, why doesn't he stop man's cruelty towards the poor?"

Papa laughed. He had, like so many others, struggled with this dilemma. "It is not God but humans that exploit and injure the weaker masses."

"But God is all powerful, why doesn't he stop it?"

"I believe that God has created and sustains the manifest universe. He is the energy and consciousness behind it. He has established Dharma, moral and physical laws of nature and has set the wheel of life in motion. Then He lets his ordinance work its way through karma, *our deeds,* and karmphal, *fruit of our deeds.* He grants us the free will with the hope that the ethical and moral jurisprudence revealed throughout human history through His incarnations, prophets and saints, will be heeded.

"It is our choice if we use the life he has given us for good or evil. Fire can be used to cook food as well as burn houses."

Vineet became immersed in his reflections for a few minutes then raised his head and asked Papa in a mysterious voice, "Chachaji, tell me, is there really a God or have humans erected a symbolic being for support when their pain is unbearable?"

"Vineet, there is no doubt that God is real. He is the master Creator. Aquinas's argument that watch necessitates a watchmaker is impeccable. His contention falls in the category of deductive reasoning. From consequence, you infer a cause. Smoke denotes a fire even if we do not see it with our own eyes. Purely physical electromagnetic forces can create subatomic particles, atoms, and molecules. But can you visualize, by any stretch of your imagination, random interaction of subatomic or atomic particles clashing in a primordial soup even with the energy of the lightening, creating highly organized, self-sustaining, energy producing, reproducing living beings? Can purely physical forces bring into being a magnificent creature called Human, with his awe-inspiring genome, incredible brain and other intricate organs that function cohesively in super organized fashion? Most importantly, matter can only create matter, it can't create 'consciousness.'

"The leap from purely physical to life systems requires a higher intelligence, consciousness, a causative power capable of thought and ideas that always come before any action. That intelligence, consciousness, and energy is God. He creates and sustains creation and is called the 'Absolute God' or 'Brahm.' We all carry part of God's consciousness within us called 'Soul,' or the 'Self.'

"By far the most consequential aspect of our being is consciousness, 'the Self', 'I,' that is the most concrete and irrefutable imperative."

Vineet listened attentively. "Chachaji, I have to spend time to think about it."

- # -

High hopes fostered by all of Meera's family were smashed to the ground with an unexpected thud. Ma moped around the house with crimson eyes, Asha avoided looking at her, Bhai's jaw was squarer than usual, eyes much bigger or so they seemed. "What is wrong with Vineet? Are you crazy? Why did you refuse his proposal for marriage?"

Dadi? All hell broke loose. "Aré, what is wrong with this befkoof, *stupid,* girl? No one looks at widows twice! They are condemned for life, doesn't she know that? Deva, I told you so many times don't give her so much chutti, *freedom,* but who listens to an old woman?" A few tears expressed her genuine distress. "Your Bauji never took a step without my advice. Bap re bap. These chokris, *girls,* have such a big mouth. We are dying with worry, and she does not even care!"

Papa was cool. "She knows what the right thing is. Leave her alone," was the only oar that saved her from drowning in the towering waves of the storm.

A smile had flitted across Meera's lightly pink-lipsticked lips, although she was unaware. It was a smile of inner glow; a galaxy of suns lit the inner spaces of her spirit.

Vineet let his breath go. "You are smiling, that is a good omen."

Meera looked at Vineet strangely as though for the first time. He was more handsome, his eyes lighter, fingers gentler as he extended his hand across the table and pressed Meera's velvety palms.

Vineet's proposal did not come as a surprise, not entirely. The three years of companionship had fanned the ember of love in Meera's heart. But she cherished their friendship, so denial was more convenient; rocking the boat with deeper stuff could have unknown and undesirable consequences.

But when Vineet posed the knotty question, it did not strike Meera as unnatural or out of place. A queer sense of unknown euphoria filled her heart. She looked up—that is when she saw him. Even after five years, there he stood behind Vineet with his seductive smile and sparkling eyes—Mohit did. His presence did not disturb her; he was not a spectator, he was a part of her. The transparency of the intuitive precognition that Mohit had come to help her find answers comforted Meera. His presence was beyond real and unreal; for her, nothing in the world was more real than the vision of her soul mate. Mohit raised his left hand and pointed to the ring finger; Meera was puzzled. He gestured again, she understood. There was no wedding ring. He smiled assuringly and stepped aside like a ripple in the wind smoothly flowing away. Meera had never seen him completely at peace before.

Following her gaze, Vineet looked behind him, "What?"

"Nothing." Her tremulous voice echoed from a far distance.

Vineet's eyes searched her face. "Are you okay? Did I offend you, Meera? I am sorry, we don't have to talk about it."

"No, Vineet, it is all right." The assenting spark in her eyes was reassuring.

But then there is history, lying in silent hibernation, just underneath the surface of life. No one knows when and where it will soar from the cold ashes and ambush the present, asserting its claim on immortality. No happening ever passes on without leaving a potent debris of the past, an invisible network of tentacles that spread far into the future; these can strangle the most alive hope or dream.

Who would have known that the ghost of Clarke would become alive twenty-three years later and stalk Meera's life?

Clarke placed his glass on the wooden bar and pulled a stool close to Avinash, Vineet's oldest brother, who turned his head and smiled cordially. Clarke responded with a sarcastic query, "This is an exclusive British officers' club, how the hell did you get in?"

Avinash turned his gaze to the dancing floor and replied coolly, "I have been invited by Captain Thomas. Do you mind?"

"Oh no, why should I mind if some people have a base taste for friendships."

Avinash ignored him and took a sip from the glass of rum that he held.

Disappointed by his inability to get a rise out of Avinash, Clark transferred his focus on another target. He started to remark loudly on Dolly's dancing skills.

"No matter how much you teach them, these uncivilized natives can never learn how to dance properly."

Tom was waltzing with his arms around Dolly; his face showed obvious joy.

Avinash liked her; the carefree frivolous charm attracted him, being a sober restrained person himself.

Tayiji was appalled, "Aré, is that Grover's daughter? He shows off his newly found wealth, all suited-booted. His wife thinks she is Queen Nurjahan! Not a Kala Dhandha, *black trade*, he has left untouched. No Deen-iman, *honesty*, money is their god? They are worst than Maletch, *low caste*, who knows who he is? Nai baba. Listen to me, Nashi, I am telling you today, she will sell us! I want a simple girl from a good family with high samskara, *predispositions*. These newly get-rich-quick have none. Dolly will have no time from her makeup. Keep away from her! Such girls can trap you in no time."

The evening was freezing; winds howled. The bearers were constantly throwing fresh wood in the fireplaces; the fire rekindled and leapt to some height before settling down to the low flickering flames.

Even excessive drinking was unable to ward off the chill in the air. Bright lights, music in the background, sound of clicking heels and shoes echoed on the wooden dance floor; young couples swayed their bodies with the beat.

Clarke was a young, hot-blooded Britisher from Lancashire, who, like thousands of others, joined the armed forces, received their commission, and arrived at the bustling port of Bombay.

The dance ended, everyone clapped. Tom kissed Dolly on the cheek. Another record was placed on the gramophone; the dance floor became alive with fresh movement. Clarke got up from his stool abruptly and straggled toward Dolly. He grabbed her arm, "I want to see how you dance with me, Dolly," and pulled her towards him.

She resisted, "Let go," tried to free her arm and looked at Tom anxiously.

Enough was enough. Tom placed his hand on Clarke's chest and pushed him, "Don't ever try to be rude with the lady. Scum like you—"

Before he could finish, Clarke punched him in the face so hard that he stumbled backward and fell against a stool.

Avinash got up swiftly. "You stupid, you think you are civilized behaving like a ruffian?"

He grabbed Clarke from the back to stop him from kicking Tom, who was trying to get on his feet.

Clarke turned around, in a flash of a second before anyone could grasp, shots were heard. Avinash staggered and fell on the floor. Blood gushed from his chest; eyes were wide open with bewilderment and closed as he fainted.

Clarke stood, with bloodshot eyes, looking down on Tom and Avinash, with a small gun in his right hand.

Storm was raging outside, roads were plugged up with piles of snow accumulated during the persistent fury of the blizzard for two days. The ambulance came too late. Avinash died on the couch of the club, with his limp head in Dolly's lap, soaked with the bright-red blood that wouldn't stop despite the towel Tom pressed on the wound in the upper chest.

Tayaji's money and influence could not buy justice. Clarke was not guilty; all of the British witnesses except Tom and Dolly testified in court that the unfortunate event was plain and simple self-defense. Tom and Dolly's truth drowned in the muck of lies. The verdict was as expected. No British colonial had ever been incarcerated for killing the Indian subjects. They were the occupiers, their power and rights were infinite, they could make or break laws at their convenience.

Clarke was sent back to the United Kingdom and welcomed as a hero.

Tayiji never got over the grief of the loss of her beloved son. She was taken ill and confined to bed for the rest of her life.

Vineet was earnest. "Meera, Biji will never accept a white child in her house. She will hate him, and I cannot give pain to her and Rishi. You do understand? We can send Rishi to the best boarding school. I can buy a house close to the school and you can spend as much time there as you want!"

Like chilly frost that decimates a vivacious bloom, an icy expression came over Meera's face. She let go Vineet's hand abruptly and leaned against the back of the wooden chair. The noises of the coffee house suddenly vanished from her consciousness; all she could hear was vibrating strings of sarod, *stringed instrument*, the sorrowful waves of music striking her ears and heart.

The resplendent moment had come and gone in the blink of an eye. She saw the pieces of her heart scattered on the damp floor.

She said, "I have promises to keep."

Chapter Three

Thousands of years ago, the powerful kingdom of Hastinapur was ruled by descendants of the famous King Bharat, after whose name the nation was called Bharatvarash, India's Hindi name.

The King Pandu died young. His five children, the Pandavs, were young boys at the time. Hence Pandu's younger, blind brother Dhritrashtr was made the king as a custodian of the state until Yudhistr, the oldest Pandav, came of age.

Pandavs and Kauravs, as Dhritrashtr children were called, were sent to the gurukul (school of the guru) of accomplished rishi (spiritualist sage) Dronacharya. During those times, brahmins, the highest priest class, were prohibited from touching weapons; their calling was to teach scriptures and spirituality to their disciples. But Dronacharya had learnt ShastrVidya, knowledge of weaponry from Parshuram, another rishi, who had picked up sword to punish power-blind Kshatriya kings who had gone astray from the path of righteousness. He defeated kings twenty-one times.

Dronacharya was a brilliant disciple and became the most adroit master of weapons in all of Bharat. He was chosen to teach the princes of Hastinapur.

Arjun, the middle Pandav boy, was Dronacharya's favorite, not only because he excelled in Shastrvidya, knowledge of weaponry, but also for the purity and humility of his character.

Dronacharya's son Ashwathama, who was also a disciple in his father's gurukul, became extremely jealous of Arjun.

"Pitashri, respected father, why do you give undue attention and praise to Arjun? I am just as able and proficient!"

Dronacharya smiled but said nothing.

The next morning, before anyone else was awake, he went out and hung a toy bird high up on a pippal tree nearby the gurukul.

After the morning prayers, Dronacharya addressed the princes and his son. "Today I wish to test your skills at archery."

"As you wish, Gurudev, respected teacher," the students chorused.

They walked on the damp grass; Dronacharya led them quite close to the tree from where the bird was clearly visible.

"Children, do you see a bird on the tree?"

They looked up. "Yes, Gurudev."

He turned to Ashwathama. "I want you to pierce the eye of the bird with your arrow."

Ashwathama was proud to have been called before anyone else. He positioned his feet firmly on the ground, placed the arrow across the bow and the string, and aimed at the target. Before he pulled the taut string, Dronacharya stopped him. "First, tell me what do you see?"

To please his father, Ashwathama replied, "I see you, Gurudev, the tree leaves, and the bird."

Dronacharya said, "That is fine, Ashwathama. Come back and stand with the other disciples."

He called all the Kaurav and Pandav princes, excepting Arjun, and asked them to perforate the eye of the bird. Everytime, just before they shot the arrow, he asked them, "What do you see?"

The responses were slightly different but along the same lines as Ashwathama.

Finally, he asked Arjun to try.

Arjun walked over to Dronacharya and touched his feet. Then with full concentration, he arranged the arrow on the bow.

Dronacharya queried, "Arjun, what do you see?"

Without any movement, Arjun replied, "Gurudev. I only see the eye of the bird."

Dronacharya commanded him, "Shoot the arrow, Arjun."

He did; the arrow perforated the eye of the toy bird with perfect precision.

Ashwathama looked down.

Dronacharya cautioned his disciples, "Jealousy is a vikar (pollutant) of the mind, it is the most formidable barrier to achievement of perfection.

"Do not be distracted, let your mind become one with your goal, you will never miss your aim."

From Mahabharat

Meera peeped in Rishi's room; he was sound asleep, a slight innocent smile flickered on his chubby face. Perhaps a nice dream; what do little boys dream about? Meera crossed her fingers, "God, please, let life stay good to us." She went right back to her cozy bed and listened to the silence.

On weekends, early mornings were marked by a dull aphony, interrupted only by the occasional jerky sound of the furnace turning on. There was a sense of void that she was still not used to.

In India, mornings dawned with certainty, noisily announced by the milkman Madho; the clamor of the bicycle bells preceded his arrival waking up the whole neighbourhood. Two dols, *big metallic containers,* of milk hung on either side of the carrier at the back of the cycle and created a perfect balance. Ma had stopped arguing with him. How could you prove it? Madho swore to all his favourite gods, God help them, "Never Maji, Mata Kasam, *swear to my mother,* Ganesh Kasam, I never do it! My Bapu told me before Yama took him away, may his soul rest in peace, 'Madho, beta, nothing goes with you except your Karma, *righteous deeds.*"

Ma quietly boiled the milk twice to kill the unsuspecting germs that found their way in the milk when Madho diluted it with pond water.

"Maji," he whispered, displaying his knowledge of the scriptures. "The cows are ominous! Our rishis had predicted thousands of years ago that in kaliyug, *immoral times,* everything will be impure, how can cows give pure milk?" Who could argue against the wisdom of the rishis?

Ma's soft voice waking up Dharma followed by clanking of pots and pans as he prepared bed tea for everyone, Dadi's loud, morning Mantra, "Om Namo Bhagwate Vasudev Vai", *a prayer,* in the backdrop like humming of bees, the mornings commenced the day with a lively initiation.

Ma's next assignment was challenging. She climbed the stairs while calling everyone, "Atul, Rakesh, Shobha, time for college. You get up late then run without breakfast. Chalo, utho, *get up.*"

Shobha would grumble, "Whose brilliant idea was it to start college at nine o'clock? Why not eleven o' clock, eh?" as she pulled the sheet over her face.

Atul would whine irritatingly and whisper, "My first period is free. Leave me alone," something that was hard to prove.

Rakesh pretended to be dead. Ma would shake Atul, "Get up, Beta. I will send Dharma to help you with Rakesh," which consisted of dragging him to the bathroom and turning cold water on his drowsy head. His yelling served as an alarm for the surrounding bungalows.

Meera was already in the front yard, full of curiosity to check on her garden. She jumped out of bed and ran out while Ma shouted behind her, "Aré, put some sweater on! This girl is going to get chill!"

Manu's verse floated in the air in Papa's gentle voice, birds chattered in their languages, the pink color of dawn enchanted Meera to no end.

In the kitchen, Ma and Dharma discussed the menu; Shoba and Rakesh fought noisily for the use of the bathroom upstairs.

"Ma, Shoba does not get out of the bathroom, can I go first?"

Sounds of different pitch and tenor drifted from neighbours' houses to lend a nostalgic tenderness to those mornings.

The phone was ringing. Meera was annoyed at the intrusion into her ownership of the only quiet morning. The other days she leapt out of bed in panic, forced a reluctant Rishi to dress up, eat breakfast, and drop him at school. The rest of the time was spent on catching up with the fast-paced day, constantly half an hour behind schedule.

Kanchan sounded excited, "Be ready, I will pick you up."

How could Meera decline the rare treat of an Indian movie even though most contemporary movies were cheap romantic trashes? Gone were the days when film directors like Bimal Roy, Mehboob, and Guru Dutt created memorable pieces of artistry. Bimal Roy, a Bengali, immortalised Sharat Chander Chattopodhyaya's books that revealed the multifarious faces of village life to rest of the world of cities. The Nobel Laureate poet, another Bengali, Rabindranath Tagore had exclaimed, "I write for the world, Sharat writes for me."

During those years, going to movies was a full-scale family adventure to which a whole Sunday was dedicated, starting with dressing up, that for some like Shoba was the most consequential act of the whole event. After dragging Shoba away from the mirror, they started to trek to the movie theater, which was a good forty-minute walk from Meera's house. Trails connected all houses to a narrow dirt road that finally merged with the main road.

Dadi mounted the rickshaw that was pulled by four strong muscled, pillar-legged, robust rickshawallas. Sometimes one of them was a weakling and had to put up with much swearing all day "Sale, bhar utha, *pick the load,* theek se, *properly,* kamzorilal kahin ka, *weakling*."

The group would not fire him; they were cognizant that no one would hire a feeble man. They also figured that their vigor may betray them sooner than later. While they ran in unison up the high mountains and down the precipitous valleys, their dark crunched bellies craved food. In the winter, the chill froze their bones and every part of their body; during monsoons, they were soaking wet with the slashing downpour of the rain, the burlap sac they used as a raincoat being a totally inadequate protection. All the gods seemed to be angry at them for what sin they dared not ask.

The rickshawalla's wife, with a frayed cotton saree over her graying head, waited for him to come home to their small, smelly, damp hut. She laid scrawny children to sleep on a single cot huddled in a worn-out blanket that may be a few generations old; in all likelihood the rickshawalla's ancestors practiced the same livelihood and were just as destitute. He would return home after dark, exhausted and hungry, his mouth fowl with the smoke of a cheap bidi, *cigarette,* that he inhaled all day to energise his cold, famished body. The wife would quietly spread his drenched, thick, brown cotton pajama and kameez on a broken rack of wood in front of fading heat of the earthen coal stove; he had only one set of apparel. The husband wrapped his achy, shiny body with the rough blanket, air circulating freely through the gaping holes, ate a few rotis, *homemade bread,* and may be a raw onion that he broke with his solid fist and rolled into a dreamless sound sleep beside his warm-bodied, uncomplaining wife.

Dadi would join them only for some patriotic movies like *Mother India* where the charming actress Nargis was the mother of a dacoit, who later became her husband, in real life of course. She agreed to see some magnificent, historic picture like *Mugle Azam,* the story of the invincible Mughal emperor Akbar's moral defeat at the hands of a young, beautiful courtesan, Anarkali, *pomegranate flower.* The crown prince Jehangir had fallen hopelessly in love with her. Akbar offered her money to forsake her lover; naturally, as the true love stories go, she refused to betray her royal inamoratos.

Akbar gave orders to bury her alive in an air tight brick and mortar cubicle, where she suffocated thereby immortalizing her love, much to the chagrin of Mugle Azam Akbar who wished to hush-hush the whole affair. Dadi cried for whole two days at the untimely extinguishing of the ill-fated Anarkali played by the screen queen Madhubala, who was indisputably the fairest of them all.

Meera and family would arrive at the theater rosy cheeked or frozen-faced, depending on the level of the mercury that evening, got pushed around and squished, intentionally of course by rowdy young boys before they could take ownership of their seats. Potato chips and Coke were bought over Papa's objections due to poor hygiene. Interval was even more fun; samosawalla, cigarettewala, chatwalla, peanutswalla, and last but not the least, chaiwalla, walked around the aisles of the smoky cinema hall like phantoms, declaring their product in competing voices, occasionally stepping on some feet to pass on their stuff. "Ouch, watch your step, stupid." Children whined, "Mummy Mummy, I want samosa." "I want Coke," etc. Who cared how the movie turned out? If you happened to bump into friends, all the more fun.

The next few days were devoted to discussing who acted, overacted, or did not act; who looked pretty and fashionable and who looked like trash, whether the movie could make it to the prestigious Annual Film Fare awards, which are almost as consequential as Oscars of Hollywood.

The picture was not too bad in spite of the lanky, huge-eyed new actor Amitabh Bachan, who could not walk or act, awkward at both. The movie was called Anand, *joy*. The hero, actor Rajesh Khanna, suffered from cancer but displayed superhuman courage in the face of death.

The ending was sad, Meera was not pleased. Kanchan teased her, "I have never seen anyone cry that much over a movie. It is imaginary, yar, *friend*."

Meera's point was that it does happen in reality.

Bela announced with her hands up in the air, "That is why I don't see Hindi films! They are unreal, hero, heroine jumping like children, dancing and singing in the garden, even poor heroine wears diamonds and flashy clothes, the hero beats up to fifteen gundas, *rogues*, without a scratch on himself. If they make a good movie, they create a Greek tragedy out of it that is meant to wring maximum emotions and tears out of you. Na, Bhai, that is no entertainment. Prashant would have loved it because he can make fun of everything, so he is okay."

"Thanks a lot, Aunty," Rishi waved his hand as Meera picked him up from Bela's house; she was pleased with his manners.

A piece of paper was stuck up in the mailbox. "I wonder . . .," as she picked it up.

Meera turned ashen and mumbled, "Oh boy," as she fumbled with the lock in the front door. Sheila was certainly going to hear this one with much exaggeration.

Rishi looked at her and asked, "What happened, Mom?"

"Nothing, Beta, Get your things together. I will drop you at Granny's. But let me phone first."

Mrs. Henderson was not home. Meera tried repeatedly, but no one picked the phone up. It worried her; what was she up to, now?

Monday was a holiday. Meera phoned early. Before she could explain, Helena retorted in a grating, haughty and hoarse voice, "I will send the chauffeur in an hour." Mrs. Henderson never called Peter by name, as though he had no identity other than the driver of her four wheels.

Meera sat on a chair in the dining room and called out to Rishi, "Beta, get ready to visit Granny."

He whined from his bedroom, "I don't want to go."

Meera walked lethargically to his room. He was curled cosily in his quilt, only his blond head was visible. Meera drew the window curtains. Bright sunlight, reflected on the pure snow and invaded the room.

"There is no one to play with. She does not let me play with Johny because he is the chauffeur's son. I don't like her anyway, she laughs funny."

Meera sat by his bedside, ran her fingers through his hair. "But she is your grandma!"

"My grandma is in India!"

"Yes, she is also your grandma. Granny is my best friend Jane's ma. Jane loved you like her own son. So." Meera was nonplussed, when is it a good time to tell him?

Vivian kept telling her, "Meera dear, it is best to tell them early. Later, the adjustment is harder."

- # -

"What happened, Vivian?"

Vivian's hand shook as she poured coffee in the mug for Meera. They had taken a short coffee break; the next patient was not expected for another twenty minutes.

Vivian looked away to hide her tears.

"Couldn't be that bad?"

Vivian looked at Meera. "It is dear, it is."

When Meera returned to Canada, holding a six-year-old Rishi's hand, Satish declared at the outset, "I will not let you work anywhere else. I am getting new patients, Vivian, my nurse, is overwhelmed. Learn typing, she will teach you the rest."

The Ugandan President Idi Amin's decision to throw all the Indians out of the country was supported by the public who hated them for controlling the economy and living in affluence while they struggled with poverty. The consequence was a flood of Indian immigrants to Canada.

A few families, whose relatives resided in and around Henderseville, arrived at the small airport with bags, baggage, children, parents, and sometimes even grandparents. To find an authentically Indian doctor in such a small town was considered a good omen for the start of a new life.

Vivian was a pleasant middle-aged woman from Quebec.

"How come you have come so far from home?" Meera was curious.

Vivian's parents were poor—father, Michel, was uneducated and unemployed who believed he had the birthright to take out his frustrations on his wife and child. One day, he returned home from the pub, both mother daughter and their belongings were gone.

Vivian clung to her mother on the train that took them to Quebec City. Anne kissed her blond head. "No one will ever beat you again, child." Vivian was five years old.

Anne found a job cleaning houses and admitted Vivian in a Catholic school close by.

As soon as Vivian stepped into the confounding domain of adolescence, she craved love of a man to fill the many voids of her life. She met Pierre in the last year of high school; his father was an engineer.

It was love at first sight; Pierre was kind, loving, and decent.

Anne stared at them sternly as Vivian and Pierre crouched together on the couch, holding hands.

"How old are you? Seventeen? How can you even think marriage? You don't marry the first guy who comes into your life and tells you that you are pretty?"

She glowered at Pierre, who was duly intimidated as intended.

"Boy, you should get education first, get a job, then ask for Vivian's hand! What do your parents think about this crazy idea?"

Pierre looked down. "We have not told him yet."

Anne looked away, tears shone in her eyes; she softened.

"Vivian, child, I don't want you to ever have to clean people's houses! A career is the only way to a good life!"

Vivian cried. "I hate you, you don't understand!" and ran out of the house. Pierre followed quietly.

He took Vivian's hand and spoke patiently, "Let me talk to my father. He is very understanding. Maybe he will find a way."

Paul was a practical man but one with penetrating intellect who could instantly grasp all the angles of an enigma. Being an engineer, he had mastered the technique of balancing all forces to create stability.

He went to see Anne.

"You are absolutely right and rational in your response. I believe kids should focus on their studies. But."

Anne looked at him questioningly.

"Unfortunately, we cannot force our children to be rational too, that quality comes with experience and age. If they do not get married, Vivian and Pierre may sin. They will. I know my son. He loves your daughter with a true heart."

Paul proposed that they get married, live in his huge house, and pursue their careers.

"Actually, after Pierre's mother died two years ago, I feel very lonely. Your wonderful daughter will bring warmth to my cold abode. What do you say?"

Vivian already had admission in nursing school at the university. Pierre started to work in the wheat mill.

After marriage, Vivian and Pierre moved in with Paul; Vivian found the father she never had. Studying late at night for her exams, she could hear gentle footsteps approach her. He would say, "My girl, brain does not work well when starved," and place a plate of sandwiches and mug of steaming cocoa on her study desk. He patted her shoulder for encouragement before sneaking out of her room noiselessly.

Soon after she graduated, Vivian gave birth to a blond, green-eyed, handsome son, Jacque. Life was perfect.

But then.

America and Canada had already joined allied forces to defeat the evil of Hitler in Europe. Pierre joined the army and was immediately shipped to France.

He never returned. Army could not find his body in the midst of maddening chaos.

Paul died a year later of heartbreak. Jacque was only two years old. Vivian never dated again.

Anne and Vivian raised Jacque who, much to their gratification, turned out to be a brilliant student at school, then at the university.

All of a sudden, once again, life turned upside down.

Police knocked at Vivian's door at midnight. Anne's health was deteriorating; she had gone to bed early.

They asked for Jacque.

Vivian had not seen him for many days, he came and went at all hours. Who could keep track of a young man?

The police left without explanation.

Vivian was gripped by unknown fears. Jacque was a good boy; he couldn't have done anything wrong, could he? All night nightmarish thoughts crawled in her mind.

Next morning before Anne woke up, Vivian took a bus to the university.

Professor Quin threw up his hands. "I told Jacque that he was crazy! He is a brilliant scholar, after his master's degree, he can easily get a teaching position in our department!"

Jacque had quit school; he was a student of the political science department.

Many French Quebecers carried a sense of grievance over the conquest of 1760. Nationalism was always a force, however meager, in their minds. In the 1940s and 1950s, they gave expression to their nationalism by defending Quebec's rights against Ottawa's centralizing tendencies.

Suddenly in the 1960s the idea of independent Quebec gained credence. What was happening on the international stage might have been the trigger. European colonialization was slowly collapsing after the Second World War. The conception of the struggle for independence attracted attention in Quebec especially after the overthrow of the French in Algeria in 1962. In 1963, Front de Libération du Québec (FLQ) was created. Employing Algerian methods, they resorted to terrorism to achieve their goal. Over two hundred bombs went off between 1963 and 1970 causing loss of property, injuries and deaths.

However, FLQ never attained a large following in terms of manpower; it remained a collection of scattered radical cells. Yet the mainstream French gave them quiet support.

Jacque was nowhere to be found.

In 1965 Vivian, received a letter from him. He just wrote, "Mama, I have joined the FLQ. I will not contact you for your security. I shall see you when we are victorious."

Anne died the next year from cancer. Vivian felt completely lost and lonely. Her friend Leanne lived in Hendersville; she moved there for emotional support.

De Gaulle, the French president, visited Montreal to attend Expo '67, the celebration of one hundred years of Canadian Confederation. His impassioned speech in Montreal and the provocative slogan "Vive le Québec libre" fanned the flames of yearning for Independence in nationalistic youth. In Paris, de Gaulle's colleagues held their breath at the fear that de Gaulle had lost his mind.

In 1970, the year Meera returned to Canada, the FLQ had become desperate; one of their groups kidnapped the British Consul James Cross and Labour minister of Quebec, Pierre Laporte.

The kidnappers demanded freedom for separatists who had been imprisoned for terrorism and total Independence of Quebec nation.

Trudeau, who was the prime minister, not only refused to negotiate but also declared War Measures Act and Martial Law in Quebec. Canadian army moved in to keep order; five hundred Quebecers, suspected of supporting FLQ were arrested.

Jacque was one of them.

The priest of Vivian's church who was an old friend called. "Jacque is fine. He swears he had nothing to do with the kidnapping, and I believe him. Prisoners are not being mistreated. Have faith, Vivian dear, and pray."

Vivian looked at Meera tearfully. Wwhat should I do? I want to see him!"

"No." Meera held her hands firmly. "He is with his friends, they will be released if they are innocent. Your safety will become an additional worry for him."

Laporte was brutally murdered. Police raced with time; James Cross's life had to be saved to avoid international furor. Finally, a tip led the police to the place where the kidnappers had kept James Cross. He was freed, the captors were exiled to Cuba.

The "October Crisis" ended in three months. Most of the prisoners, including Jacque, were freed. He called Vivian immediately, "Mama, I am sorry to put you through this. I am back to the university. Come home and make my favourite soup."

At the airport, Meera and Vivian hugged and pledged to keep in touch forever, a promise that neither could keep. Life took over, perhaps.

- # -

Bela was outright angry. "Don't be silly, you are not living in slums." She took a sip of masala tea to placate herself.

Meera looked wistfully out of the dining room window. She had bought this small bungalow for its unimpeded view of the mountains across. The tall, frigid peaks pierced the skies in daring fearlessness.

Just to bring home to Meera the perennial, impeccable law of imperfection of the world, Meera received a call from the good old, what Prashant called "snaky eyes," "two-faced" Sheila. Without exception, her call augured dismal foreboding.

"A few disturbing facts have come to our notice. I would like to meet you."

Satish was a doctor, Anil an engineer, Sunil a teacher; all of them were caught in inflexible professions. Prashant, the car salesman, was the most willing escort, whenever she needed one.

Sheila wore the usual paste of solemnity spread on her face like butter on a slice of crumpled bread. Her lips were twisted in insolence, "We have to listen to Mrs. Henderson's complaints because she is the only blood relative Rishi has! You know, you were awarded the custody, but we have to ensure that you take care of him as a mother should."

Prashant's forehead developed instant horizontal creases, his mouth opened but shut quickly like a fish in a pool. Meera had warned that he was not to, in any circumstances, open his mouth. Normally cool, he possessed immense potential for stridence. Meera had fully grasped the fragile dynamics of her predicament; trapped in a sinuous maze where the "goal" was blocked by the wall of Helena's cunning, unsavory confrontation with her stooge was a no-win situation.

Kanchan, who wore Western apparel religiously, had advised, "Aré Meera, you should wear expensive Western dresses to these meetings, otherwise, they believe that you are an uneducated woman from a remote 'rat worshipping village.'"

Meera bought pantsuits but discovered that it did not work.

"I am raising my son." Meera's eyes flashed as she emphasised on the words *my son*. "As well or better than most mothers."

"Well, it says here," Sheila feigned to concentrate on a sheet of paper on the desk, "you are abandoning him to a babysitter. You spend no time with him. Rishi has no father, and if the mother is also absent, how do you think the child will develop, eh?"

A white, nebulous blizzard swirled in Meera's head; she was extremely weary of having to prove her innocence. She looked across the table and saw a pitiable human, if Sheila could be called that, shrunken under her own weight, staring with vacuous dispassionate eyes. What would turn a sentient into a Sheila, devoid of a heart and soul, who knew exactly what she was doing?

Meera responded in a phlegmatic tone that even surprised her. "I have gone back to school to be able to earn a better living. I am not away all evening. We spend three thirty to seven thirty together. I leave him with a trusted and dear friend, not a babysitter. I love my son very much, and I am not obliged to prove it to you or anyone else. If you can prove otherwise, go ahead."

Sheila was jolted out of her complacency at Meera's unexpected, newly acquired robust posturing.

Her flesh slumped deeper into the chair, her pitch mellowed, "Mrs. Henderson has requested that Rishi could stay at her house after school and you can pick him up at night."

Meera maintained the strategy of unyielding, laconic locution, "I told you, I am home until seven thirty. If Mrs. Henderson is that worried about Rishi, she is welcomed to come to my place at seven thirty and take care of her grandchild. I want him in bed by nine. I will not disrupt his routine by hauling him to and fro at night. I will act only in Rishi's interest. And, Sheila," Meera continued, "you are supposed to do the same."

She stood up abruptly and rendered a wry thank-you in Sheila's direction. Her feet staggered as she walked toward the car.

"Are you all right?" Prashant asked gently when they settled in the car. She nodded in the negative, honestly. He wanted to comfort her. Entrenched in traditional Indian values, to hug her could bring about embarrassment. He patted Meera's left hand and reassured her, "You were good, hey, well said. Hurray, Meera!"

The words meant to assuage, triggered unleashing of pent-up emotions; Meera broke down and cried.

Prashant was at a loss. He did not know how to respond to Meera's outburst. To be useful, he extended his right arm toward the back seat to retrieve the box of Kleenex. Just then Meera bent downward toward her left leg to pick up her white leather purse that had a handkerchief. Prashant's right arm brushed against her left cheek. In utter confusion, he mumbled, "Oops, sorry," took her face in his hands and rubbed her cheek gently. An instantaneous surge of solace overwhelmed Meera, a soft light engulfed her; she let go and shut her eyes. Within the endless span of a fleeting moment, life was transformed. Gently, Prashant wrapped her in his long arms. Meera rested her bewildered head on his shoulder. The unacknowledged emotions simmering under the surface of their unconscious broke through and shattered the fetters of collective, ancient, forbidding traditional forces—freeing them, if momentarily, to just be. That moment, she was not Prashant's best friend's widow to be revered at a distance; she was a woman.

Overwhelmed by suffusion of feelings of embarrassment, guilt, confusion, her heart thumping against her chest uncontrollably, Meera parted in quandary. Prashant took a deep breath and took his arms away.

A silence replete with unspoken cadence prevailed on the way home. Meera let out a stifled "Thank you," avoiding his eyes; he responded with an equally nonplussed, "You are welcome," looking away with equal zeal.

Still in a daze, Meera sat on a dining chair with a steaming cup of tea in her hand. Outside the window, a gray sky above and pure white earth below presented a serene reticent world. No wind, no movement; life was slumbering almost like the solemn stillness after pralay, *doomsday*, when the clamor of uproarious manifest existence mutely dissolves into the "Neumenal womb," the absolute "Om." Om embraces itself within its own bosom with abandoned repose, waiting to unfold into another cycle of creation, beginning of a new yug, *era.*

The cognizance of her feelings for Prashant was too confounding for Meera; these could lead to intricate sequels of perilous consequences. Hence, she had steadfastly denied her feelings for him.

But when Prashant hugged her, in a flash of intimacy, a thousand jasmine blooms had lit her heart, maddening her with the ambrosia. The raga, *musical composition*, of Shingar Ras, *music of passion*, resounded in her spirit; how was she to deny the truth now?

But she had to push her emotions away and shelve them in a remote corner of her unconsciousness. Larger, more complex, labyrinthine meanderings confronted and challenged her daily life.

Mrs. Henderson had dedicated her life exclusively to hurting Meera, much like a sadistic villain in Indian movies. Crude hostility was not enough to make her day, telling on Meera at the child welfare department seemed to be a more gratifying activity for her. An insignificant bruise on Rishi's small body would prompt accusations of neglect or downright abuse.

The last time Sheila was harsh. "We are concerned about Rishi's education. You should ensure that he is raised with progressive ideas, befitting modern times."

Rishi had dropped a book on the floor and was playfully trying to pick it up with his feet. Meera stopped him, "Rishi, don't touch the book with your feet! It is disrespectful. Please, pick it up and touch it to your forehead." Rishi laughed nonchalantly. "Mom! It is only paper that is made of wood pulp," simultaneously dissipating his recently acquired insight.

Meera was serious. "No, Rishi. Demi goddess of knowledge Saraswati resides in the words of the book. There is nothing more sacred than gyan, *knowledge*, . . ."

She was about to lecture him on how knowledge is the sure path to enlightenment and absolute freedom but realized that Rishi was only six years old.

Meera was tough. "I was teaching him to honour erudition, if that is not progressive, I don't know what is."

Rishi pushed Meera aside rudely as he walked through the main door, stamped his feet, and headed straight for his room.

"Rishi?" She followed him into his bed room. He threw himself on the bed, lay facedown, and cried.

Meera's heart shivered; a thousand scary thoughts crawled in her head like poisonous snakes. Had she been reckless? Jane had warned her about Mrs.Henderson.

Meera sat beside Rishi, slowly protracted her right hand and started to stroke his blond silky hair. "Tell me what happened?"

"Don't," he shouted and pushed her hand away. The anguish in his voice shook her.

He just sobbed. Meera sat on the bed silently with a panic filled heart.

Dark crept in from the window claiming every corner of the room and weighing heavily on the still air. The furnace clicked in breaking the silence.

After a while, Meera stretched her arms and gently picked up Rishi. He did not resist this time, just bent his head in despair and hid his face in her bosom.

She held him in her lap with one arm and extended the other to turn the lamp on. The room became alive with magic and hope, but Rishi's chubby, fair face remained clouded.

He looked at Meera with his big, blue tortured eyes and almost whispered, "Granny told me, Mom."

"What did she say?" Meera's voice was full of stifled tension.

Rishi just hugged her tightly.

Meera repeated, "What did she say, Rishi?"

"She said . . . she said . . ." He hesitated.

"Go on . . ."

"She said that I am not your son! That is why I look kind of different. I am her daughter Jane's son. No one knows who my father is. He is not my dad!" Rishi cried and pointed his finger accusingly at Mohit's photo frame that was standing on the dresser, as though Mohit was to be blamed for not being his father.

Meera let go her breath; sudden relief loosened her body. At least he is not molested or abused. Then a sense of betrayal gripped her.

She pressed Rishi against her warm body and kissed him in the forehead. "Yes, Rishi, you are my best friend and sister Jane's son! She wanted me to raise you, and I wanted a special, sweet little baby like you, so it worked out."

Rishi appeared placated, his body felt lighter. "But . . . but why did you adopt me really?"

"I told you, Beta, I love you so much."

"But Granny says you adopted me for money."

Meera felt a fire burning in her gut, flickering flames rose to her throat; she gathered herself. "Didn't your granny tell you that Jane had no money?"

"No, Mom! Not my ma's money, but Granny's money."

Meera choked on her tears. "Rishi, I didn't even know your Granny or that she was rich. No, I did not make you my son for money. You are my life, and I love you more than anyone else in the world."

Meera turned her face away to hide her tears, moved Rishi from her lap to the bed, and walked out of the room.

"Why on earth did you tell Rishi? We had an agreement that I will tell him in my own way—"

Mrs. Henderson's harsh and insolent voice interrupted her, "I do as I please! Don't try to bully me." The phone at the other end was banged down with much flourish.

Meera looked at the phone hopelessly and put it on the receiver. She slumped on the couch, to gain her bearings. The yellow light of the street lamp, fell on the wall across the bay window of the living room.

Bright-yellow sunflowers in Van Gogh's painting, that hung on the wall, became alive. Incredulously, in spite his lifelong struggle with severe depression, his creations stand above life; the whole ambiance is transformed with a deepened sense of reality.

But tonight, Meera craved the coolness of jasmine. Many varieties of jasmine inhabit the subcontinent of India. The most popular are chameli, a vine, and motia, a shrub. Chameli blooms have simple but graceful symmetry; more or less flat ivory petals are arranged in a circle around a center where ovary and stamens huddle together.

Motia is a compact flower with many curled petals crowded in a small head. In the summer, the fragrance of a single blooming Motia shrub is carried by the warm breeze and wafts up to the corner of the street.

Meera leaned her throbbing head on the back of the sofa and closed her eyes.

Motia flowers stitched on to the deep-green foliage are sparkling in the soft light of the full moon in moisture-laden monsoon night. Everyone else is sleeping peacefully in their cots, on the roof of Tayaji's house in Delhi. The mali, *gardener,* had carried huge pots of Motia shrubs up the stairs and installed them on the roof for Meera's pleasure. The sweet serenity of the motia perfume is perfusing Meera's heart, the high turbulent waves in the Mansarovar, *a lake in Kashmir,* of her chit, *mind,* subside gently. Tranquility returns.

Meera felt restored, refreshed, bathed in Jasmine much like the Mughal emperors' queens who were the epitome of grandeur and aesthetics. If you visit the palaces and forts of Agra, that was the hub of early 'Mughal' rule, the tourist guide will explain to you, "Mem Saheb, *madam,* this is the bath area where the queens sat on pure marble stools while their maids scrubbed their body with fine muslin packs that were soaked in herbs and flowers imported from the far western mountains of Turkey." Why Turkey? The ancestors of the Mughals reigned in Turkey before they were chased out by surrounding kings. The drops of the attar rubbed on the queen's fair smooth skin lent a fragrant sheen to her body, that evoked Badshah's lust and passion, thus creating countless princesses and princes. It is a different matter that generally the princes tried to kill one another to grab the throne. One of them, Aurangzeb, killed all his brothers by a variety of means and imprisoned his father, Shahjahan, the famous lover who erected Taj Mahal in memory of his dead queen Mumtaz. Such was the power of blossoms that shaped history!

But Meera had to open her eyes and not only face the ugly realities of life but also transcend them.

She took a deep breath, walked over to Rishi's room with calm and poise. She sat down on the floor with Rishi, who was playing with his red car that Meera had given to him on his birthday.

Meera took his soft face in her hands and said lovingly, "I love you the most, my son. You are more real than the real. I will always love you no matter what. Please remember that."

Rishi looked at her complacently, a lock of his golden hair fell carelessly on his brow. "I know, Mom."

"But," he continued after a pause, "Granny also said that I don't have to live in slums. I can live in her big house."

This was a blow below the belt; Meera spoke unsteadily, "But this is your home Beta! I am your mom!" Her eyes shone with tears.

Rishi turned toward Meera and said amusingly, "Oh Mom, I am not going there! I don't even like her, she laughs funny. I like it when you laugh, you look pretty."

Even at that tender age, he understood her pain. He left his car on the carpet, got up, and hugged her. "I love you, Mom!"

Meera had believed that coming to Canada would make her life easier, better. Was Tayaji right when, in his usual, placid voice, he had told her, "Make sure you are not running away from your shadow? It will follow you."

- # -

When Meera raised the idea of returning to Canada, Atul had looked at Meera in shock, visibly irritated and impatient, raising his voice a few notches up. "Are you crazy? How can you even think about it?" Papa had just looked at her with consternation.

Rishi came back from school, dragging his feet, buried his wee face in Meera's soft, silky lap, and whined bitterly, "I don't like school. I am not going!"

It was Rishi's first day at school. Taken from a cozy and secure home and hurled in a jungle of strangers, the uncertainty of shadowy, changeable relationships, having to prove their worth on a daily basis when they have very little idea what that worth is about, can be a punishing experience for children.

Meera did not pay much attention initially, though mornings had metamorphosed into a battleground. "You have to go to school, otherwise, how will you help the world when you are grown-up?"

At this point, Rishi did not care much about his future utility to a world that scared him.

He hated school. Why doesn't Mummy understand?

Mornings were normally like a scene from a railway platform; the hustle-bustle, confounding din of clashing, competing voices.

"Asha, where is my tie? I can never find anything, yar, *friend*!"

"Mummy my ribbon does not match my frock!"

"Can I have some money, the teacher asked us to bring five rupees for the féte next week."

"Aré, chalo, drink your milk first, Nishant. Neeti, eat you eggs." Etc.

That morning, no one noticed Rishi's absence. Meera came out of the bath and announced, "Rishi your turn, hurry up, please."

There was silence. "Rishi, Rishi?" she walked around her bedroom, "You cannot play hide-and-seek now. Let's go! Get ready!

Meera started to search the whole house, "Neeti, did you see Rishi?"

"No, Bua, should I help you look?" She made an attempt to miss school and be helpful at the same time.

"Neeti . . .!" Asha admonished her, "No excuses!"

There was no sign of him. Meera's heart throbbed with fear. She immediately phoned her school and took half a day off, wrapped herself in a woollen shawl and stepped outside. It was early July, not cold but cool in the early hours of the day. The sky was still pinkish, dewdrops shone on the leaves. Meera did not notice. "Rishi, Rishi," she called out while walking around the garden.

Asha turned to Dharma. "Kaka, I will clean up the dining table. Go see where Rishi is. Oh God, I hope he is okay." She quickly prayed to Shivji, *Lord Shiva,* who is considered the easiest God to please.

Dharma was thoughtful as he walked out to the garden. "Choti Bibi, Rishi baba couldn't be out of the house. After Madho delivered milk, I locked the main door. Rishi cannot open it. Let us look inside the house again."

Well, they found him crouching behind a suitcase under Papa's bed.

Meera pulled him out gently, "Come, come to Mummy." He pouted then started to cry. "I don't want to go to school, Mummy!"

Meera placed him on her lap and kissed him on his red, chubby cheeks.

"Okay, but tell me what happened, Beta."

The story of pain and humiliation was delivered amidst sobs and tears, flushed face, and sweaty fists.

The very first day, Rishi started school on a wrong foot. The class teacher asked him, as he had inquired the other boys, "What does your father do?" A banal and inane question as Meera saw it. "What kind of question is that? If someone's father is poor, is that bad?"

That is precisely what it is about. It is customary for the school teachers to probe, right on the first day, into the ancestry of the students and their hierarchical status in society. Once in the possession of the captious insight, they designate the child to his pertinent place in the scheme of things. If the child is descendent of an affluent judge, minister, businessman, or actor/actress, it is imperative to treat him or her with respect and much tolerance; otherwise, the teacher may, soon, receive the papers of his transfer to a remote village where bullock carts are the only transport and mail comes once a month. On top of it, there may be a total lack of medical doctors and facilities for miles around the village. If, however, through the unknowable divine manipulation of stars and planets, the student is born to lowly parentage, the teacher can conveniently and felicitously employ him as the kicking ball to vent whatever frustrations the offspring of the rich are springing on him. Hence, far from being inane, it is the most consequential and exigent question of his career, as far as the teacher is concerned.

Rishi was scared and dumbfounded.

"I don't have a father." He looked down sheepishly.

The teacher was cruel. "Everyone has a father, what happened to yours?"

The handsome man, with a winsome smile, standing in the framed photo on Meera's dresser, was his Papa who died in a car accident in Canada. He felt sad many times when Neeti and Nishant played with Atul and climbed on him for a "horsee" ride.

"Why did my Papa have to go away forever, Mummy?" he'd ask. Meera had no answer to that perpetual question of her life.

Rishi spoke sadly, "He died in Canada."

"Oh . . . Oh . . ." The teacher now seemed more interested in the Canada part.

"So . . . you are a Gora, *white person,* from Canada? Well, all people in Canada went there from some other country! So, your father was from England?"

Rishi swallowed his fear and replied hesitantly, not understanding the relevance of this line of questioning, "My Papa was Indian."

The teacher's eyes shone with mischief; he smiled widely, "Oh, I see. So he was an Indian! How come you look like a Gora?"

There was encouraging laughter from the other kids who were thoroughly enjoying the drama.

"My mummy says I just look different. God made me this way."

"Oh, I see!" the teacher was sarcastic, simultaneously suspicious.

Little Rishi held back his tears at the confusion of not knowing what he had done wrong.

The children, having found grounds for an age-old, sadistic pleasure of teasing and humiliating others, started to chant, "Go-ra, go-ra," when Rishi passed by them.

He came home in tears and asked Meera, "Mummy, what is *gora*?"

Rishi looked undeniably, indisputably from a white race with blond hair, pale white skin, and big blue eyes. People gawked, generally made the worst assumptions, but never asked. Meera had taken Rishi to her school party once. Everyone—staff, students, clerks—took one good look at him and Meera become an instant butt of gossip.

"She must have married a gora."

"God knows what these women see in them."

"She was in Canada, Bhai, she must have met him there." Etc.

Santosh, a good friend of Meera, knew her past. She set out on a mission of much hard work to dissipate the rumors. But Santosh's elucidations and insistence only served to deepen the suspicion and fueled the probing, interrogation, and challenge. "So, where did she get the Gora child from, if her husband was Indian?"

Santosh expounded painfully, "She adopted him."

"Who knows, Bhai," accompanied by shrugs, raised eyebrows, rolling eyes and clicking of tongues! "Who knows what happened in Canada! You were not present! Santosh, you are so gullible! You believe everything, yar, *friend*."

The derisive rumors, true to their nature, diffused in the four directions like scent in the air; with each successive blow of wind intensifying nefariously as well as achieving greater and greater distance. Soon other schools were talking about her too.

Meera was looked down as suspect from then on. She felt bruised and humiliated.

Papa was clear. "Humiliation is theirs who are spreading lies. Stay upright and centered. You know the truth and your God knows it, that is enough. Rumors generally have a short life span because they are borne out of thin air and die of their own weight dissolving back in the thin air. Don't take it personally."

Meera even reminded herself to be like the elephant who walks calmly, majestically, and lets the dogs bark, a strategy taught to them as kids.

It was hard work but she was determined to remain unruffled. Santosh was able to recruit some other sensible teachers to defend Meera. Indeed, quite swiftly, the whole shenanigan faded away.

But Rishi was not let off so easily. The fact that he was not British was deemed irrelevant. During post-British era, in India, anyone who looked white was automatically pigeonholded into the category of the oppressive race, Angrez, *British*. When an authoritative figure like a teacher decides to crucify someone, the devout students display an uncanny loyalty and follow suit.

Meera decided to speak with the teacher.

An elderly man, perhaps in midforties, looked at her from behind his dark-rimmed glasses.

The noise of students playing in the playground just under the window of the teacher's office on the second floor barged in, so did the cold air.

He said, "Excuse me," and shut the window.

"Well?" his tone was defensive, prepared.

Meera was polite, "Mr. Gupta, has Rishi done anything wrong like disrupting the classroom or being disrespectful or disobedient to you?"

Mr. Gupta was taken by surprise by her gentle and nonaccusing demeanor.

"No, he has not," he blurted out.

"He is refusing to go to school because he tells me that you mock him, and other children join. I find it difficult to believe that a gentleman teacher would act thus. Rishi is not a liar, but sometimes children misconstrue or overreact. I want to know from you what is going on."

Meera's open and sincere face disarmed Mr. Gupta. He did not know what to say; unbeknownst to him, a film of tears blurred his vision. He looked up at the wall of his office where a framed photo of Gandhiji hung. How could he lie sitting in the shadow of the great champion of Truth?

Mr. Gupta coughed and cleared his throat, "I will tell you the truth, Meeraji. I have the feeling that you will understand. Yes, I admit I have been treating Rishi unfairly."

"Please, call me Meera, I am much younger to you."

Moist eyes and trembling hands fidgeting with the pen, Mr. Gupta reminisced the story of humiliation and anguish, oppression and tyranny.

He was a young schoolteacher in this school during the British Raj. The principal, administrators, and many teachers were British or Scots.

"Meera, you are lucky you were borne or raised after Independence. I started to work when I was eighteen years old. For long seventeen years, I suffered like millions of other Indians. Slavery is the most sordid and grotesque creation of man. We, 'natives,' were made to feel like worms of sewage. The British treated us as though we were brutes living in jungles and they obliged us by 'civilizing' us. They were always right, and we were always wrong. They had no idea that thousands of years ago, when Indian civilization was at its peak, England was a tribal land where people roamed around in animal skins. Our ancient culture laid the foundation of earliest civilization, the learned and insightful rishis propounded principles of astronomy, mathematics, metaphysics, medicine, grammar, poetry, music, etc. They showed man the way to the highest principle, God, expounded His nature and qualities in the Upanishads. It had been forgotten. I was reprimanded for teaching my students our true history. I applaud western philosophers like Max Müller, who appreciated the Hindu philosophy and translated our scriptures for the western mind. Carl Jung, a German psychiatrist was greatly influenced by Rishi Patanjali's, *a sage 1500 B.C.,* writings about the conscious, unconscious, and superconcious states of mind. Rishi Patanjali was also the founder of yoga and meditation to achieve union with God. But the West was in denial, they did not wish to believe that our civilization had ever been that advanced. They enjoyed the claim of superiority when they beat us with wooden bars, shot us for the crime of looking at their wives or daughters. My nephew was shot because he was talking to a white girl. I did come across many good and moral Englishmen. But too many were intoxicated with power and forgot to follow the Savior Christ's teachings of love and humanity."

Mr. Gupta took a break to wipe his tears with the corners of his sleeve. His face softened. "I feel extremely sorry that I treated your son wrongly. I admit it. Every time I see him I remember the principal's son who had insulted me in front of the whole school. The wound of that humiliation at the hands of a child is still raw, I guess. Please send Rishi to me, I will apologize. How could I forget how it feels to be demeaned? I am so ashamed."

Meera sat still, touched and pained, tears shone in her eyes. "Mr. Gupta, I did not realize that even after twenty-two years, the anguish of slavery is not erased from the Indian psyche. Perhaps the future generation could live at peace with the past because they have not lived the era the way your generations did. I will talk to Rishi and explain your life. He will understand as long as you treat him well."

The unforeseen commiseration he received humbled Mr. Gupta. He lowered his gaze and stood up with folded hands. "King Yudhishthre, *the oldest of the Pandavs,* the cousin of Shri Krishna, was right; forgiveness is the greatest Dharma, *righteous duty,* of man.

Maybe if I could truly forgive the British, I could live at peace. Rishi will have no reason to worry. I assure you."

However, the ball Mr. Gupta had set in motion now rolled on its own, propelled by its intrinsic momentum. The other children, some of them bullies, had no reason to stop their heartless fun. Meera was deeply worried. Damaging experiences at that tender age could injure Rishi's psyche for life. The last straw came in the form of the principal's call informing her rather caustically that Rishi had a fight with a bunch of other kids and got hurt.

It was high time Meera looked for another school in earnest, but in the middle of the school year, no good school would accept him.

In the meanwhile, menacing clouds loomed on the horizon of her days, with imperative foreboding.

All well-meaning relatives—Mamas, Masis, Chachis, Buas, all the friends of Papa's—were making a concerted attempt to straighten her life, with the irrefutable belief that it needed immediate mending. Matches were suggested, proposals brought from Chachi's sister-in-law, Mami's brother-in-law's nephew, Masi's son's mother-in law's cousin, etc.

Meera's repeated recalcitrant rebuttals placed Ma in a precarious predicament. How could she be creative with her excuses without hurting anyone's feelings, the in-law relationships being so delicate? Ma was getting more and more angry with every refused proposal. Tensions rose in the family. Nalini had been unhappy, her wonderful cousin having been rejected unceremoniously. "I was doing you a favor, Choti. You don't know how hard it was to convince him. He is older but is a magistrate. He can find ten unsoiled girls if he wants. He took pity on you and agreed."

Meera suddenly realized that marriage had somehow soiled her.

A storm was brewing, and Meera had no idea how to save herself. Papa was complacent; he knew that storms never endure for long. "Faced with tempest, all we have to do is to keep the stern of our boat straight. It will pass."

Ma lashed out at him, "I am the one who has to hear people talk. She is so young, Rishi is a child. He is not a support for her. But what about once we are gone? Na-ji-na, *no*, you cannot just sit calmly. You have to put pressure on her. She will only listen to you."

Papa refused. "I taught my children everything I know about life. Now, they have to make their own decisions. I will stand by her as long as I am alive. Then her brothers are there."

Ma was flabbergasted. "You are joking! Brothers have their own lives and problems. They are good to her so far, but when some crisis arrives, they will relegate her to a second priority."

She was right. But then who knows how Meera's new husband and his relatives would treat Rishi. Stepfathers generally treat the stepchildren harshly, and his family may not accept a gora child.

Papa took a deep breath and put the newspaper down. He was startled to find Meera sitting across, looking out of the large living room window. Snow-covered peaks looked frigid; spring was on the way, but it was still chilly. Asha still lit the fireplace in the evening.

Meera smiled sadly, "Papa, I have become a worry for you."

"Oh no," he braved. "My children have been a pleasure and pride. I am very lucky. But life cannot always be kind to anyone, Meera. Happy times are followed by challenges and the cycle goes on like day and night. We all have to carry our crosses with forbearance and puissance."

Meera felt lighter. Yes. He is right.

But she noticed the lines furrowing his previously smooth face. Papa had retired last year. A pang of pain tugged at her heart. At this stage of his life, he deserved to live a detached and content life, the Sanyas Astram, *ascetic phase of life.* Instead of giving him happiness, she was the cause of growing tension between him and Ma.

Meera was overcome with sudden fatigue; she came to her room, knelt in front of her small temple that stood in the corner of her room, and prayed.

"Maybe I should go back to Canada." Loving faces sprang up in her mind.

A few months earlier, out of the blue, Meera had received a call from kanchan. She was visiting India and asked Meera to come to Delhi. Unfortunately, she could not leave in the middle of the school year. But it was great to hear Kanchan's shrill, high-pitched voice and catching up with the local gossip. At the mention of Prashant's name, Meera blushed for no reason.

End of April, spring, with its opalescent colors and fragrant zephys, awoke the glum mountains. Rishi came and jumped up and down, "Mummy, Neeti Didi and Nishant Bhaiya are not playing with me! Tell them to, please, please."

"But they are doing their homework, Beta."

"Then you play with me."

"I cannot right now. How about ask Nani, *maternal grandmother*, to read a book to you."

Meera had just returned from a self-reflecting walk in the woods. The slanted, dimming rays of the setting sun passed through the translucent clouds, endowing them with multicolored hues. By the time she was returning, the clouds faded, losing their individuality and blended with the grey skies. The deodars stood upright, unmoved through all the transitions, just bent a little to salute the setting sun.

"Papa, Bhai, I have been thinking. I should go back to Canada."

Atul's eyes widened, forehead crinkled, jaw dropped in incredulity. His voice was sharp. "What is wrong here?"

"There are problems, Bhai."

"But children always have one problem or another." He assumed that Meera's abrupt proposition had roots in Rishi's problems at school.

"No, it is not just that, Bhai."

"Then?" He fixed his penetrating gaze on Meera's eyes in an attempt to intimidate, as he always did when someone disagreed with him. It might have been a beneficial, manipulative skill in a courtroom.

Since Meera had been exposed to Atul's intimidation tactics all her life, she was not affected.

She spoke firmly, "I received a letter from Rishi's grandmother." To soften the expected blow of the words, she intentionally did not say Mrs. Henderson.

"So?" Atul was angry. Obviously, it did not work.

"Well, Rishi is her only grandchild, in fact, her only blood relative. She does love him, Bhai, I have no doubt. Maybe seeing her will do Rishi good."

Atul shook his head in an "I don't believe it" nod. Meera was subdued a little this time for she knew that the amplitude of his nod indicated the potency of his "Over my dead body" remonstrance.

Before he could steam his annoyance, Papa intervened, "Meera, it is a serious decision. Take time to think it over. There are problems here, but we are here to help you. Different issues will face you there, and you will be alone."

Atul interrupted brusquely, "And this grandma is the one your friend Jane wanted you to keep Rishi away from. Didn't she?"

"Bhai, I will never let her hurt Rishi. He is not going to live with her. They can visit in my presence. But her love will nurture him. Someday I will have to tell Rishi that he is adopted. A blood relative close at hand will give him more grounding."

Meera continued sadly, "I must admit, I feel sorry for her. She is alone in her old age, she has reached out and wishes to connect with her grandson."

Mrs. Henderson had apologized, poured out a couple of tears on the letter, describing herself on an old dying, lonely person who would like her grandson's love to brighten her last days.

"I also want to make up for the pain I conferred on my beloved Jane," Mrs. Henderson had added.

Meera lay in bed many nights with Mrs. Henderson's stern face haunting her. Quite cleverly Granny had thrown a carrot in a letter. "Of course, Rishi will inherit my estate. My soul will be at peace to know that my dear grandson will have a good life."

Could Meera deprive Rishi of that legacy? Would that be right?

She recognized that Rishi was not a genius; he showed average intelligence. Who knows how he would do, academically. She also knew that she would never have enough money to help him start a good business of his own. With Granny's inheritance, Rishi will have future security.

And then, Granny has repented, asked for forgiveness. As a moral human, Meera could not deny her another chance.

Also, Rishi would enjoy the sense of belonging amid other white children. His difficulties at school will disappear. A weight lifted off her heart at that thought.

To have the relatives off her back would be an added benefit.

It was over everyone's objections that Meera left for Canada. The night before Meera's flight, Tayayi cautioned, "The nature of life is such that it never frees us of entangles. Decisions should be made on the basis of whether they are right according to the rules of Dharma. Do not choose any path as an escape because no path is free from thorns and sharp-edged stones. Where will you abscond again? But if your step is to serve the 'Truth and Dharma,' the thorns in your path will turn into flowers. Then I bless you."

She was doing everything in Rishi's best interest, that was her foremost dharma, wasn't it? The fact that she expended much energy to convince herself made Meera uneasy. But she did not wish to scratch the surface, because she had to go.

- # -

Bela was understanding. "It is all right, Maalti, you can go. Should Sunilji give you a ride?"

Maalti had looked at her watch, "Oh God, I have to go home for puja, *prayers.* I have to give bath to Govind Gopal, *another name for Shri Krishna,* and give him bhog, *food that is offered to God.*" Her utterance was cloaked with the faith of certainty. Asha suppressed her laughter, pressed her lips hard, her eyes twinkled with amusement.

"No, Di, I will walk."

Spring had finally arrived with much fanfare; the sun shone with the excitement, the sky was bluer than before, trees swayed dizzily with the pleasantly cool wind. A carpet of pristine soft green grass veiled the brown earth. Birds expressed their joy noisily while hopping on the buds-laden tree branches.

Five of them—Bela, Meera, Maalti, Kanchan, and Asha—had made a solemn pact to go for a long walk on the weekends. Bela's house was closest to Henderson river trail; they gathered there. Expanding waistlines and much-ado about the godforsaken chole-something was behind the newly discovered health conciousness. Cutting back on delicious chicken curry and gulab jamun was not an option. "Aré, we cannot let the quality of life get ruined!" So, there was no choice but to burn the culinary excesses by exercise, before it turned into the heart-attack-inducing lethal-chole-something.

Normally, they parted company after the walk. Today, men folk rebelled; they felt grossly neglected by the new alliance of women folk that rudely excluded them. They demanded *channa puri* lunch for appeasement.

The greediest exotic food lover, Prashant, had disappeared again, much to Bela di's chagrin. "Let him come, I will show him." Show him what was left unclear; Meera knew Di would deflate in one minute by Prashant's chikna, *smooth*, chamchagiri, *buttering*.

Asha rolled on the couch with mirth until tears floated in her black, snaky eyes.

She wiped her happy tears and rolled her eyes in adolescent contempt. "My God, I don't believe it! The stone statue bath, Bhog, in this modern age? Height of ignorance!"

Meera countered, "Well, if God is omnipresent and permeates all manifest existence, why not the stone statue, then?"

Asha hated Meera's untimely, inessential philosophizing, taking all the fun out of making fun of others.

Bela took note of rapidly evolving frown on Asha's shining-with-makeup forehead, and before it could translate into obnoxious vociferation, she spoke hurriedly, "Let us go and start lunch, Bhai, men must be hungry."

Arun retorted, "Where have you been, ladies? We are starved!"

Arun thrived on agitation: "I am because I agitate." He acted civilized in social gatherings, but Maalti had dropped hints of his pugnacity.

Anil looked at Arun. "Yar, *friend*, let them enjoy whatever they want to do. They don't exist to serve us!"

Anil wore a perpetual expression of embarassment, a quiet guilt, in his dark-brown fluid eyes. Meera was sure he was not aware of why; he had never hurt a fly!

Chachaji floated above like a buoyant playful cloud; the mere fact of its lightness rendering it unreachable and unsullible. He was cognizant of the unabated fluidity of kal, *eternal time*, the relentless concatenation of caravan of moments that comprise human existence. He maundered unimpeded into past, present, and future in his search for Truth while resolutely recusant to adhere. Truth in its infinite glory cannot be embodied within determinate units of time. How do you really fathom truth of the present moment that is an offspring of past and the seed of future?

To grasp the whole Truth of anything is impossible for man due to the limitations of time and space. Because of the time-imposed changeability of empirical world, what seems to be Reality outside of us is in fact Real but not True. Truth is absolute and eternal. Every object in manifest world is in constant flux because of the electromagnetic forces that move electrons and protons, etc. Is the object we perceive now True, or it's transformed state five minutes later?

According to Dr. Radha Krishnan, an eminent philosopher, "What is naught in the beginning and is not in the end is naught in the middle. Hence there is no true existence that can be assigned to the empirical world."

Our pursuit of Reality is not only hampered by time but also by the limitations imposed by space. Dr. Radha Krishnan pointed out regarding human understanding, "There is a Real but we are unable to see the whole. We only view parts of it at one time. We are doomed to contend with fractured Reality, depending on where we stand in relation to it."

Four blind men were loitering in a dense jungle. They came upon an elephant who was sitting complacently on the ground. Attempting to identify what obstructed their pleasant walk, one man happened to touch the elephant's leg. "It is a tree!" he exclaimed. The other touched the elephant's ears and contradicted, "Oh no, it is a big-sized fan." The elephant, somewhat irritated by the human touch, hit his long nose against the third man who panicked, "You stupids, it is a big snake, run." The all-wise fourth man groped the torso and told them all to shut up. "It is only a rock."

To further complicate our search for empirical Reality, there is space between the object and our "perceiving mechanism," namely our senses and brain. The rose bloom is at a distance from our eyes and brain. Our eyes see the object and send the corresponding message to the optical nerve to the brain where real perception mechanism is located. Hence, we do not really know the Truth of the object because all we have seen is its image in the mind. That is Maya, illusion.

Having grasped the nature of Maya, Chachaji did not judge. He forgave Asha. So did Meera for a different reason, even after the khichri, *cooked rice and lentil,* episode.

Asha stared at the steel container that Meera was holding in her right hand.

"And what is that, may I ask?"

"Oh, some khichri. I thought Chachaji may like it. How is his flu?" Meera made a gallant attempt to divert Asha's attention from the troublesome container.

Meera had prudently planned to arrive at Anil's mansion after Asha should have left for work. She was taken by surprise when Asha stood at the main entrance and stared annoyingly at her.

Asha queried stridently, "Aren't you working?"

Meera tried to laugh off her discomfort. "I was about to ask you the same question, Doctor Sahiba? What is happening to your patients?"

"I was late last night, there was an emergency. I am just leaving."

Meera had chosen to endure Asha's sinuous tongue because she did not want to lose Anil and Chachaji. Also, she suffered from a genetically inherited fatal flaw; she lacked the talent of pernicious speech.

Asha retorted with unhidden dissonance, "Why do you have to bring food? Do you think I don't feed him? People believe that I am not good to him. Why don't they"—her pitch elevated with each word—"take him, he can live with them?"

Meera smiled to pacify Asha. "No, I don't think that you don't feed him,"

Asha scorned, "Yes you do! I make lunch for him every day before I leave for work. Can you imagine the hassle? I work like a dog all day."

"Of course you do, I know that. But I had made khichri for Rishi so bought some for him. There is no harm, Asha, I also love him."

Meera had no idea that her utterance was akin to a diminutive spark that could burn forests. Asha's face turned red, her eyes flashed fiercely; she spitted poison. "I have no idea what people see in him! He is an uneducated, uncultured villager, a lowly schoolteacher. My God, he thinks he is a philosopher or a rishi. He spent all his life teaching filthy, ill-mannered children from chamar, *untouchable*, families."

Meera had no curiosity to find out Chachaji's background. His transcendence and poise dazzled her; wherever he was from was a holy place for her.

Now she understood why the first time she touched his feet at Bela's house, Chachaji's eyes had moistened.

Asha continued and flew her arms in the air with dismissive callousness. "You know my daddy was deputy commissioner, we only knew Anil was well educated and settled abroad. My masi brought the rishta, *proposal.* Who knew what an illiterate background he comes from? To love that stupid, ignorant man, you can do better than that!"

Meera was speechless.

Asha did not stop there. "And you? You love to put others down to show that you are somehow superior! Well, you are not. And I refuse to put up with your façade of goody-goodyness. Go away and do not come to visit Anil's father unless we are here. We do not want people filling his ears with stuff against us!"

Chachaji had heard Meera's voice from his bedroom upstairs and called out excitedly, "Meera, is that you, Beti? Come on up. This old fellow cannot get out of bed."

Asha yelled angrily, "She has not come to see you, so don't shout."

The injured silence upstairs dug into Meera's heart. She turned around without a word and walked away. That was the beginning of the end of her friendship with Asha.

- # -

From the living room came a shout—Sunil's voice, "Come quickly you kitchen crowd!"

It was pitch-dark outside, days were too short, the sun having been rudely pushed beyond the horizon quite early in the evening. Children were quiet for a change because they were watching a movie in the basement.

Bela, Kanchan, Maalti, and Meera moved en masse toward the living room with swift steps.

"What? What?" they queried in unison.

The response from the men was at least three "sh sh sh's"; their eyes were affixed on the TV screen.

"Aré, isn't that Mr. Bhandari, the high commissioner of India?" Kanchan exclaimed.

"Yah, Bhai, stay quiet, let us hear him!" Arun's irritated, boisterous voice stomped in their ears.

"Why is he . . .?" Bela wondered aloud.

Meera set her momery to work. "Today is Republic Day!" she whispered to Bela while scanning the room to find a suitable place to sit.

Meera was abashed. How could she forget such a momentous day?

Republic Day meant a trip to Delhi, if they were not already at Tayaji's house for the winter break. All the cities, towns and villages of free India celebrated Republic Day by organizing mini parades of their own plus the usual speeches by the political leaders that no one paid any attention to. But Delhi parade and festivities were naturally the most fabulous of all. Special trains and buses overflowing with humans, hanging precariously out of doors or perched dangerously on the train and bus roofs, converged on Delhi starting from a few days before the big day.

In the early fifties, Republic Day was celebrated with much grandstanding; the masses were intoxicated with rapture, India had finally taken charge of its destiny. A committee of veteran leaders, who had fought all their lives for this glorious day, burnt midnight oil, bent over constitution of other developed, Democratic nations seeking ideas for carving out the framework for a just and humane society. The fruit of two years of toil, the Constitution that emerged was lauded the world over because it not only incorporated the modern concepts of law, justice and freedom but also the essence of ethics and morality that were the pinnacle of ancient philosophical thought and wisdom of India.

Overwhelmed by frenzy, undeterred citizens lined up under ancient pippal, mango, and kikkar trees that lined the cordoned off route that the procession was to take. Cold water dripped from the shivering leaves from a recent or current shower of rain; overcast skies spewed an occasional drizzle. Blessing of the demiGod of rain is considered auspicious by Hindu priests, which explains adequately why the fathers of the nation did not choose a bright, sunny, spring day to proclaim India's coming of age. People would arrive at the scene the night before, bundle up and doze off beneath the dripping trees on the hard, cold ground to secure a good view of the parade.

The first president of free India, Dr. Rajendra Prashad, a quiet, behind-the-scene head of the country, was a dedicated freedom fighter. He was the lawyer who won the case against the British Raj who forced farmers to grow indigo, a much-valued dye that was a lucrative export, while they starved because of lack of food. This happened in Bihar, the poorest province of India at the best of times.

Dr. Rajendra Prashad would be wearing a simple white cotton kurta, pajama, beige cotton vest, a white Gandhi Topi, *cap,* and be seated on a horse-driven carriage with perfect poise. During and after the struggle for independence, Gandhi Topi became an essential component of Congress members' attire as a symbol of devotion to Gandhian principles. It was ironic that Gandhiji seldom used it; he only wore a shine in his bald head, perhaps his brilliance oozed out of his brain on the skin.

Preceded by the top military head honchos riding in jeeps, Dr. Prashad's carriage slowly passed with people cheering slogans, "Rajinder Prasad Ki Jai," "Bharat Mata, *Mother India,* ki Jai."

He would alight from his carriage in front of a raised podium, take a few steps up, and stand upright. Carriages carrying Nehruji, Molana Azad, Moraiji Desai, and some other esteemed Congress leaders followed, and they joined the president on the podium.

A stunning display of India's military might kicked off the parade. Young, healthy, strong sepoys, dressed in forest green crisp uniforms, marched upright in utter dignity, eyes shining with pride of responsibility, their heads held high piercing the shroud of the crisp January mist. Their left hand held a rifle that leaned against their broad shoulders, the right hand raised in salute. Sophisticated, intimidating armaments like huge guns, cannons, tanks, models of fighter planes, etc., were propped and displayed on floats, giving Indians a neoteric sense of chivalry and fervor, a tangible audacity that they could take on all enemies and drive them into the Arabian Sea without qualms.

Music bands dressed in slick uniforms walked in step and played the many patriotic songs harmoniously with their instruments.

Other pageants from all the fourteen states that constituted the Republic of India, followed depicting landmark historical events, played out in still by actors and actresses wearing gaudy, flamboyant raiments, riding on floats that passed smoothly by. Elephants of Rajasthan, decorated with embroidered, deep-red, orange, purple, yellow, deep-blue, brilliant-colored mantles walked majestically, curled up their trunks and saluted the leaders of India standing proudly in the podium as well as citizens lining the street.

Loud nationalistic slogans by the citizens who would be moved to tears, scattered in the skies. This was their India, their Republic Day, they could shout, dance, jump with joy, and they were free to do it. They deserved it. Crowds constantly jostled to get a better view. If you were lucky to be a small child, you would be propped on your father's, older brother's or uncle's broad shoulders and ask in a whine "Who is that? What is that? What are they doing? I like the trumpet, Bapu, *father,* can I have it . . . I want a rifle like those men in green shirts, Bapu? . . . I want to be a soldier? Can I, can I, please?" Bapu's eyes would glisten with tears of pride; he would raise his hand and pat the gallant son on his tiny head. "Yes you will, you will, son. We must protect our Bharat Mata. Never again shall we be slaves."

Many glances of approbation, smiles, and nods. "Shabash, *expression of pride,* Beta. We need brave children like you," would be passed on to the courageous son-father team temporarily and then of course turn to more flaunting scene on the street.

Those were early fifties. Meera would stand in front of the whole school and lead them in singing nationalistic songs as well as the national anthem or act in plays for Republic Day functions. Excitement prevailed for weeks.

And today she forgot it! Without her cognition, slowly, imperceptibly, the sharp-edged-Kal had sliced and banished her from her roots, the very font of her existence. Here she was, a shadow of her true self, wandering in an alien desert chasing mirage.

Bela Di had spoken wistfully, "Meera, do you realize that we can never go back home? Our children are here: they will settle and have families. These ties are much stronger than the ones we left behind. Also, slowly, our parents are passing on." She wiped her tears with the palloo of her saree.

Bela's mother had died recently. Tragically, she had to apply for a visa to enter her own motherland. That took time; her siblings had to cremate the body before Bela could reach India. Towns and villages do not have cold storages; the bodies of the dead are incinerated within twelve hours of their departure from this world.

Bela could never forgive herself for being so far away.

"In the last twenty-six years since we won our independence, we have made unprecedented progress, not only materially but also morally. We have given Indians a much better life compared to the last millennium of slavery . . ."

Anil mumbled, "Nonsense." No one noticed. The speech went on with much exaggerated flourish about the leaps of advancement India had taken.

Speech ended. Anil could not soften his pungent retort. "Progress? Progress? I will tell you what has progressed in India. Corruption! You will not believe it!" Anil had just returned from India; his sister had a lung surgery. He had gone after seven years.

He continued with much angst, "You cannot get anything done at any Government office from buying railway ticket to cashing travellers' checks in a bank, unless you grease some palms, many palms. You cannot move one inch without paying someone for the space for your foot. Story is the same in other business offices. People have become so morally depraved that they do not feel any shame. They ask for bribes openly and grin."

It was impossible to contest that statement. Satish remarked sadly, "You know what bothers me the most? Thousands of patriots sacrificed their lives, quit their comfortable jobs and families, took bone-breaking lathi, *long sticks used by police,* charges, went to jail—many died of diseases or torture there. All that for the love of their motherland. Now, they will sell their mothers for money."

It was harsh, Bela admonished. "Satish!"

"It is true, Bhabi! Money has replaced God. Even relationships have become victims of greed. Some people do not see their relatives who are poor. Siblings fight for their share of inheritance even while the parents are alive! Cheat, rob, hurt—no one has any qualms about degrading behavior for money. Why do supposedly civilized humans behave so depraved, Chachaji?"

In desperation, Satish turned to the most sagacious person in the room. Chachaji's forehead furrowed. "What an eternal enigma, it is as irresolvable in kaliyug, *immoral times,* as it was in tretayug, *an earlier more moral phase,* thousands of years ago. Standing on his golden chariot that was driven by white horses, in the middle of two seemingly unconquerable armies poised to annihilate each other, Arjun, the bravest Pandu, had turned to Shri Krishna and lamented,

'Keshav, why do people sin knowing full well that this cataclysmic path can only lead to bouleversement and perdition?'

"The Maha Sanyasi, *the greatest ascetic*, unruffled and self-possessed, Shri Krishna had replied, "Arjun, all sinful acts emanate from one of the five 'vikars', *pollutants of our minds*, the worst enemies of man: ego, lust, anger, greed, and attachment—ego being the fountain head of the rest. Hence, in most religions, man is advised to subjugate ego, the other enemies having lost their font, will die a quiet death.

"The ancient sages declared, 'Whoever has conquered his ego and vanquished his five enemies, is Sidh, *self-fulfilled Spiritualist*. Do not conquer the world, conquer your 'self.'"

Satish objected, "But even if I conquer my ego, I am still besieged by those who have not. The Pandav crown Prince Yudhishthre was the most righteous, truthful, forgiving, and kind soul, yet demonic Kaurav Duryodhan inflicted so much pain, injustice and cruelty on the Pandavs that Yudhishthre was forced to fight the bloody war of Kurukshetra."

Sunil resigned, "Well, if every one of us clean up his act, maybe there will be a ripple effect."

It was surprising that Arun had not spoken a word for so long. He found himself and spoke ferociously, "Forget it! What are you talking about? India has millions of stupid, greedy, vulturous, creeps who will never change. There is only one answer."

He got everyone's attention.

"India needs a dictator who would be tough enough to clean up the country. Democracy is too soft a concept for such rogues!"

Anil laughed softly. "You mean another Hitler who will just send millions to gas chambers, finito. That's it, good idea."

Everyone in the room could barely muster a hollow laugh.

While Rishi dozed in his car seat, it was quite late when they left the party, Meera quietly mourned the loss of the beloved homeland of her childhood.

What did *Republic* mean to indigent masses who were stomped upon by "white sahebs" before independence and "brown sahebs" after? Had the promises made to jubilant, hopeful masses, on that much awaited, fateful first Republic Day of free India on a chilly, January 26, 1950, been realized? If not, should we celebrate or grieve the forfeiture of Mahatama Ghandi's vision, a hapless victim of the egomaniac and venal human nature?

- # -

Meera looked around in puzzlement, "Have you lost your way, Ji?"

Prashant gave her a strange glance, "No, I have finally found my way."

The queer reverberation in his voice frightened her. Meera tried to laugh. "Come on, don't look so serious."

Prashant quietly steered the car toward the edge of the railing that ran along the river. The lights on the bridge reflected and quivered in the moving waves of the river water. It had been raining; the water level was unusually high. Clouds above deepened into dark grey, threatening more rain.

Prashant turned the engine off and leaned his head against the headrest. A silence, heavy with weight of subtle foreboding and a turning-point-in waiting, hung in the car.

"How lovely the river looks." Meera had to break the ice to calm her palpitating heart. The faint mumbling of the river created a mysterious backdrop.

Prashant did not respond. Meera's head felt dizzy with unknown emotion.

After a few minutes, Prashant spoke hesitatingly. "I need ambiguity of darkness around me to give me courage to say I want to tell you."

Meera had hardly stepped into the house when she heard Rishi on the phone talking excitedly, "Yes Uncle! I would love to . . . promise? Mom is not home yet. Oh no, I can hear the garage door open, she is here . . ." He shouted, "Mom . . . Prashant uncle is on the phone."

Prashant's voice was even. "Hello stranger, have you left the country?"

Embarrassment had stalked Meera ever since the car episode. Prashant's casual dismissive tone relaxed her.

"See who is talking! You pulled your disappearing act again, this time, Bela Di has plans to punish you. Where do you go anyway?"

Meera regretted the moment those words spilled out of her mouth.

Prashant's voice was unusually mellow. "I will tell you, Meera." Then, his intonation took its usual tenor. "In the meanwhile, I have two tickets for a concert tonight. A black blues singer from Tennessee is touring Canada. We will drop Rishi at Bela Bhabi's. I have already talked to her."

A warm assuaging cheer rose in her heart. It was very much like him to arrange everything beforehand; others were left with no excuse to decline his proposition.

"Please, do not say no. You need a change, or maybe I do. And who else will be able to enjoy Western music but the 'music master' herself?"

Meera was astounded to find how akin Western classical music was to Indian classical music in its intricate rendering, infinite expanse yet chastity of expression that touched the spirit. The Western orchestras awed her; the flourish of different sounds building up to the climax, all instruments in synchrony, expressing different tonalities yet in harmony, crisscross of many silver yarns to create one stunning mantle.

Centuries of black suffering in his liquid deep dark eyes, Noel Cross's heavy base and velvet smooth voice expanded at a wide range with a touching quiver that rendered the anguish in his eyes all the more poignant. All the songs were about human suffering, cruelties, lost lives, longings, and in spite of all the above, beauty. Isn't that what all this is about?

Meera discovered that not all but some pop music presented a luscious coupling of mellifluous tunes and powerful lyrics to create euphonious songs. Meera and Rishi listened to Beatles, Elvis, and Nat King Cole. More thorny years of Rishi's adolescence were ahead of them; he needed every shred of shared beauty of the past moments to pull him through when life would be perplexing, tangled with clashes of expectations and demands of an enigmatic outside world.

Meera was worried. How would Rishi forge his identity without the male role model to provide him with a tangible hub to build himself around? Maybe it was God's plan to bring Prashant, in her life in which case, she should stop sabotaging the hand of destiny.

An ambiguous hazy darkness suddenly arose around them, Meera held her breath; her hands were cold.

She forced words out of her mouth, her tongue having been stuck to her palate, "Go ahead, Prashantji."

Meera could hear herself speak as though she was the witness of a drama. At all the crossroads of our lives, we abscond ourselves and stand aside.

Prashant waited. The lights on the bridge flickered in the dark like jugnus, *fireflies.*

"I was married twelve years ago. Kavita's parents and my parents were great friends. When I came to Vancouver, I stayed with them for the initial few weeks while I looked for a job and accommodation. Both sets of parents decided to turn friendship into a relationship; Kavita and I got married soon after. Bapu, *father,* was not well so my parents did not come to Canada for our wedding."

His voice resonated from the past, an echo striking against the rigid walls of the stygian tunnel through which Prashant was stumbling with a weary hope of light at the end of it.

Prashant paused for a few minutes then continued, "Kavita was a sweet, shy girl. I liked her a lot. The first month was glorious; it was spring, we were surrounded by immense natural beauty, it was easy to fall in love. I had a good job, life was perfect—at least I thought it was. Generally, I came home late. Clients wanted to see cars in the evenings. One day she had a fit of rage when I came home late. I was totally shocked. I explained to her the nature of my job, she seemed to understand, cried, and apologized. But it started to happen often. Bir Chachaji, her father, talked to her. It was as though she did not hear us. The rational part of her brain was overwhelmed by a savage frenzy. She blew up like a 'volcano' on small issues. I did my best not to do anything that would displease her. I was walking on broken glass, Meera."

The mention of her name, just the act, brought home to Meera that it was her own story; she belonged there not as a witness but as a participant. What occurred then had everything to do with what was happening now. Past, present, and future are an unfractured continuum.

"Slowly, I realized that it was more than plain anger. Sometimes Kavita looked like Kali, *the demi Goddess of destruction of evil,* with wild fiery eyes, a red distorted face, and clenched fists. I was scared that she would hurt me.

"An agonizing year passed. One day I came home to find that Kavita had a broken glass bottle in her hand, curses poured out of her twisted lips. 'I am going to kill you. I know you want to get rid of me.' I struggled to get the bottle from her hand, we both got cuts all over our hands, arms and faces. I managed to retrieve the bottle, pinned her down, and phoned her father.

"Bir Chachaji is a decent man. He worked in a lumber factory all his life and raised his three children, one girl and two boys. He came, and we called 911 and took her to the hospital. Chachaji sat in the waiting room, looked at me with moist eyes and spoke in a trembling voice. 'Kavita has been having fits ever since she was fifteen. We did not know anything and hoped that a married life and a good husband could cure her. I was wrong, and I am ashamed that I did not tell you, Prashant. Will you ever forgive me?' He fell on my feet. I picked him up and hugged him. 'Chachaji, you do not make or break destinies. The one up there has that job. We will do our best to get her treated. She will be fine!' I had faith. We had heard in India medical miracles happen in the West.

"We took Kavita to a well-known psychiatrist who told us without flinching, "She has a rare 'intermittent explosive disorder.' You must institutionalize her, otherwise, she could kill herself or someone else." He admitted regretfully, "There is no treatment, though research is being pursued actively."

"That did not help us. It was so painful. I spent nights agonizing over what else I could have done.

"She is in a psychiatric institution in Vancouver. Still unstable, violent sometimes, she cries when I visit her especially when I leave. It breaks my heart, Meera. I am so weary, I could just lie on my bed and sleep forever."

In the dim light of the streetlamps, Meera saw a broken man crushed by the mills of God.

His sad black eyes gleamed with tears, like two lost stars. Their tormented light seeped into Meera, melted her away till she was nothing but Prashant's shadow. Was this the destination she was constantly running away from?

She did not know that truth is pompous and ruthless; you cannot snub it for long. It will hound you no matter which remote wilderness you hide in. One fine day, it will find you and bare you to yourself.

Meera was wonderstruck as she felt the glow of truth shine in her heart. She stretched her hand and touched Prashant's wet cheek and gently wiped his tears away.

It had started to drizzle. Tiny droplets shone against the windshield of the car, coalesced into larger drops, and slid down in streaks. Headlights of another car fell on them. In that bright light, Prashant's face looked stony and ashen. The car parked at a distance, the lights were turned off, and everything was black again.

Meera took Prashant's masculine hand and wrapped it in her warm palms tenderly. "Whatever happened in the past, you cannot change it. It has ended. Do your duty, but do not carry the burden, Prashantji."

Prashant left his hand in Meera's and looked away searchingly. "Nothing ever ends, every event itself, being part of the chain, propels further actions leading to consequences that chase our present like a sleuth hound."

It was a stinging truth of life. Meera could not contradict it. She just kissed Prashant's hand gently.

Prashant extended his strong arms, wrapped her, and pressed her head against his broad chest where his aching heart had longed for the touch of her body. The audacious scent of his body immured her; a surge of tepid fire that arose from her loins set her ablaze. Meera quivered at the rapturous force of the long-forgotten passion.

Prashant bent his head down, his lips searched for hers. Meera shut her eyes and raised her flushed face; Prashant kissed her impetuously, deeply on her open lips.

Meera floated helplessly in a glowing river of lava that was warm, soothing but demanding. She had no clue where it was taking her, and she did not care.

A smiling, contented face of Mohit rose up in Meera's eyes; she kept her eyes tightly closed, tears welled, she pleaded, "Mohitji, you understand, na?"

Prashant hugged her tight and asked desperately, "Meera, will you walk with me?"

"Yes, yes," she whispered. She knew that Mohit had come to bless her, once more.

The watchman was about to close the doors of the conservatory. He smiled when he saw Meera; she was a pleasant regular. Before she could say anything, he said, "It is okay, ma'am, you can spend some time. I will do other stuff in the meantime." Meera grinned broadly, "Thank you so much, Peter, we will not be long." Peter looked intently and curiously at the dark and handsome man who smiled at him but did not ask anything; he nodded to Prashant's pleasant "Hi."

Meera was transformed into a spirit gliding smoothly amongst the rows of blossoms, her face glowed with inner peace and pulchitrude. Holding Prashants's hand, she bent unselfconsciously to sniff some flowers, looked at others with infatuated eyes, and nodded her head incredulously at their unparalleled grandeur. Prashant watched her, half amused, half in wonderment. Meera's love affair with beautiful blooms was eternal; a smile flitted across her serene face as she spoke to them silently and listened to their colorful music. They were her loyal friends forever; Meera had to share all her moments with them. She had come to them to borrow their embalming grace in order to lend some semblance of beauty to her embattled life. She owed them this visit. Meera touched, caressed the flowers tenderly as she passed by maroon dahlias, multicolored pansies, radiant white, pink, red roses. With uplifted faces, they had waited for her.

- # -

"Thank God," Maalti looked up at her invisible God. "He is merciful, Vivek got admission in medical college."

All immigrant Indians, friends of Meera, hankered for their offspring to be doctors. It was quite obvious that the zeal had nothing to do with compassion for the suffering humanity. Of course, no one admitted it directly, but it could be deduced rather quickly that money had much to do with their ardor.

The second disappointed choice was law then engineering. Commerce was a dubious choice because of the uncertainties involved in the economic sector.

The youngsters, who were not chosen by gods to have a future in the most favoured professions, only received a reluctant nod, "That is nice, Beta," when they announced excitedly, "Uncleji, Uncleji, I am going to major in sociology!"

On the other hand, the med-school admittee was honored with Temple Puja and lavish, curried langar, *meal,* afterward. The celebration was incomplete without the full-blown party of rejoicing in the evening with outpourings of congratulations and drinks in that order.

Bela was wistful. Rohit was not doing well in studies and was also rumored to be doing other unsavory activities like going to bars, staying up late, going around with white girls, and all that forbidden stuff.

Arun interrupted belligerently, "What do you mean Thank God the Merciful? What does He have to do with anything?" He turned to Meera hopefully, "This is what has sunk Indians. This decrepit reliance on Gods, Ganesh, Shiva, etc., such nonsense. They do not work hard and then blame it on gods!"

"Don't talk like that, Ji," Maalti whined. "You are not thankful, but let me be!"

Meera came to Maalti's rescue. "Direct proportionality between hard work and reward is not a consistent fact. Toil is not always equal to success. Other factors, beyond human control play a significant part in fruition of our actions in life. Maalti calls them God, what is your problem?"

Arun threw up his large, arborescent hands in a gesture of frustration at the dim-witted females and stomped out of the kitchen to join supposedly a more sagacious crowd in the living room.

Men were as always deeply engrossed in the ponderous task of resolving all the world enigmas, instantly, the amplitude of the pandemonium being a direct measure of consensus or deep divisions amongst the masses. While the living room was alive with conflicting voices, the kitchen air was perfused with the flavor of peppery spice and tantalizing tattle—who went to India, what are the current fashions in jewelry and apparel, what are the latest tricks of the trade to escape the Customs when you are bringing twenty-two-carat gold jewelry, were morsels of intelligence that were of plenary consequence for the next visitor to India who could be anyone.

The basement resounded with sometimes playful sometimes combative uproar of children.

Meera only attended small parties of close friends now. The earlier years, after Mohit's death and after she returned to Canada, she attended colossal gatherings where practically everyone belonging to the small Indian community was invited. People regarded her with a condescending posturing, an unpalatable amalgamation of pity, and feigned sympathy that was especially distasteful when they called her bechari, *poor thing*. Their commiseration soon vanished, giving way to malevolent excoriation; no one could fathom Meera's battle for Rishi's custody. She could not explain because no one asked her; their snide, grating remarks were always voiced behind her back.

Meera's self-proclaimed well-wishers benevolently furnished her with an exaggerated version of what someone allegedly said about her. Jyoti made an empathetic holier-than-thou face, "I don't know why Usha does not understand your problem! I told her frankly, it is Meera's decision! Poor thing, she has lost her husband, she needs someone. But Vimal said, 'Meera is young and pretty, why does she not get married again?' But what! Neelam is right 'It is easier said than done, who marries widows?' I am sorry, Meera, you are such a nice lady, but men can find unmarried young girls by the dozens, why should they marry a widow? Eh? We know these men! They can do whatever they want to, who can stop them, but they will not take a woman who has been . . . you know what I mean."

Neelam was the ringleader of the gossip club. Her daughter Vimmy was Anita's age group. Sometimes Bela invited the Neelam family. Her husband had a dubious export-import business, dubious because no one knew what he imported or exported. But he was congenial, hence forgiven.

In the kitchen, around the cooking pots, the women congregation stood. Neelam's eyes rolled, lips twitched, eyebrows danced with the intensity of the issue; her hands flew in all directions for maximum effect. "You know what, Gupta's Vijay was found dancing in a bar with, what do you know, a gori, *white*. He is gone, hooked, finished. God knows what these goris have. Our boys reject such goody-goody girls of our community and run after them with their tongues hanging out and tails wagging! Gosh! These good-for-nothings would sleep with, God knows, how many boys before they get married and how many after. No Dharma, no culture yar, this gori race."

Meera's face flushed with the awkward realization that her son was gora. Bela shushed Neelam. She was unyielding, glanced at Meera critically, and blurted out gallantly, "Bhai, I am very frank kind of person. I don't know how you can feel in your heart that Rishi is your son."

Meera's blood rose to her face, not in anger but defiance against the sheer turpitude of such a remark. "But I do" she said calmly.

Bela tried to divert the attention. "Food is ready. I will call the children first."

Chachaji was comfortably perched on a dining chair right across from where Meera stood in the kitchen. Their eyes met. He smiled and coughed for attention. He faced Neelam with his usual halcyon placidity, "Beti, we are children of the same God. Why this hostility?"

Neelam's eyes sparkled with venomous odium, her voice assumed sinuous acerbity, "Lest you forget, Chachaji, these children of God tyrannized us, as slaves. How can we love them while they hated and humiliated us?"

"But, Beti, Rishi is Canadian not British. Even the present-day Englishmen cannot be held accountable for acts of their ancestors."

Chachaji continued sadly, "This is precisely what is wrong with anger. It blinds people's sense of discretion to distinguish between guilty and innocent. Like a forest fire, it scourges indiscriminantly, reducing to ashes anything and everything that stands in it tenacious path."

Neelam despised Chachaji's unflagging allegiance with Meera; both stood on seemingly higher moral ground. She let out a cold "Umph" of disgust and turned to Seema and Kanchan, hopefully for a more agreeable communion.

Completely oblivious of the drift of the contentious logomachy between Chachaji and Neelam, Seema was busy with what she did best, brag. She was the one with dancing eyes and eyebrows that must have been raised for a purpose sometime in her life time but forgot to come down. She was from Bangalore hence held the ownership of many prized and enviable bright-colored, brocade-bordered Bangalore silk sarees.

Most friends avoided commencing a conversation with her because once the floodgates were unlatched, there was no stopping the torrent of vaunting. "Oh, Kanchan, did I tell you that Pramod has been promoted to gifted class? His teacher, Mrs. Robinson or some such name, I forget these English names, Bhai, she said to me 'Mrs. Ramaswamy, Pramod does not belong to the ordinary class! They are all duds, no matter how much you teach them, they just don't learn. But your son? Very bright, very bright . . .' You know, he learnt his ABC when he was two years old? Can you believe it? But I am not boasting, Ji, don't misunderstand me, a lot of people misunderstand me, na. I spent so much time to teach him when he was little. My Daddy Ji, he works in the secretariat, big big officer, so many people work under him, na, you know, he said, 'Children learn best when they are small, Seema . . .' So, I had to do it. My Pramod knew how to read and add 2 + 2 when he went to kindergarten! The principal was so shocked! He told me, 'Mrs. Ramaswamy, this is fantastic.' It is not common, na. My voh, *husband*, is so happy that I put in so much work. I tell him it is my duty, Ji, my children are my whole life! Not like some other women! Play cards, go shopping, have kitty parties all day—no one is home when kids return from school. They just dress up like dolls, do all the nakhra, *pretension*, when hubbies come home, then they want to go out for dinner because they are tired! Working hard all day? You would think men would have some brains to figure them out. But no! They are so entranced by the decked-up, nicely scented with perfume from Europe, lovey-dovey dolls that they believe them! What do you know? Poor children have homework to do, so they stay at home! My God, I cannot believe it, the selfishness? Of course their children are not in the gifted class, are you surprised? I am not."

Seema looked triumphantly and fixed the palloo of her yellow, gold-bordered saree. Contrary to her intention and belief, no one seemed impressed, bored maybe, because they had heard it so many times before.

Bela, being the hostess, although her kids had just been enlisted as duds, was gracious and forgiving, "You are right, Seema."

Neelam, one of the "other women" Seema had so contemptuously referred to, smiled maliciously and replied snarkly, "You, Sati Savitri, *a devoted wife,* will remain backward. What is the point of coming so far away to a foreign land? You will never learn how to enjoy life. At least let others do it. What is your problem?"

Seema was so taken aback at what she thought was an unprovoked rebuke that tears filled her large black eyes.

Di cancelled Neelam from her guest list after that.

- # -

Meera was surprised to see light in the living room. She was heading towards the dining room with high hopes that food would put her to sleep. She had been tossing and turning for hours. It was one o'clock at night.

Atul was speaking tersely on the phone. Meera lifted the curtain that hung between the dining and the living rooms; she stood there, undecided whether to leave or stay.

Asha appeared on the other side of the living room in her pink nightie, with disheveled hair and half opened eyes, "What is going on?" She was startled to see Meera.

"I am sorry to wake you both up." Atul spoke without looking at either of them. He put the phone down.

Two sets of eyes focused on him questioningly.

He dismissed them without looking up. "Go to bed both of you."

Asha walked toward him. "What happened?" Atul looked up at Asha accusingly, "Do you know that your son's bedroom is empty? It is one o'clock, and he is not home!"

"Oh," Asha's voice dropped. Whatever the children do wrong is always the mother's fault.

"I thought he was back. He had said he will be a little late . . . but . . . ."

Asha attempted to be useful, "Did you try Ajay, Toni, Prakash?"

"Yes. I am going to call Nakul. But I don't have the telephone number, Asha. Nishant must have left his diary at the hostel in Chandigarh."

"No. Because most of his friends are in Simla, his diary is here. I will get it."

Nishant had come home to Simla for a few days to be with Meera.

Meera looked at them. Asha was paler than before; sweat hung on Atul's forehead in spite of the cold and rainy weather. Strange foreboding tucked at her heart.

Atul was apologizing softly. "Khanna Saheb, please forgive me. I was wondering if Nishant is at your place?"

"Yah? . . . Nakul came back? Can you ask him please if he knows where Nishant went?"

Atul nodded at Asha assuringly. At least some connection had been found that could lead to answers.

Meera could not help. "Bhai, why are you so worried? You used to come home late!" she laughed. "Of course, Ma did not sleep until you came home."

"Really? I didn't know that!"

"Boys! They are so clueless!"

Asha smiled and then became sad. The boy of her childhood was gone forever.

"Yes? He doesn't know? Thank you so much . . . I hope so too."

Atul's face was ashen.

Ever since Meera had come to Simla, this time she noticed that Atul had metamorphosed into a different person altogether—estranged and self-absorbed. He hardly ever raised his voice.

"Bhabi, what did you do?" Meera teased Asha. "You have successfully domesticated a lion after all these years."

Asha did not laugh, just looked away sadly.

Something serious was up. Meera mentioned to Ma and Papa; Ma got up abruptly and started folding clothes that did not need folding at that very moment. Papa knew he had to answer. "Meera, just as you have matured, he has too."

"But, Papa, it is not maturity. It is as though a he is displaced from his center. He looks disconcerted, too soft to be himself."

Papa smiled faintly.

"It is nothing, Choti, life is like that. Things happen, people change, it is normal."

What things might have happened to Atul that took away his very essence, leaving behind a shadow, a stranger?

Asha sat on the sofa, her gaze fixed on the beige kaleen, *Persian rug.* Atul stared vacantly at the darkness outside through the glass pane of the window. Like Meera, Asha generally left the curtains open.

Meera asked, "I am going to make tea while we wait, Hahn, *yes*?" Asha and Atul nodded resignedly; it did not matter.

When she returned from the kitchen with a wooden carved tray in her hands with two steaming mugs and a glass of milk on it, they were still sitting the way Meera had left them. She passed on the tea mugs to them and picked up the glass of milk from the tray that she placed on the center table. Tea at night was sure invitation for palpitations.

"Bhabi?" Meera was restless. "What is going on? Why are you so worried? He is a big boy! I am sure he is okay."

Atul's irascibility surfaced for a moment. "Choti, go to sleep! I know he will be fine, but it is normal for parents to worry about their children. You know that!"

"Yes, of course." She knew the truth of that statement firsthand. Somehow, she could not leave them. The clock ticked on, they sipped the beverages in silence; the clock struck three.

Atul got up. "I am going to call the police. I cannot take it anymore. I have to do something." Asha did not stop him.

"No, he has not been gone for twelve hours, but he has never done it before, Sergeant! Maybe something bad has happened, am I supposed to just wait? Yes?

"All right then, I will call the DSP, *District Superintendent of Police,* Saheb, who is my father's close friend, maybe he will order you to start the search." Atul banged the phone on the receiver, but his hand trembled a little.

Asha got up with determination. "No! You are not calling Mishra Uncle. Let us go to bed and pray. Nishu is fine, my heart tells me." Atul got up obediently, quite unlike his younger self, looked at Meera, and ordered her, "Go to sleep. Do not tell Ma and Papa."

"Of course not, Bhai."

Life had changed ever since her last visit. Dadi had passed on, victim of old age. She had smiled at her last breath and whispered with her debilitated mouth, "Bauji ke pas jati hoon, *I am going to my husband.*" Ma wiped her tears. "She looked so peaceful at last, Choti."

But that was a normal conclusion of a normal life and was acceptable because of its universality.

But this was frightening. What was happening to her family? This time, Papa appeared weary, Ma pained, Atul lost, Asha worried, Rakesh more stooped than before. Nalini was the only one who was unchanged; she was still obnoxious.

Within the half hour, Nishant sneaked in the front door. He was surprised to see Meera sitting on the sofa all curled up with a shawl wrapped around her body.

Meera felt so relieved that she forgot to scold him. "Are you okay?"

"Yes, Bua. Are Papa and Mummy really mad?"

"Yes, but go to bed straight and pretend to be fast asleep. They will deal with you tomorrow, you naughty lad!"

Meera walked softly to Atul's bedroom.

"Nishant's home. He is fine."

Before Atul could get out of bed to dish out some severe punishment on him, Meera spoke quickly, "Bhai, he has gone to sleep already. There is still tomorrow."

Papa had commented sadly to Meera, "I have become pessimistic. The value system is deteriorating fast, children talk about money and materials. Relationships are weighed on the scale of profitability. No one is interested in the larger concepts of society, nation, or world. The emphasis is on 'me' and 'mine.' People have circumcised themselves in the smallest possible space, and all spaces are disconnected from one another."

Meera had perceived an explicit change in the domestic climate. There were more tensions, sparks, loud mouthing, much less respect for the dignity of relationships. Sometimes, irreverence appeared to be directed at her, but she dismissed it and smiled, hoping Papa and Ma did not notice.

Notice he did. But Papa sounded gratified. "I see a lot of maturity in you. Meera, those of us who do not know how to strike back have to develop lofty mechanisms to transcend life much like a lotus that is borne out of mud and water but remains untouched by it." He continued, "These are times of inner and outer turmoil. We have to detach ourselves from the negativities of the present-day world, find our inner nave, a refuge that radiates beauty to cushion us from the ugliness around us. There is no other way to live happily."

Yes, Papa, there is no other way. Meera gazed through the large window of the living room, scanning the mountains, deodars, azure skies and fluffy clouds for relief, as much as to escape Papa's scrutinizing eyes.

He looked at her keenly and queried softly, "How is Rishi doing?" This was the first time he had not accompanied her to India.

"He is growing up, difficult sometimes, but adolescence is tough in that country, too many pressures to deal with."

After she visited the conservatory with Prashant late that night, Meera had knelt in front of her temple and prayed.

Rishi thought of Prashant as cool and funny; both the attributes achieved great significance if you wanted to be respected by a young boy.

But. In the propitious attendance of the demi God of fire, Agni Dev, Meera had vowed to be Mohit's shadow for seven janams, *births*. She did not even make it the very first! Wasn't it immoral? Shameful? She was Hindu, after all.

Drenched by Meera's copious tears, sleep decided to abscond to safety; she got up with red eyes, heavy head, and a confused heart.

Peter had picked up Rishi quite early. Granny knew that he liked to sleep in but did not seem to concern her.

Meera plugged the kettle to make tea when the doorbell rang. Prashant looked freshly bathed, groomed, skin glowed, sparkling eyes, smiling lips, and bouquet of red roses in his hands as he stood in the doorway.

"Hello," he beamed.

His visage clouded as soon as he laid eyes on Meera. Without a word, she stepped forward, put her soft arms around his strong neck and rested her head on his chest. He placed the roses on the table in the foyer and held her in his arms calmly, knowingly, stoically.

Meera knew instantly that she could never let him go, not even if Hindu priests burnt her alive? That was taking it too far; she broke into a smile. Prashant looked in her eyes. Meera felt that he understood.

Tears duly wiped, an affectionate kiss stamped on Prashant's cheek, Meera took his hand and led him into the kitchen. She picked up the roses, closed her eyes as she always did, and sniffed the perfume of the beautiful satiny blooms.

"I will put them in a vase, Prashantji. You have not had your breakfast, na? I will make it right away."

At times of distress, Rishi's eyes turned fluid like two burning lakes.

"I knew it. I knew it there was something fishy going on. How could you do it, Mom? How can you leave me?"

Two months had passed. After much reflection, Meera and Prashant decided to let him in on the goings-on. It was obvious that he had intuitively apprehended some transposition in the cosmic order within the house; more smiles, softness, some hand touching, something intangible between Meera and Prashant. Meera paid more attention to him, and that infuriated Rishi for a reason he could not construe. He acted rambunctiously, stomping his feet often to express his disapprobation.

"But I am not leaving you! Prashantji is joining us in our life journey. He loves you, Rishi, and you adore him, you've said that often."

"That was before! You don't even spend any time with me!" He fumbled to justify his feelings.

"But both of us do."

"It is not the same! I want it like it was!" He was becoming louder.

Prashant had been silent so far. He looked straight in Rishi's eyes. "Rishi you are and will remain the most important person in your Mom's life. But I love her and want to help."

Rishi burst out insolently, "She is my mom, I will help her! We do not need you."

Meera spoke firmly. "You are being rude and unfair, Rishi. I love him and want him in our lives."

Tears trickled down his adolescent cheeks where a slight stubble of hair was trying to take hold; he kicked the chair with his feet and stormed out of the front door. "I hate you both."

Meera and Prashant sat in silence. The tea got cold. Outside, wind was catching on; the bare birch tree swayed with the gelid wind, dark clouds promised the first snow of the season.

Prashant attempted to lighten the air. "Come on, Yar, *friend*, this is a perfectly normal reaction on the part of a child who has had his mother to himself all his life. To share you with me will take some adjusting on his part. Maybe we will cool it for a while."

Meera turned her face away to hide her pained eyes.

Papa noticed. After a few minutes of silence, he spoke in a calm voice, "Meera, Rishi has to find himself, and it is not an easy task when his place in the world has been obscured by his past."

"I don't know why you are wasting your life raising someone else's child!"

Papa and Meera were both startled to hear an acicular voice emanate from one corner of the living room. They did not notice when Ma had come in and sat knitting Papa's sweater.

Meera was jolted, "Ma, he is not someone else's child! He is my son!"

Ma's voice became loud, "No, he is not! So much lafda, *complication*. You cannot even get married. That buddi, *old woman*, Grandma is giving you so much distress. Look at your health? Dark circles around your eyes at such a young age?"

Ma softened. "Why should you go through so much pain, Choti? Let Granny have him."

Meera was exasperated. Never before this issue had been raised because Rishi was always with her. This was the first time she had come to India alone. Rishi wanted to attend a summer camp with his friends. There was yet another reason for his reluctance; he did not need to spell it, Meera knew.

A chasm seemed to have grown between Rishi and his cousins. Whether it was his adopted status or the fact that he spent very little time with them, relatively speaking. Rishi came to India, for a month, every two years; all his cousins evolved into quite diverse individuals in the meantime. Rishi, being the only one absent during this adolescent transmutation, he was not in tune with their idiosyncrasies; he was alienated and just did not fit.

"Ma", Meera tried to explain, "I promised his mother!"

"No!" Ma was unusually tough. "His mother was dead. You could have refused. You are just being stubborn. You don't know how worried your Papa and I are! This boy of yours will kick you one day and leave you. What will happen to you in your old age? You cannot remain young and strong forever. And we are not going to live forever to support you. What after us?"

With jaded step, Meera walked over to her, sat down on the floor, and held Ma's face in her soft palms. "Ma, I am sorry! I did not realize that my decisions would cause you so much grief! Please forgive me." Meera buried her face in Ma's cozy lap.

Mother and daughter hugged, sharing mutual pain. Ma whispered in a reeking voice, "I am so afraid of your future, choti!"

Meera looked helplessly at Papa, through her tears. Suddenly she saw two dark somniferous birds soar from Papa's eyes and glide smoothly into hers; their avoirdupois weariness weighed her down.

She jerked herself up and turned to Ma resolutely, "God has always taken care of me. Let us not be ungrateful and doubt His love. My health is good. I am fine, please Mama, do not worry."

Meera wanted to tell them about Prashant but could not.

She stood up and walked away slowly, leaving Papa and Ma in silence. Ma picked up her knitting, and Papa picked up the newspaper he had already read twice. Meera stepped outside on the covered veranda next to Papa and Ma's bedroom. That is where Papa sat on an armchair every summer morning. Shawl wrapped around his shoulders, he savored the morning cup of tea that Dharma would bring in a wooden tray.

At dawn, even before the dull orange silky chiffon spread on the waiting skies, the birds wake up and express their amazing energy for loquaciousness, to warble different songs, tunes, pitches, words; as many songs as birds. Before life begins and the intruding hubbub of the unmusical world disrupts their communications, their ballads of love and expectation ride on the soft wings of breeze to inform the perspective mates where their territory of hope begins. The birds wait in the freshly dewed boughs, hidden in the fluttering leaves tinted with the pristine glow of dawn.

Of course, Papa appeared on the scene after dawn; small birds like maina, hopped on the humid lawn in front of the Verandah. Papa broke some glucose biscuits and threw those on the cement floor of the veranda. He would then watch the birds hop cautiously, their tiny eyes blinking rapidly observing the whole world at once. The birds stretched their jerking head as far as they could safely to pick up the goodies.

Some brave birds, having faith in Papa, came close to him boldly, picked up biscuit crumbs with their sharp beaks, and ate those right there, with gratitude in their sharp eyes.

His vision gliding on the garden, Papa relished the fresh awakening of colorful blooms, enjoyed the musical murmur of leaves shining in the slanting rays of early morning sun. The layer of glowing diamonds of dew on the grass, with the hue of pink of the dawn reflected in their lucidity, invited Papa to walk barefoot that he dared not venture with due respect for his aging body.

Meera did not mind the sprinkle of tiny raindrops that fell on her body. She wrapped up the palloo of unprotecting chiffon saree around her shoulders and stood her ground.

Felicitous at the much-awaited rainshower the nocturnal creatures held a noisy celebration; their din shattered the dark silence into pieces. A lone frog daringly croaked at Meera as he squatted wide eyed on the wet grass, close to the cane garden chair on which Meera was sitting.

She felt alone, maybe lonely. "Mohit, if you had not left me so abruptly, I did not have to go through the struggles alone." She smiled sadly at the foolishness of her thought. "If" does not respect our desires and dreams.

Suddenly, Meera felt the strangest, intangible sensation of not being alone. She turned back her head to look if someone had stepped in the veranda; no one did.

Mohit? An ache of longing awakened in her heart.

Quite abruptly, the rain stopped, a soft touch on her shoulder sent a shiver through her body. Meera shut her eyes, she understood that eyes were an impotent instrument for seeing Mohit; inner vision had to be employed to capture his presence.

Tiny droplets of rain shimmered in the dim light of the streetlamp that stood behind the fence creating a halo around the bulb. Some stray fireflies hurled themselves against the light bulb in a futile attempt to merge with the seductive fire inside, idol of their eternal passion. The trees, bushes and flowering plants abided at the threshold of existence, vaguely visible in the hazy semidarkness like ghosts of themselves.

She opened her eyes. There was no one.

- # -

Papa leaned back on the cold wooden bench. His vision perused the hazy sky above, the long-limbed deodars and the rugged peaks that were partially embraced in the gentle coolness of fog. He was looking at something beyond perception.

"I shut my eyes, and the most beautiful and noble woman materializes. Her raw flesh is gleaming through the holes of her tattered raiment, her slaty, disheveled hair is covered with a frayed discolored palloo, *edge part,* of her white saree. Kneeling under a barren, disconsolate pippal tree, face buried in her parched hands, she is sobbing. She is bruised, bright-red blood is effusing from her wounds. People just walk by without even glancing in her direction. No one shows empathy to hold her hand and ask 'Mother, why are you crying?'

"She is our Bharat Mata, *Mother India.* She is weeping because her own children have traumatized her mercilessly with daggers of immoral conduct, debauchery, rapacity, cruelty, and selfishness. They have unscrupulously plundered all her jewels of tradition and value that had adorned her body for thousands of years. She is abandoned on the frigid harsh earth, bound to the earth under her feet, where can she escape? Her deliverance is insuperable because her brutalized womb has lost its virility to procreate great children like Gandhi, Nehru, Patel, Tilak, and Ram Mohan Roy. Enervated, she can only muster morally deformed offspring whose only talent is to bring perdition to her existence."

After a painful pause, Papa lamented, "Meera, it breaks my heart."

Monsoons had arrived in Simla late but stayed on vengefully. A cloud floated smoothly, embracing Meera and Papa, who faded in thin air.

"Aré, Yadav Saheb, is it you?" The clouds effectively hid the person behind the voice for a few seconds.

"Hahnji, Guptaji, have not seen you in a long time!"

Guptaji emerged victoriously out of the fog, "Beti, when did you come?"

"Namaste, *greeting,* Chachaji, I came last month."

"How is your son . . ."

"Rishi!" Meera helped him out.

"Yes, how is he?"

"Good, growing up. How is Didi?" The memory of the early years brought a smile on Meera's lips.

"Fine, fine."

Guptaji turned to Papa. "How is your health?"

Papa smiled congenially. "Same as yours."

Both laughed.

"Where is the Missus?"

"Where is yours?"

They chuckled.

Papa said, "Gupta Saheb, take care, don't slip!"

"Bye, Uncle."

"Bye, Beti. God bless. Give my regards to Bahenji."

"You do the same."

Gupta ji moved on.

"Papa, let us go home." It was humid and chilly. "I don't want you to catch cold."

Papa sighed and made himself more comfortable on the frigid wooden bench; catching cold was least on his mind.

"Where are all the moral giants like the Mahatama Gandhi, a saint, Dr. Radhakrishnan, our president, the philosopher king, Nehru, a statesman whose love for his country was unsurpassed. There are no more intellectuals like Tilak and Ram Mohan Roy who fought against the evil traditions like Sati, *when a woman burns herself in the pyre with her dead husband,* picked up the banner for women's education and uplift, iron man Patel and saintly Pant. Every drop of their blood carried the Sanskriti, *tradition and values,* of ancient India of the 'rishis,' Truth, charity, honesty were taught in gurukuls, *school of the guru,* before boys stepped into the world. These leaders restored our Mother India's lost honor and dignity—a glorious vision of the future of their nation shone in their eyes. Under their rule, the progress India made in the first decade after independence is beyond belief. They moved the world in spite of the world, their greatness lay in transforming the ordinary masses. An intrinsic momentum drew them towards their goal.

"Then came the petty politician Indira Gandhi, daughter of the noble statesman Nehruji. No one knows how and when the mutation occurred. She destroyed the virtue and essence of Democratic principles that her father's generation had laid down as the foundation of Independent India. She centralized the authority in her own hands and the Congress party. Indira did not allow any non-Congress state government to function! The members of the ruling party were allured with promises of ministership if they defected. Of course they crossed the floor en masse. State governments broke down, fresh elections were called, same stories. Indira initiated political corruption that has become a pattern now. Hence, Indians have lost all the benefits that normally stem out of Democracy. Some philosopher said aptly, 'Wisdon has its limitations, but folly has no such handicap.'

"The sole aim of the elected politicians is to keep their seats somehow and make quick money for their next seven generations. No one expends any energy and time for public good, hence evil of poverty is still stalking millions of Indians. Palkiwala, the great academician and philosopher, concluded wisely, 'A nation progresses gloriously when knowledge and power coexist in the same individual. It faces great danger when some have knowledge and others have power.'

"I am disillusioned because I think of the height man is meant to attain. Instead of evolving, Indians have devolved. Civilization is an act of the spirit. Modern man with satellites is less civilized than ancient Indian living in a simple hut."

Papa leaned back exhausted after the outpouring of his pent-up emotions.

Meera's heart ached for Papa. She took his cool hands in hers. "Papa, don't be dejected, life is not fair—you taught me that. When life situations do not make sense at a closer, narrower level, look for broader themes, principles that may form the underpinnings of what we see. What we are observing is an inherent retrogression of our civilization. All civilizations of the past—Indus Valley, Egyptian, Greek, Roman, Islamic and British—attained the summit of their development whereby all possible potentialities came together to consummate fully. But then all those fell from the peak of glory. Hindu civilization flourished for thousands of years during the Vedic era, when the sages, rishis, were the guiding forces who defined our society by creating moral systems. The kings had a cabinet with a rishi as the highest advisor. We have witnessed gradual decadence over the centuries, but we will have to plunge to the very bedrock of abyss before we can scale the heights once more. Papa, do not grieve the demise of our moribund civilization. It has to die before it can be reborn into something refined and venerable!"

Papa's face turned pale. "Meera, we have hit the rock bottom, already."

She looked at him questioningly.

"You do not know about Vineet, we did not tell you."

Papa wrapped the quilt around his ears, his weary voice echoed in the silence of the night, "It is cold today, check on Beji, *Mother*, if she has the extra quilt on. She forgets everything these days."

Ma got out of bed reluctantly, wrapped her shawl around her shoulders and groped in the dark, too lazy to turn the lamp on. In a few minutes she came back. "Beji is fine. I turned the room heater on."

The night was tenebrous, bleak dense clouds hung low. Silently, it spoke of dangers of precarious slipperiness of slopes, of times, of life. Deodars listened and bowed helplessly.

Papa tossed and turned in his cold bed that stubbornly refused to get warm. Every day they heard dreadful stories from neighbours and friends; there was no way to tell if these were rumours or truth.

Gelid zephyr wailed and banged its head against the wooden doors, rattled the glass panes of windows, trying to awaken people's spirits in futility. Papa thought he heard a knock but dismissed it, at this God forsaken hour? It had been a cold, seemingly endless winter.

But there was a louder, more persistent and desperate knock. His heart froze. He looked at the radium needles piercing the darkness; it was two a.m.

This cannot be good. Who could it be? What news?

His old hands fumbled with his night gown. He heard voices in the living room; Atul must have opened the door. "I don't have to get up then," Papa thought fleetingly but immediately changed his mind. No, this must be important.

Papa stepped slowly in the darkness, Ma raised her head with a jerk and got up worriedly, "What is it, Ji?"

"I don't know, let us see." He could hear a loud and agitated female voice, then Atul's high pitched retort. Papa walked slowly towards the living room. Usha was hugging Atul tightly and crying aloud while standing in the foyer. Her black overcoat was clammy, her cheeks were red with frost.

"What happened, Beti, *Daughter*?" Papa could not control the quiver in his voice.

No one noticed Bhola, *the servant*, shivering in the open doorway; a gust of wind drifted snow unimpeded into the foyer.

Usha looked at Papa, her big black eyes were full of anguish, bewilderment, disbelief, "Chachaji, *Uncle*, they came at night... he should not have opened the door... I told him not to....," Usha could not compose herself, her whiny words came out jumbled and incoherent.

Papa was shaken, he could intuit a horrible tale behind Usha's bumbling.

Atul was loud with impatience, "Who Usha, who came?" Simultaneously Ma and Asha entered the living room from opposite directions. Asha asked worriedly, "What is going on? Usha, this late, is everything okay?"

Asha looked around and took charge, "Aré, close the door, Bhola, come inside Bache, *child*, do not freeze." He looked thankful.

Asha said, "Usha, come in first, sit down then tell us."

Ma spoke warmly, "Beti, change your clothes and dry yourself first."

"Nai Chachiji, *no Aunty*, there is no time." Ma went in to get a towel to dry Usha's hair. Asha helped take off Usha's overcoat; they all moved to the living room.

Usha slumped on the edge of the sofa, her face was covered with tears. She gathered herself, "The police came! Knocked at the door loudly, again and again. I told Vineetji not to open. He said it may be someone who needs help. He opened the door, four police men barged in. I was still inside the bedroom putting on my nightgown. When I came out they were pushing him insisting that he change his clothes and come with them." She started to sob.

Atul retorted brusquely, "They did not have a warrant? He did not have to go!"

Usha wiped her tears with her handkerchief and stammered.

"Vineetji kept his calm, kept asking them on what charge, where is the arrest warrant? He kept repeating, 'I have done nothing wrong'. Bhaiya, *Brother*, they pushed him on the floor, insulted him, kicked him, he looked at me and told me to change, take Bhola and fetch you. I went in to change quickly. When I came out they were all gone. What is going to happen, Chachaji, *Uncle*?" Usha bawled uncontrollably and doubled over on her knees.

Papa was aghast. So, the rumours were true; the Government was arresting people illegally. Overwhelmed with intense apprehension, he lost his voice.

Atul asked the obvious question, "Usha, did he do anything or say anything against the Government of Indira Gandhi?"

"No Bhaiya, he did not", she stressed vehemently. "He told me 'Usha, I am mad at what she is doing but I am not getting into any Lafda, *complication,* of politics. I have to think about you, Raju and Biji, *mother.*'"

Atul's face turned red, his ears were hot and throbbing. No one was sure but whatever was happening around them was perplexing, hopeless and tangled. News were grotesquely twisted, truth was shred into pieces, rumors poisoned the air people breathed. A stygian darkness had engulfed the whole nation and there was no Mahatama Gandhi this time to lead the lost masses out of the ugly quagmire.

TV, radio and newspapers were in the Government's control, hence, useless to impart any real information regarding the truth. Indians turned to BBC but news on India were generalized bulletins. Of course, broadcasts of the world Leaders' reactions to India's political turmoil, were aired all day; what President Nixon, Prime Minister Trudeau, and other Western leaders stated regarding the suppression of liberty in the largest democracy of the world.

Of course, they had no idea that in India, corruption and democracy were synonymous and interchangeable. Even before Indira Gandhi undid it completely, democracy was a sham, whereby votes could be bought by one bottle of homemade brew, or a blow of the Lathi, *long sticks used by police.* Any candidate standing against the established hierarchical order could land up in a ditch, dead.

To save herself from getting humiliated and ousted from power due to charges of wrong doing during her elections, India Gandhi declared 'Emergency'; overnight she turned into a brutal dictator, a slap on the noble face of her dead father, Jawaharhal Nehru. Every excess was carried out by her, all democratic rights and freedoms were taken away and suspicion hung around people like dark, foul, shadows.

A few days after the 'Emergency' was imposed, Bombay edition of 'the Times of India' carried an obituary that read, "D'ocracy, beloved

Husband of Truth, Loving father of L. I. Bertie, Brother of faith, hope and justice, expired on June 26, 1975."

The Courts were suspended resulting in lawlessness and totalitarianism, people were put in jails in the tens of thousands; anyone who spoke against Indira's actions was arrested, jailed and sometimes disappeared from the face of the earth. A rough estimate of number of Indians who were arrested during the 20 months of Emergency was 140,000.

Having lost their freedom in one fleeting moment, people's greatest fear was that Indira's 'Raj', *reign*, may even turn out to be worse than the 'British Raj'.

This was no time to lose nerve. Papa shut his eyes momentarily to summon his failing courage. To give in to timorousness at this critical juncture would amount to losing the battle even before it commenced. If this was some sort of test they could not afford to fail; Vineet's life was at stake.

Firmness returned to his jaw. "Atul, get ready and go with Usha. Leave her at home then go to the police station. I will call Bhatia, he is a great friend of Misra." Then he turned to Usha, "Tell Bahenji, *sister*, we will not let anything happen to Vineet, go and sleep well. Leave the rest to us."

Color returned to Usha's fair face.

But he knew in his heart, it was going to be formidable task to take on a Government turned against its own people.

Papa looked at the clock ticking on the living room wall. It was 3.00 a.m. but this could not wait. He called his friend Bhatia.

The servant told him that he was out of town. He called Misra, the District Superintendent of Police; he was away to Delhi.

Who else could he call? Papa had retired now from his job as Secretary to the Education Minister, Mr. Dyal. The latter had moved to Bombay on a better position with the Government of Maharashtra. The new Education Minister in Himachal Pradesh was young, cold and arrogant. Nakul, Papa's old friend from Amritsar, was now with Central Government in Delhi. But there was no point to call him because he could not pull any strings in Simla without connecting to others who were all slumbering at that moment.

Papa took off his gown and got into bed. Ma looked at him questioningly.

"No, I could not get hold of Bhatia or Misra. Just pray real hard and try to sleep."

It was easier said than done. Little Vineet, clad in this tiny shorts and T-shirt, jumping amidst flowers, running away after pulling little girls' ponytails, hiding behind trees, his black naughty eyes dancing with mischief, came to her mind all night. Then, as a tall handsome man, at his wedding, his somber empathetic eyes seemed ready to take on the pain of the whole, anguished humanity. Papa was haunted by the image of Vineet's sad face behind bars attempting to make sense of this blind whirlwind that folded him in its moving labyrinth and dumped him on a hard, cold, cemented prison floor.

Around six o'clock on the dismal morning, Papa could not wait any longer. It was still dark. Ma got up when she noticed Papa sitting at the edge of the bed, a chiaroscuro silhouette in the dim light of the bathroom coming to the bedroom through the crack in the door.

"I will make tea", she uttered quietly. Atul had not returned, all night they waited for the rumble of the main door.

When Ma entered the kitchen, Asha had a tray in her hand with three cups, sugar pot, teapot, milk pot and a plate of Papa's favorite biscuits; she knew no one had slept.

"Dharma, *the servant*, is still sleeping?"

"I did not wake him up. Today is Sunday, kids will sleep in."

Ma and Asha walked into the dining room with lifeless steps; Asha placed the tray on the dining table and started to pour tea without a word, her gaze fixed on the cups.

Papa looked disheveled as he sauntered in slowly. "You could not sleep either, Asha?"

"No, Papaji," she did not look up.

Papa looked at the clock, it was still too early to wake up Nakul. The squall had quieted during the night. Pale, sickly light of the light bulb hanging from the ceiling with a brown glass shade, fell on them; three doleful, yellow, clay statues trapped in a strange twist of time warp, unable to free themselves from the clutches of Kal, *time.* What next?

"I hope Akku is fine", Ma wanted to say just to breach the unbearable silence, but did not. She looked at Asha disconcertedly, who was stirring the spoon in the tea cup, sunk in thought. A lock of black hair with a sprinkle of grey, fell carelessly on her crinkled forehead. She was wearing a black Kashmiri woolen gown that Atul had bought on his business trip to Sri Nagar last year.

Asha suppressed a sigh. She knew Atul's temper, he could not stand injustice and this crisis demanded tempered tending. She kept stirring unconsciously, praying for her husband to come home safely.

As though an answer to her prayers, there was an impatient knock at the door. Spontaneously they all glanced at one another, three sets of eyes shone with restored hope. Asha got up and walked with animated steps towards the foyer.

"Must be Atul", Ma looked at Papa anxiously.

Asha opened the wooden door; frosty draft wafted in with a few lone flakes of snow sliding from the roof. Atul stood tall at the door against the backdrop of the umbrageous night. His ashen face, blood shot eyes, drooping lips, forehead frowned in familiar eloquence, made it obvious that the news was not good.

Atul took off his wet overcoat and handed it to Asha to hang, without a word.

He slipped his feet in slippers, dragged his exhausted legs to the dining room, sank in dining chair, rested his elbows on the table and held his damp head in both hands. Papa looked at him, "Atul?"

He remained taciturn for a few minutes and shut his eyes hoping to obliterate what he had just experienced.

Ma called out to Asha who had gone into the kitchen to fetch extra tea cup for Atul. "Get something for Akku to eat, Asha."

Atul looked up. His normally fearless eyes were shrouded in undisguised despondency. "Papa, Vineet is in big trouble."

"But, I am Vineet's lawyer and I have the right to know on what charges he is being detained!"

The Police Inspector was a macho looking young guy, with oily slick hair pasted on his pointed head, chubby well fed shining face and downwards slanting eyes that spelt meanness.

He retorted querulously at the interruption of his nap; his feet were on the table and back leaned comfortably in a large cushioned chair. He opened his eyes slightly like slits, "I only have orders to arrest him. They have a file on him but I have not been given the detail. Tomorrow they will deal with it."

"And who are 'they'?" Atul was sarcastic, an obvious blunder.

The Police Inspector got his feet on the floor, opened his eyes fully, and glared at Atul, "Don't try to be a smart with me, Mister. 'They' are my superiors. Are you satisfied? Now go away."

"But I have to be present for the 'hearing', when and where is it happening?"

The Inspector ignored Atul as insignificant, settled his feet back on the table, sunk in the chair, made an attempt to find the most comfortable position for his much coveted nap.

Atul was not going anywhere, his face reddened with building anger, "Inspector Saheb, there is something called law in a civil society; India is not some barbaric country. I want to see my client if he has been taken care of and I want to know what the charges are. You cannot throw anyone behind bars without telling him why..."

"He has been told," Inspector looked wicked.

"Told what?"

"Treason."

"What" Atul gasped, "I do not believe it!"

Inspector appeared triumphant at having achieved the desired effect. "Yes", he remained reclined with his feet resting on the table, but raised his head a little. "Your client has been charged with plotting against the Himachal Pradesh Government; others of his group have been arrested, too."

Atul slumped on the nearest chair. An acerbic fear pierced his normally intrepid heart; something dreadful had been meticulously planned and so far executed with precision. Atul understood the futility of communicating with this poor excuse for a human, who was sprawled behind the formidable desk on which human destiny was piled, tucked away fastidiously in neat brown colored, labeled files. Hapless citizens were at the mercy of scums like him. 'They' may need concrete evidence whoever they are, but 'they' must have already concocted enough corroborative props to underpin their false incriminations. How difficult could deception be at a time when the pharisaical leaders were covered with mud of prevarication from head to toe? Simple scare tactics were enough to transmogrify an upright truthful man into a fibber on the stand in the court. Such dismal times had befallen the nation that unveracious witnesses were a dime-a-dozen, forgery, perjury, and mendacity were the orders of the day.

India was a lawless country, now. Afraid of jail or losing their jobs, good people learnt to seal their lips and look the other way. They even spied on one another. "I have to take care of my children and family, what can I do?" Their Machiavellianism was adequately rewarded by promotions.

Atul just sat in shock for a few stony moments. He looked up at the inspector, swallowed his pride and softened his voice, "Okay, tell me when and where the hearing will be, I would represent Vineet as his lawyer."

The Inspector's newly acquired power had not only dehumanized but also demonized him; he was deriving sadistic pleasure at Atul's plight. His pointed moustache that looked like a fatal edge of a virulent arrow, quivered with deep sense of tintillation. He glared at Atul petulantly, "You have wasted so much of my time, Mister. You realize there is 'Emergency' in place; we can hold people in jail without hearing for three months. So, the hearing will be in three months. Now get lost before I lose my temper." He let his head limp back and closed his eyes obliterating Atul out of existence.

Atul's gut twisted with ferocious rage, he pushed his chair back clamorously and got up. He chewed each word to underscore his disgust, "I am going to find out what is going on right today. You have no idea but the D.S.P. Saheb, Mr. Misra, is a close friend of my father's. I will see to it that your insolent and contraband behaviour comes to his notice. You have forgotten that you are paid to serve the people not destroy them."

Atul turned around and headed for the door stomping hard on the wooden floor. Atul caught the Inspector off guard, who could not decipher if Atul was bluffing or he really was in possession of the formidable link in his pocket.

The Inspector's eyes were still shut; he felt trepidation, a slight shudder in his hardened heart but made a brave attempt to dismiss the image of D.S.P. Saheb humiliating him or worst still, firing him in front of all the constables who would immediately lose respect for him if they had any in the first place.

He opened his eyes courageously, stared hard at Atul's departing head and growled with much exertion, "Don't try to scare me, Mister, my orders are from Delhi High Command. I only answer to them. I don't care about D.S.P. Saheb." His voice lost its spunk for a second but recovered quickly; after his explicit show of power he could not look weak. "With due respect, D.S.P. Saheb must already be aware. Oi Nathu, show this man the door, and tell him never dare step here again", disregarding the fact that Atul was already out of the door.

"Papa, call all your connections at Delhi. It seems orders came from the Central Government. We need to move fast."

Papa turned to Ma, "You and Asha get warmly dressed up and go to Usha and Bahenji. They have cut their phone lines. Tell them we will get Vineet out, not to worry."

Ma prayed hard, "O God, please help your child who helps your children! How can you let him get hurt?"

Papa got Misra's Delhi phone number from the servant.

Papa was earnest on the phone, "Misra Saheb, I can give you a written guarantee that Vineet has not done anything wrong. I will bet my life on it. He is like a son, I know him. I will be indebted to you for the rest of my life, please help him." Papa's voice quivered.

Misra was suave, promised to look into it immediately.

Papa phoned all possible avenues in Simla to get the local information. No one had a clue. Finally, after several trials Papa managed to get Nakul in his Delhi office.

"Deva, don't worry, we will find out right away." Nakul assigned the fact finding mission to his secretary. Nakul was adviser to the Central Education Ministry after his retirement but had contacts with Internal Security Department. The truth unfolded.

Vineet was member of the Communist Party, not a forgivable position considering the current, highly inflamed political climate. A year ago he had written a scathing report against the Ministry of Social Welfare in Himachal Pradesh and sent it to the Central Government.

Vineet had given a detailed account of how grants conferred to the poor farmers were plundered like a booty amongst the Social Welfare Department's high officials, their stooges, the landlords of the region and their families. Vineet attached affidavits by the victimized farmers who received nothing but were made to imprint their thumbprints on papers stating that they had, in fact, received thousands of rupees in 'assistance'. Vineet had appealed for an enquiry.

Of course, no action was taken, except a slight slap on the wrist of the Indian Central Services officer in charge of the 'assistance' funding; he was transferred with a promotion to another lucrative location for further pillage. Vineet, on the other hand, was served notice for a transfer to a remote, secluded area of Himachal Pradesh that was almost completely cut off from civilization, where mail arrived once a month, the transport was bullock carts and the only doctor worked in an unhygienic shack.

Vineet was able to pull strings to get the transfer orders revoked.

Now, the opportune time for nemesis had arrived. In the venomous atmosphere of suspicion and shifting loyalties, favours were exchanged, vengeance had become an inexpensive commodity that could be bought cheaply.

Fabricated letters were willed into existence, proffered as a proof of Vineet's scheme to burn down the Legislative Building in Simla. Three Gundas, *rogues,* signed the deposition that Vineet had hired them to do the job. As simple as that.

Mr. Misra was candid. "If you can prove that the Gundas are lying, Vineet can be freed. Otherwise weight of three persons' claims against his assertion of innocence is not going to fly."

Atul cast away his practice. It was clear to him that his Kurukshetra, *an historical righteous war,* had actively sought him; impromptu he had been thrown in the midst of the battle between good and evil. Stakes were high, he buckled his armour for a protracted war and began by tracking down Gangu.

Gangu was not even a professional Gunda. He had earned the unsought for appellation when he hit his boss and his two puppets eight months ago when they refused to give him his salary. Gangu was well built and strong unaware of the puissance of his own punch; he was charged with assault and spent six months behind bars.

However, he became an instant hero amongst his fellow labourers.

When Gangu was released from prison, much to his surprise, a throng of cheering labourers welcomed him, adorned his neck with marigold garlands, lifted and planted him on their shoulders. The procession then proceeded to gherao, *surround,* the boss's mansion with much commotion; inflamed slogans, enraged abuses were hurled in his direction while the boss and his family hid under their expensive rose wood bed.

Ever since Gangu had punched him, the boss was a bit scared of the authority Gangu held amongst his fellow workers. Quite unbeknown to him, Gangu was transposed from an artless worker to a crafty leader of the proletariat, capable of dealing fearlessly with the exploitive bourgeoisie. The common labourer sought his advice and protection. The show of unity shown by the factory workers petrified the boss who started to treat him with feigned respect thereby exalting Gangu's peerage to greater heights. Since this situation made his life less onerous, Gangu did not protest his newly acquired nomenclature, 'Gunda.'

Gangu explained defensively to Atul who was sitting quite uncomfortably on the charpoy, *a bed of knitted straw mesh*, "Saheb, *sir*, I am not a violent man. I had no money, my children were hungry. My own hard earned money was due that day but the boss refused just because I missed one day of work due to illness! I lost my temper and hit the boss. His Chamcha, *stooge*, Manager and his son came to help him and I punched them, too; I also cursed at them. But I did pay for it and went to jail. I was wrong in hitting anyone.

"Two weeks ago two Constables came to my jhuggi, *hut*; I was frightened, maybe my boss sent them. It was cold outside so I asked them to come in and sit on the charpoy, the one you are sitting on." The information caused Atul to feel more uncomfortable. Gangu continued, "I asked Champa to make hot tea. It is safe to keep these haramzadas, *swear word*, happy, Saheb. I hate them but what else can a poor man do? They just talked this and that and told me they had heard of me. I felt panic rise in my gut; police does not make friendly calls. But I pretended to smile and show cordiality. After drinking my tea, one of them bent down and extended his hand under the charpoy and pulled a small brown paper bag. 'Oh, what is this?' I was horrified, 'I don't know, I have never seen it before, Constable Saheb!' He opened it with twinkling purposeful eyes; there was some white powder in a plastic bag. The other Constable feigned shock, 'Oh… oh… so you take drugs and sell them?' I cried, fell on his feet and pleaded innocence. Champa begged them too. They handcuffed me and threw me in a stinking jail cell, kicked me and hit me for mere pleasure. For two days they did not give me food, just small amounts of water. The third day a hefty, cruel looking thanedar came to my cell and said, 'You are a criminal, drugee, we have proof. But I feel sorry for your family. I will let you go, just sign this paper.'

"I asked him with a beating heart, 'What is it, Saheb?' He kicked me in my belly with his huge boots and roared, 'You want to get out or not? Sala, *swear word*! Argues with me; I am trying to help him!' Thanedar turned to his sheepish junior.

"I signed and swiftly fled before he could change his mind. I had no idea, Saheb? Thanedar also told me that I will have to come to court one day. They will tell me what to say. And if I buggered it up, he will break my scrawny legs."

Atul was appalled. It was obviously an adroitly woven web, how could he cut the deadly threads without hurting Gangu? Atul deliberated for a while, then raised his head. "Gangu Bhai, they have falsely accused my brother of plotting to set fire to the Legislative Building. Thanedar will ask you to tell the Judge that my brother asked you to do it and promised to pay you ten thousand rupees."

Atul leaned forward and spoke intently. "Gangu Bhai, will you help me, an innocent life and family will be destroyed?"

Fear surfaced in Gangu's sad eyes. "I swear Gangu, I will not let anything happen to you and your family." Gangu looked at Atul and bent his head. After a few excruciating moments he raised his head, his eyes glistened, "Yes Saheb, I will speak the truth. I will not be the cause of pain to your brother and his children. That is my Dharma, *duty*."

He pleaded, "Just make sure, Saheb, that my wife and children are not hurt. I will send them to my brother in MotiGaon. Tell me what to do."

Gangu was strong and determined.

Atul extended his paw, took Gangu's crude, rough hand in his palms and touched it to his forehead. "Gangu Bhai, I will be in debt to you for the rest of my life and do everything to give you a good life. I may have to move you out of Simla temporarily until this 'Emergency' is there. It should not last long. Now listen carefully. The police will show you my brother's photo, so that you can identity him in court; go along with them. Once you are on the stand, tell the Judge that you want protection and want to tell the truth. Don't be afraid, I will be there with a couple of people who will whisk you away after your statements, and take you to Mehto, my peon. You stay in his hut until

I arrange to send you to my Tayaji's, *Uncle,* house in Delhi. He will find a job for you."

Gangu pondered and appeared satisfied.

Atul emphasized, "Bhai, tell your truth bravely. You are on the side of Dharma. God will protect you."

Atul did not realize that in Kaliyug, *an unrighteous epoch,* such assertions can be overridden by the ferocious, murky forces of evil swirling around good humans.

At the court hearing Gangu stood confidently and told the truth. However, the other two Gundas testified against Vineet, produced letters that he had supposedly written to them, asking them to do the job. A handwriting expert testified that the signature was Vineet's. Hence, there was enough overriding evidence to try him for sedition. The trial date was set after a month.

Right after the court hearing, Dharma and Mehto, sneaked Gangu out the court and sprinted to Mehto's small hut; Champa was already there. Mehto moved in with Dharma at Atul's house. Gangu and Champa were affirmatively told not to open the door to anyone except Mehto and Dharma. The code of knocking was established.

A few days passed without incidence. Gangu and Champa felt safe but bored. Gangu asked Dharma for some straw to keep them busy; they made straw mats to be sold later.

One morning, according to a wailing Champa, Gangu had gone out for his morning routine. There being no indoor bathroom, they went out before dawn just to ensure invisibility. Behind Mehto's house, a dense jungle provided for safety; a small stream solved the problem of baths.

That morning Champa came back but Gangu did not return. She waited anxiously with fear rising in her heart. Dharma brought food for them in the morning as always; Champa was sitting on the damp floor of the hut and crying uncontrollably. Dharma rushed towards the woods. There was no wind, darkness still reigned, and even birds had not woken up. Dharma stumbled on something solid, a fallen tree he thought at first. He looked down and found the bloody body of Gangu, beaten to pulp; his open eyes looked surprised.

Dharma's stomach convulsed at the wretched sight. Atul was having breakfast ready to go to office. Panting Dharma, tears rolling down his rugged face, told Atul the horrid news. A lead weight of guilt fell on him like a mountain, acrid feelings of remorse, impotency and betrayal demolished him. Atul could not get up from his chair. How was he going to show his face to Champa? And Vineet? How would he pull him out of the morass, now?

Atul had been allowed to see Vineet only once, that too with Misra's help. He looked pale and gaunt. Dark shadows under his big eyes accentuated the sorrow lurking behind a brave front. His hands were bruised and swollen; obviously they were torturing him. A teary film blurred Atul's vision.

Vineets's eyes were defiantly dry.

"Are they torturing you?"

"Yes, that is usually the case, Bhaiya, *Brother*," he was stoic and casual. Atul took both his hands in his and pressed gently, "I swear, I will get you out. Just hang in a little longer."

"I know you will", Vineet smiled reassuringly.

After Gangu's murder, Atul sent petitions of protest to Central Government Congress High Command, and Justice Department. Nothing came out of it.

Papa's connections in Delhi and Simla had become worthless like forged Bank notes. Everyone in the Government felt precariously uncertain regarding their position in the scheme of things. Alliances shifted overnight like sand dunes in a desert, new leagues sprung up within the hours; engulfing vacuums under people's shaky feet sent them deep down the daunting abyss of incertitude. No one was quite sure who was pulling which strings, therefore no one was willing to endanger their security by seeming to side with the wrong people. And of course, no one knew who their friends were, if any; the line between friend and enemy had dissolved unpretentiously.

Vineet's fate hung on a chance goodwill somewhere, somehow.

Papa knocked and walked in Atul's study slowly; it was late at night. Atul was working bent on the study table; auramine light of the lamp fell on his sad face that had suddenly wrinkled. He looked much older than his age.

"Akku, find the handwriting expert who testified that the letters were written by Vineet."

Atul looked up, hope glimmered in his morose eyes.

"He is obviously lying. Why not try to trace him and work on him? He will have perjury on his hands but you can argue in the court that police coerced him."

The next morning Atul met the grumpy looking Judge and filed for an extension for one week; he had a lead that would prove his client's innocence.

The Judge looked displeased but granted three days. Papa called his friends in the Secretariat, and for the first time in his life, asked for a favour. He asked for the name of the handwriting expert who had testified at Vineet's court hearing.

Shastri took off his glasses and wiped them, looked at Atul intently and asked, "What would you have done? Tell me what could I do?"

Atul sat speechless. Yes, what would he have done?

"When the Gundas told me what they wanted me to do, I could not sleep for many nights. My soul was on fire; I am a Brahmin, *highest priest class,* I never lie. I read and follow Gita, *Hindu's Bible,* I asked Shri Krishna, *incarnation of God,* 'What would you do? This is not Kaliyug, *immoral times,* but Ghor Kaliyug, *intense kaliyug.* When you took Avatar, *incarnation,* on this earth, it was Tretayug, *an earlier more moral phase,* and more people were pious. Come down to this wicked world now, be a Shastri and tell me what would you do?"

Shastri's anguished voice broke. He continued, "I was scared to death, was Savita hurt? Was her honour spoilt? Do you have a daughter? Yes? You know then how I must have felt! She ran to me, hugged me and cried. I asked her if she was all right? She said 'Yes'. What a relief, God, I cannot describe it. Then I turned on the two men. I grabbed the neck of one and said, 'Why did you take her away?' They were strong, ruthless looking, ruffians, one of them pushed me and said harshly, 'Let us talk'.

'Talk about what?' I was exasperated. They spoke casually as though they were planning a tea-party. 'We will rape her, if you don't do what we want; we have police behind us.' What could I do?"

Atul sat stunned. What is the answer if any?

The area was ordinary, small houses had lost their paint, the wooden gate was chipped and rough.

Shastri was an elderly, timid and decent looking man. When Atul knocked, he opened the door. He was wearing a cream colored Dhoti, *a long cloth covering waist and legs,* beige Kurta, *loose shirt,* and a green shawl wrapped around his stooping shoulders. It was end of April, yet quite cold.

Shastri recognized Atul, a brush of pain swept over his calm face. As soon as Atul laid his eyes on Mr. Shastri's face his heart cringed. Gangu's dead face rose up in front of his eyes like a ghost. He promised to himself, no matter how, this man was not going to be a martyr to Vineet's cause.

"Please, have a seat," Shastri's voice was soft and gentle. He turned his face towards the curtain that hung on the door that opened to the rest of the house. "Savita, bring a cup of tea."

Shastri was polite, "Beta, why are you here? You will endanger my life, you know that." Atul took a deep breath, he wished there was some way he could run away from this quagmire.

"Baba, you must know why I am here. You know it and I know it, that handwriting is not Vineet's. Why did you say it was?"

"But it was!" Shastri stressed but looked down, then his voice broke, "As far as I could tell." He got up and paced the room like a caged animal. He nodded again and again and mumbled to himself.

Savita, a young girl about fifteen or sixteen years old, clad in an ordinary cotton Salwar and Kameez, *pant and long shirt,* entered shyly, carrying a wooden tray with two mugs of tea and a plate with some saltish biscuits. She said namaste, *greeting,* in a quiet voice without looking at Atul, stood in front of him and bent a little to offer him the mug.

He smiled, "Thank you."

She smiled back, placed the tray on a small wobbly side table and left.

Shastri took a deep sigh. "Take a good look at my daughter. She did not come home from school one evening. It was like a nightmare, I felt so sick in my heart that I cannot express. I looked all over, went to police station. When I came home two young ruffians were waiting outside my house. Savita was sitting on the steps and crying."

"Baba, he is my brother. He is innocent, help me please."

Atul spent three long hours with Shastri; the night crept up on that tiny house without their awareness. They were only cognizant of the safety and dignity of their loved ones.

Savita cried and begged Shastri. "Baba, someone innocent will be sent to jail! Think of his wife, child, and mother!"

Shastri relented.

Atul focused with all his brain power to cover all grounds for their protection. The memory of Gangu had become a thorn in his heart that bled relentlessly. He could not take any chances. Before he left Atul placed his strong hand on the head of a fearful and scared Savita, "I swear, I will not let any harm come to both of you even if I have to die to protect you."

The next day, Atul produced two witnesses in the court. Shastri told his story and a weeping Savita supported. He looked at Vineet and asked for forgiveness. He turned to a horrified Judge and asked, "What would you have done?"

The Judge had sweat on his brow, took off his glasses and squeezed his forehead. "Yes, what would I have done?"

In the stunned courtroom, everyone looked at one another, "What would we have done?"

Right after their testimony Shastri went to the men's bathroom, Savita to the women's; windows at the back had been broken, they jumped out. Satish, Atul's assistant, his wife Leena, and Dharma were waiting. They ran behind trees, on small paths and arrived at the railway station just in time for train to Kalka. Satish and Leena travelled with Shastri and Savita, and deposited them at Tayaji's, *uncle*, house in Delhi.

Overnight Shastri became Mr. Bhave and Savita turned into Savitri.

Nitin was released the next day. Even in Indira Gandhi's crooked regime, there was at least one Judge who still preserved his soul. Nitin hugged Atul in the courtroom and wept for the first time.

Police were reprimanded sternly, a case was filed against the two Gundas for perjury and conspiracy to cause bodily harm. Since police was a major participant in the plot, that was, of course, commanded by some unknown higher power, the Gundas, *rogues,* escaped punishment and were hired immediately for the next job.

Atul never told anyone about the threatening letters he received, the dark shadows that stalked him, about someone attempting to hit him with a Lathi, *long stick,* on a lonely path. He took major streets then on, walked with groups of people, travelled on different routes, came home early and worked at home.

Atul's reality was changed forever. He lost faith in the system, humans, life. A lurid shadow of hopelessness followed him where ever he went; anguish became a fixture in his heart. Is this life? Is this humanity? Where are we going? What is to become of all of us? What kind of society we live in where poor people are used as pawns and discarded like garbage? What about Gangu? Where is God?

Asha knew. One night while he tossed and turned, she placed her hand on his chest and said softly, "You cannot change the ways of this world. Don't torment yourself over something that is beyond you, Ji. Papa, Ma, children and I need you. Stay at peace, please."

Atul threw his arm around her and wept in her bosom.

- # -

"She is a maharani, *queen.* We treat her so well, but she does not care a damn about us!" Asha grumbled while stirring the dal, *lentil soup,* on the stove.

Rakesh and family were coming; the maid found out and declared herself ill to escape the extra exertion.

Meera was cutting vegetables. Asha continued, "Dharma Kaka has also spoilt us." Dharma aged, as is the case with all humans. With his life savings, he purchased a small brick house in the village where his extended family lived.

Meera made an attempt to assuage Asha. "Don't worry, Bhabi. They are not begane, *outsiders.* Nalini Bhabi can help."

"You think so? You live so far, what do you know?" Meera was surprised by the bitterness in Asha's voice. She looked at her intently. Dark circles around her apprehensive eyes; her lips that were always curved upward in readiness for a smile were curved downward with wrinkles at the edges.

Meera was puzzled. She believed that Asha had everything: a great husband, loving in-laws, healthy children. On the other hand, Nishant was twenty-one but still struggling at Punjab University at

Chandigarh; having dropped B.com. midway, claiming that it was dry. He had joined Law College. Nishi was finishing bachelor's degree in arts. The future of your children can be worrisome.

Meera felt guilty and ashamed at her own self-centeredness. She had never asked Asha how her life was! "Bhabi, is something bothering you?" Asha was not expecting that little girl in frocks, long braid flying behind her, to pose such a solemn question.

She looked at Meera curiously. "No, Choti, why do you ask?"

"You look too tired. You do so much, and I come from Canada and sit on my butt like another *maharani, queen.* I am so sorry, Ji, I should help you." The truth was that life drained her in Canada; her India trip had become a therapeutic escape. Before Asha could reply, the doorbell rang, impatiently, repeatedly.

Ma opened the door to a gush of raucus. "Pranam Mama, Papa, how are you?" Rakesh looked happy.

"Pranam Dadi. Krishan Bhaiya said that he will throw me out of the car if I talk too much. You tell him, na Dadi!" Keshav complained. He was eighteen years old, but being the youngest one, the older sibling and cousins bullied him habitually.

"I have to change my saree, it is so crumpled!" Nalini's voice rang.

Asha became worried. "Choti, we will have to serve tea first, we will deal with dinner later."

Meera came out of kitchen and hugged everyone then moved toward Nalini, who was leaving the room, "Hello, Bhabi."

Without looking at Meera, Nalini retorted, "I'll be back," and left.

Nalini's obvious disrespect for Rakesh's family did not allow for good relations between Meera and her. How do you relate to someone who does not wish to relate with you?

The nonexistent bond was further damaged during Meera's visit to Chandigarh the month before.

A volcanic explosion in the kitchen brought Meera out of her reverie. *I hope it is not a fire*, she thought as she ran down the stairs.

True enough, there was a sizzling fire, but it was emanating from Nalini's red eyes. The outline of a small shadow immured in the adumbrate corner of the kitchen was barely visible. As Meera approached, she recognized Kewli, the maid's daughter; she was pale with dread pasted on her trivial physiognomy. Her black doe eyes shimmered with tears and stood out as disproportionally colossal.

Nalini's shrill, strident voice attained an acicular edge. "What are you hiding in your hand? Show me, show me! My god, such a small thing and a 'big deed,' stealing! I should have known, you mother-daughter team are no good. Sushma warned me to be careful, but I am befkoof, *stupid*, I trust. In kaliyug, *immoral times*, trust a maid? I say open your hand, or I will slap you!" Nalini's threat was real.

Meera looked at Kewli kindly. "Come on, Bhabi, I am sure she hasn't stolen anything!"

Nalini's fury found another target. "And you, you are the one who spoils them! It does not work here, this is not Canada! These low people can only be dealt with joota, *shoe*!"

Meera walked up to the little girl. "Kewli, I know you did not do anything wrong. Show me what you have in your hand."

Kewli's tear glands that had been gripped by fear found a sudden release at the touch of a rare trust. With a loud sob, Kewli sat down, placed her face between her knees, and bawled.

Meera controlled her tears; she saw the vast colorful land of India with millions of Kewlis sobbing with their tiny faces buried in their knees out of fear, shame, and untold pain.

Meera sat down on the floor and opened Kewli's little brown fist, gently.

"Kewli, this is the piece of burfi, *sweet*, I gave you! Why didn't you eat it?"

Pallor swept over Nalini's red-with-anger face. "Did you give her this burfi?"

Meera turned to Kewli and questioned her, "Why didn't you tell Bhabi that I gave it to you?"

Tears kept flowing; Kewli was mum. Robbed of confidence in herself and faith in the cruel world at an early age, how could she expect her truth to be believed?

Meera lifted her chin with her right hand. "Look at me. Look at me, Kewli." Kewli slowly raised her head and looked deep into Meera's gentle eyes. In her liquid black eyes, there lurked a portentous shadow of the knowledge that she would always live in this world in fear of being crushed unjustly.

"Kewli, listen, never fear. Tell your truth, people will believe you. Bhabi would have understood and believed, wouldn't you, Bhabi?"

Nalini had not yet recovered from the humiliation of losing face; she issued a disdainful and defiant "umph" and left – whatever that meant was left for Meera and Kewlei to decipher.

Meera wiped Kewli's tears with her palloo, gave her a glass of water, patted her head affectionately, and said, "Now, eat it."

Kewli did not move, just fixed her gaze on the floor.

"What, you don't like the delicious burfi?"

Kewli shook her head in a slant that in those parts means yes.

"Then?"

Kewli was emboldened; she replied hesitatingly, "I want to take it for Bhola, my little brother."

An unearthly softness and glow enshrouded Kewli's face. A rare glimpse into the soul of a child revealed to Meera a yet unbeknownst truth; rich people may possess all the material opulence, but it is the poor who hold the real wealth of the spirit of love and selflessness. Who is the greater pauper? she wondered.

An intangible tension always hung like a fog in the ambiance of that house; Rakesh often looked dissipated. This time, Meera noticed that he was stooping a little while walking and sitting; it hurt her deep inside. What was eating him?

There was animated and noisy reunion of cousins; Nishant had come with Rakesh too, in spite of rude hints from Nalini that the car would be too crowded. Keshav and Krishan squeezed him at the back happily. "Mummy, you have all the space that you can handle, so, stop whining. We are fine at the back."

Nalini looked angrily at Rakesh, who was silently maneuvering the heavy traffic. It was expedient for Rakesh to seem busy and remain silent at such times; otherwise, there was much scope for unending peril.

All the youngsters missed their Par Dadi, *father's dadi*. They used to sit around her to please her. They figured that she was rich and could include them in her will. Keshav was the only one truly in love with Dadi. He would sit on the floor with his head on Dadi's warm lap; her frail fingers caressed his curly black hair. Maybe his innocence reminded Dadi of Dadaji's chastity.

Amidst the chaos of clashing voices, kids teasing one another, Rakesh's worried query about Papa and Ma's health, Atul questioning Rakesh about his job, dinner was served.

Even before the dinner was over, Nishant, who was the leader of the pack, raised his voice and declared, "Let us go, friends," motioning to Neeti, Keshav, and Krishan.

Neeti said excitedly, "But I have to change?"

"Aré, that is the lafda, *complication*, with girlie-girls! What is wrong with what you are wearing, eh?" Krishan complained.

Atul raised his hands for attention. "Hey, hey, wait a minute! Where are you going? It is late already, man!"

Nishant was irritated. "Papa, I am twenty-one, I cannot have a curfew now."

"Why not!" Atul smiled wickedly.

"Ma, tell him." He turned to the regular conciliator. "What can happen in the mall? There are hundreds of witnesses!"

"Okay," Atul relented. "Don't be too late. It is not safe, Bhai."

Summer evenings at Mall Road were exotic. Diwali of neon lights sparkled in the eyes of the young decked-up-girls and whistling naughty-eyed, teasing young boys. The crowd was mostly young people sprinkled with seemingly out-of-place older people and younger children. The Mall Road was so tightly packed with humans that it was impossible to walk at will; you moved en masse with the procession.

Of late, it had become customary for the Bombay moviemakers, to bring hero and heroine together in Simla and film them sauntering on the Mall Road or walking on small paths in the valleys or peaks of the green lush mountains. A macho villain with huge tattoos on his bare muscular arms, murderous-staring eyes, and a red scarf tied around the thick neck would appear on the scene to create an authentic triangle. Mostly, one of the hero-heroine team is rich and the other is poor. Does not really matter what transpires in the middle of the movie; eventually, villain is beaten up and put in his place, which is generally behind bars. The happy couple ties the knot, heroine wears red bangles, brocaded saree, and stroll arm in arm on the mall, where they met the first time. The end. Whether they live happily ever after is left to the viewer's imagination.

Many times, a crowd gathers like honeybees around a lovely film actress or handsome film star, talking and giving autographs, sometimes on young girls' hands or blushing cheeks, cherished and protected for a couple of weeks until the respective mother threatens suicide.

The Mall Road had become even more crowded ever since Simla became the capital of a new province called Himachal Pradesh that was carved out of Punjab territory. Instantly, it ceased to be a holiday resort; Mall Road became littered with cans, bottles, paper, cigarette butts, discarded food, etc.

On occasion, the chief minister and other ministers of Himachal Pradesh or ministers from the Central Government were seen strolling on the Mall. They went home humiliated and disgusted, brought down to earth by the lack of attention that defined their relative place by the citizenry.

The young foursome were not coming home anytime soon. After the "fashion parade" on the mall, a *dosa* at coffee house, and a movie at the Regal Theatre, that was located on the slopes behind the Ridge, were imperative to consummate the evening successfully.

Meera and Asha cleared up the dishes on the dining table and piled under the sink for the maid to clean the next day.

"I hope the Maharani, *Queen,* shows up tomorrow!" Asha sounded worried.

"Or an imported maid from Canada can be called to replace her, not to worry!"

"Choti, keep your promise tomorrow." Asha laughed.

Suddenly, Asha said, "Choti, only seven days for your flight. Have you done all your shopping?"

"Mostly. Just one is left." Meera spoke shyly.

"What?"

"I want to get an embroidered kurta for Prashantji."

Asha smiled at Meera affectionately.

"Yes, Papa, he is a very good man."

Papa was reclining on the sofa chair in front of the large window of the living room; his eyes were half shut. Papa and Ma had started to think of moving to Chandigarh with Rakesh; old age was not conducive to cold, wet weather.

Meera came from behind with soft steps. "Papa are you sleeping, dreaming, or hallucinating?"

"All at once, Choti, at my age what else can one do?" Meera pulled a footstool close to him and took his hands in hers; his long fingers seemed frail and longer.

"I have to tell you something, but promise not to worry."

A gleam of satisfaction filled Papa's deep eyes after he heard Meera. He coughed after a pause. "So, is there any possibility of marriage?"

Meera's eyes moistened; she looked away. How can she tell him? She can't even tell herself! Crossroads were a constant in her life. The possibility was and wasn't at the same time.

- # -

"Ma'am, can you pick up Rishi!" There was panic in Kelley's voice.

"What happened? Is everything okay?"

"No, ma'am. Madam is hurt, and Peter is taking her to the hospital."

"I will be there soon."

Rare as it was, Prashant and Meera were sitting cozily on the couch; Meera's head was on his broad shoulder as he folded her in his embrace.

Meera looked up at Prashant anxiously. "Granny is hurt."

Rishi was already standing outside the gate; Kelley stood by the main door to watch him. He ran toward the car, opened the car door with a jerk, planted himself on the passenger seat next to Meera, and banged the door shut with zeal—all in a few seconds.

Meera attempted to hug him, but he pushed her away and shouted, "Let's go!"

"What happened?"

"Let's go." He was getting angry.

Meera drove home in silent prayer.

Rishi went straight to his room and slammed the door.

Meera knocked gently.

"Go away, leave me alone."

Meera spoke as calmly as she could. "You have to tell me what happened. I am in the living room whenever you are ready."

Meera phoned Kelley.

"I don't know exactly what happened. Madam and Master Rishi were watching TV in the living room. I heard voices go up then a crash. I ran in. Madam's head was bleeding, the pieces of a green china vase were scattered all over, and Master was standing on one side, crying."

It was hard for Meera to keep her palpitations in check. Her head swirled with anxiety, apprehension. What is happening to Rishi?

Meera phoned the hospital and spoke to the nurse in the emergency. "Mrs. Henderson has some stitiches on her head. But she is feeling fine. She will go home soon. But who are you?"

It took Meera a few seconds to figure out her relationship with Granny. "She is my adopted son's grandmother."

"Oh! No problem, ma'am, thank you."

Apparently, Meera's social status elevated even if her connection with Mrs. Henderson was indirect.

Meera walked to Rishi's room and announced, "I am coming in."

Rishi was lying down on his, bed pretending to read an *Archie* comic book. His fair face that was developing a harvest of stubble was red with anguish, confusion, and defiance.

Meera pulled a chair close to the bed, sat down, and said, "I am listening."

He knew there was no getting away, "I threw the vase at her because she made me so mad!"

"What did she say?"

"She called you a slut." He continued, "And said that if you loved me, you wouldn't be running around with men. I felt blood rush to my head, and I don't know the rest."

Meera let him finish, kept her cool though pain of humiliation pierced through her heart.

"I hate her. I do not want to see her, ever."

Meera got up calmly from the chair and sat by Rishi on the bed.

"If you do not want to see her, then you don't have to. But you must understand that no matter what she says, I am the same, and I am not a slut. And I love you more than anyone else in the world."

"Even more than Prashant uncle?"

That was a tough but critical test; she did not hesitate. "Yes."

Rishi's face relaxed, and he looked at her with strange satisfaction.

"But throwing the vase at Granny was a very bad idea. What if she died of the wounds?"

Rishi's eyes became tearful. "I felt awful when I saw her with blood all over her face. I am not a bad kid, Mom."

Rishi's innocent and desperate self-appraisal hurt Meera. "Of course not, you are a good kid." She emphasized, "You are a wonderful child of God, just going through a difficult time. Rishi, never forget that I love you and will always love you no matter what. We will work through it. Don't worry." Meera got up and hugged him. Rishi did not resist.

Mrs. Henderson's bedroom was like a hazy antiquated room from British royalty's palaces: silver, gold vases, and marble statues for decorations; velvet dark curtains; a flowery Iranian silk rug covered every inch of the floor; large framed paintings of the Impressionist era hung on all the walls. Granny was lying on a pompous bed overshadowed by a satiny canopy supported by dark mahogany pillars. She looked like a shriveled, squeezed wet doll.

Rishi walked cautiously toward her. Granny smiled and extended her old hand. "So, how is my Roy?"

Meera had picked Rishi from his school and drove him to Granny's mansion.

Rishi's fear was dispelled by Granny's soft words. He inched toward her bed and spoke stiffly, "I am sorry. But you should not have hurt my feelings."

He turned around and ran down before Granny could respond.

Kelley came after him briskly. "Master Rishi, Madam wants you to stay and have dinner here."

"No, thank you, Kelley, tell her I don't want to," he said in an agitated voice.

Tension in the air became a fixture after that. Rishi moped constantly, looked at Meera accusingly, as though it was all her fault. It was obvious that he was attached to Granny; she was his real mother's mother, a tangible and consoling kinship.

Rishi had mixed feelings about his visits to Granny's mansion. He was bored to death, but the special affection, expensive gifts, lavish lifestyle in a colossal extravagant house almost made up for that.

Meera felt trapped, yet she knew what she had to do.

Chachaji said placidly, "I know you will decide on a moral path."

Satish said, "Be careful. Don't let your idealism hurt you."

Kanchan's words, "You are crazy."

Sunil said, "I will advise you against it, you cannot swallow poison knowingly."

Anil added, "Meera, I am so afraid you will get hurt."

Prashant said, "I will go along."

Asha, in the gossip circle to Neelam, "Meera tries to show to the world that she is very pious. You don't know how low her character is, oh God."

Bela did not chew her words, "Don't, don't send Rishi to that buddi, *old woman*. Please. We all know that she is going to give you grief."

"Di, Rishi loves me, no matter what Granny says, in his heart, he knows me. Truth will win in the end."

"In the meantime, you will suffer, badly, stupid."

"Di, Rishi loves her, and she loves him, that much I am sure about. I cannot take away that source of joy from him."

Bela hit her forehead with the palm of her hand gently, a gesture of utter frustration in Indian body language. "That rakshsi, *demon*, has no love for anyone. Why don't you see the truth?"

"Doing one's Dharma, *righteous duties*, is mostly inconvenient, but we cannot abandon it because of that." Tayaji's voice echoed in her spirit.

The situation was still in limbo when Meera decided to visit India.

Rishi declared, "I always miss the sports camp. I don't want to go to India."

The counselor advised her, "Mrs. Maitra, it will do him good and channelize his frustrations."

"Rishi, call me every week. I have given enough money to Mr. Robert."

Rishi was ecstatic, even gave Meera a much-craved hug that had been a rare gift.

"Promise to be careful, keep yourself safe, and do as Mr. Robert tells you to. Take care, Beta. I will miss you." Meera became emotional. Rishi laughed. "Mom! It is only for six weeks, and so many of us are going. What can happen?"

Meera gave Mr. Robert a list of phone numbers for emergency contact. Mrs. Henderson's phone number was not included.

- # -

"What I do not understand is how a horrible, inhuman construct like untouchability could be a part of Hinduism, Tayaji?"

Vineet looked gaunt; the vision in his dark solemn eyes had sunk farther inward. Fingers of his right hand were twisted, a long-lasting gift of a short-term emergency.

Krishan had come home from the Mall that night, all excited. "Who do you think we met at the Mall today, Bua?"

While Meera was exercising her mind in futility, Keshav could not hold the precious information that he knew would delight her. "Vineet Uncle!"

"Really!" Meera felt a wave of thrill. Not only he was a companion of her childhood, she had fallen in love with him—sort of. Sort of because she had not been able to freely admit to herself that she could love another man so soon after Mohit's demise.

Krishan glared at Keshav admonishingly. "Stupid. You cannot keep anything," then turned to Meera. "Bua, I told Vineet Uncle that you are leaving for Delhi in three days and you will be at Tayaji's house for two days before leaving for Canada. He was happy because he has a meeting in Delhi. He said to tell you he will see you there."

Meera looked at Vineet sadly and asked, "Sugar in your tea?"

"No."

"Since when?"

"I got used to having no sugar."

Meera understood.

In Bihar, the most backward and indigent province in Indian Confederation, one young achhoot, *untouchable,* in his yearning for social justice, dared to stand as an independent in provincial elections against a wealthy landlord. He refused to give in to the threats; his charred body was found in a ditch a day before the elections.

Hacking and killing the poor achhoot labourers who defied the landlords was quite frequent in the villages of Bihar; no one would raise an eyebrow. But burning alive? The incident sent waves of horror in the hearts of all decent Indians all over India.

Tayaji announced with certainty. "Untouchability and Hinduism are completely incompatible."

"How?"

"Simple reason. Hinduism stipulates that Brahm, *Universal God,* the Absolute, pervades all manifest existence. The same spirit of God is present in all living beings as Atma, Soul, the 'Self,' our Reality. Soul is the same in achhoot and brahmin, *highest priest class,* only the external apparel of the soul, the body that is constituted by nonliving matter, looks different. Hence there is an unbreachable unity amongst all humans and God. That is the Advait Sidhant, *the philosophy of Advait, only one Existence.*"

"What is meant by Advait? I do not understand." Vineet looked puzzled.

"Advait is the highest pinnacle of spirituality. It means 'not two.' Only God exists. He is the fountainhead of all 'Souls' as well as their destiny because ultimately, all spirits merge with the Absolute God. Hence, there is an absolute, unviolated unity in existence. This principle is the fountainhead of all morality and ethics in Hinduism. Since you and I are one, I love you as I love myself. I cannot possibly harm you. Altruistic and selfless humans are living examples of consummation of the principles of Advait."

"But how did caste system creep up in Hinduism?"

"All societies excepting Marxism have working hierarchical classes. The creation of a Varn system, *division of society,* was a socioeconomic necessity for proper functioning of villages in ancient times. In absence of trading schools, the vocation of a father was passed on to the offspring. Hierarchy was there, but it was more functional than oppressive. It was the brahmin, *highest priest,* class that, over thousands of years, accentuated the ranking distinctions to be able to justify oppression and exploitation of the least powerful class, the shudras, *the lowest class.* Untouchability is a more recent aberration that stretches the tyranny of priest class to the extreme. There is no mention of untouchability in Hindu Scriptures.

"Shri Krishna ate food at the Shudra Vidur's simple house and rejected the invitation of the Prince Duryodhan in his palace. Shabri, a Shudra devotee of Shri Ram, who was an incarnation of God, tasted each ber, *a fruit,* to ensure that it was sweet, before offering to her Lord. Shri Ram devoured each one of the fruit with utmost pleasure and told Shabri, "Mother, today after a long time, I feel content." With these examples, how can anyone claim that Shudras are low class and not to be touched?"

The evening had quietly slid into darkness; there were sounds of happy birds going home, children playing in the playground across from Tayaji's house; some night creatures had already come out of their slumber and shrieked to vanquish the tired voices of the day life-forms. Clanks of utensils in the kitchens of the neighbourhood pierced the darkness. The deep silence in Tayaji's living room somehow maintained its tranquility.

Vineet shifted in his sofa chair restlessly. Gangu came in to announce dinner. Meera smiled faintly. "A bit later, Kaka," who then looked at Tayaji for support.

Lack of response was considered unanimous; Gangu went away, disappointed and mumbling, "No one understands! I have to clean up everything then go out to the presswalla, *the man who irons clothes,* to pick up clothes."

He did not know, of course, that their discussion was unworldly, not as immediately pertinent as dinner, but pertinent nevertheless.

"Tayaji, what is the purpose or meaning of life? The everyday changing paradigms around us defy the notion of any unflagging, enduring Truth. At least I cannot find it."

"Some philosophers believe that God created this existence for the 'Soul' to evolve to be able to Realize its unity with God. But Hindu sages believe that Soul is already evolved, perfect and Absolute because Soul is a wave on the sea of 'Absolute Brahm' and is not distinct from it. Hence, it is fully evolved in not only man, but in all living sentients. It is the mind and intellect that needs to evolve to be able to grasp the Reality of God and His inseparability from us. Lower life-forms have a 'Soul' but do not possess the mechanisms of cognizance to understand or recognize God. *Homo sapiens* are the only animals with sufficiently evolved intellect, reasoning power, and logic to conceptualize God and Soul by removing the obstacle of 'ignorance' that stands between man and God. Once ignorance of the nature of Reality is removed and the illusive bondage with the material world is severed, man's final act is to discard his intellect for a purposeful union of his Soul with God."

Vineet was doubtful. "Tayaji, I do find this whole concept interesting, but is it really true?"

"The fact that you are asking questions means that you have reached your frontiers. But you are not the end of this *Samsara* or the Reality. When we reach our *finis* point and cannot go any farther, we are ready to let our egos go. Only then can we step into the transcendental realm of Truth. Learn from learned sages like Vivekananda, Dayanand, Shankara Charaya, Sri Aurobindo, Dr. Radha Krishnan, and many more who have spent their life time pursuing what you are seeking in your free time. The ideas and reflections of these spiritual giants will reveal to you a fraction of the Truth and give you a craving for the whole. Make sure to seek Reality within you. Like Tibetan Buddhists, who continuously spin the prayer wheel that contain strips of paper on which are written the words, 'Om Mani Padme Hum,' meaning 'the jewel is within the Lotus.'

"'To seek and understand life is to seek satisfaction, for there is nothing to match the satisfaction of understanding.' Socrates said that, so it must be true."

Three months after Meera returned from India, she received a sorrowful letter from Papa.

"Your Tayaji was born a saint, lived like a saint, and died a saint."

Meera was shattered.

Tayaji was one of her gurus from whom she had learned that life's beauty is defined by three words: truth, love, and compassion.

Chapter Four

In ancient Vedantic times, a young aspirant sought a guru who could guide him to Moksh, the ultimate freedom, that is a blissful union with God.

Sitting on a woven mat that lay on the mud floor of his straw hut, the guru was absorbed in the scriptures attempting to find his own way to Moksh.

The seeker knocked at the door; the guru looked up. He knew.

Silently, he got up from his straw seat, picked up a metallic pail from an obscure corner of his hut, opened the door, and handed the empty pail to him.

The young man was puzzled. As he was about to query, the guru said somberly, "Go fill this pail to the brim with water from the Ganges river," that flowed by the hut. The seeker did the guru's bidding.

The guru stood at the doorway. "Can you see the mango tree at the end of the garden?"

"Yes, Guruji."

"Take this pail, walk over to the mango tree, and water it." The lad was intrigued, "Could Moksh be that easy?"

"But," the sage cautioned, "make sure you do not spill a single drop of the sacred water."

"And," he continued, "you have to recite 'OM' without interruption. Otherwise, you start all over again."

The youth laughed to himself. He could have Moksh in less than fifteen minutes and become a renowned rishi, instantly, before the evening meal.

He held the pail firmly with his sturdy right hand and set out toward his goal.

Out of nowhere, a man appeared and bumped into the disciple, who lost his balance.

"You stupid man, watch where you go!"

Ah, but the sacred water lay disgraced on the ground and "OM" scattered in the winds. He went back to the river Ganges, filled the pail, and focused on "OM" with greater concentration.

The young man did not notice a rope lying on the ground; he tripped, water spilt. He was enraged, "OM" forgotten.

Next time, he was distracted by two fighting men, a comely lass passing by swinging her hips rhythmically, a snake crossing his path, a barking dog wanting to drink the water from the pail—it went on and on. Years passed.

Slowly, without his cognizance, the young man became more centered within himself, less aware of the happenings around him.

One beautiful, sunny spring morning, wildflowers bloomed, grass was lush, sky clear and deep, but the young man did not know whether he was distracted or not. He reached the tree with "OM" resonating in his consciousness; the pail was intact.

The seeker of Truth did not need to pour water at the base of the mango tree. His guru stood there smiling with his blessing. "Now, you are ready to tread the path toward God and get Moksh because your 'ego' that is attracted and affected by the external world has been annihilated. Your heart and soul are pure, unblemished, and ready for an encounter with God."

Rishi stared at his plate, hoping to find answers to all his life enigmas.

"Rishi." Meera looked at him across the dining table. "Do you want to tell me what happened?"

He remained quiet and pulled up his usual wall of silence to defy her.

Thorny bushes and iron fences with sharp claws stood between Meera and Rishi. He was bleeding; she wanted to embrace him and embalm his wounds. But as soon as she got closer, he ran farther away, like a mirage, in sight but out of reach.

Mr. James, the principal's tone was condescending. "I don't know what is happening in your life, Mrs. Maitra, but Rishi's grades are slipping. He is more disruptive. Today he had a fight with Neil and punched him. I would like to arrange some counseling for him."

"No!" Meera was appalled. "He is stepping into a challenging domain of adolescence, I will talk to him."

Mr. James was not impressed. "As you wish."

Meera waited for a few minutes then asked in an even voice, "Why did you hit Neil?"

Rishi looked up and spoke insolently, "What do you know, what they say to me?"

"You never told me, Beta? What do they say?"

"They tease me that I am a Paki's, *Indians and Pakistanis,* son."

In her remotest dreams, Meera could not imagine that Rishi could be a victim of racism. Why, but he is white?

"Come, Rishi, we cannot be affected by what people say. Remember the story of elephant walking calmly while mad dogs bark?"

Rishi was furious. "You don't know anything! They call me a bastard, you got from a white man!" Meera was horrified. "I didn't know that! Why didn't you tell me earlier?"

A pungent fire flickered in his tormented eyes; it scared Meera. "How could I? You are busy running around with Prashant uncle!"

Meera's face reddened. "I am always here for you, you know that."

"How does it matter? What would you do?"

"I will make sure that you know and believe the truth."

"But they don't!" Rishi was becoming louder.

"Do you tell them that you are adopted?"

"I do, I do, but they laugh in my face and call me a liar!"

Meera was dumbfounded. *Jane, why did you leave him without identity?* But Jane was not there, and a ruthless tornado had conjured up in her path.

Meera suppressed a breath of exasperation and spoke with a composed daring, "Rishi, what can we do except to ignore rubbish? We know the truth, God knows it, people who love us know it, and the rest do not matter."

Rishi shouted now. "But they do matter! I have to see them at the school every day! They hate me, and I hate them!"

His words pained Meera. "Beta, hate is a very strong word. I do understand how hard it must be . . . I will talk to Mr. James tomorrow. But I need some names."

"Are you crazy, Mom? They will really torture me then. Don't do anything please, let me deal with them myself."

"Not the way you dealt with Neil. Look at me, Rishi."

Rishi looked up reluctantly. "What?"

"Let us be strong and dignified. Even if someone provokes you, just walk away, look the other way. If you don't react, they will stop doing it. Rishi, please, do not use violence in words or actions."

Rishi looked up at her desperately. "Even if someone hurts me?"

"Yes! You tell the teacher, principal, me. Please do not stoop to their level. Otherwise, what is the difference between them and you?"

"Mom," he protested. "They hurt me and make me angry. I cannot take it like a sissy. I don't care what you say. I will do what I feel like."

"Please, don't. If you act deplorably, you will lose your self-respect. Don't you understand ultimately that is what matters?"

Rishi was not ready to surrender his right to protect himself for dubious principles.

"No!" He was really mad. "It is easy for you to say!" Rishi pushed his chair noisily and stomped out of the room.

Meera did understand that a sixteen-year-old boy's daily survival in a cruel world required more than inner knowledge of righteousness. She left the kitchen and the dining table in a mess, walked over slowly to the living room, and collapsed on the couch. She rested her aching head on the back of the sofa. *What now?* She looked up knowing fully well that only time will answer her question. God does not reveal future, for good reason.

In the past years, racism had raised its ugly head; vandalism and rude remarks had become common. Umesh's shop was broken into, stuff was stolen, merchandise strewn on the floor, glass items were shattered; a sign on the glass window written in orange lipstick said, "Paki, go home."

Meera also had a firsthand experience of racism.

Two seemingly middle-aged women, dressed fashionably in reasonably expensive top pants, were chatting cordially with a man who looked about the same age. The women's hair were neatly set like a frozen halo, faces were heavily made up to cover their age that did nothing of the sort. They were gesturing profusely, vying for his attention; he talked to one then the other about the weather, economy. Trudeau's arrogance, breaking of his marriage, blaming his young flirtatious wife, Maggie. Last but not least, the conversation turned to the selfish immigrants who come to Canada and have no qualms whatsoever in snatching jobs from the locals.

Meera was sitting in the principal's waiting room that was furnished with five chairs, a couple of side tables with piles of magazines, and a coat hanger on one side that was loaded with heavy coats. The glitter of Christmas was over; January, as usual, was chilly and bleak; people had exhausted their pool of good cheer as well as funds. Conversations generally turned into grumpy complaints about the misery of the weather and more of the same to come. It was pleasant to hear the cheery voices of the two women and the man.

The ladies went into the principal's office, and Meera was left in the room with the gentleman. He was casually dressed up, in blue jeans and beige jacket. Meera attempted to strike a conversation, "What a cold day. It may snow tonight."

The man smiled forcefully then picked up a magazine, obviously to avert her encroachment in his space.

The man who, a few minutes ago, was the embodiment of social grace, suddenly turned into a dry autumn leaf, unable to impart any oxygen or moisture to his environ.

Meera had experienced similar aversive attitudes of some white individuals. She let it pass because it was easier to deal with such unsavory situations by not dealing with these at all.

People in the West, generally, avoid acknowledging other humans in their surroundings by either introverting attention toward their inner life or busy themselves with a magazine they may not even be interested in.

In India, in any kind of waiting room, especially a doctor's office, the woman next to you would look at you, smile self-consciously, slowly tilt her head in your direction, make eye contact, and whisper, "Bahen, *sister*, what is wrong with you?" Indeed, it is an intimate question—that is, if you are from the West. If you are an Indian, you feel touched, take a deep breath, and spill all your beans. The woman takes your hand, says encouraging words, and tells you that she will pray for you. You are further moved, ready to ask the woman about her plight. She may weep, her sweaty hands squeeze yours in her anguish; she recounts her illnesses, twisting lips with each description, eyes fixed on your face to see your reaction. You have to say, "Oh, really," "Ahh . . ." to express your empathy. The woman may go farther and inch toward you, lowering her saree to show you the scar from the appendicitis operation she had, or may raise her blouse bottom to reveal the cut that was made to get her sick gallbladder out of her abdomen, as the case may be.

You are duly impressed; she gets teary eyed. "Behan, it still hurts, you know!"

"Oh, that is bad, very sad." You keep searching for possible phrases to express your sorrow at her predicament. There are hugs, exchange of addresses, promises of letters that are sometimes kept up until you die.

Naturally, counseling or psychiatry is not a popular profession in India. Who needs the mind doctors when experienced, free counselors are available in every corner?

Of course, men do not participate in the process of free mutual counseling; hence more men than women get heart attacks!

"I wish to point out that some boys are mistreating Rishi with racial undertones in their attitude," Meera blurted out quite directly to Mr. James.

Mr. James was an older man, with gray hair and a small stoop. His eyebrows scrunched toward his eyes, and his mouth developed an unhappy downward angle at the corners; he looked at her intimidatingly through his thick glasses.

"I am shocked!" He feigned surprise and lay an unlikely claim, "There are no racial problems in my school, Mrs. Maitra, at least I haven't heard any."

"You have heard now, from me. The impact of racism is spilling right in my home. Please look into it. I can provide you with some names."

"Oh, oh no! The children in this school are from good families, er . . . like you. The parents are mostly educated and have good values."

"I am not questioning their value systems, I am talking about the children's behavior. Look, I am a single mother, and Rishi is an adolescent going through many problems. He does not need extra blows to his fragile self-esteem. I will appreciate if you could speak with the parents of Peter Kent, Joshua Kramer, Neil Peek, and John Rogers. They are all in Rishi's class, tenth grade. Thank you." Meera got up before Mr. James could continue with his mumbling, fumbling remonstrance, indicating that he was not going to do anything about it.

- # -

For once, Parshant did not blow the situation into a colossal bubble of burlesque for fun. He even donned a rare doleful expression.

Anita was reading the mysteries of existence in a philosophy book while eating a sandwich at the cafeteria. She was studying for a degree in arts and science at the University of British Columbia in Vancouver. She was startled by a shrill, "Hi there, how are you?" Vimmy placed her plate of hamburger and fries on the table, sat down authoritatively, bent forward, and batted her eyelids with excitement, "So, how's that flirtatious aunty of yours? Your family is quite close to her, na?"

Anita was taken aback. "Which aunty are you talking about?"

Vimmy winked wickedly, "Now, now, the aunty with that *chitta* son she claims to have adopted."

Anita was beside herself with rage; she shouted, "She did adopt him, stupid!" The students at the other tables looked at her. Anita lowered her voice but maintained the acicular tone. "She is not flirtatious, she is the finest person on earth. Where do you get your gossip from, anyway?"

Vimmy smiled a Neelam smile, all knowing and base, the source of her information being beyond doubt.

"Everyone knows excepting your simpleton family. Come on, don't pretend, she has been running around with . . ." Vimmy fumbled for the name. "That uncle who looks like actor Dilip Kumar, *a famous actor*?"

Anita felt trapped. Meera Aunty and Prashant Uncle were together a lot, but she never thought of it as flirting; there was dignity in their relationship. When Mohit, her "most favorite" uncle disappeared suddenly from the face of her world, Anita transferred her affection to the closest substitute, Meera. Bela, being old-fashioned, dealing with a young girl's milestones fell in Meera's lap. She was the one who calmed a hysterical Anita the first-time blood spotting appeared on her panty that naturally led to the most disconcerting topic of sex. The feat was accomplished with much redness of faces,as well as shock on Anita's part.

"No, Aunty! That is not true!"

"Yes, it is!"

"You mean my mom and dad?"

"Yes! Where did you think you came from?"

It took Anita a minute to recover from the newly acquired information, and then they both started to giggle that lasted for extended period.

Meera had taken Anita to buy her first bra. She had been an unsuccessful advocate of Anita, who wanted to be in step with her peers and date. Di looked at Meera as though she was crazy.

"Meera, how can you even suggest that? You know in white culture there are no limits? Anita will do what others do. We cannot take a chance. No dating!"

"But, Di. They can go to movies, restaurants, and friends' get-togethers. What can they do there? Communicate your fears, values, and limits. She loves you, she will respect your boundaries. Otherwise, she may rebel, and situation may go out of hand!"

Anita told Meera, "Aunty, I am going to UBC next year, I will do what I want."

Meera laughed. "Do what is right. Don't go haywire."

Anita perked herself and looked deep into Vimmy's dark and mischievous eyes. "People have dirty minds. My aunty and uncle are just good friends, that is all. Why don't you show some respect to your elders and stop spreading lies?" By the end of the sentence, Anita's throat choked at her aunty's humiliation; she was not doing enough to defend her.

Vimmy sneered, "Don't get upset, yar, *friend.* As to the source of my gossip, your Asha Aunty is telling everyone the gruesome details. But who cares? This is Canada. not India." She moved a little forward and whispered, "Guess who else is flirting in our town?"

Anita did not hide her disgust and started to collect her books.

Vimmy was disappointed. "You are such a bore."

Anita felt disturbed. Could it be true? She went to her dormitory and called Bela, "Mom, guess who I ran into in the cafeteria today?"

Bela was thrilled to hear Anita's voice. She shouted to Sunil, who was sitting in the living room reading the newspaper. "It is Anita, Ji? Yes, Beti, how are you? We miss you so much? Are you coming over the long weekend? Otherwise, I will come!"

"No, Ma, don't come, I promise I will come. Mama, I ran into Vimmy today."

Bela was not impressed. "You stay away from her! Both mother-daughter are bad news."

Recently, two best friends had turned into bitter enemies, thanks to Neelam's skillful maneuvering.

"You know, Sushma, I like you a lot—that is the only reason I am telling you. This is a wicked world. You think someone is your friend, even best friend, and you are ready to die for them. I know, I know you are that type of a person. But the so-called friend? She will stab you with malicious lies! Toba, toba, I could not believe it when Sarita told me that Sushma's family in India is not as rich as she claims, and the jewelry sets she gets from them are not real gold, they are fake! Then she tells me not to tell you! By God, I was so upset for days, my husband told me, 'Neelu, you should not worry so much for the world! You will kill yourself!' But I can die for friendship! I am your friend, na? Am I not? Then how can I hear your disgrace and stay quiet? I told Sarita not to tell lies and left."

Sushma and Sarita never spoke to each other ever after, much to Sarita's chagrin because she had no clue why Sushma had started to hate her.

Anita was getting impatient. "But, Ma, listen! She was saying awful stuff about Meera Aunty and Prashant Uncle," and started to cry.

Bela became serious. "Tell me, what did she say?"

"I know they are both so nice, I love them. But . . . I hope what Vimmy said is not true."

Bela was firm, "Anita, they are good friends who are helping each other in difficult times. Tell this to anyone who points their fingers at them."

Sunil was on the other line, listening silently. He spoke at the end, "Don't pay attention to people, just focus on your studies. We will talk about it when you come here."

Air was heavy, Bela was worried. "Meera, your reputation should not be soiled, na?"

Prashant spoke in an unruffled voice. "I will not do anything that would jeopardize Meera's life. Maybe we will stop seeing each other?" He looked at Meera keenly.

Meera looked defiant. "No! We are not doing anything wrong. We will keep doing what we are with heads held high!"

Her words were tough, but the underlying tremor in her voice did not escape anyone's notice.

Prashant clapped. "Hurray, that is my brave girl!"

Bela admonished him, "Don't joke, buddhu, *silly*."

Sunil listened attentively as usual. He was in the habit of reflecting on all arguments before opening his mouth. He looked at Prashant and Meera. "Get married. We will arrange everything. What do you think?"

Meera leaned back on the sofa. "Bhai, we would have it if we could."

Prashant's face became clouded, but his smile shone through, "I agree with Meera. The time for marriage has not arrived yet, Sunil!"

Meera was anguished, was it the right decision? She missed the one man who could guide her.

One month after Chachaji left for India, Meera received a letter from him. He wrote, "I am reading the book *The Speculative Philosophy.*

Baruch Spinoza, a seventeenth-century philosopher, concluded, in the essay 'Foundations of a Moral life,', 'But human power is very limited and is infinitely surpassed by the power of external causes, so that we do not possess an absolute power to adapt to our service the things which are without us. Nevertheless, we shall bear with equanimity those things which happen to us contrary to what a consideration of our own profit demands, if we are conscious that we have performed our duty, that the power we have, could not reach so far as to enable us to avoid those things and that we are a part of the whole of nature whose order we follow. If we clearly and distinctly understand this, the part of us which is determined by intelligence, that is to say, the better part of us, will be entirely satisfied there with and, in that satisfaction, will endeavor to persevere; for, insofar as we understand, we cannot desire anything excepting what is necessary, nor absolutely can we be satisfied with anything but the truth. Therefore, insofar as we understand these things properly will the efforts of the better part of us agree with the order of the whole nature.'

"Meera, Malcolm Muggeridge said in his autobiography, 'In all the larger shapings of a life, there is a plan already into which one has no choice but to fit.' We don't run this place, it runs itself. We are part of the running. Our will is bent by some higher power, which often saves us from ourselves. Surrender to that omnipotent being.

"Life does not ask too much from us for the blessing of form, only courage and love. Then its grace falls on us. It chips away the unnecessary, unreal and gross and exposes the subtle, the spirit, and the real in all its glory.

"Holding a chisel in its deft artistic hands, life confronts us. With every stroke, gentle or hard, it attempts to fulfill God's vision to create something sublime out of us. Ignorant of life's purpose, we wince, withdraw, resist, bend with every blow rather than stay upright with courage. As a result, the strike that is meant to create a soft curve produces a haphazard contortion. In the end, instead of a genuine piece of art, we become distorted statues of ourselves left standing naked, counting the marks of the wounds and cursing life and the Creator.

"Michelangelo was able to create David, a symbol of grandeur of human form, because marble did not wince to avoid the blows.

"If only we could stay equipoised through life's sculpturing blows, the pulchritude of the end product would surpass any piece of art created by man's hands.

"The tragedy of modern man is not that there is chaos around him, but there is void within him because we have lost touch with our true selves. We believe that we are this body, the material world the sole reality and happiness lies in fulfilling our worldly desires. Because everything is subject to everlasting, pervasive law of change, happiness is transient. We are forever in the pitiful bondage of desiring happiness, not getting or losing it if perchance we have it.

"When unfavourable change hit us, we cry but have nowhere to go, no shelter from ruthless transformations and transmutations of matter. Unfortunately, most of us do not know that man has a refuge that is unchangeable and constant. The visible world is multidimensional, the four dimensions—length, width, height, and time—are open to our sense perceptions and make up the empirical world. However, there is another dimension that is beyond observation, sensation and empirical analysis, hence not apprehensible to most humans.

"And that is the radiant and blissful sphere of the 'Fifth dimension,' 'I am,' our Real Self, the 'Soul'. We can only step into its ubiquitous dimentiality by transcending the other four dimensions. We come home to it because we belong here.

"Once we are conscious of and live in the protecting sanctuary of the Fifth dimension, without delay, the other illusionary dimensions disappear. The Truth at the center of our existence is the Fifth dimension, the only Reality, where we find total freedom from the clutches of form and ego that cause the misery in our lives.

"I know this about the workings of nature, that after a dark formidable night, no matter how long, the arrival of day is inevitable. Nothing can stop it. The courage and charisma of nature will bring it. But sometimes long, dark nights break us—the darkness imbues and rests so deep within our eyes that we lose cognizance of the possibility of light. Whether there is dark outside or light, we sit in darkness all our lives, then we are truly lost and defeated. And not to let it happen is victory. And by far, the greatest, profoundest triumph is when irrespective of darkness around us, the inner light of our spirit enables us to live as though it is all light.

"And that is where we need to abide, in the realm of the *Fifth Dimension*: once you are there you know that nothing can be lost, it is all there."

- # -

Bela furrowed her forehead, wrinkled her nose, and twisted her lips. "You should have stayed out of this lafda, *complication*. Budhu, *silly*."

"Maalti, sit down with Arun and talk. Tell him how he is hurting you."

Maalti was appalled at the mere suggestion. "Are you joking? As soon as I bring up any contentious issue, he shouts, throws things around, and stomps out of the house after banging the door. Lately, he slaps me for good measure."

Meera had been cautious. She knew that Maalti's education was limited to matriculation from India; her skin colour also stacked up against her like a red flag. How could she find a decent job? Like millions of women around the world, Maalti was stuck in the deadly quicksand of poisonous violence and domination all because of economic dependence. Not only history of nations, as Karl Marx had aptly concluded, but also history of individual relations depends on economic realities.

After Independence of India, Papa had vowed that his girls would not become victims of perpetual tyranny of men. He was shaken to his core by the indescribable disgrace of women that he witnessed during the darkest hours of Partition, *the time of Independence of India, it was partitioned into Pakistan and India.*

"Ram charan, Bhai, shut the door," Papa said without raising his head from the files. The small dark room had a cold, bare cemented floor; the rotted wood of windows had cracks that allowed chilly drafts of wind to enter at will. Ram charan had somehow procured, for those days nothing was easily available, an ancient room heater that decided on its own when to shut and start again.

Ram charan's coat was obviously not as warm as Papa's tweed overcoat that a friend had brought for him from England. He would sneakily shut the door often, hoping Papa did not notice. Papa wanted the anguished men to walk in without obstruction, without having to knock. But that was a chilly, misty morning. January in Delhi was generally overcast, sometimes rainy, but always gelid.

Papa smiled sadly as Ram charan leapt to close the door promptly.

During those excruciating dim days and never-ending cimmerian nights, miserable, fearful humans fell on their knees and prayed for the safety of their daughters, mothers, sisters, wives, and grandmothers. They looked up at the heavens for mercy. God, incredulous at the brutal and inhumane scene below on earth, just could not bear it; He shut His eyes. Neither man nor God took pity on the sweaty, benumbed bodies that crouched on the filthy floor of the truck. The bruised, bleeding, flesh peeped from their torn kameez, *shirt*, veils were shred into pieces during the struggle to save their honor; the young and old women alike arrived on both sides of the Indian border, crammed in trucks like animals.

Tortured faces were buried between their trembling knees, burning tears soaked their bosoms; cries of different pitch and tenor, the requiem of the tortured souls, formed a thick, black, liquid backdrop in which they wanted to dissolve and dissipate their disgrace.

Army barracks, where Indian sepoys once slept in anguish at having to beat their own brethren, became the temporary destination of the trucks. Three females were crammed in each barrack; the fact that they had no luggage helped because there was no space.

With each truckload, spilling with hapless, broken-up females that arrived in the camp, the lists of missing women were checked and relatives informed through defying channels since postal services had ceased to exist, much like everything else.

Papa was the chairman of a committee of three that was hurriedly set up because no one had expected humans to mutate into devils without conscience. Papa's two helpers ran around to organize the minute detail of day-to-day workings of the camp, the most tiresome task being to gather up enough rations to feed the females who had been starved for who knows how many days or weeks.

Women were medically checked, physical wounds were treated; everyone knew there was no cure for the emotional lacerations. They were fed, clothed, and sent to their barracks to share their excruciating past with the roommates. Warm friendships were moulded in the dark, dingy, cold rooms; shared encounters were the founding stones cemented by hot tears, held together by the locking of bruised achy bodies hugging and huddling together to keep away the dark shadows of fresh memories of indescribable, undeserved torment.

Papa's office was furnished with an unbalanced wooden worktable with uneven legs, a wooden chair that defied laws of physics by mutating into freezing, unyielding iron. A rusty filing cabinet with one missing drawer sat in one shady corner of the room where Papa was supposed to keep all the lists of the missing women that relatives had filed with names, descriptions, rarely photos because they were part of the possessions left behind in Pakistan.

The names of incoming women were published daily in some unknown newspaper that was still operating. The joyful and tearful union of some families was the only dim light that gleamed in the dreary atmosphere of the camp.

But another unimaginable tragedy awaited many of the women.

There was a hesitant knock at the door. Papa had just arrived, seated, and balanced himself on the precarious chair and was looking through yesterday's lists.

People rarely came that early in the morning. The refugee camp was relocated at the purlieus of the city as thousands then hundreds of thousands of exhausted, wounded, hungry, half-dead humans staggered into the western frontier of Delhi. The camps were far from everything including the barracks. Bus services had not been organised yet; horse-driven tongas, taxis, and scooter rickshaws were too expensive for the displaced humans who only had their battered bodies and minds they could call their own. Most of them trodded the dusty roads all day, starting with looking for missing relatives, searching for jobs, hunting for a roof for shelter because refugee camps were not permanent abodes; as new arrivals flowed in incessantly, space was needed to house them.

The forlorn men also stood in long lineups at the various offices where the new Indian government had set up committees to grant money for the displaced and to register for compensation for the property the fleeing refugees left behind in Pakistan. These haggard men dragged themselves back to their camps late at night utterly consumed since they were also underfed.

The barracks were the very first stop for the heartbroken relatives who trekked several dusty, stony miles before starting to trickle in Papa's office, even before the reluctant sun appeared on the horizon.

It was seven thirty. Ram wrapped up his faded muffler around his ears and opened the creaky door. A zephyr of chilly air hit him before he noticed a tall man standing at the door like a ghost. He was relatively well dressed by the current refugee standards; he wore a woolen coat whereas a vast majority of displaced population wrapped their underdressed bodies with the rough, woolen blankets they received at the camp. The man staggered in and slumped down on the wooden chair across from Papa, bent his head on the table, and started to weep like a child. The scenario was hardly new. Papa consoled him calmly with empathy. "Please, do not lose hope, your daughter, is it?"

The man nodded without looking up.

"We are expecting two truckloads today."

The man continued bawling, unabashedly. Papa motioned to Ram, who poured a glass of water from an earthen pot into a steel glass and offered to the man. Papa got up and placed his hand on the man's shoulder. "Talk to me, please. The name, description, we will find her for you."

The man lifted up his gray head, tears flowed down his unshaven rough cheeks, his lips quivered. "It is not what you think, sir. You already have my daughter."

"Then?"

Papa took his hand off his bent shoulder.

The man broke down again, "My God what should I do?"

Papa was in shock and reclaimed his icy chair.

The man took out a dirty handkerchief from his coat pocket and wiped his face. He drank a few sips of water, composed himself, and spoke in a drowning voice.

"You see, sir, my biradari, *community*, and my neighbors have told me clearly that if I bring the impure girl home, they will ostracize us. My other daughter's engagement will be broken, my son will lose his job that he found with great difficulty. He has a wife and two little girls. I do not have a job yet. My wife has sold all her jewelry so that we can eat. I have three young daughters to raise and marry, who will marry them? What shall I do?" He fixed his glistening eyes on Papa's face, hoping for some miraculous words of wisdom that could resolve his dilemma.

This was the first time Papa did not know what to say; he was immobile with disbelief. His stunned silence provided the man with the inevitable answer. He regained composure by the mere affirmation of his own decision. He dug his hand in his inner coat pocket, retrieved a crumpled, small brown paper bag and placed it on the table. His hands trembled fiercely. "This is all the money I have. Please do something for her. Marry her to someone you find, get her some training, or place her somewhere. I don't think God will forgive me."

This was the first in a chain of many other similar cases that followed. The relatives came and hugged these tortured women with lowered, ashamed eyes, unable to face their shocked-filled gaze and went home. To the world, they announced that "she is dead," followed by regular mourning process full of spiritual rituals, kirtans, *devotional songs*, praising the Good God who took their beloved away from the wicked world. The statement regarding the loved one's death was not entirely untrue because fathers or husbands had themselves dealt the final death blow to the ill-fated women by deserting them.

Many courageous humans did embrace the unfortunate women in spite of the dark storms raised by their community.

Another committee was formed in a hurry to organize the placement of the abandoned women. Much brainstorming resulted in a scheme. Cash rewards and job training were promised as incentives for young men to step forward and take the hand of the young girls.

Marriages were hastily arranged, five at a time, in a tent that was instantly erected on the grounds in front of barracks where once-young Indian *sepoys* marched to the tune of British rulers. A few strangers were the witnesses to the wedding ceremonies that consisted of an unostentatious pyre for the fire God to bless the couple, performed by an insolvent, humble pandit, *priest*, a displaced human himself. In an all-pervasive mist of grief, there was no room for mourning the crushed dreams of the bride of a grand wedding in gold and silk, lights and laughter, music and chatter.

The weary groom placed cheap sindoor, *a red powder,* in the parting of the girl's black hair and unceremoniously led her away to a supposedly new life.

Only some of those weddings claimed success; the rest terminated in even greater calamity. Some depraved men pocketed the money and disappeared in the confusing, chaotic fog of new India. Some disapproving, angry in-laws threw the girls out of their homes, alleging that they were bad charactered. Some husbands could not bear the sting of the realty of a wife impregnated through rape by some unknown devil. Innocent newborns, wrapped in rags and newspapers. were discovered in gutters, garbage, front doors of orphanages. Some were smothered to death or aborted even before they saw the light of day by usage of crude unhygienic means that often killed the mother as well as the unwanted offspring.

The girls and women who remained in the camp were taught pottery, sewing, basket making with straw, and employment found for them.

Many girls were seen dancing in kothas, *prostitutes' places,* in the red districts. How many innocent lives were destroyed, there was no accounting. Historians only pen the upheavals, the thrones turned upside down, the invasions, the wars; history never acknowledges its complicity in concealing the truths of ordinary humans' anguish through the many catastrophes that fill the history books.

The unpropitious well was located in front of the kitchen area, its pure, cool water being the only supply for the refugee females. It was not too long before it became stained with the hot blood of the first girl who made a decision that the echoing obscurity of the well was safer than the lurid labyrinth of a future life where one could not even trust one's very own.

When Meera grew up, she went to pay homage to the infamous well that came to be known as Kumari Kuan, *maiden's well.* The new government did not own up to how many young girls and women found refuge in the cold, numbing bottom of the water font.

If Jinnah, *the first Prime Minister of Pakistan,* had not died of tuberculosis in 1949, Meera would have gone to Islamabad, might have been taken inside the prime minister's house at gunpoint, and asked him, "Was it all worth the price in human suffering, really?"

History is clear on that. Jinnah did not fight for creation of a religious nation, Pakistan, for Allah's sake; he is said to have never stepped within a mosque or follow any of the rules of the Koran. It was his insatiable hunger for power that destroyed millions of lives.

Papa had insisted that Shoba get a master's degree in sociology, when one fine morning, she declared, "I don't want to waste time with stupid classes and horrid exams. What is the point? I am going to land up as a wife and mother. Papa, please."

Meera determined to go for her master's degree in music that would qualify her to get a professor's job in a college.

"Please, stop crying, I cannot understand what you are trying to say!" All Meera could hear was an inaudible blurb mixed with sobs and heaves.

Maalti's voice trailed off slowly to a reasonable pitch. "He hit me hard again! I cannot take it anymore! What should I do, Meera?" She started to weep again.

Meera felt forlorn as never before; her own kurukshetra, *an intense historical war between good and evil,* was relentless. How could she take on someone else's battles in such a wounded state?

"I can't stay here any longer. I feel poison in the air."

"Maalti, listen carefully. If you want to leave, let it be your own decision. My house is open if you want to come here, but . . ."

"Meera, you are so good! Asha had been telling me all the time to leave Arun, but when I asked her for help, she refused." Maalti sounded a bit relaxed.

Meera ignored the information regarding Asha. "Do not run away like a coward. Face Arun, tell him clearly how much he has hurt you and why you are leaving."

"Oh God! No! You don't know him! He will stop me physically, hit me again. I want to pack up and get out before he comes home from the office."

What is, if any, right way to deal with wrongful people? After a brief pause, Meera spoke firmly, "Then leave a letter. Also tell him where you are, he will find out anyway. He will surely come here, but Rishi and I will be here."

Maalti hesitated. "Should I take a taxi?"

"Yes, I have to pick up Rishi from school, but I will leave the key in the mailbox. Come in and lock the door. Don't open it if Arun comes." There was a fearful pause on the phone. "Maalti, if you have to fight injustice, you have to be strong. Pray and overcome your fears."

Maalti sounded defeated. "But I am not strong. My brothers always teased me as dumb, and my parents just laughed. Biji, *mother*, Bauji, *father* favored them. My younger sister and I felt low and worthless."

"You have all the strength. Just awaken it, Maalti, and use your will, please." Meera knew it was useless.

She arrived home to find a heaving, broken Maalti resting her head on folded arms that were set lifelessly on the dining table. Veena sat timidly, with swollen eyes, watching TV in the living room. Maalti rushed toward Meera and hugged her like a child running away from bhoot, *demon*.

Rishi exclaimed, "Aunty, what happened to your face?"

He was only informed that Maalti and Veena would be staying at their place for a while. Rishi was not inquisitive about such irrelevant matters; at his age, life was too full of other grandiose stuff. Grown-ups are stupid anyway, what can you expect? Meera motioned to Rishi to pick up the brown leather suitcase that still sat at the entrance where the taxi driver might have left it.

Rishi turned his blond head toward Veena in the living room and announced cheerfully, "Hi, Veena, your room is downstairs." He was not too fond of Vivek and Veena. He found them plain and colorless—no fizz, no fun. Vivek was bookish, and Veena lost in her own world that, he figured, was not a happy place.

Veena spoke awkwardly. "Hi, thank you," and proceeded to watch *I Love Lucy* on TV.

Meera sat down on a dining chair and examined Maalti's bruises; her eyes were black and puffed up, her left cheek was blue where Arun had slapped her. When he pushed her, she fell on her right arm. The elbow was swollen with blood oozing from the cuts. How can a man brutalize someone he has promised to love, honor, and cherish?

"Sit here, I will put some hot oil with haldi, *turmeric*, to get the swelling down."

In the kitchen, Meera's hand trembled as she heated oil and haldi in a small pan; she just stood there staring at nothing. This was the first time she had witnessed from close quarters the sheer ugliness and cruelty of violence against women.

Meera took Maalti's battered face in her hands and dabbed haldi poultice on the wounds. "I am glad you left!"

"Ah . . ." Maalti flinched in warm pain. "Meera, he is going to come after me."

"I am here, Veena and Rishi are here. If he tries to hurt you, I will call the police."

Maalti's despair flared up like a fire. "Oh no! Then he will really kill me!"

"I will lock the door. You go down and rest."

Meera needed a quick repose. Suddenly, the question of supper cropped up in her foggy head. "I will order pizza. Rishi, is it okay?" She walked toward his room as she spoke.

Rishi was on the phone, "Mom, you are always interrupting? What is it with you? You know that I am going out!"

Meera was patient. "Beta, don't go today, we may need you."

"You never need help!" He sounded bitter. Rishi did not know why; Meera did not know either. "I cannot stay, anyway. I have to meet Joshua and Mike at the library. We are doing this science project together that is due tomorrow."

"Don't leave your assignments until the last day, Rishi." He pretended that he did not hear her.

Meera wanted to believe him so much, but in her gut, she knew that he was lying. How do you tell your child, "You are lying because my gut tells me"? A mother's intuition would never hold up in any court of law.

Rishi had lied before; Meera had caught him. But something, maybe her sense of decency, stopped her from confronting him right out and cause ugly embarrassment. She did communicate with him on this issue, what he called a lecture, and hated it.

"Rishi, I want you to know that I will never be angry no matter what you tell me. It will hurt if you do some serious wrong, but we will deal with it. But I will be devastated if you lie to me. I trust you. I know you will speak the truth. We must have integrity."

At such times, he looked down, his face reddened a little; he would get up and leave, abruptly. Rishi's reactions, unpredictability, outbursts, and cruel silences were like a glass wall; no matter how cautiously she penetrated it, inevitably, shattered glass resulted in cuts and wounds.

Arun called around seven in the evening; they were just finishing pizza. Maalti looked at the phone as though it was a poisonous snake. Maybe in her reality, it was.

Meera took a deep breath to brace herself for the much-expected onslaught. Why was he so bitter? In spite of his abuse, Maalti and the kids were loving and obedient. Maybe he was the fruit of a choler tree, a dysfunctional family.

Arun bellowed in her ears, "How dare you? I can't believe you could do this to me."

"I didn't do anything . . ."

"You take my family away then act innocent?"

"Arun Bhai, listen . . ."

He continued the vilification using some swear words that Meera had never heard before.

Maalti stared at Meera's face to gauge what Arun was saying.

Meera let him fume then spoke resolutely. "Now that you have said what you wanted to, it is my turn. Maalti took the decision to leave you completely on her own. I only let her stay with me because she had no other place to go. Instead of wasting your breath on blaming me, why don't you sit down with her calmly, without shouting, and sort out why she ran away from you?"

"Don't tell me what to do! You don't have a husband, how do you know how to deal with domestic problems? I know all about you. You pretend to be so pure, 'Sati Savitri,' but in reality, you are someone else. I don't want to talk to you. Give the phone to Maalti."

Meera instantly figured out it was "Asha speak." She asked Maalti in a tired voice, "Do you want to talk to him?"

"No!" Maalti shrank into herself in a demeanor that expressed disgust as much as diffidence.

"She does not wish to talk to you. Why don't you leave her alone for a little while? She will cool down, and then you can both talk."

"No!" He screamed so loudly that Meera's whole head vibrated along with the eardrums. "How dare she leave me? We are not Angrez who marry and leave whenever they please. We are Indians, we have our culture and traditions."

Meera could not help but say, "Do we have a tradition of beating our wives and children?" She slammed the phone down intentionally. *Obnoxious* word was coined for the likes of him.

"He is going to be here, soon. Veena and I are with you. Let him shout and say what he wants, but do not let him force you, physically, to go with him. If he touches you or Veena, I will call 911. Let us agree on that strategy, now." Like Maalti's true daughter, Veena started to sob. "Aunty, what will happen?"

Meera was at the brink of her patience with the mother-daughter team. "Veena, have courage for your Ma's sake. Do as I said."

They both shook their heads in unison. Meera knew for sure they were both going to fall apart as soon as Arun arrived.

In desperation, she called, Sunil, Anil, and Satish. No one was home.

Fifteen minutes, later there was a knock on the main door. Meera straightened herself, tucked the palloo of her pink saree in her waist in a posture of readiness for war, and opened the door.

It was a chilly night; seven thirty was already pitch dark. Arun looked like a huge wolf, with red twisted face, disheveled hair, piercing murderous eyes, ready to pounce and tear flesh with his sharpened claws.

Meera was not afraid. What do you feel for someone who trampled his own beautiful garden without any realization that he was part of what he destroyed? She felt sad, stepped aside to let him in, and spoke politely, "Come in, Bhai."

Arun looked down at Meera disdainfully then charged past her. "Where is she?"

Maalti and Veena were huddled together, holding hands, on a couch in the corner of the living room; their homely, artless faces were pale in terror.

"Get up, now, get your stuff. Let us go," he ordered.

Maalti looked hopelessly at Meera, who gave her a resolute look of encouragement.

Maalti found her voice and nodded sideways. "I don't want to go with you! You hurt me all the time. Unless you see a counselor and change, I cannot live with you."

"Counselor, counselor," Arun roared. "What does a counselor have to do with anything?" He turned to Meera angrily. "This must be the idea you have stuffed in Maalti's thick head."

Meera was cool. "Everyone knows that a man who abuses his family needs help to change his behavior."

"It is none of your business, anyway. Stay out of it. You've got an Angrezi son, you think you are Angrez, *British*? Our women, don't leave their husbands. Maalti, did you hear, let us go."

Meera's voice was now cold, hard. "It becomes my business if you treat my guests disrespectfully. This is my house, and you know the tradition that we Hindus must give our lives to protect our guests."

Arun was mad like a dog that was unleashed after a long detention; he stomped toward Maalti, grabbed her by the arm brutally, and pulled her up. Maalti started to bawl and struggled to free her arm. A terrified Veena got up, stood aside, and squealed, "Dad, don't do it!"

Meera walked briskly toward Maalti to help her. Arun pushed her with his free left hand; savagery of his emotions conferred him with such brute strength that Meera fell down and hit her head against the corner of the glass center table.

Veena shouted, "Stop it, Dad. Stop it. You are hurting Aunty."

Meera was on the rug for a few seconds, in shock, but recovered quickly and tried to get up. Without looking at Maalti or Arun, she told Veena firmly, "Veena, pick up the phone and dial 911."

Veena did not move; she was bewildered and deaf with inner turmoil. Meera forced a tough voice; she did not know why it took so much effort. "Veena, do it now!"

Meera touched her forehead with her hand; something warm stuck to her fingers—it was blood.

Arun shouted ferociously, "Veena don't you dare! How dare you poison my daughter against me, asking her to act against her father?"

Meera got up slowly. She said to Arun disgustedly, "You are no father or husband until you act like one."

Veena's feet were frozen; she just slumped on the sofa chair that lay behind her, buried her face in her knees, and yelped.

Meera walked languidly toward the phone that hung on the wall between the dining and living rooms. Arun dropped Maalti on the floor abruptly and lunged toward Meera to stop her.

Maalti held on to Arun's legs tight and shrieked, "Meera, do it fast! Do it! Let them get you, bastard. You've ruined my life. You have hurt me so much, you will burn in hell. God will never forgive you! I hate you, I hate you." A flood of tears covered her anguished face.

Maalti's rage, bottled up for eighteen long years, unleashed like red hot, molten lava of a volcano that had erupted after a superficial calm of a thousand years. The loathing and repugnance in her voice shook everyone in the room.

Arun was stunned; he looked at Maalti in disbelief and stood there speechlessly.

Meera had a moldy heavy voice. "Twenty-three Adler Street. There is a man beating his wife. Please hurry."

Arun looked at Veena, Maalti, and Meera in turn, as though they were strangers. Maalti let go his legs, slumped on the floor, covered her face with shaking hands, and bawled in agony. Veena still sat doubled up on the sofa chair, sobbing out of control.

Meera walked toward the dining table and almost collapsed on the dining chair with her head in her hands. Blood flowed from her forehead to her hands and then down her arms. She felt dizzy and had no energy to get a towel to press on the wound. Outside, from the dark gloomy skies, soft snowflakes floated onto the white ground, indifferently. Three minutes later, two cops walked in through the main unlocked door and found four humans frozen in time; a heart-wrenching drama of age-old tale of dagger and blood, power and invalidation, woman and wolf. *But the wolf must be hurting too,* were Meera's last thoughts as she passed out and fell on the dining room floor.

One of the cops, Russel, walked over to Maalti and asked, "Ma'am are you all right?"

Maalti kept weeping. "Can you tell me what happened?" the other cop, Gary, asked her.

Russel held Meera and sprinkled some water on her face; she gained partial consciousness and attempted to sit up. He pressed a wet kitchen towel against the wound on her forehead. Gary approached Meera now, being unsuccessful in squeezing any statement out of the two women in the living room.

"Are you able to talk?" he asked Meera sympathetically while helping her sit on the chair. In a dreamlike state, slowly, unemotionally, flatly in a weary tone, she explained everything.

They asked Maalti. She corroborated with a teary nod.

Arun had, in the meanwhile, sat down and stared into space.

Russel asked him twice, "Sir, did you hit your wife?"

Suddenly, he recovered and looked at the cop in disbelief; his defence mechanism awoke instantly. It was not important what he had done; it was important what was being done to him! Now, he had to fight a different enemy, the one who had much more clout than Meera and Maalti.

Arun straightened himself and glared at the cop. "This is my domestic problem, husband and wife fight, don't you?"

Gary and Russel looked at each other, discomforted by the onslaught on their personal life. Russel replied with a forced courtesy. "I do not hit her, ever."

Arun got on his feet in anger. "I am leaving now. This is gone out of control. Maalti, I will pick you up tomorrow after office. I will forgive if you come home to me."

Gary looked at Maalti. "Ma'am, you wish to press charges?"

Maalti was in a daze' she did not understand. All her energy was spent in awakening of the slumbering volcano. All the lava had already flowed out; there was emptiness of hot rocks and an echo of what was. She looked at Meera blankly. Meera was still half dizzy. "It is up to you to decide."

"I don't know. Tell me what to do."

Arun growled and started to walk toward the door. Russel stood in front of him to block his way. "You can't leave yet, sir."

Before he could bellow, Gary, who had enough of Arun's belligerence, said sternly, "Sit down, sir. Don't force me to take my gun out."

Arun was nonplussed. What is this? He is the victim being treated so unfairly! Gary's threat seemed real; his hand was on the butt of his gun that was hanging in a case on his waistband.

"I don't have to sit! I will stand."

"Whatever, as long as you don't leave the premises."

"Actually, I am going to call my lawyer."

"You can do it at the police station."

Russel thought for a second. Maybe it was a good idea to get Arun out of the way so they could proceed with their business.

"All right."

"You can use the phone in my bedroom if you wish, Arun Bhai." Meera's voice was resigned and polite.

She looked at Maalti with detachment. "I will not tell you, but I can advise you. Press charges, let the cops take him to the police station. They can ask him to commit in writing that he will see a counselor, stay away from you for two weeks until you are ready. Otherwise, they will press charges of assault and that you have okayed the deal."

Maalti appeared pacified. "Maybe that is the best." She still did not look at the policemen.

Meera turned to them. "Can you do that?"

"Yes, ma'am, we can. But she will have to sign some papers. Can you bring her to the police station at 9:00 a.m.? After her written statement, we can proceed to pick him up."

Arun returned triumphantly from Meera's bedroom. "My lawyer will see you at the police station."

"You can go now, sir. But we will have to pick you up tomorrow. You can phone your lawyer to come to the police station then."

Arun looked at the whole crowd pitifully and stomped out of the main door.

Meera, Maalti, and Veena looked at one another; they knew that Arun did not have a lawyer.

"Yes, I will bring my friend to the police station tomorrow. Thank you so much for your help," Meera attempted to smile faintly.

"By the way, ma'am, do you wish to press charges for the assault on you?"

"No!" Meera said calmly. "It was an accident. I am okay, I think."

"Let me see if your bleeding has stopped."

Gary bent over her and took off the towel from her forehead; the towel was drenched with blood. Meera felt weak in her knees; if only she could crawl in her cozy bed and never wake up again.

Gary looked at Russel, "She needs stitches," then turned to her. "I am worried about your wound, ma'am, we will take you to the emergency."

Meera turned to Maalti. "Go to sleep now, be at peace."

In the police car, sitting in the rear seat, Meera felt a sickening sense of déjà vu overwhelm her—a sharp nostalgia of a catastrophic journey long ago, though it felt that it happened yesterday.

The doctor closed the wound with six stitches and warned, "Please keep the wound clean and come tomorrow to get the bandage changed."

Russel offered to help Meera into the house.

"Thank you so much, I am okay." Meera's voice was feeble. She dawdled in, collapsed in her bed, and prayed. She wished Prashant was there to help her.

Maalti and Veena were asleep downstairs, or more likely, pretended to.

- # -

Meera left a note on the kitchen table for Rishi and left.

The door was ajar, Meera just walked in. Prashant was sitting in front of an opened suitcase with unfolded clothes stuffed haphazardly, mismatched socks lying on the bed for their partners to show up.

The strongest of men turn into powerless children during an emotional crisis; maybe women are more evolved after all. Their existence is intricate because they are emotional creatures, drawn into others' life demands that propel them to give perpetually. They learn to rise above their own sensibilities to heal others.

Meera dumped a load of laundry in the washing machine, started to fold the clothes that lay all entangled in the suitcase, motioned Prashant to sit on a chair and tell her what happened.

"Meera, I have no idea what to expect. Just received a telegram that Baba, *father,* is not well, to come soon. Knowing Baba, he would not have allowed Ravi to send a telegram unless he is very ill. I am so far away, could never do anything for them. I feel so guilty! I'll never forgive myself if anything happened to Baba!"

Prashant's eyes looked like two wounded birds; only once before Meera had witnessed such agony in his eyes—when he had talked about his wife.

Meera stopped folding clothes, stood up, and caressed his stubby, unshaven cheeks with both her hands. He extended his long arms and wrapped them around her supple body; she fell in his lap with a start.

The stars twinkling high up in the faintly lit summer sky witnessed the incredible grace of the merging of pathos and love, pain and pleasure, hurting and healing. It was the willful annihilation of the opposites culminating in the ultimate state of transcendence called Shunya by Buddhists and Brahm, *Absolute God,* of the Vedantists.

Meera finished the packing, kissed his cheek, touched his feet, and left silently.

Rishi was pacing up and down in his nightshirt. He pounced on Meera as soon as she entered the house.

"Where were you? Do you know what the time is? I was worried!"

Meera was surprised. "I left a note. I was at Prashant's . . ."

"Gosh, you don't have to sneak out? I knew you were sleeping around with him . . ." He was disdainful.

"Rishi!" Meera was stern. "I did not sneak out, I left you a note. You were asleep when I received a call from Prashantji. His father is critically ill. I went to see him off and support him. I don't like your tone. You have no right to shout at me."

Rishi did not care. "Granny is right. I should have moved with her."

"Rishi, I love you more than anyone else, and you know it." Meera was depleted; it was a losing battle, but no matter how wounded, she did not have the prerogative to fall in the battleground until it was truly lost.

"Focus on your studies. When you are eighteen, you can choose to live wherever you wish. But I thought Granny was not talking against me anymore?"

Rishi did not respond. He stomped out of the room. "I hate you, I hate school, I hate everyone. I also hate Granny and you. You are all selfish, no one cares about me!"

When she returned from India, much to her chagrin, Meera discovered that Rishi had been staying with Mrs. Henderson the whole time she was gone. At the camp, he had tripped on a stony pathway and bruised his knees and hands. He had called Bela, Satish, and Anil, but no one was home. Mrs. Henderson sent Peter to pick him up.

Palpitation, tensed-up nerves, and pungent headache were the initial reactions of her body. Yet Mrs. Henderson was there to help Rishi!

A certain sense of foreboding settled in her heart; she was trapped in the silky threads of a web. Irony was that Meera could not even sever them; they were her life.

How could she intentionally take away something that was precious to Rishi? People did not understand because she was the object of their worry. But Rishi, not her, was the main concern of her life.

Rishi had sounded happy. "Mom I have told Granny that I will see her if she stops badgering you. She has not so far. I do love her."

"He left us, Meera, and left a huge mess." Prashant broke down on the phone a week later.

Meera controlled her tears. "I will pray for all of you."

"Listen, before the phone lines die, I need money immediately. I have already mailed . . ."

"What?" The crackling in the background increased.

"Cheque! Cheque!" Prashant elevated his pitch. "I have mailed you. But it will take time to reach you. Get help from Sunil and send me fifty thousand dollars right away."

"Fifty thousand?" Meera was surprised.

"Yes."

"I will send telegraphically . . ."

"No . . . there is no such connection here . . . Register . . . Can you hear me?"

"Yes, I will. Hello . . . Hello?" The phone line broke off.

The plane had landed at the New Delhi airport at eight in the morning.

The airport smelled of sweat, smoke, dirt, and many other unidentifiable odours. The air conditioner was habitually out of order. People stood restlessly in lines, wiping the sweat off their necks and faces, bent down by the weight of huge suitcases, obviously containing many gifts for the relatives. Obstreperous shouts of joy welcomed people emerging from the exit door.

Prashant spotted a gaunt, ashen Ravi standing on one side of the crowded exit area. He ran toward Prashant, pushing some people, ignoring annoyed looks, touched Prashant's feet, and broke down in his arms. "Baba left us last night at one o'clock, Dada, *brother*."

A rock hit Prashant in the chest and shook him. It occurred to him that he was flying over Europe, maybe Poland at that time. Ravi clung to him like a child and wept. Prashant's quiet tears fell on Ravi's curly black hair. The mob around them did not notice the silent grieving.

Prashant wiped Ravi's tears and said in a jaded voice, "Let us go home, Beta. Has Kanti come?"

"No, Dada." Ravi picked up Prashant's suitcase and started to walk toward the taxi stand.

"Car?"

Ravi pretended that he did not hear him.

The taxiwalla Sardarji, *Sikh,* welcomed them cordially, "Sat Sri Akal, Bhaji, *Sikh greeting*! Let me keep the suitcases in the dicky, *trunk.* Oho, you travel so light. People bring so many big, big suitcases from Vilayat, *England,* sometimes I have to tie them up on the roof of the taxi. Ha. Ha." He laughed freely at his keen observation.

The highway between Delhi and Meerut was lined with ancient, shady kikkar, mango, pippal trees on both sides. Sardarji drove aggressively on much fissured, potholed road, competing ruthlessly with carts, bullock carts, cycles, trucks, cars, scooter rickshaws, pedestrians, cows, dogs, and rarely cats, for space. He maneuvered, overtook, honked, gestured with his right hand, occasionally poked his face out of the window, and shouted obscenities at his cotravelers if they got in his way.

Prashant wanted to ask him to slow down but felt almost paralyzed; nothing was important—the unbearable heat and dust, the taxi with broken windows, seats with springs protruding out, digging into his flesh. All he knew was that he would never see his Baba again. His childhood at the green fields at home, laughing, teasing, sleeping on the roof, and whispering until Baba announced, "No more talk, bachas, *children,*" passed in front of his eyes like a motion picture.

At the Delhi airport, Baba was teary-eyed but proud the last time Prashant saw him, when he left India.

It was not fair, Prashant chided God. He was not even given a chance to do anything for Baba, look after him in his old age. Baba wasn't even old yet. Prashant held Ravi with his left arm and fumbled in his pocket for a handkerchief. Ravi leaned on his strong shoulder; they both cried.

The taxiwalla looked in the rearview mirror and saw them. His face fell; he mellowed, slowed down the taxi out of respect for their sorrow.

Someone honked from behind; Sardarji stretched his right arm out of the window and motioned for the driver to pass him, who threw a few curse words toward the taxi as he drove past.

"Sale, *swear word,* I am letting you pass, and you curse?" Sardarji poked his face out the window and shouted back. His face softened again. He sighed. "Lost someone, Bhaji?"

Prashant looked into the rear mirror and nodded.

"It is too sad, life is so harsh. Only Wahe Guru, *Sikh name for God,* knows why we have to lose our loved ones. But He knows! We have to accept His will. No, Bhaji?"

It occurred to Prashant that in Canada, no one would ever express themselves to strangers. Even friends were expected to make sure that the aggrieved was not offended by the intrusion of uninvited sympathy. In India, there is no formality, no boundaries, only the common ground of shared grief since no one is a stranger to the notion of death.

"Yes, Sardarji. We have no choice but to accept God's will."

Prashant's house was in a suburban area of Meerut, close to their farms. Prashant paid Sardarji and asked him to come in for a cold drink and lunch.

Sun was beating down on the house. As they entered the gate, Prashant saw men, with bowed heads, sitting in the veranda, *covered area in front of a house,* on the dari, *woven rug,* that had been laid out. The mango trees surrounding the house shaded this area. Dead silence prevailed, excepting the sharp chirping of some birds hidden in the clusters of mango tree leaves.

As Sardarji, Ravi, and Prashant approached the house, all eyes turned toward them. A wave of lament rose in the veranda and flowed inside the house; the woman's cry was more piercing and dark.

Sardarji folded his hands and bowed his head out of respect for the deceased.

Ravi turned to him and said, "Come in please and eat something." He led him around the house toward the kitchen that also opened at the back of the house.

Lying in the center of the veranda on a raised wooden platform, Baba's lifeless body lay covered from head to toe with white cloth; garlands of fresh marigolds had been placed on top. Prashant staggered toward Baba's body, hugged him, and let go of his emotions.

The crowd of men sitting around, joined Prashant in his ululation. After a few minutes, someone came from behind and tried to shake Prashant away from Baba's body.

He looked back. "Gopu, what happened? Why did you not tell me?"

Gopal wailed as he wrapped Prashant in his burly fold. "Bhai, it happened suddenly. But you have to be strong for everyone."

Prashant's legs felt like immovable iron posts.

"Where is Biji, *mother*?" Gopal led Prashant by the hand into the living room that had been darkened by thick curtains to block the summer heat. It took Prashant a few moments to get used to the gloomy obscurity. Slowly he made out many white dupatta, *veil,* covered heads of women sitting on the carpeted floor. His eyes searched desperately for Biji. Perched in the far corner of the room, holding Neeta's young hand, Biji sat like a statue surrounded by other familiar faces of Mami, Masi, Chachi, Bua, neighbors, and cousins. Neeta got up and ran toward Prashant, crying loudly, "Dada, what will we do without Baba?"

As he held her against his chest and kissed her head, it hit him. Baba had left the whole family under his care. He had to gather himself bravely; he wiped her tears with her dupatta. "It is okay, baby, I am here, na."

He walked toward Biji, stepping carefully through the crowd of sitting women and touched her feet. He sat on the floor, took her face in his moist hands, and wiped her tears. She looked up at him vacantly; there was no sign of recognition in her eyes. It scared him. "Biji, it's okay. Your Shantu is here."

She suddenly came out of the trance and cried out, "Shantu, kya ho gya, Beta. *What happened*? Why, Why?" He pulled her in his sweaty arms and stroked her gray head; Neeta, Ma, and Prashant wept for a while in one embrace. Prashant shut his eyes and saw Meera's serene face. It did not seem odd that he felt her presence.

Prashant was jolted out of his state of mind; there were preparations to be made!

Ravi was standing right behind him when he got up; he held his arm and walked out of the room. When they were in the veranda, Prashant asked Ravi in a low voice, "What is to be done for the cremation? Where is Bhavani?"

Ravi looked grown-up. Prashant had left him a young boy; now, he was a man with a moustache, a small beard, and a husky voice. "Dada, Krishan Mamaji and Bhavani have gone to arrange for wood, and priest. They should be back soon."

Little Bhavani's preferred choice of playing was to hide somewhere in the house and make everyone look for him; it was tedious because Bhavani knew some corners of the house that no one had visited before. At his tender age, Bhavani is getting wood for his father's cremation! The thought broke Prashant's heart.

He was not going back to Canada, Prashant made a solemn decision. Meera will join him here. But Rishi? He stopped himself.

"Where is Kanti? He should be doing all this?"

"We sent the telegram. I don't know." Ravi shrugged.

Ever since Kanti tied the knot with his boss's only daughter, his visits became rare and short. Baba laughed, "Ghar-Jamai, *a man who lives with his wife's family*, is no one's son. He only remains jamai, *son-in-law.* Let him be happy."

Baba was a bodybuilder; no one could beat him in a game of *kabaddi* when Prashant left for Canada. Six years later, his long, consumed, shiny body was lying on piles of sandalwood that was sprinkled with pure ghee. Prashant, held a long stick of wood with fire raging at its tip, walked three times around the pyre, and lit it. The mantra "Ram Nam Satya Hai", *God's name is truth*, resonated in the warm, still night air; golden flames of fire leapt and burned Baba's material body to ashes. The priest chanted mantras for Baba's peace; the smoke ascended to the cimmerian skies above and carried his soul to the heavens.

Prashant's legs trembled as he stood holding Ravi and Bhavani in both his arms. Kanti arrived with his decked-up, bejeweled wife, Sujata, while they were away cremating Baba's dead body. Every part of Prashant's body and mind throbbed with pain. Ram, Doctor-Chachaji, *uncle,* had given Biji an injection. She succumbed to an interrupted restless sleep. Neeta was rolled on the floor with her head on Biji's arm. Woman relatives sprawled in different corners of the living room covered with white sheets. Although it was hot and the fan was swirling on the ceiling at full speed, for women to lay uncovered was immodest.

Mamiji, *mother's brother's wife*, forced everyone to eat a few bites. Prashant suddenly realized he had not eaten anything for almost twenty-four hours. In the plane, a pretty, saree-clad air hostess had offered dinner with a pleasant smile. Prashant's heart, gut, everything was in turmoil; he did not want to look at food.

Mattresses were laid out on the floor in the two bedrooms; all of them huddled together. The third bedroom was given to Kanti and his rich wife, at his insistence.

"How will Sujata sleep with all the other strange women she doesn't even know?"

Whether it was for his wife's comfort or his own, he got a bedroom for himself; he was not used to thinking about anyone else. Baba would have created a joke out of the situation.

Light from the streetlamp sneaked into the bedroom through the large windows; mournful shadows of small trees and shrubs fell on the exhausted human torsos.

Prashant, with Ravi and Bhavani lying next to him, slid into a disquieted sleep; his turbulent unconscious wove many nightmares of flames and smoke, anguished faces, Baba walking away.

For the next four days, amidst the sobs and tears, condolences and hugs of visitors, family priest read the Shrimad Bhagavad Gita, *Hindu's Bible*, chapter 2, that speaks of using wisdom during occasions of loss and bereavement. Everyone in the house ate, slept, and wept. For Prashant's family, life had ceased; there was no living, only breathing and hurting.

On the chautha, *the fourth day after death*, Prashant, Kanti, Ravi, Bhavani, and Gopal went to the cremation ground to pick phul, *remains*. Five of them proceeded to Haridwar and offered Baba's last relics to the sacred river Mother Ganga.

Mamaji, *mother's brother*, his son Amol, Ravi, Bhavani, and Prashant sat in the veranda after returning from Haridwar in the evening; they were utterly spent. It had rained during the day; some other time air would have felt pleasant.

Kanti had left right away on the night train to Jabalpur.

A jeep stopped in front of the house. All heads turned spontaneously; Mohan Chachaji, *father's younger brother*, and his two sons, Kewal and Karan, got off the jeep. Kewal ordered the driver hoarsely, "Park it on the side, oi."

Prashant stood up to greet them as they walked toward the veranda. Ravi and Bhavani looked at each other; their faces tensed up. Prashant did not notice, "Bhavani, get three chairs from inside."

Mamaji and Amol said a cold "Namaste." MohanLal did not bother to look at them, indicative of an unsavory past.

"Beta, too bad you were not here. Bhai suffered a lot." Mohan wiped his imaginary tears. "We helped as much as we could."

Red-faced, his piercing gaze resting on Chachaji's eyes, Ravi stood up. "Chachaji, you are Baba's brother and are standing in his house. I don't want to insult you. Please, leave and never show your face again."

Prashant was out of his mind with shock and confusion. "Ravi! What are you saying to our respected Chachaji?"

"Dada!" Shaking with rage, he turned toward Prashant. "You don't know anything! I have reasons. I will explain. We do not want to see so-called Chacha's shadow in Baba's house." Prashant looked at Bhavani. He just nodded in the affirmative.

Mamaji and Amol sensed a storm, excused themselves, and headed for safer quarters inside the house. Prashant could not believe it.

"What happened, Ravi?"

Ravi gathered himself, spoke with unexpected vehemence. "Why don't you ask Chachaji what happened to our car, most of the furniture, land, and Biji's jewelry?"

"What does that have to do with him?"

Chachaji pretended to bow his head in injury. Kewal spoke angrily, "Bapu tried to help you people! You ungrateful bastards!"

Prashant held his hands up. "Stop, Kewal, please. Chachaji, I am sorry, please go home at this time. I will see you later."

A piqued Chacha and his fuming sons stomped toward the gate. "I swear we will never step here again to be insulted."

Prashant slumped in his chair and said sternly, "I am listening."

In the full view of the rising moon, the moist air hanging still around them, Ravi narrated the heart-wrenching saga of their Baba's last years.

Lung cancer assaulted Baba two years ago; breathing became hard work. Ram Chachaji understood. "Kedar, I cannot diagnose it properly, you better go to Patel Chest Institute in Delhi. I will contact my friend there, he is a competent surgeon."

Ravi and Bhavani paced in the waiting room while Dr. Ramesh operated and took out the tumor and a section of Baba's right lung. Nauseating and debilitating chemotherapy followed.

Six months later, Dr. Ramesh finally smiled and told Baba, "You are free from the wretched virus. Go home and enjoy life."

A bald and slimmer Baba alighted from the car with Ravi's help. Biji looked through the window, tears filled her eyes; she knelt in front of her temple and thanked God.

The truce only lasted for six months. Most of the right lung had to be sacrificed to the cold-blooded invader. Slowly, Baba was left with half a lung, making it difficult for him to breathe.

Doctors' bills, hospital bills, expensive medicines, Ravi's stay in the hotel in Delhi—money started to slip down a gluttonous, ever-hungry abyss.

Ever since Baba became ill, the income from the land evaporated in thin air. The manager, NeetiLal, concocted endless array of novel excuses. "The tube-well broke down, had to get it fixed, so little rain this year Babuji, *sir,* bulls died in the epidemic, manure got wet, the laborers are causing problems . . . the crops are not yielding that much money . . . I don't know what to do . . . I know you need money . . ."

Baba knew NeetiLal; he was a cheat and a liar. As long as Baba was active and fully in charge of the farming, he could keep a check on him. Now, how could he challenge him lying in bed? To find another manager could be risky; what if he is worse?

One morning, Ravi brought the tray of breakfast for Baba. He smiled weakly, "Where is Ramu? Don't you have to go to work?"

"I will, Baba."

Ravi placed two pillows behind Baba to prop him up, straightened the blanket in front of him, and placed the tray. Baba looked at Ravi keenly. "Don't look sad, I will be fine. Have faith."

"I know, Baba, I am not sad!" He made a brave attempt to smile.

Baba leaned on the pillows. "What is on your mind?"

Ravi's new job at the insurance company did not bring much money, yet Neeta and Bhavani were still in college in Meerut living in hostels.

"Baba, we should ask Prashant Da for money."

"Oh no! He does not have much income and has to support his wife in an institution in a foreign land."

"Then let me sell the car. There is a good bus service."

Baba sighed and looked away at the hazy sky. A few birds flew across the window.

Ravi let the word out that he was selling his car. Customers were already waiting; MohanLal bought the car at dirt-cheap price because Ravi could not bring himself to refute and insult his Chachaji.

One sunny morning, Kaushalaya Chachi, Mohan's wife, came to visit Biji, which was not often. She hinted to her crudely, "Bahen, *sister,* I know you are in trouble. I want to help. We women keep jewelry for such hard times! I don't really need it, My Beji-Bauji have given me so much? But your jewelry should stay in the family, na? I had a bad stomach ache, I cannot even walk, but I said, 'If we don't help who will, eh?'"

Without consulting, anyone, Biji quietly accepted the offer of pilferage of her ancestral jewels. Kaushalya paid her a measly amount. "Bahen, we don't have much money! I cannot tell you how I am doing it for your sake!" It was insulting, but Biji swallowed it; only she knew how food was put on the table.

Baba decided. "Ravi, let us put the land as collateral and borrow money from the bank."

The bank manager's wife could not hold such significant gossip in her weak belly; by the next day, the whole village knew. Minutes after the rumor arrived at Mohan's doorstep, he appeared at Baba's bedside. In spite of or maybe because of Baba's illness, Mohan had not visited him. With sad irony in his smile, Baba said, "Maybe Mohan is afraid I will ask him for help."

Mohan appeared innocent and harmless as he gestured with his rough hands in the air. "It will be a hardship for me, Bhai, but I am thinking of our Bapu. If someone else ploughs his land, it will break his heart wherever he is!" He wiped crocodile tears with a white cotton handkerchief.

Baba smiled. "But, Mohan, I am not giving the land away, after I pay the debt, the land will be mine."

Mohan shook his head. "But how will you pay? Ravi's job is new! Bhavani, Neeta are still studying. The income from the land is dropping, mine is too," he lied fluently.

Baba became thoughtful; Mohan had a point. Mohan saw Baba softening.

"Bhai, I can buy from you. That way, the land will stay in the family."

Baba knew his scheming brother.

Their father died of malaria when Baba was sixteen and Mohan was ten. They had already lost their mother to typhoid. Baba dropped out of school, toiled hard at the farm Bapu had left behind, but sent Mohan to a good school then college in Meerut. At the end of each harvest, Baba split the income and deposited Mohan's share in the bank.

Baba arranged Mohan's wedding and gave him half the land as well as a fat bank balance, since all of Mohan's expenses were financed by Baba including the wedding.

"He is like my son, I have to do it, yar, *friend*," he said proudly to his friends.

Stories of Baba's honesty and brother love became the stuff of storytelling in those areas.

Baba looked at Mohan hopefully. "Mohan, let me keep some of the land with you as collateral and give me the loan."

Mohan's shameless eyes looked at Baba. "Then I will take half of the harvest as well." Baba was shocked. "I will be paying you the loan back with interest in increments. If you take half of the harvest, how will I ever pay you?"

"Bhai, my sons insisted that if you agree, I have to ask these terms . . ."

"Mohan, this is not the way it is done."

Baba felt exhausted. Neeta was home for the holidays; she came in with a tray in her hands with two cups of tea and a plate of biscuits.

"No, no Beti, don't bother."

Baba spoke in a tired voice. "Mohan take it." He sighed, and then looked at Mohan, "I am happy Bapu is not alive to witness this."

Ravi and Bhavani were mad. "Why should we deal with that leech who would fleece his own brother who raised him? I will get the money from the bank fair and square!"

Baba was grim. "Once we use the land as collateral, if we need more money, we will not be able to sell it. Beta, let me sell a small piece of land to Mohan. I will be better soon, we may not need to sell any more."

A myna sat at the windowsill looking at them curiously. The curtain fluttered. Baba looked at the fearful myna fly away.

"Ravi, did Kanti write back?"

Ravi's gut twisted with revulsion. Can he tell Baba that his own wealthy son cannot help his ill father because he has to buy a new car? "I have to keep appearances you know. I work and socialize with rich people. You understand, Ravi?"

Ravi suppressed his anger and replied calmly, "Baba, he wrote that his business is not good. Let us ask Prashant Da."

"No!" Baba was resolute.

"Then let us sell to someone else," Ravi pleaded.

Baba shook his head. "Let Bapu's land stay in the family. Maybe . . ." He paused uncertainly, "He will let me buy it back?"

Ravi felt like laughing aloud but could not destroy the serenity of Baba's simplicity.

Mohan suppressed his excitement, spoke with a solemn face, "Bhai, I cannot pay the going rate. I am a poor man, how can I raise so much money? This is between brothers. We don't want to haggle like strangers, do we? I am making this sacrifice only for our Bapu!"

"Mohan, don't tell anyone what you are doing! I don't want people to find out how low you can fall."

While Prashant's family was busy fighting with death, the land, slowly, piece by piece slipped into Mohan's dirty hands.

The night creatures became alive, the night had deepened. Suddenly, heavy dark clouds gathered, veiling the moon; monsoon had come a little early. There was a momentary dazzle of lightning and thunder followed by outage of power; all lights went off. Neeta stepped out and fumbled while trying to get accustomed to the umbra that shrouded the veranda. She asked in a low voice, "Dada, should I bring the food out? But . . . it is dark unless I bring a lantern . . ." It occurred to Prashant, *Who is doing the cooking and the housework?* Yesterday, he noticed Mamiji hanging the washed clothes on the line. He had seen Ramu only occasionally.

Bhavani explained after a few minutes of hurt silence, "Da, we had to let him go. He has another job but has been coming the last few days to help."

Neeta stood patiently waiting for an answer. Tears rose in Prashant's throat; he got up, approached Neeta, and scanned her from top to bottom. Moon had temporarily made an appearance; in the dim light, he saw holes in her dupatta, her salwar-kameez was discolored with wear and tear, her sandals lacked one strap. But her face was serene, like Baba's. He pulled her toward his chest and hugged her with intensity. "I promise, all will be fine, baby."

Neeta looked up at Prashant with bewildered, tearful expression in her young, pure eyes.

Prashant called Meera the next day.

Mohan got up and instantly pasted a fake grin on his face. "Come, come, my son! I am so happy that you have remembered this Chacha of yours."

He turned his face in the general direction of the kitchen and shouted crudely, "Oi, Lalu, bring chai, *tea,* and sweets and tell Bibiji that someone special is here."

"Don't bother, I am not staying," Prashant said dryly.

Mohan was sprawled on a garden chair in the veranda, reading *Times of India.* The news was bad; in the aftermath of emergency, the wounds were still raw; Raj Narain was like Mahatama Gandhi, a saint but no politician. Ambitions, infighting, power struggles became an obstacle in India's democratic renewal after a dictatorship of three years by Indira Gandhi.

But Mohan was a content man; what happened to millions of Indians did not concern him a bit.

He refused to be another victim of Neetilal's unscrupulous conduct and fired him; Mohan and his two sons managed the whole operation themselves. The land was producing gold; he extended his house, bought a new car and tractor—what more can one ask? His affluence was noted by all the surrounding villages and towns. Many fathers bowed to Mohan and offered the hand of their beautiful and homely daughter for his sons. He was now in a position to bring home a rich man's daughter who will, of course, bring a huge dowry and accentuate his glory. Mohan was about to fold his hands and thank Goddess Lakshmi, *demi Goddess of prosperity,* when his eyes fell on Prashant walking tall with a steady step.

Prashant made himself comfortable in the chair, his eyes flashed with unfeigned contempt, yet he spoke with restrain. "I have come to buy my Baba's land back. I know everything my Baba did for you and how you repaid him. I will pay you exactly what you paid my Baba so that you do not profit from your black deeds."

Mohan was in shock, his hair stood on their ends in fear; how could he part with the gold mine just like that?

"Prashant Beta, even if I agree, Kewal and Krishan will never let me!"

"If you refuse, I swear, in this and other villages every child will know what kind of human you are. You have a good reputation because my Baba loved you and did not break a word about your greed. You will have nothing left by the time I am finished with you, excepting the land and your useless sons who will never be able to find a bride. And I mean it."

What could he do?

- # -

Satish sat on a stool next to Meera and examined her right hand. The palm was red and swollen; she had tried to break the fall with her right hand.

"I cannot believe it, silly girl. You work in a doctor's office and act so careless? The wound is infected now!"

"But I did dab it with alcohol!"

Satish was furious. "You should charge that bastard with assault and send him to jail."

Meera picked up milk and bread from a corner store and walked toward her car. It was semidark; the parking lot was quite empty.

Arun materialized out of nowhere and grabbed her left arm from behind; Meera was startled and turned around. Arun looked lost; he was disheveled, unshaven, and wore just a plaid shirt in the cold February weather.

His desolation touched Meera.

Arun had declared, after Maalti and Veena left for India, "She will come crawling. I am not going to beg her to come."

"You ruined my life! Why did you give Maalti the money to go to India?" His grip was tight while he shook Meera. The bag of groceries opened up—milk carton, bread tumbled on the concrete parking lot.

Meera struggled to free herself. "Arun, Bhai, you are hurting me! You know fully well that you are responsible for what happened."

Arun was deaf with anger, if that is possible. He hit her head with his huge fist. Meera lost balance and fell on her right side.

A man inside the store happened to look out of the window and noticed the commotion. He shouted, "Someone is hitting a woman!" and ran out. Many others followed. They yelled at Arun in unison, who jumped into his car and drove away swiftly.

A young boy, perhaps Rishi's age, helped her up, "Are you hurt?"

"Not bad, I think." She rose to her feet and stabilized herself. Good thing she was wearing slacks that day, Saree would not have stayed in place in such an absurd situation.

"Do you know him?" A middle-aged man was curious.

"No, he must want money. Thanks for showing up just in time!"

Everyone slowly dispersed, commenting upon the evil that had unleashed on humanity by the devil himself. The young man gathered up the milk carton and two loaves of bread. "Should I get another bag?"

"No, it is just a few items. But thank you so much."

Meera wondered if Rishi would be that thoughtful and helpful. The very fact that she asked that question made her uneasy. Was she losing faith in him?

Meera phoned Robin the next day. "Arun needs help!"

Robin was emphatic. "You must file charges."

"But he is not a bad person."

"Well, if you charge him, he will be forced to receive counseling as a condition."

"But you will put him in jail first, right?"

Robin had a big laugh. "Meera, if it was up to you, all the criminals would be out on the streets doing what they do best."

"Let me think."

Satish got up from his stool. "I will get antibiotic cream." He opened a cabinet and started to read labels.

"There it is." Satish pulled his stool close to Meera, took her right hand, and dabbed a cotton swab moistened with alcohol to clean the wound. Meera suppressed an "Ouch."

A loud bang of the entrance door startled them. They spontaneously looked up at the clock. It was five-thirty. "No more patients, I hope," Meera mumbled to herself. She had already stayed longer because Rishi was a school, rehearsing a play; she was fagged all the time.

Satish bent his head over Meera's bruised hand and spread the antibiotic cream evenly. Before they could blink, the half-open door of Satish's office was rudely pushed open with a thud.

Meera turned her head to see who it was. What met her eyes sent a tremor in her spine. Kanchan stood there looking like a real incarnation of Goddess Kali, *demi goddess who destroys evil,* the same red angry face, yellow fiery flames shooting out of huge, bloody, bulging eyes, threatening, ferocious furrows on the forehead, and clenched fists; only the hanging out red tongue was missing.

Satish glanced toward her briefly. "Hi, nice surprise," and continued bandaging Meera's hand.

Kanchan roared, "You slut, how dare you, how dare you?"

Meera's jaw dropped in shock and disbelief as though someone had pushed her off a cliff.

Satish was jerked into looking up, "What the hell, Kanchan?"

She aimed her poison arrow at him now. "Don't you shout at me! How could you?"

Meera was horrified by the gratuitous obloquy. "I don't understand!" Her voice was inaudible.

Satish was breathing hard in rage; he finished bandaging Meera's hand, stood up right in front of Kanchan, and bellowed, "Do you know what you are saying, stupid woman?" Sanity had absconded on both sides, Kanchan looked crazed.

"Yes, I do! How could you let her trap you? She has no husband, but you have a wife!"

Satish held her by both her shoulders in a manly grip, "What are you saying? Say it clearly because my *sister* and I do not understand."

Meera sat like a marble statue; agony gripped her mind and body like a black cobra that oozed out deadly poison in her blood.

Kanchan pushed away Satish's hands from her shoulders and screamed, "You two are having an affair!"

"What?" Satish shouted in shock.

"You come home late, you two laugh together, hold hands?"

Satish was out of mind with fury; he clenched his teeth and glared at Kanchan. Before Meera could stop him, he raised his right hand and slapped Kanchan hard on her left cheek. The unexpected onslaught caught her off guard; she lost her balance and tripped on her left side but did not fall.

A dagger pierced Meera's heart; she meant to get up and come between them, but her body was frozen. "No, Bhaiya, please," she pleaded.

Red finger marks surfaced on Kanchan's fair cheek. She was bewildered. "Oh God, you hit me, for her?" She did not even look at Meera.

Satish looked at his hand then Kanchan's cheek; he did not back off. "I consider Meera as my sister, and she always treated me like a brother. How could you, in God's name, even think of such lowly ideas?"

Kanchan's eyes shone with tears of humiliation. She lashed back in a weepy but choler voice, "And what people have seen and heard is all false? Can there be smoke without fire?"

"Yes, if people, whoever they are, are crazy enough to imagine both!"

She wiped her eyes with her chunni, *veil.* "Now even I have seen you both holding hands and sitting so close. Can you deny that?"

Meera's arm with bandaged hand was hanging on one side of the stool she was affixed to. Satish took it and jerked it toward Kanchan. "She had a wound that needed antibiotic cream. That is what I was doing sitting on a stool close to her!" He let Meera's arm drop gently.

A baffled Satish was a bit softened. "I don't believe it! When did you become this suspicious mean creature?"

Kanchan responded with a loud whine, her steam having been dissipated with the slap. "Yes, I am mean. Throw me out, get her in. She is pretty, I am ugly."

Meera's chest tightened; she couldn't breathe. What did she do to be at the center of this absurd drama? She had to say something, now. "I swear to God, Satish Bhai is like my brother. Please, believe me. But I will stop working here."

Satish interrupted loudly. "No! No! You will not do any such thing. When Mohit left us suddenly, I promised to myself that I will take care of you. Prashant said to me before he left, 'Meera is tired. Be there for her.' I will keep my promise. Kanchan, you go and look in the mirror, what you have beome? And whoever is your informant, both of you cleanse your hearts. That is where the real problem lies."

In a flash, it occurred to both Meera and Satish who it could be. In the last one year, Kanchan and Asha had become bosom buddies; simultaneously, the former had become cold and rude to Meera.

"Asha! Our dear Asha. Isn't it?"

"Yes." Kanchan was defiant. "At least she is a good friend." She pointed at Meera with disgust. "I did so much for her, like my own sister. This is how some ungrateful, low people repay kindness!"

Satish opened his mouth, but Meera interjected. "Kanchan, you have my word, I will not work here. Just be happy, both of you." Emotion stopped her from going further.

Satish was vehement. "You can't leave, you are innocent, Meera!"

"Bhai, Kanchan is a good woman. You can't blame her for being human."

Kanchan couldn't stand it, she bellowed, "Don't try to be goody-goody. I know your reality!"

In a daze, Meera got up slowly and walked away. Kanchan twisted her face, moved on one side, and let her pass.

Meera left with torment on one and triumph on the other face. Is that victory?

- # -

Footsteps and voices slowly pierced the fog of Meera's mind and became audible. She attempted to open her eyes.

"Can you hear me?" An elderly lady in white, with lines of anxiety on her visage, was bent over her.

Meera struggled to rise above the confusion and figure out where she was.

A young man with a stethoscope hanging around his neck peeped from behind the woman. He was certainly a doctor; the lady had to be a nurse. She turned her head back and spoke softly.

"She is partially awake."

"Mrs. Maitra, how do you feel?"

Suddenly, Meera became keenly aware of the debility of her aching body and a sharp pain in her chest; her heart beats pushed at the chest.

"What happened?" She looked into the doctor's blue eyes for clarity.

The doctor was cut and dry. "I am Dr. Heggie. No bones are broken, there are only some cuts and bruises on your chest and forehead. Do you remember someone smashing into your car from behind?"

Still in a daze, Meera looked up and nodded in the negative.

"Try to remember if you had dizziness, chest pain, or a blackout before or after the accident?"

In desperation, Meera wrinkled her forehead and concentrated on recent past. All of a sudden, Rishi's face emerged, "Oh no, oh God!"

The doctor patted her hand. "You will be fine. There is nothing to worry about."

Meera shut her eyes to rally her strength. "Please listen, call Anil at 604-298-4415, tell . . ."

Before she could finish, Anil and Bela made an appearance from behind the doctor. Anil shook his hand and asked anxiously, "How is she?"

Dr. Heggie scanned him. "Are you a relative?"

"Yes, she is my sister."

Di walked briskly toward the bed and took Meera's hand. "How are you? What happened?"

The doctor explained to Anil. "She was unconscious when the paramedics brought her in. I want to find out whether she fainted before the accident or after. We are going to do CAT scan to make sure she does not have any internal bleeding. Also—"

Meera called in a pathetic whine, "Anil, listen!"

Bela interrupted the doctor, "Sorry, but, Anil, she wants to talk to you."

"Go to Rishi! Please, now! Downtown police station."

Anil turned toward the door. "There is no danger?"

"No, I don't think so. But the condition of her heart needs to be checked."

"Why?" Anil was startled.

"Did she ever . . ."

Meera tried to scream, but only feeble staccato words came out of her mouth. "Anil, I will tell the doctor, you go."

He looked at the doctor apologetically. "I will be back soon."

After he left, the doctor turned to Meera. "Just a few questions."

Meera nodded; she held Bela's hand tightly with anxiety.

"Have you experienced chest pains, short breath, sudden sense of weakness, palpitations?"

Meera was astonished. "Yes! All of them." The doctor scribbled something on the chart he was holding, "Well, we can handle it." Dr. Heggie assured Meera as he noticed intense fear in her half-opened eyes. He did not know that Meera's trepidation was not for her own safety but for her son's.

The doctor left with deep furrows on his forehead. Whether it was fatigue or worry, Meera could not tell.

A deluge of warm tears covered Meera's face. She turned toward Bela.

"Sh. Sh. Have faith in God, Beti." Bela stroked her hair.

"How did you find me, Di?"

"We waited for you then started to drive towards your house. We saw your car and the police and asked them. They told us that you had been taken to the hospital."

The nurse gave Meera a white pill. She turned to Bela in curiosity. "Family problems?"

"Yes," was all Bela could utter.

"Di, Rishi?"

Meera was shaken out of her reverie when the phone rang noisily. She debated if it was worth the trouble to answer it; generally, it was the telemarketeers trying to impress you into buying their stuff, whether you need it or not. Just out of reflex, she picked up the phone.

A matter-of-fact female voice asked for Mrs. Maitra. "Speaking."

Meera's face dropped as she consolidated her focus to make sense of the utterances at the other end of the phone. She said, "Pardon me?" several times, prompting the lady to ask if she knew English. "Yes, of course."

Meera's heart pulsated furiously, her limbs felt numb; she attempted to get out of bed in panic, but the force of gravity pulled her limp body back. Rishi was at the police station. "What, why? . . . No! He could not have done it! Is he okay?" Meera stammered without commas or full stops, affirming the lady's suspicion that Meera was an FOB, *fresh out of the boat,* still learning the language of her new homeland.

"Please come and bail him out!"

"Can I speak with him, please?" she begged.

Rishi kept repeating in a scared voice, "Mom, I did not do it! I swear!"

"I know that, don't worry, Beta. I am coming." Meera tried to stay cool.

Rishi sensed it.

"Mom, you believe me, na?"

"Yes, son, I do, I do. I will be right there."

Meera's head swirled like a whirlwind; with fumbling hands, she called Bela.

"Di, phone Anil and ask him to be at your place. I will pick you both up."

"What, what happened?" Di stammered nervously.

"I will tell you later." Meera picked up the keys and purse and scurried to the garage.

It was a frosty late afternoon, snow drifted on the road in smooth waves, dense fog caged her in the car. Meera's angst was that she was not sure of anything anymore. Could he have done it? She burst into tears. *Where did I go wrong?*

The counselor, Ryan, had told her frankly, "Rishi is a complex young man. He has a love and hate relationship with both you and his grandmother. Lost in the maze of conflicting emotions and unable to comprehend his inner turmoil, he gets angry and violent."

"Tell me what to do," Meera asked earnestly.

"The fact is that you are doing everything right. You are showing tremendous patience and love. But his grandmother has to learn to love him without stirring negative emotions against you. You are an idealist, because you still let him see his grandmother. It is laudable. But I am worried about the impact of her nefarious attitude towards you. Also, she never shows up for the meetings I arrange, that indicates her indifference to his welfare."

"I am sure that there is great love and bonding between them. I cannot deny Rishi his rights."

Rishi's identity was in a state of crisis, what was going to happen to him? He was battling demons outside as well as within him.

As Mahtama Gandhi had said, "Real 'Kurukshetra' is within us, a constant battle between good and evil."

Meera wiped her eyes; visibility was very low because of the dense fog and she needed to focus on the road. The brown trees that became visible when the car was close, looked like shadows of themselves in a strange land.

Sharp pain in Meera's chest took her breath away; a sense of suffocation was tightening her lungs. She took deep breaths and chanted, "OM," in an attempt to take the edge off the excruciating malaise.

All of a sudden, the car was pushed from behind, and it hit the curb, throwing Meera toward the steering wheel.

Anil came back within the hour without Rishi but with a cop. Meera felt nauseated; the hospital smells and the extreme mental anguish created a storm in her gut.

For one agonizing hour, Rishi had waited at the police station. Finally, he called Mrs. Henderson, who came herself and bailed him out.

The tension in Meera's body unwinded. At least Rishi was safe and not caged in a jail cell. But the sense of impotency wounded her heart; her son needed her as never before, and she betrayed him.

"What happened, Anil? Why did the police charge Rishi? He did not do anything!"

Anil glanced at the cop meaningfully. "There must be a mistake, Meera. It will be clarified soon."

"Bring him to me, please, he must be in anguish. I want to hold and console him."

Anil stressed, "He is fine, Meera. Please don't worry. I will keep calling Mrs. Henderson. He will come."

Meera felt a little better, but the thorn of her helplessness kept scratching at her heart.

The cop approached her; he was courteous and polite, "Ma'am, I need to ask you some questions regarding your accident." The sedative was taking effect. Meera was sinking into herself.

"What accident?"

The elderly nurse admonished the policeman authoritatively. "Mrs. Maitra should not be agitated. I am sure your questions can wait. She is not going anywhere!"

"I'm sorry, ma'am. Of course, I will come back."

He asked Anil softly, "Sir, can I speak with you?"

"Of course, Officer." Anil smiled to assure him that he was actually not doing anything wrong contrary to the nurse's implications.

The cop tiptoed out of the emergency ward, trying his very best not to arouse the patients by the noisy clicks of his shoes; Anil followed.

The rainbow colors floated in Meera's vision; God's blurry face smiled at her. But Meera could not find any consolation.

"God, this is too much, my pail is almost full, please help me," she wept in the vagueness of a dreamlike state.

Satish had called late one night, about a month after the Kanchan episode. "The clinic has been set on fire, Meera," his voice choked.

"What?" Meera sat up in her bed.

"The police just called me. Fire was blazing, everything is burnt," he couldn't go on.

"There is insurance, na?"

"Yes. Thankfully. But to start from scratch . . ." Satish sounded drained. "I want to know the name of Prashant's friend in the police department."

"It is Robin Williams, he is wonderful. So, so sorry, Bhai. Please don't worry. God will help you build an even better clinic."

"I don't know about God." Meera could visualize his sad smile.

"You are always in my prayers. I don't care if you don't believe in God. He believes in you."

"Meera, how are you feeling?" He changed the topic.

"I am fine. Don't worry about me. But who would have done it?"

"I found the hard way that I have at least one enemy," Satish laughed. "Racial perhaps."

A tide of racism had arisen again from the Pacific Ocean and splashed eastward all the way to Ottawa. Also, Sikhs' Khalistan, *Sikhs wanted their own country, named it Khalistan,* movement was heating up in India; its flames leapt across the many oceans and reached Canada.

It was arson. Police suspected that some Khalistan supporter was responsible.

Satish was Hindu.

A month later, Rishi was arrested. Anil started to look for a good defence lawyer to fight Rishi's case.

Balwant and Surinder had gone to India for six months.

Meera was released two days later. Bela said, "I will not let you go to your house. You are going to stay with me." She had no energy to resist.

Meera kept phoning Mrs. Henderson's house. There was no answer. Meera wished to drive over to Mrs. Henderson's, but Bela put her foot down.

"No! I am sure she is there. And any confrontation with Mrs. Henderson is going to be injurious to your health. I will ask Anil to go instead." That sounded like a reasonable proposition.

Anil stopped at Bela's house around seven in the evening. He had just visited Mrs. Henderson's mansion.

"Wow, what a beautiful place she lives in! Anyway, the housekeeper was shocked to see me. I asked her where Rishi was, she was hesitant. I explained to her bitterly how hard it is for you not to know where your son is. The expression on her face told me that she worries about you. She said, 'Tell Ms. Meera how deeply sorry I am. Mrs. Henderson and Master Rishi have gone on a cruise.' I was shocked! I told her that Rishi was not supposed to leave town. She smiled with irony. 'Madam has reaches to the top, she can do anything, sir.'"

"Tell Rishi to call when they return."

- # -

The nurse wiped Meera's tears with a Kleenex and murmured in her ears, "Now, now, don't lose courage."

The cool touch on Meera's burning forehead comforted her even in a delusional state of mind. A round blurry face was bent over her; Meera fluttered her eyelids that felt glued together.

Meera woke up in a stony dark prison of hollow silence; she panicked with the sense of suffocation by the compression around her mouth and nose.

Bela detected terror in Meera's half-opened eyes. She stepped back and whispered to the nurse, who immediately checked Meera's vitals on the many screens; the blood pressure was high, pulse raced, and heartbeat was erratic. The nurse frowned, hurriedly filled a syringe with a white liquid, and injected in the IV tube hanging on the left side of Meera's bed.

Bela held Meera's sallow, gelid hand.

"Di . . . ." But there was no sound.

Bela hid her anxiety behind an assuaging smile, "Shush . . . don't talk."

Another blurry face propped up from behind Bela, but Meera could not focus; she struggled to keep her heavy eyelids from sliding back over the eyeballs.

Bela and the dim face left the room; Meera screamed for them to stay, but they could not hear the mute entreaty. Tears filled her eyes in desperation.

Meera sank in the world of delirium again. Papa stood outside a large red-brick mansion that was surrounded by trees of different species. Dried, faded flowers stuck to the brown branches of shrubs; the needles of the evergreen trees had lost their luster.

Rishi came running out of the main door; he was about seven or eight years old. Papa became Prashant. Rishi ran past him; he flailed his arms to catch him.

Dabs of vivid coloration splashed in Meera's vision. She half-opened her eyes that fell on a huge bouquet of red roses, white carnations, pink dahlias, yellow lilies with green leafy shoots interspersed in the bunch. In spite of the material inanimation of the bed, tubes, and machines, the flush brought sanity and melody to the smelly and murky hospital room. The ostentatious pulchritude drenched Meera in a fountain of tranquility. She looked searchingly beyond the blooms; a docile face smiled sadly at her. The wounded eyes, filled with innocence of a child, could only belong to Anil.

He held her right hand gently and asked in a low voice, "How are you?"

Meera could not hear him and became agitated; she shut her eyes to escape the sense of overwhelming conundrum.

The nurse motioned to Anil to leave.

He came out and walked briskly toward Satish, Bela, and Sunil; they were talking intensely in the hallway.

"Bhai, what is going on?"

Kelly was startled when she saw a frail and gaunt Meera standing at the door, leaning against the wall.

Meera did not wait to be asked in; she stepped in and told Kelley flatly, "I am here to see Rishi."

"I saw Mrs. Henderson drive away from Parktown Hotel! They are back!"

Bela had just returned from a shopping spree. Meera was lying listlessly on the sofa in the living room, staring blankly at the roof.

There had been no word from Rishi.

Meera sat up in excitement. "I will go and get Rishi!" Her eyes shone with hope.

"No, you will not!" Bela's stern voice prompted Meera to slide back on the sofa.

"Anil will accompany you to that churhel's, *female demon*, house."

Anil was away, and Meera could not wait.

She dressed up and slipped away when Bela was upstairs resting.

The freshly painted dark-brown gate creaked as Meera stepped into a finely manicured garden. The cedars as well as shrubs had been pruned into triangles, globes, square and some other shapes; the garden looked like a blackboard on which all the geometric forms were permanently affixed.

Meera abhorred trimmed gardens where plants were mutilated at the altar of conformity—the imposition of man's conceit entailing rude violence. Such gardens reminded her of uniformed, regimented, replicas of Hitler's youth who walked like robots and uttered slogans that sent millions of innocent humans to gas chambers.

Meera felt at home in untamed, untouched wilderness, where freedom was an inviolable right; trees, bushes, creepers, ferns, mosses, and wildflowers thrived with civilized camaraderie, making room for all.

Deep-emerald tall pines and spruce trees of unknown age surrounded the mansion as a protection from the curious onlookers as well as noises from the streets. Waterdrops hanging on the needles were aureate with soft rays of the setting sun. It had rained earlier that day.

A gray stone path, lined on both sides by brown rose bushes led to a covered porch and the humungous, high, dark wood main door. Even before Meera rang the doorbell, Kelley opened it and poked her dark face out. She had noticed a car parked in front of the mansion when she was dusting Rishi's room on the third floor.

Only one lamp in the far corner diffused pale aggrieved light in the expansive living room. Meera stepped in carefully, fearful of hitting into the furniture in the faded semidarkness.

As shapes and colors materialized, the living room appeared grandiose; heavy polished dark mahogany furniture, red velvet curtains, expensive Iranian flower-patterned rugs, vases, statues, and other immaculate decorations filled all spaces that were not occupied by the heavy furniture. Tall, artistic portraits of Mrs. Henderson's ancestors had an overbearing presence. A tall, middle-aged man wearing military uniform with many gold medals pinned close to his heart stood upright with a robust confidence; Meera gathered that he must be Jane's grandfather. Quite in contrast to his army apparel, his bearded face reflected a mature tenderness that only comes from compassion and forgiveness for an imperfect world. A same-size painting of a vain, lavishly dressed woman hung next to his. Her Victorian long gown was tight at the chest and frilly and fluffed up with wires at the bottom. She was exorbitantly loaded with gold jewelry of exquisite Oriental designs that she must have bought in India. The stiff aspect of her posture and the rigid features indicated a disdain for all living beings; she was definitely a true mother of Mrs. Henderson.

As Meera turned her gaze around, an exceptionally handsome young man—simply dressed in brown jockey pants, white shirt and beige vest—looked down at her. His aquamarine, melancholy eyes were affixed on a serene face; clearly, Jane had inherited the tranquility of her dignified father.

"Yes?" A crude hoarse voice resounded in the room.

Mrs. Henderson was sitting upright in a huge antique red, velvet sofa chair. The pink floral chiffon dress failed to ameliorate her harsh appearance. The dark circles around her colossal eyes, pale, sagging, dotted skin, and a sordid expression on her uncompassionate face entitled her to be the "queen of Halloween."

She glowered at Meera to intimidate her and looked annoyed when Meera refused to oblige. Meera asked politely, "May I sit down? I am not well."

Mrs. Henderson motioned toward a chair at the far corner of the room, the farthest distance between them.

Without wasting time, Mrs. Henderson growled, "You cannot even bail out your son when he needs you? What kind of mother are you?"

Meera had expected this very line of attack, yet it injured her; her chest tightened.

"You are omniscient, so why don't you know that I had an accident and landed up in the hospital? All my friends were trying to contact him every day. Where is he? I wish to speak with him."

Mrs. Henderson's voice was sinuous like a bramble bush. "If I have any power, he will never see you. Leave him to me."

A sense of fatigue drained the prana, *life force*, out of Meera's body. She had set out on a crucial battle in a weary and wounded state. To make matters worse, her adversary had no qualms in using poison arrows while Meera carried no weapons for offence or a shield for defence.

And yet how could she lose? Her very life was at stake.

"I promised your daughter that I will raise Rishi." Tears shone in Meera's brown eyes.

"To hell with your promise! Jane was crazy, she did not know what she was doing! Also, you pledged in a courtroom full of witnesses that you will raise Rishi as a Christian. How come I do not see him at the church?" Mrs. Henderson's words dripped with bitter sarcasm.

"You do know why. I tried my best. The church rejected him."

Life was simpler when they lived in India. Meera and Rishi went to the tall grand church located on the Ridge in Simla. Some relatives and close friends were shocked.

"Yadav, sahib, we are Hindus! How can we pray in a church? We should not discard our Sanatan Dharma, *infinite religion*, for any other faith, na."

Papa smiled. "Meera has not abandoned Hinduism. She is augmenting her faith in one and only God. I need not remind you of the wise words of Hindu sages thousands of years ago: 'All paths lead to the same God.'"

That was not the end of it, though. Some people, especially women who had nothing better to do, circulated their two bit in gossip circles, "Do you know Mr. Yadav's daughter, Meera? She goes to church! Meena told me na . . . why would she lie yar, *friend*?"

"Gosh, some people think just by going to church, the color of their skin will change and they can pass for a foreign *memsahib*."

"Toba Toba, if my daughter did that, I would have sliced her throat, na."

Since her family was firmly behind Meera, the world at large did not matter.

When Meera returned to Canada, complexities laid snare in her path immediately.

Pastor Smith called her in his office. "We would like to baptize Roy as soon as possible. Once chastised in the 'fire of Baptism,' he will be purified from all sins and start a good Godly life."

Meera did not expect the conundrum this early in Rishi's life. Pastor Smith added, "Actually, Mrs. Henderson wants us to go ahead."

Meera understood. "Please let me think and speak with Rishi."

A few months passed.

One day, Rishi came upstairs after attending Sunday school in the basement of the church. Meera was talking to Susan, who led a committee for arrangements for all functions of the church. The potluck for Thanksgiving was being organized.

"Sure, I can bring something. I think I should not use any spice."

Susan laughed. "Yes! Good idea. Most of us are only used to salt!"

Rishi clung to Meera's legs and started to cry.

"What happened?"

"I want to go home!"

"But why are you crying? Are you hurt?"

"Let's go!" he shouted. Some people turned their heads to see what the commotion was about.

Meera picked Rishi up and hugged him. "Okay, let's go." She walked to the car with Rishi clinging to her shoulder.

"I am not going to church anymore!"

"Why? I thought you enjoyed the Sunday school and the interesting stories you learn of Abraham and his sons?"

"No! I hate everyone. They tell me I am a sinner."

"Why?"

"Because I have not taken a dip in that tub of cold water. Jesus will never forgive me!"

"Okay, that is not hard. Do you want to take a dip?"

In one corner of her heart, Meera was happy; the issue that had been haunting her seemed to have resolved itself.

"No! I don't want to see the mean boys who hurt me."

Meera called Pastor Smith. "I think it is better if we wait until he is grown up enough to make a decision himself."

Rishi refused to go to church after that incident.

Meera composed herself. "Look, next year, Rishi will be eighteen, he can decide himself. In the meantime, we can both give him our love. Let him focus on his studies. He has to make a life. Please, don't destroy him." By the end of the sentence, Meera's voice broke.

Mrs. Henderson straightened herself and roared in anger, "You incompetent native! You don't know how to raise a child and blame me? Go burn in hell. You natives destroyed Jane's life! Leave Roy alone."

Meera was stunned by the unexpected onslaught; the possibility of not getting Rishi back suddenly became real. Mrs. Henderson knew that she had defeated her opponent; now she proceeded to finish her for good.

"Don't you realize Roy does not want to see you? I have not tied him up! You are deceiving yourself. He hates you!"

Like a massive rock, Meera was dislodged from a high mountain peak and rolled toward a cold, blind, bottomless pit. Her heart became heavy; shooting pain arose from the left area of the rib cage and diffused radially.

For the first time in her life, Meera experienced a wrenching emotion that was unfamiliar and undefinable but agonizing. All she knew that it would kill her if not dealt with, immediately; her pail was full and ready to spill with just one more drop of water.

Outer and inner grotesqueness had no place in Meera's heart; she could not stand the hideousness of negative emotions. She knew that compassion and forgiveness needed to be summoned, instantly; there was no other way to maintain the purity of her heart.

Meera looked at Mrs. Henderson seated defiantly on her red throne, bent and spent like a withered flower that was devoid of any fragrance. Her dehumanized, pathetic existence contained no semblance of beauty. She was a cactus with acute thorns that lacerated everyone who happened to cross her path; how could she invoke love in others? And life without love is like a searing, sandy desert where even mirage of an oasis is reluctant to ingress.

How could Meera be angry at someone whose life was bereft of any meaning, who had nothing? Meera's heart filled with pity and compassion.

She recovered her inner equilibrium, but the sense of despondency remained. The pain in her chest was excruciating, and drops of sweat oozed on her tepid forehead. She got up and staggered toward the main door. Kelly appeared from somewhere to help Meera with her coat.

"Are you okay, ma'am?" Kelly was worried.

"No! Call an ambulance, I will be in the car."

Meera could barely speak. She crossed her arms across her chest and pressed hard.

Kelly held her, "I will walk you to the car."

"No, ambulance . . ."

Meera could not remember anything except the tall deodars bending over her as she lay at the back seat of the car, writhing in pain.

- # -

Bela bent over Meera. "Rishi is fine, he has been found innocent. We have to give Mrs. Henderson credit for taking care of him."

Meera let her head sink in the blue pillow of the hospital; tears of relief trickled down the sides of her face.

The prosecutor Joe Candell's discomfort was obvious; John Radley Jr. sat next to Rishi and Helena. He was a brilliant lawyer and practiced law in Vancouver.

Radley sauntered in the courtroom casually and shredded the testimonies of the police as well as the witnesses.

The defense was impeccable. Rishi's gold chain that had his name engraved on it was clasped when the police found it in Satish's burnt clinic floor. If it had fallen from Rishi's neck while he was setting fire, the chain had to be unclasped; it happened to be too small to go over Rishi's head.

The proposition that Rishi may be carrying it in his pocket was ridiculous.

As to the two witnesses who claimed that they saw Rishi around the clinic at the time of the fire, two other witnesses were produced who testified that both of them were somewhere else. Case closed.

Bela cried openly when the judge dismissed the case. Rishi shook Radley's hand. "Thank you, Uncle."

"You are welcome, son."

He turned to Helena. "I am having lunch with Joe, we went to law school together. See you later."

Rishi was sitting with his back toward Bela and Sunil. He stood up, turned around, and started to walk toward the door with triumphant Helena on one side and Peter on the other. He was pleasantly surprised to see them.

"Hi, Uncle, hi, Aunty. I did not know you were here!"

Helena stared at the happy couple, hoping that they would melt away in the fire of her hatred.

Sunil did not notice; he stepped forward and said with obvious glee, "Rishi, son, I am very happy that you have been cleared. I wish to talk to you about your mom."

Mrs. Henderson commanded harshly. "Roy, keep walking."

Bela was angry; she stepped right in front of Rishi, looked straight into his pure blue eyes, and spoke emphatically, "Your mom is very ill in the hospital and wants to see you."

Rishi was visibly shaken and looked at Helena questioningly. She bellowed, "You are a pack of liars! Why don't you leave him alone?"

Helena pushed Bela aside brusquely, gripped Rishi's arm, and charged on like a military commander. Bela staggered; Rishi looked back apologetically, but she did not notice.

Meera's stay in the hospital was prolonged to two months. Vitality of her heart returned slowly, but bacteria invaded her lungs. The antibiotic meant to kill the trespassers also wiped off the friendly bacteria that were living in a happy symbiosis in her gut.

Pain ravaged Meera's body; her mind was in torment. Rishi was nowhere to be found. Anguish of Rishi's loss gripped her like death. She wanted to curl up and die just like that.

A quintessential domain of Meera's consciousness reminded her that her real Self was unscathed; she had to hang on to that truth. Sensibility of Meera's mind swayed between the invincibility of her soul and the cachectic state of her suffering body and mind.

When all attempts to reach Rishi failed, Bela decided to stand outside his classroom.

Rishi was astonished, "Aunty, hi? Is my mom okay?"

Bela took his arm and pulled him on one side. "Your mom is very ill. That is why she could not come to the police station or at the court hearing. Please believe me, I don't lie."

Both of them saw Peter walking toward them with long strides since he was fairly tall. Rishi looked at Bela and Peter in turn; he was hopelessly confounded.

Bela figured that she had just a few seconds; she spoke hurriedly, "Your mom is going to India. Please come to the airport." She handed him a piece of paper with the date, flight number, and departure time.

Rishi held his tears and spoke with determination, "Aunty, I will come."

Meera could almost see Rishi, looking taller than the rest of the crowd, rushing toward her and hugging her. "You cannot go, Mom!"

Bela took Meera's hand. "I know he loves you."

Meera made a sincere effort to smile. "I know, Di."

Sunil had parked her wheelchair on one side of the waiting room for the disabled passengers. The airport was exactly like all other airports in the world—tired, irritable adult populace carrying the dual burdens of family and luggage. The suitcases becoming heavier by the minute, children more cranky. Muffled, incoherent announcements prompted anxiety attacks in many people; what if the information being broadcast was that their plane had just left?

Sunil assured Meera, "I will keep trying to contact Rishi." Then turned to Atul. "We are planning a visit to India next year!"

Atul's clouded face brightened. "Please come and stay with us. I have no words to thank you both. I can never repay the debt! If ever we can do something for you, please, give us an opportunity."

Sunil, being a miser with words, just smiled, "No need, Bhai."

Meera took a few deep breaths to release the tension in her body and leaned against the back of the wheelchair. She closed her weary eyes, "I know Rishi will come to me one day. He is always in my heart." Meera rested her right hand on the left area of her chest where her heart lay in agonizing pain.

Atul glanced disconcertedly at his hunched sister sitting in the wheelchair with her trembling bony, white hand on her heart. How could he ever forgive the ungrateful world that inflicted deadly wounds on his chaste sister? Atul moved closer to the wheelchair and stroked her black thick hair.

It did not seem long ago when a little girl in short frock would jump up and down, her ponytail following the body motion, and ask him, "Bhaiya, are you going to the mall?"

"Yes."

"Then you know what?"

"What?"

"Bhaiya?"

"No, I don't know what, choti!"

"Oh, Bhaiya, how can you forget? Chocolate! Remember?"

"Oh . . . of course!"

Meera would giggle happily and jump higher.

If he could, Atul would reverse the direction of kal, *infinite time,* and fixate it to the time when innocence and joy bubbled in the little girl who was his favorite.

- # -

Leela entered Meera's bedroom and mumbled something incoherently. Meera did not understand.

Leela repeated a little loudly, "Didi, someone is here to see you."

"Who?"

"I don't know. A sab, *gentleman*."

Meera whispered, "Ask him to come some other day."

The shadows of dusk fell on Meera's bedroom and brought a sense of tranquility and stillness by dissolving the background noises of the neighborhood.

As a little girl growing up in Simla, she could be found standing in silence, hypnotized by the breathtaking view of the setting sun. The transforming rainbow colors of the clouds hung over the overwhelming stature of the Himalayans; trembling silhouette of the deodars faded in the grey dusk before dark swallowed them completely.

Rishis of ancient India instructed their disciples to pray and meditate before sunrise or after sunset. According to them, when the collective physical activity and cognitive vibrations of the world subside, the unruffled mind flows, without any obstruction, to merge with the Soul that is the gateway to the realm of God.

Leela returned a minute later; Meera was about to tell her to get lost when she noticed a tall shadow behind her. In the semidarkness she strained her eyes to recognize the face above Leela's head.

Meera's heart beat intensely; she did not know how her hands synthesized enough sweat instantly to make them cold and soggy.

Leela complained in a nasal voice, "It is not my fault. He is not listening."

Meera's dull introverted eyes shone. She smiled weakly. "It is okay, Leela. He never listens to anyone. Now pull a chair close to my bed, turn the lamp on, and get strong tea for Sab. Get a plate of mithai, *sweets*, also." Her voice trailed off by the end of the sentence.

Leela turned the lamp on and left, intentionally dragging her feet to express her annoyance. Not only the man paid no attention to her authority, Didi, *sister*, smiled and encouraged him.

Prashant pulled the chair next to Meera's bed and sat down. His normally unfathomable eyes looked deeper and troubled; his complexion was darker, the heat of India perhaps. He also looked older. Meera was embarrassed at the thought that she must appear much older due to her illness.

Prashant extended his hand under the sheets, groping for hers, pulled it out, and kissed it fondly.

All of a sudden, a flood of tears burst forth from Meera's eyes, "Papa . . .," she whispered hopelessly.

Asha bent her head toward Atul and murmured, "Did you tell her?"

"No." The car splashed water from the potholes on to the windshield.

"Oh, ji!"

The car jerked; they all bumped upward almost hitting the roof.

"Sorry, guys, I cannot see the potholes. Water is covering the highway, man!"

Asha turned her sleepy head back and looked at Meera. "Choti, you are very obstinate. We should have taken the flight to Chandigarh. The car ride is so straining for you, na?"

Meera wanted to say, "Bhabi, *sister-in-law,* I want to feel the water-laden breeze against my burning cheeks, the music of the rain to awaken my silenced songs. I wish for golden sunrays of dawn to lift the veil of darkness from my spirit. I crave for my life to come back to me again, I am fighting for it, Bhabi, don't you see?"

When Atul wheeled Meera out of the New Delhi airport, umbrageous clouds looked threatening. Atul stopped the car at Karnal; a brand-new restaurant had been erected just recently on the right side of the highway. As Atul parked the car and went inside to access a wheelchair, it started to pour. He came back quickly, running in the rain, "Meera, you cannot get out. I suggest you both stay in the car. I will order breakfast, and a bearer can bring it."

"But he will get drenched, Bhaiya."

"Meera, I am sure they have raincoats for the staff." He was a bit irritated.

"I hope so," Asha mumbled.

Half an hour later, a young man in a white uniform stepped out, with Atul holding an umbrella over his head. Since the small umbrella could not cover two people, they both got drenched.

"Oh no." Asha was upset and ordered the bearer, "Beta, change your clothes."

He smiled at her kindness. "Bibiji, we are used to staying in wet clothes for a whole day. We *garib, poor,* are tough!"

Meera frowned to express her concern.

Needless to say, the young man profited much from his wetness; a huge tip in dollars immediately brought warmth to his clammy skin. He bowed several times to express his gratitude and became more soaked with rainwater.

Meera said impatiently, "Bhai, run in, thank you," and shut the car window to prevent any further display of thanksgiving.

After they were well fed with toast, jam, omelet, and tea, Meera lay back in the backseat to mollify her aching body, Atul drove, and Asha planned to pick up clothes for Atul from Karnal. However, it was too early; shops were closed.

Asha looked back. "Meera do you have any shawls in your luggage?"

"Yes, Bhabi." She got up with worry. "Let us stop the car, we can get those out. At least Bhaiya can be warm."

Atul nodded sideways to dismiss their anxiety. "Yar, *friend,* I will not catch cold because it is still summer! Don't fuss, please."

Asha kept quiet. Meera looked out through the glass window, beyond the streaks of rainwater, at the landscape. A rich verdant vista—that blended variegated shades of emerald belonging to the foliage of trees, twiners, tall grass, bushes, unfurling ferns and the wheat crop in the backdrop—ran past her like a fast-forwarding film. She drank the potion of life with thirsty eyes.

As soon as he heard the car pull in the car porch, Rakesh came out of the main door in his pajamas. Tears streamed down his stubbled cheeks as he opened the car door for Meera; he pulled her torso toward him and embraced her tightly. "I am sorry, Choti, you are so sick, Papa has gone. What is happening to us?"

Meera did not get a chance to get out of the car that morning; she had another heart attack.

Atul drove the car at a crazy speed; early in the morning, streets were empty and the constables slumbering in their wives' loving arms.

Within a few minutes of their arrival at the Post Graduate Institute of Medical Sciences at Chandigarh, a team of doctors, nurses, and machines surrounded an unconscious Meera.

Manik came briskly to emergency. "What happened, Atul?"

Atul's muscles relaxed. Manik was Godsend; he was a great friend who happened to be a heart specialist.

"I am not worried now, mere bhai, *my brother.* I know you will save her."

Manik pressed Atul's hand and joined the medical team immediately.

For three seemingly endless days and nights, no one slept as Meera fought with Lord Yama. Ma flew from Simla. Shobha could not come; her mother-in-law was also critically ill. She phoned every two hours, her voice submerged in guilt. "Ma, I have never been there to help Choti! If she does not make it, I will never forgive myself."

"Shobha, no regrets. Pray for her with a pure heart."

Atul, Ma, Rakesh, and Asha took turns to lie on a small sofa in the waiting room. The rest of the time all of them sat at the edge of their chairs.

On the third night, Meera's pulse, blood pressure, breathing stabilized—she moved her hand.

Exhausted, Manik came to the waiting room and touched Ma's feet. "Aunty, your daughter is safe."

Atul embraced Manik, buried his tortured face on his shoulder, and wept.

"Atul, now is a time for joy. All of you, go home and sleep. I will spend another night in ICU. She is out of danger, Bhabi." He turned to Asha.

Ma just nodded a firm no. "Manik Beta, I want to be here when she opens her eyes."

Asha and Rakesh left, Atul stayed back. Manik allowed them inside the ICU. Ma swallowed her tears at the sight of all the tubes coming out of Meera's sickly body. She lay peacefully like a withered flower.

Only one person was allowed to sit beside Meera. Hours went by, Ma's lips moved in constant prayer. Meera's eyelids fluttered for a few seconds. Ma held her breath and bent over Meera, who closed her eyes and dozed off.

Meera woke up more alert and saw Ma wrapped in a plain-white saree with no jewelry; it was unbearable. Tears flooded her eyes. Ma wiped Meera's tears, held her hand, and smiled, "But I am okay,

Choti." Meera wanted to embrace Ma and console her but could not move. She rolled into sleep again.

Doctors transferred Meera out of ICU to a room after a week; sun came in through the window. Asha had brought roses for her that virtually transformed the ambience.

Ma sat on the bed, took Meera's hand in hers, and spoke with utter equipoise, "Your papa would cringe if he saw you like this. Pray to your Lord and get up."

Shakuntala had lived under the shadow of her husband's overbearing wisdom and puissance. She was content because Papa respected her as his better half. Now, she had come to her own; the power that rested within her awoke and replaced Papa's stoicism with full capacity, for the sake of her children.

Meera wanted details. She wanted to know what happened to Papa. Ma pointed her finger toward the heavens and said, "Time had arrived for him to go."

"Let us stay in a hotel overnight," Ma cried.

Papa wrapped the scarf around his neck and head, "I am warmly dressed, are you?"

Ma's hand trembled, the cup fell on the kitchen floor with a crash; thick woolen socks saved her feet from getting scorched. As she stooped to pick up the pieces of the china, Hari hurried toward her, "Maji, I will do it."

"No, you will not!" Nalini bellowed. "Hari, finish whatever you are doing. Go! Don't look at my face!"

Rakesh already knew Nalini's reaction to the idea. So he picked up the phone, not to ask but to inform her.

"Nalini, I am bringing Papa and Ma. It is too cold here in the winter."

Expecting loud vociferation, he distanced the phone from his ear to avoid getting hit by her choler speech.

"Okay then, we will see you tomorrow." He did smile wickedly, having escaped the immediate consequence of his highly provocative actions.

After waiting for a few minutes, Rakesh picked up the phone again and assumed a tough stand. "Do not, do not create any hangama, *noise,* and spare everyone the pain. It is only a matter of a few months." He hung up the phone before she could shout.

Rakesh's activism was an act of bravery. Over the years, he had learnt the technique, often used by husbands in trouble, of tuning the wife out as a survival mechanism.

He did not foresee that Ma and Papa would have to pay the price for his daring.

At the outset, Ma made an attempt to take care of Papa and her own needs including cooking. She knew that Nalini had very little capacity and no willingness to exert herself for anyone.

The very first morning, when Ma went into the kitchen to make tea for Papa, Nalini glowered at her, "Why can't you wait until Hari is free? You want people to think that I don't take care of you?"

"No, Nalini Beti, I don't want to be a burden?" Ma was horrified at the accusation.

"Of course you are! Why pretend?"

To appease her, Ma stopped going to the kitchen with disastrous consequences. Meals for them were habitually delayed, sometimes by a couple of hours. Ma brought fruit and cookies to survive in the meantime. Their laundry, cleaning was not done for days. When she took her daily bath, Ma got into the habit of sanitizing the washroom.

Nalini complained to her friends, neighbours whoever provided their friendly ear, "There is so much more work with their fussy demands. Maid has so much to do, she cannot just serve them, you see?"

Snow fell on the Himalaya mountains that are a mere fourteen miles from Chandigarh, sending a wave of freezing temperatures. Papa was half lying in bed; quilt covered most of his torso. He was deep in thought, reflecting on the nature of life that sometimes brings so much of undeserved perdition on good humans. Perhaps the theory of karma, *our deeds,* that we pay for our past births' mistakes is the only logical explanation.

Ma came out of the bathroom, shivering. Papa glanced at her, "You don't have to take a bath every day." Ma just smiled. Papa knew she would not face her God for prayers unless she was pure in body and mind.

When Papa and Ma were a young married couple, he would sometimes argue, "God only cares about chastity of your heart and mind. Rituals take us away from Him!"

After a lifetime of retrospection, he had comprehended that at their very core, every human has designed a reality that is all his own; that creed is the only truth he can believe and live by. Who was he to question others' verity while he was still striving to ascertain his own? Papa wished he had the absolute surrender and belief in God that his brother possessed. It was not that he did not believe—he did. But there was a core realm of his mind that was constantly shadowed by the agony of the poor, oppressed victims of wars who do not start the conflicts yet pay the price with their lives. He could not transcend it and reach the state of culmination of his faith.

"Should I make soup for you?" Ma asked as she put on her saree.

Papa nodded in the affirmative.

She felt anxious, almost nauseated at the thought of facing Nalini's insolence, but she had to venture to the kitchen.

Ma's prayers were answered; Nalini was not there.

Hari looked at her, "Maji, I will make the soup as soon as I finish rotis."

"Nai, Beta, I will do it. You finish lunch. Rakesh and Keshav are coming home for lunch."

Ma placed a steel pot on the burner of the gas stove that was not in use. She added water to the pan and picked a pack of dry soup from the pantry and prepared it in hurry while thanking God for modernization; she did not have to cut vegetables and cook soup from scratch.

As soon as Ma poured the boiling soup in a cup and turned to leave the kitchen, Nalini walked in. She yelled, "Why can't you eat whatever everyone else eats? If you want your own stuff, go to your own house."

Ma sat at the edge of the bed and wept for the first time.

Papa had heard everything that had precipitated in the kitchen since their bedroom was located right next to it.

It was not that he did not know, but he had learnt to ignore. But it was becoming unbearable to face not only Ma's pain but also Rakesh's anguish. He carried a perpetual guilty shadow in his eyes; a stooped back and graying hair were becoming conspicuous. He was painfully silent most of the time.

Papa had reconciled to the reality that all humans have to carry their crosses themselves. Even though Jesus's cross was the most grievous, He was the Son of God and knew it; the Divine insight endowed Him with power to uphold it with grace. But mankind, unaware of the tenacity and puissance of their "Real Selves," is bound to suffer more profoundly. The tragedy of parents' destiny is that they not only shoulder their own crosses but also those of their beloved offspring, who are often stumbling with avoirdupois burden of their lives. It is impossible to gauge which is the source of greater misery.

Papa put aside his quilt and got out of bed. "Pack up the essentials in an airbag. Rest will come later."

"What?" Ma looked up in bewilderment. "No!"

Papa walked slowly toward the kitchen and called Hari. "Papaji, I will get your soup, soon."

"Nai. Call mali, *gardener*." Hari was puzzled but went out and fetched him.

"Beta, get a taxi." Mali looked at Ma's and Hari's faces to figure out if the request was genuine.

"Go, now, Bhai. We have to get the bus to Simla."

Hari was stunned. "You are not well, you will get worst, Papaji!" He held Papa's feet. "I cannot let you go. What will I tell Rikku Bhaiya?" Papa stroked his hair. "It is okay, Hari."

Within fifteen minutes, Mali came back. "Papaji, I could not find a taxi. I got a scooter rickshaw."

In the scooter rickshaw, the chilly, rainy wind hit them like frozen arrows. The bus to Simla had left just as the scooter rickshaw pulled into the bus stop.

Papa approached a taxiwalla Sardar, *Sikh*. "Bhai, can you take us to Simla?"

"Sab, *gentleman*, roads are not safe."

"I will pay you double. Just drive slowly and carefully. We will make it."

Rakesh came home for lunch. Nalini was lying on her bed facedown, weeping. She elevated her bawling to an appropriate pitch to be heard by Rakesh as he entered the house.

"Ma shouted at me! I only asked her to wait for Papaji's soup! They just left without even telling me, as though I am nobody. They always treat me shabbily. Asha is the only one they love." A few tears fell.

Rakesh's heart sank; without a word, he went to the kitchen.

"Hari kaka, what happened?" Nalini followed Rakesh and glared at Hari; he looked down. "I pleaded with Papaji not to go, Rikku Bhaiya!" His voice broke.

Rakesh picked up the phone, his voice dripping with anguish. "Bhai, I just came home. Papa and Ma left for Simla. They have taken a bus. I am sorry."

Atul was flabbergasted. "What happened?"

"I don't know, but I will find out soon."

Atul understood. "Rikku, stay calm. I will call you as soon as they arrive."

Atul's words of understanding did not mollify Rakesh. He shook with rage, went into the bedroom where Nalini had reposited herself on the bed and continued her part of the drama.

Rakesh pointed to the door, barely able to speak in fury. "Go, get out, or I will hit you."

Nalini left for Kanpur by Howrah Mail, swearing never to come back.

Atul waited for Papa and Ma at the bus stop; the passengers got out excepting them. Sick with worry, he inquired about the next bus.

"Sab, *gentleman*, there is no bus now. It is late and the road is not safe to drive in the dark."

Atul slumped on a bench slowly. A thin drizzle fell on him. Where are they? Horrible scenarios visited his consciousness. At the best of times, the highway from Kalka to Simla was full of dangers. On one side, there was solid rock, steep upwards slope of the mighty Himalayas and on the other precipitous, steep cliffs. Often, bus drivers become reckless, overconfident, and try to display their skillful maneuvering to the passengers, most of whom, especially the first-timers, develop palpitations and anxiety disorder.

As Atul passed by the taxi stand, he spotted Ma and Papa getting out of a cab. He was so relieved that he could kiss Sardarji's face, but the dense beard and moustache was not conducive to the idea.

Ma hugged him and wept in his arms.

Papa spoke calmly. "Akku, get a rickshaw."

Cars are not allowed on the city roads in Simla; taxis drop people at the bus stand or the nearby railway station. Rickshaw pulled by four sturdy men is the transport for the weak and the old; young have no choice but to walk even miles.

By the time they arrived home, Papa was burning with fever. Papa's frail body could not withstand the chill of wet clothes for hours. He developed pneumonia, stayed in the hospital for two months. After that, he remained vulnerable and feeble, not quite himself. A part of his heart remained broken; there was no remedy for that malady.

Early March, Lord Yama came in the form of bronchitis, collected Papa's soul from his ailing body, and took him away from a world that he did not belong to anymore.

Papa expired the same day, same time when Meera had a major heart attack outside Mrs. Henderson's mansion.

Prashant bent over Meera, held her damp face in his hands, and kissed her gently on her pale lips.

She felt aggrieved, failed, lost—she could not stop crying. Her loved ones had been snatched away irretrievably; there was nothing left, except a consumed, doddering body and impotent mind. What was she going to do with it?

Footsteps came closer. Prashant took a handkerchief from his khaki pants pocket, wiped her cheeks, and sat back. Meera murmured, "I am sorry." Prashant smiled reassuringly.

Leela walked in, plunked a small table in front of Prashant noisily, and left. Meera and Prashant looked at her back and suppressed a smile. She came back a minute later with a tray that she deposited on the table with great flourish.

Meera spoke slowly, "Thank you, Leela. Can you now pour tea in a cup, one spoon of sugar and some milk? Then pass the cup to Sab, *gentleman.*

"Also, give him a quarter plate."

Prashant interrupted, "We can manage, thank you. Save your energy!"

Leela was tensed up, stiff like a wooden plank. Didi is smiling too much, talking to this Sab she had never heard of! The whole situation was highly suspicious. He was certainly not good news. Why? Didi cried when she saw him. The fact that Leela did not know anything about this new development added to her aggravation.

When she left the room, Prashant released a deep sigh, "If she was to approve me for your hand, I will be dismissed in a hurry."

Meera laughed softly at his mock distress.

She asked him, "How is Mataji, Bahen, Bhai?"

Prashant became serious. "Everyone is fine except you. Why did you all keep me in the dark?"

His distress was justified. Meera looked worn, thin, and gaunt in the diffused, pale light of the lamp. Yet he noticed a dull glow in her brown half-opened eyes and a slight smile on her quivering lips. Of course, belonging to the male subclass of *Homo sapiens*, who are retarded in the territory of their brain that enables understanding of womens' emotions, Prashant did not know that the origin of Meera's smug contentedness was recent, after she saw him.

A car entered the porch; a few minutes later the car door slammed. Meera looked at Prashant meaningfully.

He got up, touched her forehead lovingly with his hand. "You rest now, I will see Bhaiya and Bhabi." He turned the lamp off and walked out on tiptoes.

Meera heard the loud, "Aré, what a wonderful surprise! I did not know you were coming? Meera did not say anything! Anyway." Without waiting for any reply, Atul continued, "Have you seen Meera yet? Yah? We'll let her rest. We will go to the living room."

Suddenly, Atul became aware of Asha's surprised presence. "Meet my wife, Asha. Bhai, get us some tea. You have had it? Dinner then?"

Prashant folded his hands in greeting. "Meera has told me wonderful things about you, Bhabi."

Asha laughed. "Prashant, I am very happy to meet you too. I am sure Meera's recovery will be faster now."

Meera could not hear Prashant's response, but she could visualize his reactions; he assumed a self-conscious shyness with strangers.

Meera's head was hazy, but a small light twinkled in her heart.

Prashant spoke as soon as they were settled in the living room. "Bhai, I am so sorry about Papa's passing away. It is my misfortune, I did not get a chance to be in the presence of the noble soul."

Atul looked down to hide his tears; it had been too recent for him to come to terms with the tragedy.

He raised his head. "Please accept my condolence at Baba's death. Meera had written to us. How are Maji, your Bahen, and Bhai doing?"

The golden fire that had reduced his Baba to ashes still raged in Prashant's heart; his sense of guilt did not let it extinguish. "We are trying to cope as you all are."

Atul poured drinks. "Prashant, gin, scotch?"

"Bhai, I don't drink alcohol!"

Before Atul could comment on Prashant's queer confession, Prashant queried, "Where is Ma?"

"My Masiji in Kanpur is not well. She is visiting her."

Asha passed biryani to Prashant. "Prashantji, take more. Don't be shy. This is your own home, na?"

He responded by pouring a large helping on his plate.

"That is good! I like that." Asha expressed much satisfaction.

Having ensured that Prashant was being fed properly, the first rule of Indian hospitality, Atul now turned to more consequential political issues as men always do.

Indira Gandhi had regained power, thus affirming the well-known adage that voters suffer from short political memory. Citizens had forgotten the atrocities of emergency years. The masses did not give the new government of Janata Party a chance to govern because they sought instant gratification that is impossible to deliver in a massive, highly diverse and populated democracy like India. The infighting for control did not help.

A moderate police inspector's dead body was found in a ditch in Amritsar, yet another victim of Bhindranwale, *the leader of the Khalistan movement.*

"I cannot believe Bhindranwale has become so powerful! He is killing all the moderate Sikhs. It has come to light that he has long lists of people he wants to terminate, no one knows how to stop him. All our Sikh friends do not want Khalistan and call him a fanatic. He is playing on uneducated Sikhs' religious sensibilities in the name of Sikhism," Atul retorted.

"Bhai, Indira Gandhi's game was to empower him against Longowal, who was a balanced, moderate, and popular member of the Akali Dal party. She was afraid that Longowal would win the election, which would have meant an end of Congress rule in Punjab. Indira created a Frankenstein to divide the Sikh vote. Now, we will have to wait to see if she exterminates him, or he annihilates her first. But we are all suffering the consequence of her blundering!"

Atul became pensive. "Yar, *friend,* this debacle has caused a schism between Hindus and Sikhs. Extremists on both sides are having a hay day."

"Prashantji, have more chicken." Asha smiled complacently. "Don't lose your appetite over it. We Indians are experts at inventing perplexities, as though the nature's calamities are not enough to challenge us. There is drought in Bihar, hundreds are starving. In the north, floods have destroyed much of the crops. Villages are under water in UP and parts of Punjab. We should focus on dealing with these problems. I don't know what is going to happen to our India," she ended with dejection.

Asha changed the topic. "I am sorry, I had wanted Nishi and Nishant to have dinner with us, but as usual, they already had their plans written in stones. So much for wanting to spend time with your children! They always find excuses and disappear."

Prashant laughed. "Bhabi, they are young, and by their standard, we already fall in the category of old."

Atul complained, "Bhai Prashant, you have treated us like begana, *stranger.* You should have visited us before. You have been in India for one and a half years."

Prashant felt embarrassed. "Bhai, I did want to. But it has been all consuming to sort out the mess of last years of Baba's illness."

Atul's face fell. "Really?"

Leela came with fresh chapatis. "Bibiji, should I bring more chicken and *bhindi*?" She did not look at Prashant at all.

Prashant attempted to lighten up the atmosphere. "Bhabi, I am eating such good food after a long time. Our Ramu is a good fellow, but cooking is not his forte. Ask him to clean, and he will shine the floors, you can see your face reflected on it. But do not expect to lick your fingers with his chicken and *bhindi.* And . . ." He lowered his voice in feigned fear. "When Meera is better, teach her some of the culinary art. Her cooking is good . . . but . . . don't tell her I said that."

Asha laughed heartily.

"Prashantji, you are not fair. Meera is a good cook, but it is not her favorite activity. By the way, I did not make all this." She pointed to the table that was covered with dongas, *casseroles.* "I better straighten the record. Our Dharma Kaka did. He came at Papa's death. When Meera became very ill, he insisted on staying to look after her. He is like family, such a support."

"Meera told me all about him. I would like to say my pranam, *greetings*, to him."

Atul interrupted abruptly. "You are staying for a few days, na?"

"Yes, Bhai, three or four days."

"We better get your luggage from the hotel."

"No, no. It is quite okay," Prashant protested uncomfortably.

"Prashantji, we have plenty of room. And we will not let you stay anywhere else," Asha announced decisively.

Atul had rented a house in Chandigarh for the winter. Meera was too weak to withstand a cold winter in Simla after her heart attack. She needed special care, and Nalini was still in Kanpur.

Prashant held on to Meera's limp hand and stayed by her bed until late at night. Occasionally, she opened her eyes and smiled faintly; he kissed her hand.

Night took charge outside. Prashant turned the lamp off. With no competition, the placid blue moon rays ingressed smoothly in the room through the open window. In the cool, dewy light, Meera's wan skin gleamed like marble. Prashant was awestruck by the sublimity of her spirit that was reflected in her tranquil face.

Asha peeked in the room a few times. She motioned to Prashant to come out of the room. "You must be tired, Prashantji. You should sleep."

"Bhabi, I will obey you only on one condition."

Asha was taken by surprise. "What?"

"You drop the *ji* part of my innocent name! You are older, you have full right to call my name sternly and order me to go to bed."

Asha laughed.

Bougainvillea sprawled across the archway of the balcony next to Prashant's bedroom; it rocked slightly with the cool morning zephyr. A few tender magenta blooms fell on the lawn below.

Prashant woke up to the usual bird gobbledygook. The silky effulgence of the morning sun radiated in the guest room through the open window; a glowing patch of light, bordered by the shadows of the moving branches of the bougainvillea, created shifting patterns on the white wall.

Prashant got out of bed, stretched himself, gave out a yawn of satisfaction, and stepped out on the balcony; the light sapphire sky of early spring looked transparent.

"Good morning," a duet of two voices startled him; he looked down.

Atul and Asha were sitting comfortably on garden chairs sipping "bed tea," as the morning cup of tea is called in India. The nomenclature is a legacy left behind by the British; the English *sahib* and *memsahib* were served the first cup of tea in bed by the "native" servants. Traditionally early risers, Indians do not stay in bed in the morning; hence they drink their first cup of tea out of bed. It is still called bed tea.

Asha looked up. "How are you? Did you sleep well? Were you warm enough?"

"Bas, bas, *enough*." Atul laughed. "Is Prashant going to drink your torrent of questions, or are you going to offer him some tea?"

Asha blushed. Prashant smiled congenially. "Bhabi, I feel perfect. I will be down in five minutes."

"Prashant, I will send Dharma Kaka to turn your geezer on for hot water."

"Bhabi, please tell me I do not have to shower right away? I don't want to!"

Asha broke into laughter. "If you plead enough, I will allow you another half hour!"

She turned to Atul when Prashant went in. "Isn't he so sweet?"

Atul smiled in agreement.

True to his word, Prashant was down in five minutes and plunked himself down on the empty lawn chair. "How is Meera this morning?" he queried in a low tone.

"She is not up yet." Asha could not repress a sigh of worry. She stirred sugar in Prashant's cup and handed it over to him. Her face was clouded. "Meera had seemed predestined for a happy life. Talented, pure of heart, immense unity with God and his creation. Nothing small could break her."

Asha continued after a small pause. "She was ten years old when we got married. I raised her like my first child. It breaks my heart to see her so ill. Life has cruelly clipped the wings of a free bird, how will she fly?"

"Bhabi, she has not lost her wings, only exhausted them. The flight was too long, sun beat on her. But her spirit cannot break. She is inseparably attached to the most profound source of power. She will never be let down."

In the backdrop, the birds celebrated the onset of spring, noisily. Atul's house was in a quiet area, close to the Sukhna lake. In the evening the lake area was crowded with people. Stalls of tea, samosas, sweets, chat, etc., were located on one side of the lake; it was like a picnic, and many people, especially in the spring and summer, made it a daily ritual to enjoy the festivity.

In the mornings, though, the lake was quite deserted, excepting retired men and women, who had lately turned into "health buffs," mainly inspired by the joggers in the West, went for walks. Asha and Atul had joined the club, whenever Atul was in Chandigarh.

The expansive house was surrounded by a well-cared-for garden. The annuals, sweet peas, marigolds, pansies, larkspur, dahlia, carnations, etc., were already flowering profusely; their perfume blended in the fresh air and lifted everyone's moods. Blooms on the shrubs like huge pearl-cream flowers of champa, pink clusters of kaner, deep-orange, substantial blossoms of hibiscus, delicate-petaled roses of different colors scintillated with lively ardor against the green of the grass and were equal participants in the explosion of color that overwhelmed the senses and the spirits.

In one corner of the garden stood an ancient mango tree that shaded a vast area of land. Wisely indeed, the mali, *gardener,* had planted low perennials with broad foliage that trapped enough sunlight to photosynthesize sufficient food using the extensive surface area.

Prashant smiled. "Once Meera gets better, I am going to fight with her."

Atul laughed. "You do not look like a competent fighter in spite of your strong built."

"Oh yes, I can fight rather well. You don't know the real me, Bhai! She did not tell me how ill she was and forbade everyone in Canada from informing me! I would not have known that she has been in India if Bela Bhabi, *sister-in-law,* did not break down on the phone. That really hurt. She had all the right to ask for my help."

Asha sighed. "She was always like that, took others' responsibilities but forsook her rights."

"Meera would enjoy this beautiful morning. Can she sit here in a comfortable chair, Bhabi?" Prashant asked.

Before Asha could reply, Leela came out. "Bibiji, Didi is up."

"I will help her with morning chores, then you can sit by her."

Meera was leaning against a couple of pillows to support her torso, gazing sadly out of the window. "I wonder what Rishi is doing right now?"

Prashant made a lively entry. He had a mischievous smile of a small naughty boy; his hands were at the back. Without a word, he knelt by Meera's bedside, magically produced a homemade bouquet of bougainvillea flowers, took one of her soft hands in his paws, and asked in a calibrated tone, "Will you marry me?"

Sweet puzzlement passed over Meera's rested visage. She laughed softly.

"Good," Prashant said in a relieved tone, "At least you can still laugh. Now, my answer?"

Meera looked at him searchingly; he was serious. Her vision delved inward in search for an answer.

Prashant let her be; he just kept her hand in his palms.

"Prashantji, are you saying it out of pity? I am useless, a cumbersome burden, and I have no idea if I will ever be strong again."

Prashant let her hand go and leaned back on the chair. Two wounded eyes looked straight at Meera.

"I thought we understood each other, and I did not even have to pose this question."

"I know." Meera was ashamed.

"I want to marry you, take you home, and take care of you." His voice assumed softness.

A flood of tears burst forth from Meera's eyes. She extended her arm, took Prashant's hand in hers and kissed it passionately. Prashant wiped her cheeks with his hand. "Does it mean yes?"

"Yes." Meera was emotionally depleted. She could hardly speak. "But so soon after Papa's death?"

"Wow, you look happy. What did I do to deserve it?"

Meera looked rested and serene, having napped while Prashant visited some friends who lived in Chandigarh.

"It is amazing how Chachaji, *uncle,* knows exactly how I feel." She pointed to a letter lying on her bed.

Chachaji wrote,

> The timeless battle between good and evil is waging in our hearts every moment. Good must conquer, even if we suffer. You have not been defeated in your kurukshetra, *war,* just wounded. We can even die in the war—that is not important. Only when man, in struggles with life's upheavals, loses his "essence" then he is truly vanquished. That should be a cause for grief. You fought with your last breath to hold on to righteousness as well as your very essence. You have triumphed. Life has caused you immense pain, but it has brought you closer to your core, "Self," and God. Our Soul is what we must protect through the toils of our lives.
>
> Your illness is battle fatigue, pertains to your material body. Even your mind is not decrepit; housed in the brain that consists of gross matter, may superficially appear to take on its cachexia. Do not confuse the debility of your body and mind with your true "Self." Your "Soul" is untouched, a witness to the ongoing of your life. Don't let that knowledge slip. Try to meditate inwards and identify your "Self" with your Soul.
>
> Meera, actually, it is our worldview and "Self" view that brings sorrow to our lives. We humans are insignificant, tiny specks in the infinite Reality, and yet we believe that we are at the center of the universe. We demand that the whole existence, other "specks," take us into account and act according to our desires and wants. We are angry if life does not work in concordance to our will.
>
> The fact is that we are no more important than grass and grasshopper existing simultaneously with all God's creatures. We humans are not the point of reference in this vast manifest "Reality."
>
> An earthquake or hurricane is not intentionally hurting us, it is nature's yawn or wink—a totally natural phenomenon as far as nature is concerned. The resultant devastation is a normal consequence of the workings of

the empirical Reality. Disease, epidemics, and death are an expression of the same phenomenon.

Billions are drowning in a sea of sorrow caused by hunger, wars, loneliness, illnesses, losses, yet we only fight for our own breath and life? It is such because we have reduced our world to our own self-interest, without realizing that self-centeredness is completely contrary to the dictates of civilization. Civilization is an act of the spirit, not a state of material development.

Konrad Lorenz, the Nobel prize winner, declared aptly, "I have found the missing link between ape and civilized man. It is us."

Individual good does not mean anything in a broader context of human survival or evolution if it is not at the same time good for all. One brick's attempt to protect itself from decay is futile. When the whole house collapses, it will land up in a heap of rubble with other bricks. Only when all the parts are intact can any functional entity consummate its usefulness.

Meera, your suffering stemmed from forgetting Shri Krishna's sermon that you must not be attached to the karmphal, *fruit of your actions.* Your moh, *too much attachment,* for Rishi clouded your wisdom. Moh is considered one of the vikaras, *pollutants of the mind,* to be conquered on the path to salvation. Mostly, we humans have difficulty in separating *moh* and *love.* Of course, moh must entail love, but love does not necessarily involve moh. Moh binds us to the object of our love; it creates a fertile ground for craving, disappointment, hurt. Giving love or loving everyone should be a goal without any expectation. Then desire ceases, pain of disappointment ends. The beauty of love is that it frees us from our own "ego" because we cease to be at the centre of our universe.

Rishi will come back to you. Give him more time to mature and grasp his own life and your role in it. You gave him your all, even though you became a pauper in doing it. You have proven your worth as a mother.

Also, remember, Rishi is not the end of your journey. Having raised him you have done your one duty, but other goals are waiting for you. Shake the dirt off, get up. No regrets, no self-pity. Be proud of your essence and live it well.

Anil is fine and enjoying the taste of simplicity of village life again, at least for now. He looks happy after a long time. He worries about you. We will come and see you soon.

Do contact Prashant. You have a right to do it, and he has a right to know. One advice: don't lose him.

God bless all of you. Your loving Chachaji.

Chapter Five

Dattatreya had answered that God's nature is his highest Guru, teacher when someone asked him how he could always be happy and cheerful.

As the Vedic story, from the ancient scripture Vedas, goes, Dattatreya was incarnation of the Hindu Trinity, Brahma, Vishnu, and Shiva—who represent three powers of the one God. Anusuya, the wife of sage Atri, was a lady of perfect virtue. In response to her austerities, all the three Gods—Brahma, Vishnu, and Shiva—appeared to her, disguised as ascetics. They asked her for a boon; she replied that she wanted "three sons, one like Brahma, one like Vishnu, and one like Shiva."

The three Gods became three little babies. Sage Atri embraced them together, and they became one child who grew to become a great rishi, spiritualist and sage, possessing the knowledge and power of the three Gods.

In his words:

"The earth taught me patience and generosity.
Ocean—to remain the same in spite of storms.
Air—to move freely, not stay in one place.
Water—how much purity is needed for good health.
Sky—to be above everything and yet embrace all things.

Moon—that the 'Self' remains the same, even when appearances change.
Sun—that a luminous face is reflected by all smooth surfaces.
Dove—love means feeding one's family.
Bee—collects sweet wisdom from places where no one suspects it.
The arrow maker—to be purposeful and always concentrated on one point.
Snake—to be content to live in a hole.
Fish—never take the bait and destroy yourself.

"Sir, I have something important to tell you." Kelley's soft eyes and gentle face was in turmoil.

Captain Robin looked at Kelley intently.

"The fire at Dr. Verma's clinic was set by Peter, Mrs. Henderson's driver. But he did it on Mrs. Henderson's orders, he had refused adamantly."

Captain Robin scanned across his desk at Kelley's honest black eyes.

"Why did Peter have to obey, Miss Kelley?"

"Where are your parents, young man?" James had watched him curled up on the park bench for a couple of days. Arms over his face, lean, famished, and dark, he could not be more than fifteen or sixteen years old.

"I . . . I . . ." The young boy looked at him and attempted to sit up.

"When was the last time you ate something, son?"

The youngster looked down.

"Come then, let us get some breakfast in you. What name would you like to be called by?"

"Abel," he spoke softly.

James and Abel walked across the street and went in a small café.

Abel's crude, dry hand shook when he tried to pick up the toast. Silently, James applied butter and jam on the toast, cut it in small pieces, picked one piece with a fork, and said kindly, "Open your mouth."

Abel's face flooded with tears. James took out a handkerchief from his coat pocket and wiped them.

"Thank you . . . sir."

"Well, I have not deserved the thanks yet, open your mouth," James ordered him. "You must eat, son, it is all right. Jesus is watching over you, you have innocent eyes."

He fed Abel toast, omelet, and bacon and then made him drink milk.

Abel ate like a hog; he found his voice. "How shall I ever repay you?"

Without a word, James got up and took Abel's hand in his, "Come, let us go home."

Kelley was not surprised; it had happened before. Young black boys had a past they ran from, they did. Kelley hugged Abel, took him to a small, room with a single bed, a table, and a lamp. "Sleep it off. Have faith."

Abel slept for forty-eight hours.

Kelley and James were eating breakfast. He walked in, still in a daze, sat on the chair, and said, "Sir, down there we call this country God's land. Now I know why. Find me some work."

Helena was still young. Joseph had already left home. Jane was a sweet little girl being raised by a nanny, Rosa. Helena got a slave for life.

How?

Because Abel had secrets, bad, sorry secrets.

Kelley and James never asked any questions. "He will tell us when he is ready." But James was sure of one thing, "My heart tells me that this boy ain't done no wrong."

But Helena was a different creature. She hired an investigator to go across the border and dig all the details of Abel's life in America.

Abel had run for days; he lost the count.

He did like Anna; she was as pretty as a lily, fair, and delicate. They played together behind Mr. Ashley's back. Mrs. Ashley was a kind lady.

Abel managed the stables; his parents worked in Anna's huge mansion. He was the best rider in those parts. Master allowed him to ride his horses, sometimes.

Anna and Abel went horse riding. "Daddy is away for two days, we can have fun." Anna danced on the grass and sang.

The breeze swept across their zealous faces; Anna's long hair flew in the warm spring air. They laughed; the sky was clear. By the murmuring river, they sat and sang under the trembling shadows of the poplar tree.

Anna spread a throw and placed fruit and sandwiches on it; she lay down, and Abel could not resist. They hugged and kissed; passion was on fire. Anna's fair hands opened his belt.

Abel sat up. "No, Miss Anna, we will not sin. You are pure, I want to see you like this."

Anna was mad. Before she could shout, Abel looked around, "Where is Lacy?"

"He will come back on his own, Abel! You come back right now and unzip me!" Anna ordered.

"No! I must look for the horse. If I lose him, Master will crush my bones, and your cook will make a stew—"

"I hate you, don't ever say that!" Anna was really mad, now.

Abel ran and called out, "Lacy, Lacy come back." He was scared; he kept running and looking around.

Suddenly, he heard screams; it was certainly Anna's voice. He turned around and raced back.

"Help me Abel, please, don't hurt me, stupid."

There was Richard, the neighbor's son, bent over Anna trying to take her dress off. Unable to take it off, as Anna fought hard, he ripped it.

Blood rushed to Abel's head, he grabbed Richard from behind and tried to pull him up. Richard gripped Anna tight. She kept screaming, "You bastard, you are hurting me, I will tell your father . . ."

Abel could not get Richard off Anna; he looked around, a few rocks lay scattered around. He picked up a large one in a hurry and threw it at him. Abel did not aim at Richard's head—no he didn't—but Richard had moved his head up to see what Abel was doing.

A fountain of blood spurted out of Richard's head, he just collapsed. Anna got up screaming and hugged Abel; her dress was covered with sparkling red blood.

"Abel, run, please, my father will kill you."

"But . . . you will tell him that I did it to save your honor?"

"Are you kidding? They will hang you anyway!"

Abel knew that she was right. He kissed Anna. "You will always be in my heart." And he raced away.

Anna watched him disappear through her tears.

With money, Helena bought the information.

For the price of silence, Abel sold himself and became Peter.

Nine months after the fire consumed Satish's clinic, the police found a suspect. The populace had been pressurizing, questioning the police department.

"What kind of security do we have?"

"Such a small town and yet no suspects."

"Oh, suspects must be there. But Police can be bribed into silence, can't they?" Et cetera.

The man was charged with arson and sent to prison for five years.

But there was someone who could not sleep at night. The face behind bars haunted Kelley because she knew the convicted man was innocent.

Peter had refused. "Ma'am, I can't do it. I am sorry. I cannot set the fire and frame Master Rishi."

Helena leaned back on her red, velvety sofa chair and sized him up. "Peter, you know that you cannot refuse."

He cried, "I have been loyal to you, even lied to Master Rishi, but this is too much. Don't make me do it, ma'am, please."

But fear of the noose was strong; he had a wife and a son to take care of.

Kelley was trapped in the web of gratitude. James, her husband, had developed tuberculosis that started with a slight persistent cough. Helena helped them with money for the treatment. Whether it was self-serving, not wanting to lose a good obedient servant, or compassion, it was hard to tell. Nevertheless, James recovered.

After a few years of remission, he had a terrible bout and died, leaving Kelley in the bondage of loyalty. How could she harm Mrs. Henderson?

She looked up at the wooden cross in the church. There He was, Jesus, piety, compassion, and truth flowing out from his beautiful eyes. Kelley knelt and wept. When she looked up, Jesus was looking straight at her, angry and forgiving at the same time. She cursed herself. Who was she answering to, Mrs. Henderson? And her Lord Jesus, who gave his life for her, didn't she owe him anything?

Kelley got up, determined and fearless. She went home and packed her bags; indescribable peace came over her heart.

Helena woke a groggy Rishi and threw him out of the front door.

"Granny! What did I do? I do not even know?"

"You know perfectly well, you swine! You plot against me, under my own roof?"

"No! No! I did not, I love you. I don't understand."

Trembling with shock, wearing striped pajamas, Rishi treaded the streets for many hours. Where was he to go? He sat under a pine tree and bawled. Bela Aunty? But she would tell Mom, and she would surely fly to Canada immediately though she was so ill.

Cold, tired, hurt, and hungry, Rishi walked back to Peter's small house that was located at the back of Mrs. Henderson's mansion.

Martha took him in and hugged him. "You are like my Johnny, Master, I will take care of you. I do not have much, but we will share."

So far, Martha did not know anything. She was worried. "Master, what happened? Do you know where Kelley is?"

"No!" Rishi shook his head.

Martha was called to take over the work in the mansion. Rishi and Johnny missed school; they just sat together on the sofa. Johnny tried to joke around to make Rishi laugh. He could not; there was a fire in his heart and gut.

Kelley sneaked in at night. By that time, Martha had found out the goings-on.

Martha was mad when she found Kelley standing at the door. "I thought you were like Peter's mother! How could you, why did you?"

"Martha, we have to answer to Jesus our Lord. I know Peter refused. I told the police that he is not the guilty one."

"But he will still go to jail?"

"How about the young man who is innocent but rotting in prison? He must have a mother too, who knows that her son is not guilty and yet suffering. Jesus commanded us to speak the truth, Martha dear!"

They both held hands and wept.

Johnny was indignant; he turned to Martha. "Mom, is it true? Is it? How could Dad do something like that? He lied to please that cruel bitch. Mom, why?" he shouted.

Martha wiped her tears and said, "All right. Maybe it is time to tell you."

Johnny and Rishi sat stunned as they heard Peter's tragic past.

"Madam will tell the police and send him to America, where surely they will hang him. Johnny, what should we do?"

Kelley left.

Peter came home late at night to a devastated family. He had been wandering on the streets all day, worried, desperate, and scared.

Martha ran to him and wept on his shoulder. He kissed her head, sat on the chair, and shut his tired eyes for a few minutes, perhaps praying for some light in the fog of his mind.

Peter got up, walked over to Rishi, who was sitting on a sofa in the living room, and knelt on his knees. "Master Rishi, will you and your mother forgive me for my sins against you?"

Rishi had heard Peter's life story a few moments ago. He hugged him and said, "Peter, it was not your fault, what could you do?"

Charles, the prosecutor, was frank, "Robin, we need more."

"We don't have anything else, man." But he phoned Kelley.

"Mr. Robin, if Peter confesses that he set the fire on Mrs. Henderson's orders, she will make sure that he is hanged in America. How can I ask him? Can you protect him? It happened almost thirty-five years ago!"

Robin was pensive. "Let me talk to Charles, maybe we can do something."

Charles laid his cards. "Peter has confessed already, you have no way to escape prison, Mrs. Henderson. I can reduce your sentence though, if you promise, in writing, that you will not disclose Peter's past."

Radley Jr. bent his head toward her and whispered his advice.

She spoke haughtily, "Yes."

Peter was sentenced to prison for two years, Mrs. Henderson for seven.

"Rishi?"

"Yah."

The room was semidark. A pale ray of streetlamp light came through the small window located at the upper end of a wall in the basement apartment.

"Who would have known?"

"What, Johnny?"

"We would both land up under the same roof."

"Yah. But it is a good roof, isn't it?"

They both laughed then became silent.

"I am sorry, Rishi."

"Why?"

"So much has happened, your life has turned upside down."

"Well, that is life, isn't it?"

"I did not know until now."

"Me neither."

Silence again.

"Do you miss her?"

No answer.

"Do you, Rishi?"

"Yes, too much. Now let me sleep, I have a class at eight thirty, crazy. Good night."

Rishi turned his face toward the wall. Tears trickled down on the pillow.

We have to be brave and pray for strength!

"Yes, Mom," he mumbled.

Martha, Johnny, and Rishi stayed at Kelley's basement apartment. She had some savings that were used up to set up the place for four inhabitants.

Kelley and Martha looked for and found jobs as household help.

Rishi applied for a student loan.

"No, Master Rishi, I will not let you. I wronged you and your mother. I stood by, watched lies, traps, meanness, and did nothing. If I do not repent and take care of you, I will never be able to face Jesus. Would you take eternal life away from me and let me burn in hell?"

"But, Kelley, I am a burden on you. I watch Martha and you try to get special food for me. It is too much. If I take a loan, I can get my own place."

"Then you will have to pay it back, Master Rishi."

Martha was cutting onions for soup in the kitchen; Johnny was watching TV. He turned his head toward the small dining table where Kelley and Rishi were sitting, arguing.

"Rishi, stay with us. We will have fun."

"Master, you have always been kind and respectful to us. Kelley and I can take care of two sons. Can't we?"

"Then call me Rishi, please."

Kelley spoke painfully, "Rishi, we must call your mother in India and tell her."

"No!" Rishi almost shouted. "No, she is ill. She will worry and try to come here." His voice softened, "Kelley, I cannot face her, not yet."

Kelley was firm. "Do not tell her any details. Just talk to her, please."

- # -

John Radley Sr. sat comfortably in an armchair with a pipe in his mouth, listening intently. When Kelley was finished, he leaned his head back and shut his eyes.

Kelley came in the main door and threw her purse on the dining table. "Rishi dear . . ." There was a tremor in her voice.

"Yeah." He turned his head and looked at her. He was having lunch in front of the TV.

"I told you, Jesus helps those who love him."

The face was familiar. Kelley had picked up the local newspaper while waiting for her appointment at the doctor's clinic. She had been feeling exhausted; Rishi, Martha, and Johnny ganged up on her to see her physician.

Where did she see him? Kelley started to read the caption under the photograph. The man, who looked about seventy-five to eighty years old, had received an award for humanitarian work in the field of law. Kelley could not believe it. His name was John Radley.

She had served tea and cake to Mr. Christopher Henderson and John Radley in the expansive garden of the former's mansion. Henry Radley had retired in the late thirties and passed on Mr. Henderson's legal, financial, and other affairs to his lawyer nephew, John Radley.

Kelley might have been fifteen or sixteen years old at the time. The legal jargon she overheard as she poured tea in the cups sounded significant because she heard the words *Helena* and *her children* repeatedly. It had puzzled her because Helena was not even married yet. Kelley's father, Timothy, was excited. "It is wonderful that Master had made a trust for Ms. Helena's offspring."

Kelley's mother, Margaret, was sad. "Isn't it terrible that Master cannot even trust his own daughter?"

"Well, if she was your daughter, would you?" They both chuckled.

John Radley inhaled a puff of his pipe and pointed to a plate of pastries that lay on the round center table. "Ms. Kelly, please help yourself. My housekeeper is a baker's daughter. You can see my big belly, eh, a result of my inability to resist!" He had a free ringing laughter.

"Now, what is dear Jane's son's name?"

"Rishi, sir."

"That is an unusual name, indeed!"

"It is an East Indian name."

"Oh, so his mother gave him that name? She is from India, you said?"

"Ms. Jane named him Rishi herself, sir."

Radley appeared entertained by the notion. "Really! Well, we have to make sure that this young man is looked after, don't we? It is very nice of you, Miss Kelley, very nice indeed, to support him. You are a good Christian woman."

Before Kelley left, he said, "Please ask Rishi to see me. We will settle everything soon. He can live comfortably then."

John Radley called out, "Mrs. Robinson, can you please bring the tea outside?"

He turned to Rishi. "We cannot waste this gorgeous spring day! We must enjoy the blessing of beauty."

Rishi smiled sadly. "Of course, Uncle." Meera would have said something similar.

John became pensive. "Your great-grandfather was a great man. I found excuses to accompany my Uncle Henry to visit him. He had great stories to tell."

Elizabeth died of malaria in Amritsar, where Colonel Christopher J. Henderson was posted during the British Raj, *British colonization of India.*

He sat by her bedside and wept. "It is God's revenge." But Christopher had adamantly refused to participate in Major General Dyer's murderous plans. "It is a peaceful gathering. Why not let people enjoy their festivities?"

Dyer's jaw became square, his blue eyes turned red, the color of hatred.

"These natives need to be taught a lesson they will never forget."

Dyer led a unit of fifty soldiers, some on foot, others on horseback and a few propped on top of a cannon. "March!" he ordered; the troops advanced toward the Jallianwala Bagh, *garden*.

A thousand dabs of multi colors rose up on the horizon as the army drew close to the garden. For the festival of Vaisakhi that celebrates the end of harvest season in the spring, every single Punjabi must wear brand-new, bright apparel.

The bazaars were packed weeks before the long-awaited day; tailors had no time to scratch their heads. "I cannot do it Bahenji, *sister*, look at this pile! Only a week left for the thirteenth of April."

"Please, I will give you double money. If you don't stitch our clothes, my family will be disgraced in the village. We will not be able to show our faces!"

Even on the day of such great festivity, men's voices were devoid of any streak of joy. They were loud and agitated, exchanged stories about their own painful experiences of slavery. Women squatted on the lush grass and spoke of shortages of food and other items of daily need, sometimes wept at the tragedy of someone's son or husband shot to death or imprisoned wrongly by the British.

The crowd of thousands, engrossed in their woes, did not notice when Dyer's troops arrived at the Gate of Jallianwala Bagh. Dyer stood on his jeep and shouted, "Take the cannon in the garden!"

The soldiers, all of whom were Indians, shuddered at the thought of murdering thousands of their own. A powerful urge to quit the army swept over all the young *sepoys*. But they knew that while they would be hanged by the noose, the army would not suffer; other young unemployed Indians burdened by the responsibilities of taking care of their parents, grandparents, sometimes siblings as well as their own wife and children would become the new unwilling recruits.

The cannon was too massive to go through the low gate of the *bagh*, much to the relief of the troops. Someone else, who was not even an Indian, was assuaged. Colonel Henderson, who stood on the same jeep with Dyer, looked at him. "God does not want you to be a murderer, don't you see? Let us go back!"

Dyer gave Christopher a deadly stare, turned his red angry face toward the foot soldiers, and yelled, "Leave the cannon, march inside the garden."

Some people sitting in the vicinity of the gate turned their heads in curiosity; they looked at one another with rising fear in their hearts. "What now?"

Dyer bellowed, "Line up . . . take position . . . aim . . . shoot!"

He gave no warning to disperse. Within a span of a few minutes, chaos descended on thousands of unsuspecting humans.

History can never shake the dust of madness that followed. The pandemonium of loud shots in quick succession, shrieks of people trying to flee to nowhere because the few narrow escape routes located at the periphery of the large garden were blocked by foot soldiers.

Hundreds of people jumped in the cool water well that had served as the only water supply in the bagh. The older people, unable to move fast, slumped in the pool of their own blood; mothers bent over their children to protect them, the flesh of their backs was torn away with the rain of bullets.

Christopher shut his eyes. Dyer roared, "Colonel, if you keep shooting at the trees, I will court-martial you!"

The massacre continued for a full ten minutes. Turbans rolled, dead and wounded bodies fell in heaps. Red blood, gleaming in the full radiance of the sun, spilled on every blade of grass.

Dyer commanded, "Retreat." The *sepoys*, tears flowing down their flushed cheeks, many bawling loudly, marched toward the cantonment, leaving behind a scene that could not have been less than Dante's hell.

At least three thousand people were dead and twenty thousand wounded.

Christopher paced in the hallway of his bungalow way into the night. Lizzy complained, "I cannot sleep with you walking in the corridor! Come on, it is okay, they deserved it."

Silently, he stepped into the garden. The stars were dim, moon was clouded, the wind was silent—or it just seemed that way.

Early the next morning, Christopher walked to Major General Dyer's bungalow and threw a sheet of paper on his face.

"Accept my resignation. God will never forgive you."

Christopher was protected by his close connections with nobility in England. Dyer clenched his fists and shouted, "Get out of my sight, or I will shoot you and call it self-defense."

The very next day of the butchery, Lizzy developed high fever, chills, sweats; malaria had struck. She died three days later.

"Uncle Christopher had spoken ruefully to me. 'John, son, I did not mourn her death. My spirit was benumbed by the grief of murders of thousands of unarmed, innocent humans. Helena has the cold-bloodedness of her mother. One time, Lizzy beat up a young girl servant so severly that she died. That was the day I stopped loving her.'"

Christopher came to Canada and moved in a small village then called Happyville. He refused to go back to England. "My countrymen have lost their conscience. Major General Dyer was greeted with garlands and a hefty pension when he arrived at the docks in London, England. He was hailed as a hero of the British Raj! *Disgust* is too mild a word to express my revulsion."

While horse riding in the wilderness of tall evergreens that shrouded the Rocky Mountains of British Columbia, Christopher decided to build a pulp factory, employed the locals especially the natives, expanded it, and became the richest man in those parts.

The small town was renamed Hendersville.

Joseph was an engineer who worked at Christopher's pulp mills. Christopher noticed his gentle and kind personality, invited him to his mansion for dinner as well as an offer of his beloved daughter Helena's hand in marriage.

"Helena was getting older and could not keep any boyfriend. She scared them all." John Radley laughed heartily.

"Rishi, you know, Uncle Christopher had proposed marriage between Helena and myself. Your grandmother was a stunning young girl, I have to admit that. Even her hauteur accentuated her beauty, somehow. Thank God, my sanity prevailed," John chuckled with a great sense of relief.

Helena had retired to her bedroom. Christopher and Joseph relaxed in armchairs close to the fireplace.

"Helena is my only child. She is demanding and a little short-tempered. I think I have spoiled her. But she has a good heart."

Helena did not put up any fuss at the arranged marriage, an idea she had scoffed a little while ago. She had a deadly fear of spinsterhood.

Joseph did not survive Helena's utterly selfish and harsh behavior; he left after two years to join the army and sailed to Europe with thousands of other brave, young boys to fight Hitler. No one heard from him again.

Christopher also left for France a little later. He was not young, but when Hitler invaded Poland, he said, "I have to fight against evil."

Due to his age, the generals of the allied armies did not let him be too close to the combat; he was appointed as an advisor behind the lines. But there was no safe distance from death in the midst of a war. In the chilly winters living in the tents in France, he caught a cold that quickly turned into pneumonia. He died a few months before D-day on June 6, 1944.

"I wished he had lived and seen the victory of good over evil." John Radley was sad.

"When, Jane, your mother was eighteen, I called her to my office and explained to her about the trust money that belonged to her. She was expressionless, shrugged her shoulders, and refused to take anything that was related to Helena."

John stopped. A bird perched on a willow tree in the corner, chirped sharply, starting up a lively colloquy with his relatives who responded immediately.

"I wish I could understand their language."

Rishi smiled. "Uncle, do you know that the ancient rishis of India understood all the languages of all the animals?"

"Really?"

"Yes, Ma was explaining that those chaste saints had submerged their spirit in the Universal Soul, God. The Souls of all living beings being one with God, they could have a direct knowledge of all other sentient beings through their unity."

John Radley was visibly impressed. "Many times, I have felt that the East has an understanding of the spiritual realm that Jesus was trying to teach the Christians. Unfortunately, Christians became stuck with sin, salvation, and eternal life. They have missed the essence of who we are and who we can be if we had heard Jesus with an open spirit and without the fear."

Rishi was astonished. "Uncle, that is quite great of you. No one else I know likes to admit that the Eastern religions are even legitimate religions."

John Radley laughed. "Son, you are young, you have much to experience. But it comes down to human ego. It tells every human that he is the best, better than the others. This huge pride is the only block between man and the other humans and between man and God."

"Gosh, Uncle! This is exactly what my mother kept emphasizing to me. It would be great for both of you to meet and exchange ideas."

"Maybe one day we will."

John Radley suddenly came back to the original topic of their conversation.

"Jane was a very comely and gentle child, much like a tender flower that could droop down with a slight wind. I am so sorry Helena harmed her to that extent. I did not know much. I got married and spent many years in England after the world war. When I returned to Hendersville, Jane was living independently. That is not unusual for an eighteen-year-old lassie. I found out later about the foster parents and the abuse she endured."

"Well, well," he continued. "We must make sure that you move forward and fulfil your ma's dreams."

- # -

Perched on the lush branches of the dense mango tree, birds conducted a group discussion, fluttered their collective wings, and flew away in noisy camaraderie. The leaves murmured, the breeze was gentle and warm.

Meera's eyes perused the vista of the golden ocean of ripe wheat panicles that glittered in the aureate rays of the sun; waves rose and ebbed with the mild wind.

A car stopped at the gate followed by clamorous slamming of the two doors.

"Who has Prashantji brought home today? What shall I serve for dinner?" Meera mused as she sank in the padded garden chair that lay under the dense shade of the mango tree. She did not turn her head, hoping that Prashant and his unknown buddy would head for the house without disturbing her happy communion with the gleaming spring afternoon.

After a seemingly endless journey in the dolor of despondence, Meera's spirit was alight with the resplendence of hope.

Manik had patted Atul on the shoulder affectionately. "Don't worry Bhai, *brother,* Meera shall live long. She just needs a lot of care."

Meera was diagnosed with congestive heart failure. The heart attacks left her with unbearable decrepitude of the whole life systems including the brain. Consequently, the cognitive functioning of her mind was impaired; thoughts, perceptions, and comprehension became a constant blur. The existential authenticity of her spirit, the font of her intrinsic potency, became inaccessible. Her angst was that the bond she had painstakingly fostered between her Soul and God became illusive.

Anil held Meera's limp hand fondly. Chachaji settled on the edge of her bed and prayed.

Meera was staring vacantly on the wall on which the shifting shadows of bougainvillea branches were playing. Sun had made an appearance after many cloudy weeks; early January was still chilly.

Chachaji looked at Meera compassionately. He bent his head toward her and whispered, "Thomas à Kempis was right. 'If you bear your cross gladly, it will bear you.'"

Tears fell silently on Meera's pillow. She murmured softly in anguish. "My son hates me, Chachaji, it is unbearable."

Chachaji stroked her hair. "Rishi's grandmother has poisoned him, but he can never forget your love, Beti."

Anil wiped her tears with his handkerchief; pain surfaced in his light eyes.

Chachaji thought for a moment then spoke softly, "We humans do not possess the power to understand God's will, but His every act is full of mercy. You could not have worked after you fell ill. Money problems were sure to come. At least Rishi is being looked after well. There is a silver lining to all our clouds of despair, we just need to look."

Asha opened the curtain of Meera's bedroom and came in. "Chachaji, breakfast is ready."

Anil smiled. "But we ate before we came, Bhabi."

Chachaji's village was a mere one and a half hours' drive from Chandigarh. They had been visiting Meera often, especially while Prashant could not come. "Biji is not well, Meera, I cannot leave her right now," Prashant had called.

Asha insisted, "But that was two hours ago. Dharma Kaka has made your favorite omelet with tons of green, hot chillies, Anil!"

Chachaji got up. "We have to appreciate a good man's efforts, Anil."

He turned to Meera. "Beti, pray for Rishi's happiness. His happiness lies with you. He will come sooner than later."

Meera stood on the soundless shores of an ocean and scanned the horizon through semidarkness and a thick layer of fog. Suddenly, a small light twinkled in the mist at the far distance; Meera took a deep sigh of relief. The light became brighter as a small boat approached the vague shore. Meera noticed Papa's gray head. It was surreal. "Oh God, I thought Papa was dead!"

Someone sitting near Papa turned his head.

"Rishi, is that you? Why did you dye your hair black?" she shouted soundlessly.

"To surprise you!" Rishi jumped off the boat and ran toward her.

Meera woke up with her frail hand on her pounding heart that was filled with an impossible amalgamation of joy and longing.

Heavy snowfall overlay the Himalayas; the mercury dipped to plus two degrees Celsius in Chandigarh and the surrounding regions.

Meera stayed in the cozy bed wrapped up in a thick quilt and brooded over the dream.

Ma opened the door slightly, "Are you up?"

"Yah, Ma," Meera spoke cheerfully. "I dreamt that Rishi has come back to me!"

"Of course he will, I do not have any doubt." Ma was certain as she opened the curtains.

It was drizzling silently; Meera felt warm and content for some unknown reason. Bougainvilla branches and leaves looked freshly bathed and stooped with the weight of the raindrops. The playground across from Meera's window was deserted; obviously, mothers had prevailed in preventing their insistent kids from playing in the rain.

Asha came in and spoke with thrill in her voice, “Bela Di has some exciting news that she wants to tell you first, Choti.”

“Is Rishi okay?”

“Of course!”

Ma helped Meera out of the bed and wrapped a blue Kashmiri-embroidered shawl around her shoulders. Meera held the walker firmly in her hands and treaded in slow motion toward the drawing room. Much to her surprise, the anxiety she always experienced at Bela Di’s call had been replaced by calm acceptance.

“Hi, Di, how is Rishi?”

“Good! Speak to him!”

“What? He is there . . . with you?” Meera stammered, tears glistened in her eyes instantly.

Asha and Ma stood still and stared at Meera’s face.

Meera forced words out of her mouth, “Hello, Rishi? How are you, Beta, *son*?”

There was a painful pause.

“Rishi, talk to me! Please, do not cry!”

“Can you ever forgive me, Mom?” Rishi wept. “I hurt you so badly!”

“No, you did not. Life did. I can hear your voice, nothing else matters . . . tell me about yourself?”

“Mom, I did not know anything. Uncle Peter told me . . .”

“Who . . .?”

“Uncle Peter told me about your accident and heart attack. I thought . . .”

“What?”

“I thought you did not love me!”

“Rishi, how can you even think that? You are my life!”

Phone lines became crackly.

“When are you coming here, Rishi . . .?”

“Not yet . . . Ma.”

“Why? . . . I said why . . . can’t hear you?”

“How is your health . . . Ma?”

“I am great, Rishi, come soon.”

Phone lines clattered, became inaudible, and got cut off.

Meera covered her face with shaky hands and cried.

Ma and Asha asked in unison, “What happened?”

"Rishi said, he did not know about my accident and heart attack! He loves me, Ma!"

"Of course he does, Choti! When is he coming here?"

"Not yet. But I want to see him!" Meera said tearfully.

"No more tears, Meera! Rishi has come back to you, that is all that matters." Ma was firm.

Chachaji and Anil drove to Chandigarh right after Asha called them.

Chachaji smiled toothlessly, his dentist had removed all his teeth in readiness for dentures. "It is an auspicious day, Beti."

Anil demanded halwa, *a dessert*, associated with happy occasions.

Neeti came home from college and barged into Meera's room. "Bua, *father's sister*, what am I hearing? Rishi is coming back to us?"

Meera laughed. "Not yet, but he will, Neeti."

Atul arrived from Simla by the late bus; he did not drive on the lofty Himalayas ever since winter arrived with a bombast of snowfall in November.

Gelid Umbra reigned over Chandigarh; the moon had escaped behind obscure clouds. Atul left icy Simla, hoping to find some relief in relatively warmer Chandigarh. He was sorely disappointed, wrapped the woolen muffler over his frigid head, and knocked at the window of a taxi.

The shivering taxiwalla had made an existential decision to snuggle in a blanket inside his taxi rather than chase prospective passengers, as he usually did. Today, he did not care if his wife deprived him of food or made him sleep on the lumpy, rough couch in the unheated outer room. How could money matter while he was battling death by freezing?

Asha had been unable to contact Atul in Simla. His secretary said in a respectful sweet voice, "Ashaji, Atulji is visiting a couple of rich clients who refused to get out of their cozy homes in the cold!"

Atul was surprised to see lights in every room; ripples of laughter floated toward him as he alighted from the taxi. Ever since Papa left and Meera arrived in India, ill shadows of melancholy had gripped their hearts; laughter had become rare.

Neeti came out of the main door and ran toward the gate when she heard the sound of the taxi. "Papa, Bua is going to be just fine," she said tearfully as they walked briskly toward the house.

The whole family, including Chachaji and Anil, who were persuaded to stay the night, were gathered in the drawing room. Without taking off his muddy shoes and heavy overcoat, ignoring everyone's presence in the room, Atul walked straight to Meera and folded her in his strong arms.

"My heart is finally free, I could not bear your sorrow, Choti."

Meera was half laid on the sofa covered with a quilt. She sat up, hid her face in Atul's chest, and cried, "Maybe I can go to Canada with Anil and bring Rishi home?"

"No! Don't even think!"

"Please, Bhaiya!"

"Let him finish his school first. He can come in the summer. In the meantime, call him as often as you want!"

Rishi was studying arts and science at the University of British Columbia, Vancouver.

Nishant sneaked home late at night as usual and tiptoed to his bedroom.

In the morning, he stumbled out of his bedroom in a groggy stupor, "Mommy, can I please have a karak, *strong*, cup of tea? I am late for my class!"

"Nishant, who told you to come home late, eh? You missed an evening of so much joy! Rishi has come back to us!"

Meera had not slept a wink, yet her eyes were bright and cheeks were flushed. Nishant hugged her tight, "Bua, I have not seen you smile in such a long time! Good for you!"

A beautiful red brocade, silk saree and traditional, Bengali-style gold jewelry with intricate designs were spread on Meera's bed. Meera crinkled her nose and looked at Shobha apologetically. "Di, it is too flashy for me, na."

Spring was slowly stepping in shooing the winter away. Meera had insisted on sitting in the covered veranda, *covered area in front of a house*, much to Leela's protestation, since it involved much exertion on her part.

"Didi, you are still weak. If you catch cold . . ."

"Leela, get me a blanket for my legs, shawl for my shoulders, and hurry." Leela grumbled and left.

Soon, Ma joined Meera. Asha gave instructions for lunch and brought her knitting; hot steaming tea and glucose biscuits were served, and there was contentment.

Flower buds were still encased within the sepals, a protection from frost bite, yet a recent rainfall had bestowed rich lushness to the garden.

Meera's face beamed as Anil and Chachaji ascended from the car. Indeed, more garden chairs, tea, and biscuits were duly ordered, much to Leela's chagrin.

It was almost one month after Rishi's call. Chachaji proposed, "Prashant and Meera's marriage should not be delayed anymore. Meera is recovering marvelously."

Ma sighed with relief. "Bhaiji, I have been saying that for a long time."

Asha explained, "Ma, Choti was not ready, yet."

For Meera's hurriedly organized, small wedding, Shobha extricated herself from what Meera called the death grip of her in-laws. The nomenclature was appropriate because according to Meera, "It seems that 'death do us part' vow exists not only between you and your husband but also with your in-laws!"

Shobha wept at the sight of a frail and sallow Meera, who had just started to walk with a cane.

"Will you forgive me?"

"For what?"

"I have been a lousy sister."

"Well yes, that is true," Meera agreed immediately.

Shobha waited for her to take the next step and forgive her.

"Well?"

"Well what? The issue is serious. I want to ponder it!"

"Meera!"

"What?"

"Are you going to forgive or not?"

"Maybe with one condition!"

"Like?"

"You must abscond your sticky family and be a part of my life, sometimes!"

The flames of the sacred fire burning in the *vedi* flickered in Meera's longing eyes. Rishi was ecstatic at the news, "Mummy, I cannot tell you how happy and relieved I am. But I cannot leave school right now."

The three brothers—Atul, Rakesh, and Anil—supported Meera while she treaded slowly behind Prashant, on the mandap, *canopy where wedding ceremony takes place*, around the vedi, *the sacred fire*. The light-pink silk saree with silver border and an elegant jewelry set of cream-colored pearls accentuated the simplicity and serenity of Meera's bearing.

Shobha had expended much time and energy on the dusty, crowded, noisy streets of Calcutta to locate the best boutique of traditional Bengali wedding apparel and jewelry. She grumbled loudly, "If Dadi, *paternal grandmother*, was alive, she would never let you get away! No bride wears an ordinary pink silk saree and pearls for her marriage! Pearls are for parties, silly!"

In Bengal, demi Goddess Durga is by far the most consequential diety worshipped with great ostentatiousness in large, ancient, Hindu temples. For thousands of years, adroit artisans have labored to create refined jewelry of confounding complexity to adorn "Mother Durga."

The divine, traditional art influences the designs of gold jewelry that Bengali women wear, especially those who are blessed with affluence. The rest, less fortunate females, contend with imitation jewelry of cheaper metals.

Prashant wore a cream silk Achkan, *long coat,* and pants, as well as a grin of rapture on his tanned visage.

The priest chanted mantras with great zeal while pouring ghee, *heated butter*, and other stuff that created much smoke to the sacred fire that leapt up toward the heavens. The fire God blessed the bride and bridegroom with a happy union for seven consecutive janams, *births.* Hopefully.

The small gathering of relatives and friends perched on the daris, *woven throws,* that were spread around the *mandap* in the backyard of Atul's house. The sky was radiant with lukewarm sunrays; the pulchritude of the kaleidoscopic blossoms shone against the lush, freshly cut, green grass. Breeze carried dizzying ambrosia of the roses, sweet peas and perfume of many other flowers. The whole of existence seemed to have joined the celebration of the union of two patient but ardent hearts.

Cups of hot tea were constantly circulated to keep the spectators warm; end of February is still cool in the morning in Chandigarh. Much catching up of gossip occurred while the solemn bride and groom made promises in Sanskrit, *sacred language of Hinduism,* that neither understood.

After the baratis, *the bridegroom's party,* returned to Meerat with the happy bride, their guests left one by one, carrying boxes of sweets and gifts bestowed by the mother of the bride. It was already dark outside; Beji, Neeta, Bhavani, Ravi, Prashant, and Meera sat and chatted in the drawing room.

Beji turned to Meera, "Beti, Shantu has never seen peace and happiness. Take care of him."

Meera touched her feet and spoke gently, "Beji, bless me that I become healthy to look after all of you."

Living in the midst of the infinitude of farmland, a perpetual landscape that transcended the very notion of transience of nature, brought an ethereal sense of aplomb to Meera's heart. Rishi's distant but sweet voice and Prashant's patient compassion dispelled the darkness clouding her spirit. And she could understand more clearly than ever before that God had not deserted her; it was the impotency of her mind that failed to experience His presence. As the scriptures have pointed out, "To receive strong light you need strong eyes."

The vividness of the scintillating colors of nature reappeared in the chastised sky of Meera's consciousness: the sweet aria arising from her heart resounded in its infinite vastness.

Prashant embraced Meera's supple body in his manly grip and demanded, "I want to hear the most romantic song ever composed."

The car door shut and the car drove away. Meera's curiosity was piqued; she turned her head toward the gate.

A tall young man, his fair skin and blond hair glowing in the warm rays of the sun, was striding toward her; his gait had a familiar rhythm. Meera stared incredulously for a few seconds; this was a reoccurring dream she had in the last years. Was she dreaming?

"Oh God, oh God." Meera struggled to get up from her lawn chair; her feet faltered, saree got entangled, and she tripped.

"Don't, Mummy." Rishi started to run toward her. "Do not strain yourself."

Meera slipped into his open arms and hung on to his broad shoulders, her face wet with flow of tears. Rishi seated her on the lawn chair, knelt by her side on the absinthe grass, and buried his face in her lap.

"Mummy, can you forgive me, please?"

Words were utterly inadequate to express the immensity of Meera's sensibilities; she just ran her doddering fingers through his golden locks and kissed his head repeatedly.

Meera could only mutter, "You are here with me, Rishi, I will never let you go."

Meera held his hands and trembled; what if this was a dream? Her apprehensive, anxious visage touched Rishi deeply. He pressed her sweaty thin hands against his forehead and said, "Mummy, I am here na, all is well."

Meera and Rishi sat on the lawn chairs silently, her wee hands in his manly clasp, moist eyes locked; a voiceless yet eloquent flow of unimpeded love between their hearts erased all misgivings. Meera's vision was directed inward and outward, simultaneously, to capture the totality of her own reality in relation to the world. In those brief moments, she experienced infinity in its fullness, its endlessness, and resplendence. Truth had fulfilled its promises, as it always does.

Some birds flew over them and headed for the coolness of the mango tree; they chirped in unison to welcome the stranger. Sunrays split into tiny diamonds and scattered the sunlight through the fluttering leaves of the mango tree that played hopscotch on Meera's face.

Meera looked calm, but Rishi could discern a layer of pathos underneath the surface that only he could intuit. Upheaval of life might have interrupted them, yet there was an unviolated continuity in their bond.

The fickle and ever-changing panorama of nature reflected in her light-brown eyes as she looked at Rishi, yet the external could not hide the underlying steadfast, the most uncomplex truth of her being. Suddenly, the realization hit Rishi. Meera had achieved the perfect equilibrium between the external and the internal, and these were both irrelevant. Her truth was beyond, a silent witness;

whatever surfaced briefly submerged back in that transcendent, potent, infinite spirit.

Rishi's tension dissipated; he did not need to worry about his mother anymore. Rishi smiled contentedly. "Mummy, I always visualized you sitting under a shady tree in full poise. You look so lovely!"

Meera blushed. "And I imagined you dancing with pretty lasses."

"No, Ma, I've turned into a geek like Vivek. I study a lot. But tell me, how are you? How is your health?"

"Rishi, I do not even know anymore! All I know is that I am content with you sitting right in front of my eyes. I cannot believe you are here! Why didn't you tell us?"

"I wanted to surprise you."

"You did that! Now tell me, how are you? How is your granny?"

"I am fine." He ignored the second part of the question, "I really am, Ma."

Meera donned a serious expression. "Rishi, I hope you give proper regard to your grandmother. It does not matter what she did to me, it was out of love for you."

A dark shadow passed over Rishi's face. He changed the subject. "Before flying for India, I visited Bela Aunty. She invited the whole gang! Did you know that Arun Uncle actually went to India and apologized? Maalti Aunty and Veena look happy for the first time. Kanchan Aunty avoids eye contact with me. I have not done anything wrong . . . so . . ."

"It is not you, it is me." Meera laughed. "How is my Satish Bhaiya?"

Rishi became animated, "Satish Uncle and Bela Aunty are just great people, Mom. I will tell you later. Bela Aunty sent tons of gifts for you."

"Oh, she is too much."

Suddenly, Rishi asked, "How is Prashant Uncle's family? Where are they?"

"They are all in Meerut. Ravi has a job, Neeta and Bhavani are studying in college. Prashantji bought a house. Beji lives with them to look after everyone."

Rishi burst into laughter. "I do not understand why even grown-up kids in India need looking after until they get married?"

"Well, they are not complaining, everything is done for them!"

Meera asked again, "How is your granny?"

Rishi looked startled and then got up. "Mummy! I am starved! Can we go in?"

Meera was embarrassed. "Oh God, I am sorry, Beta. I am so excited that I forgot that you have travelled seven seas to get here."

"Not quite," Rishi said as they walked towards the house. "I took a break in London for a couple of days to sightsee."

As soon as Meera and Rishi entered the house, noisy commotion took over. Ramu and Kaki were delighted and showered unsuspecting Rishi with many undecipherable blessings in Hindi. Rishi turned to Meera for translation; she laughed. "You have been blessed with a hundred children and a thousand cows!"

Ramu was immediately dispatched to buy Rishi's favorite samosas, gulab jamun, burfi, etc. Kaki got busy in the kitchen to start up dinner.

Meera turned to Rishi, "Beta, take a shower, then we can have tea and snacks."

Rishi looked at his watch. "Oh yes, it is quite close to your tea time."

Meera laughed. "You still remember?"

"How can I forget! Wherever you were, at four o'clock, you demanded tea!"

By the time Rishi came back to the dining room, a huge spread of his favorite snacks welcomed him. "Wow," was all he uttered before he sat on a chair and started to gulp down all the goodies. Waterdrops dripped from his freshly bathed golden hair and ran down his neck. Meera looked at him; he had inherited a graceful long neck from Jane. She looked gratified as she poured tea in her cup.

A jeep entered the gate clamorously and stopped with a jerk under the covered porch.

Meera looked at Rishi with shy apprehension. "Prashantji is here."

Hurried footsteps approached the main door that was opened and shut with a bang followed by the sound of Rashant's extralarge shoes in the hallway. Prashant had stopped briefly at the sweets shop on his way home. A giggling halwai, *sweets maker,* informed him, "Saheb, your son has come from Ca-na-da."

Prashant barged in the dining room impatiently with a boyish thrill on his beaming face.

"Rishi, my boy, what a surprise!"

Rishi got up from his chair and touched Prashant's feet while swallowing the samosa. Prashant hugged him tight, simultaneously dishing out contemporary blessings, "May God bless you with many pretty girlfriends!"

Rishi protested, "Oh no, Uncle. Right now, I want a simple blessing to get an A on my exams."

"So be it, wise choice! Look at you! You have turned into a Paul Newman! Girls must be crazy about you!"

Rishi blushed. "No, Uncle. I have been a good boy and study hard."

"I am disappointed in you, young man. Your priorities are kind of mixed up."

Amidst laughter, Meera asked Prashant, "Tea?" He did not hear her.

"How are you? Why did you not tell us that you were coming?"

"Isn't a surprise much more fun?"

"Yes, that is true." Prashant turned to Meera. "I will take a shower then have tea."

Rishi squatted on Meera's large bed, his anguished face looked up. "I have no words to express how sorry I am for making you miserable—"

Meera interjected, "Rishi, it was not your fault!"

"Mummy, please let me finish." He paused to contain the storm that raged in his heart.

"I had no idea that my granny was so wicked! She showered me with expensive gifts, took me on cruises, I truly believed that she loved me! But she poisoned me against you, Mummy. When I was with you, I felt your love and knew it to be true. But whenever I visited her, she tried to prove that you did not love me. I was so confused within myself, I could not handle my conflicting emotions and acted out in rage.

"When Prashant Uncle came to your life, Granny painted a horrible picture of your relationship and my future. My world fell apart. How could you love anyone else? I despised you both and then hated myself for mistreating you.

"Then one day I was arrested. I called you, sat on a dirty bench of the cell and wept. Maybe God was punishing me. I promised to myself that I shall never hurt you again.

"But you did not show up! I waited then called Granny. She said disdainfully in the car, 'Your mother is sitting in a restaurant with friends!' I could not think straight and believed her. Maybe she was right all along that you did not love me. I hated you, Mom." Rishi trembled with torment.

Meera sat up on the bed and took Rishi's hand in her fragile palms. Her face was flushed with tears.

"Granny took me on a cruise. I did not enjoy anything. I was tortured. On our return, I asked Aunt Kelley if there was a letter or phone call from you. She held my hand and spoke in a quivering voice, 'Master Rishi, your ma does love you. Maybe she is ill!'

I laughed and said, 'Kelley you do not have to find excuses for my mother. I do not really care!' But I did. The very thought that you did not love me haunted me day and night."

Kaki came in and asked Prashant, "Should I bring more tea, Sab?"

Prashant nodded and passed on the empty cup to her.

"The day of the court hearing, Bela Aunty told me that you were ill and in the hospital. I looked at Granny questioningly. She pushed me and did not let me talk to Bela Aunty. In the elevator before I could query her, she fumed, 'The guts this woman has lying to you blatantly! Peter saw your mom yesterday in a mall!' I looked at Peter, and he looked down and spoke in a low voice, 'Yes, Master, that is true.' I believed him! You had washed your hands of me, finally! I was devastated and wanted to commit suicide." Rishi's throat became clogged with tears.

Meera's hands quivered. Prashant bent forward from his chair and held her hand. Both of them were lost for words.

Rishi continued, "Johnny and Aunt Kelley supported me through my depression. Then one day Bela Aunty came to my school and told me that you were leaving for India. She said, 'Do not believe your granny. Your ma loves you.' I became furious. Were Kelley and Peter lying too? But I told her I will come to the airport.

When I told Granny, she became mad and commanded me not to go. But I was determined. That afternoon, Granny collapsed, and we took her to the hospital. Tests were done, nothing was wrong. Aunt

Kelley told me later that the drama was to stop me from going to the airport. Granny was afraid that the truth would come out.

Nine months after Satish Uncle's clinic fire, a young man was charged with arson. I did not care and focused on my studies.

Suddenly one morning, Granny pulled me out of bed, dragged me, and threw me out of the house."

"What!" Meera and Prashant exclaimed in unison.

Rishi summarized the agonizing past.

"Oh God. Why didn't you tell us?"

"Mom, that is when I called you from Bela Aunty's house! But you were so ill, I made everyone promise not to tell you."

He paused and looked down. "I was also ashamed. How could I face you?"

"Silly boy! What did you do?"

"Bela Aunty and Satish Uncle wanted me to move in with them. But Aunt Kelley begged them. She wanted to look after me. She said that she sinned by silently watching Granny hurt us. Actually, I wanted to live with Aunt Kelley and Aunt Martha. Johnny and I had become great friends. It was fun."

"But, Rishi, Kelley and Martha lost their jobs!"

"They both found work in cleaning businesses. We were poor, but there was immense love and caring in that house, Ma. Also, Bela Aunty and Satish Uncle bought everything that I needed."

Rishi laughed and continued, "And then a miracle happened, and I became rich overnight!"

"No, you are lying!" Meera said incredulously.

"It is an unbelievable story. I inherited the money that my great-grandfather had placed in a trust for Jane Ma. Aunt Kelley made it possible."

Meera took a deep breath. "Long ago, Kelley helped me get your custody. I am indebted to her."

"You know, Mom, I found peace for the first time in my life. All doubts, conflicts, mental anguish disappeared. I could feel the poignancy of your love and could love you with all my heart."

Rishi fell silent. He was depleted; the grievous avoirdupois of the debris of the past had been cast off. An eerie silence pervaded the darkening room. Evening was coming to an end; they had lost track of time.

"Turn on the lamp, Ji," Meera turned to Prashant.

They blinked for a few moments at the sudden onslaught of light. Kaki came in to pick up the tray and asked in a low voice, "Bibiji, when do you want to eat dinner?"

"I think we should have it soon. Rishi should sleep early," Meera spoke in a tired voice.

Rishi nodded absentmindedly then delivered the climax, "And listen to this. Granny died in prison last month. Some illness. Kelley Aunty said, 'Good riddance, she can never hurt us again.'"

Meera gasped. "What?"

Prashant shook his head. "What do you know!"

Cobwebs? Can a spider get caught in his own cobweb?

In the background, there was faraway sounds of cows returning home, the bells around their necks made chiming sounds. The music of flute floated in the air; perhaps a cow herder was taking his cows home.

"My cow herder, *a reference to Shri Krishna*, where are you? Has my Kurukshetra really ended?"

Meera did not know where to place the bizarre culmination of an equally bizarre life of Granny. She did not mean to be happy—she was not—but there was an undeniable feeling of closure of a story with an end that befitted the theme.

Conflicting emotions played in Meera's ashen face like shadows dancing with uncertain steps.

Prashant was watching her keenly. He took a deep sigh, "Yar, *friend*, let us go to the drawing room and leave your ma alone. She looks exhausted."

Rishi got up reluctantly and looked at Meera wistfully; he was not done yet.

- # -

Rishi and Meera sat on lawn chairs, in the dewy morning, under the mango tree.

"Read it." Rishi gave Meera a brown envelope.

"What is it?"

"Read it!"

Meera became apprehensive. What now?

"Uncle, I do not want to touch anything."

Radley Sr. was surprised, "Well, son, come and see me, we will discuss it."

"There is nothing to discuss." Rishi was brusque and did not make any attempt to hide his disdain. Radley was quiet for a moment. "I cannot force you, but if you do not want to use Helena's inheritance on yourself, you can donate it to different charities!"

The idea hit a chord. Meera had spoken longingly when Rishi was young, "Let us go to India, Rishi, I want to open up an orphanage. Do you know that orphans have no one, nothing? Evil men take them home, break their arms or legs, or take their eyes out . . ." She had shuddered. "And make them beggars. Every evening they take their collections, give them a little food, beat them if they disobey. Orphans are helpless, where can they go? They live in misery all their lives. Can you believe that?"

"Uncle, I will see you next week."

Immediately after the legal paperwork was done and Rishi became the sole owner of her estate, Mrs. Henderson's mansion was put up for sale.

"Uncle, just sell everything!"

Radley Sr. assigned Radley Jr.'s friend, Willie Smith, a real estate agent, to take charge and dispose of all the assets of the late Mrs. Henderson.

Helena's bedroom had a secret safe. Kelley knew of its existence. "But I have no idea where the key would be!"

Well, a locksmith was not difficult to find.

A treasure of diamonds, pearls, rubies, and other precious stones set in gold lay in boxes lined with velvet.

Rishi could not contain his excitement.

"Aunt Kelley, this is all for you and Aunt Martha!"

"No!" Kelley shrank back, "I do not want it."

"Then sell it and use the money. You can retire! You've worked so hard all your life!"

"No, child. I am content with the life Jesus gave me."

"But . . . but . . . this is my gift to you! You cannot refuse!"

"And what is this?" Kelley picked up a bundle of letters tied together with a red ribbon, simultaneously changing the topic.

"Rishi, you must read these."

"Oh no, you read them, I would be bored."

Kelley laughed, "Who knows there may be a letter from your grandfather."

"Or my Jane Ma?" Rishi's face lit up with hope.

Kelley was sad. "I do not think Jane baby would have ever written to Madam."

Rishi asked playfully, "How come you still call my mom, baby?"

"Well, we called her baby when she was a little girl, and all of us doted on her! You will not believe how beautiful she was with her big blue eyes and blond curls. And then . . . well, you better read the letters, Rishi." Kelley left the room abruptly to hide her emotions.

Rishi stretched on the bed where he had slept during the most excruciating period of his life, when he was divided against himself, oscillating between two states of consciousness: "My Mom does not love me," and "Yes, she does!"

Most of the letters were from Helena's friends.

But then there it was.

The letter started with *PS*. Meera looked up in puzzlement, "Rishi! The letter is not addressed to anyone! Whose letter is it?"

"Ma, you remember my Jane Ma had written a letter to you before she died?"

"Yes." Anxiety gripped Meera's heart.

"This was a part of that letter, Granny had stolen it because . . . well, read it!"

Rishi leaned back on the lawn chair and looked away beyond the horizon, at the cobalt sky, and even beyond that—at his past. Life had tread on crisscross, stony roads; he had stumbled on the rocks, his feet bled from the wounds. To escape from the dark shadows of the nightmarish memories, he brought his vision back to his mother, whose pallid visage reflected indescribable pathos as she held the letter with unsteady hands.

Rishi looked away in pain.

Kaki came out of the house and approached the mango tree under which Rishi and Meera were unfolding the past.

"It is hot na, Baba. Do you want lassi, *buttermilk*?"

"Yes, Kakiji, bring two." He smiled at her vaguely.

Kaki glanced worriedly at Meera but left silently.

PS, I have struggled with the thought a million times in the last month and dismissed it. But I am going to take my life in a few minutes, and my heart protested. I cannot leave this world without telling my truth and give identity to my sweet child. Please do not hate me.

It was last Christmas; that is when people like me sink into deep depression. My past conjures up and haunts me, I truly hate my mother and the world at such times. The office Christmas party was at Mona's house. It was stormy outside. We all drank booze excepting Mohit. He said that abstinence was easy because he did not know the taste. Mohit dropped me at my apartment. I was staggering. He held my arm and helped me upstairs. I wept on his shoulders, clung to him in my helplessness. I swear he did not do anything. I evoked his pity and stole some moments of his life.

I was so mortified that I stayed away from the office the next day. Mohit came to see me at home. His calm face looked ruffled.

"Jane, please forgive me for last night, I do not love you that way. I am so embarrassed."

I laughed, "Good, because I do not love you that way either. But I am so ashamed, I forced myself on you."

Mohit said kindly, "Jane, please do not blame yourself. We are all human, it can happen."

We decided to erase the incident as though it never happened. The next few days were a bit awkward, but soon it was business as usual.

Less than a week later Mohit received a letter from home. His mother was ill. He left for India the same day.

Mohit returned with a wonderful bride. I got a friend and an anchor. I was grateful, I can never forget the times we spent together.

I missed my periods for two and a half months but did not worry because my periods are irregular anyway. Finally, I went to see the doctor. He informed me that I was pregnant. I was devastated! I could not even look after myself. How would I raise a child? If Mohit found out, it would end your happy marriage!

I hid at home, became depressed, and landed up in the hospital.

Mohit got worried, and inquiries led him to my ward on the fifth floor. The nurse mentioned to Mohit casually that I was pregnant.

Lightning struck his world. He slouched on the chair, held his head in his hands, and stared at the floor.

I begged him, “Do not tell Meera, please. I will go away, get an abortion, and never show up in your life.”

Mohit spoke after a long agonizing silence. “Jane, on our first night together, Meera and I promised that we would be truthful, always. I must tell her. She will surely make me marry you and go away to India . . . Oh God.” He broke down.

I was stunned. “Why?”

“In our tradition, it is my moral duty to take care of my child and the mother.”

I bawled. I could not bear his anguish, he could not face mine.

Before he left, Mohit placed his hand on my head and spoke in a quivering, yet sure, voice, “Do not worry, Jane. I will never shirk my responsibility. Get well now. We will talk later.”

Next morning Mona broke the horrible news of Mohit’s accident. I was shattered. I felt responsible for the tragedy and cursed myself for being weak. I wanted to commit suicide. But the baby?

I decided to tell you everything, but when you hugged me and wept, I knew I could never do that and wreck the beautiful memories of your short marriage. I needed you but could not face your grief; I felt guilty and tortured. I left, changed my name, and lived in Green Acres, that is quite close to Hendersville.

When I held my son in my arms, I knew that he is yours. You are his real mother.

I cannot live because I cannot forgive myself, I took away Mohit from you. But I feel at peace at the thought that his son will grow up and take care of you.

Make sure that shadow of Mrs. Henderson does not touch him. His name is Rishikesh.

Please forgive me. Good-bye.

Jane

The letter slipped from Meera's hands. She looked up at Rishi in a daze, as though for the first time. He had definite resemblance with Mohit, the same square jaw and full lips with an upward angle at the edges, the dimples and broad forehead. Rishi's eyes were unmistakably Jane's endowment.

Meera's heart pulsated furiously and shook her light frame; tears shone in her mystified eyes. She spread her arms. Rishi got up from his chair abruptly, knelt in front of Meera, and wrapped her torso in his strong hold. Mohit's scent effused from his youthful body.

Anguish surfaced on his features, "Mama, the shame of feeling like a bastard has been lifted from my heart. For the first time in my life, I feel purified. I know now how great my father was."

Rishi looked up, he was troubled by her long silence. "Are you mad at my dad?"

Meera kissed his flushed cheek. "Of course not. This happened before we got married. And Jane and your dad gave me such a precious gift, Rishi!"

Meera smiled tearfully. "I cannot believe it, Rishi. You look so much like Mohitji, I should have figured."

They sat silently, happy but with a tinge of sorrow at the losses of their lives. Kaki had brought two glasses of lassi and placed them on the table. Rishi picked up one and took a few sips. He looked away and started to pace on the green grass. Sun was now up above their heads, but they were protected by the shade of the mango tree.

Rishi fidgeted with his long fingers.

"What is on your mind, Beta, *son*?" A wave of warm breeze ruffled his blond hair. The chirping of the birds seemed accentuated by their silence.

Rishi stopped and looked straight into Meera's eyes. He did not hide his agitation.

"Mummy, you are so perceptive. Why could you not figure out Granny's vicious personality? Sunil uncle told me that everyone else knew and stopped you from letting me be with her? Truth might have saved us na, Ma?"

Meera suppressed a sigh. In the last years, she had confronted this dilemma frequently.

"Rishi, in my world, grandmothers are a sea of love. Helena showed love, wanted to spend time, gave money and material pleasures to you. I knew she hated me, but I felt that she did love you. How could I deprive you of her love? She was your real mother's mother?"

"But Ma, Bela Aunty said there was ample proof that she was wicked?"

"Rishi, a life of pervasive mistrust is not worth living. Against all odds, we must maintain faith and trust in humanity in general. Only when someone is proven guilty beyond a shadow of a doubt, we can cast guilt and that is fair. My problem was that I did not find a definite proof of her lack of love for you."

Meera paused briefly. "Rishi, much happens in our lives that is beyond our control. It is most unfortunate, but that is the way life works or does not work."

Rishi sat down on his chair, dejectedly. "Ma, is that destiny?"

"Yes, I believe so. Helena and I belonged to contrary worlds, bound by our Sanskaras, *built-in mind-sets and beliefs*, that are based on our past karma from previous births. She could not grasp my reality any more than I could fathom hers. So . . ."

"But it is a horrible predicament that we cannot escape from the grip of our destiny, Mummy?"

"Fortunately, for humans, it is not true. We can break the shackles of the past by our willingness to make a commitment to face our flaws, follies, and weaknesses and change our very core. When that happens, we cannot help but have good 'intentions' and do good karma. Therefore we determine our fate in the next birth. We are the creators of our destiny. Many times, we see good actions leading to happy consequences right in this birth. Hence, not all the happenings in the present life are predetermined by the past. The most important, immediate consequence of our evolution into better humans is that we transform the world into a better place. That fulfills our destiny because that is the reason for our very existence in the universe."

Prashant's jeep rumbled and created a noisy dust storm. He jumped out, opened the rusty gate, and walked toward them briskly. "Am I late?"

"Late for what, Ji?"

"Your alu parathas, *homemade bread stuffed with potatoes,* what else?"

Meera stood up excitedly, held Rishi's hand, and presented him, "First, I'd like you to meet your real son."

"What?" Prashant gasped.

Meera laughed. "Rishi, give him the letter and enjoy the reunion. I better get started on the parathas for your bhukar, *glutonous*, uncle."

"But, Mummy, there is something else we need to talk about!"

"What?"

"Do you want to help the orphans or not?"

"What?"

"Granny had left a huge amount of money that I do not want to touch. With that money, you can open up the orphanage you always talked about."

"Oh my God. I cannot use her money, child!"

"Not even if you can give a good life to the poor miserable children who are otherwise doomed to suffer?"

Meera sat down. She was drained; her legs felt weak.

"Oh, Rishi. I will have to think about it. Also, I do not have the energy anymore."

Prashant, who wanted his parathas soon, concluded, "Well, there is a good solution. Rishi, you finish your degree in Canada and then come and live here. We can all pitch in efforts and open up an orphanage. We can hire a manager to manage the day-to-day work to run it."

Meera looked up at Rishi expectantly.

Rishi was excited. "I would love to."

"You mean you will live in India?"

"Yah!"

"What about the heat?"

"What are air conditioners for?"

"Flies? Mosquitos?"

"Mosquito repellent during the day, nets around the bed at night?"

Meera grinned with disbelief. She turned to Prashant.

"Prashantji, I have a confession!"

"Go on."

"With all the exciting good news, I am feeling emotionally drained. Can Kaki make the *parathas* today?"

Prashant feigned disappointment.

"As long as there is a promise that you will make them soon!"

Meera said, "Fair enough."

"Mummy, I am a witness, you cannot back off."

Glossary

Aangan	Covered area in front of a house
Abba	Father in Urdu (language of Moslems in India and Pakistan)
Acha	Really
Achkan	Long coat
Achoot	Untouchable
Advait	Unity amongst existence
Agnividya	A religious ritual using fire
Allah	Moslem name for God
Allah-o-Akbar	Allah is great
Alu parantha	Homemade bread stuffed with potatoes
Amin	Amen
Amir	Rich
Anand	Joy
Anarkali	Pomegranade flower
Angeethi	Mud stove
Angrez	British
Antra	Middle part of a song
Appa	Sister in Urdu
Ashram	Abode of Guru, teacher

Ashwas .... Horses
Atma .... Soul
Atam Vidya .... Knowledge of the Soul, Self
Avidya .... Ignorance
Azadi .... Freedom

Babuji .... Sir
Bache .... Child
Bacho .... Children
Badi Bua .... Father's older sister
Badshah .... Emperor
Bahen .... Sister
Bahenji .... Respected sister
Bap .... Father
Bapu .... Father
Baraat .... Groom's party
Bas .... Enough
Bauji .... Father
Bauji ke pas jati hoon .... I am going to my husband
Bawa .... Child
Bechari .... Poor thing
Befkoof .... Stupid
Begane .... Outsiders
Ber .... A fruit
Beta .... Son
Bhabi .... Sister-in-law or friend's wife
Bhagwan .... God in Hindi
Bhagwat mantra .... A verse from Hindu scriptures
Bhai .... Brother or friend
Bhai Bhai .... Brothers
Bhaijan .... Brother in Urdu
Bhai Saheb .... Respected brother
Bhaiya .... Brother or friend
Bhaji .... Brother or friend
Bhang .... Opium
Bhat .... Cooked rice and lentil
Bharat Mata .... Mother India

Bharat me sikhi thi .... Learned it in India
Bharat Varsh .... Ancient name of India
Bhog .... Food offered to God
Bhoot .... Demon
Bukhar .... Greedy
Bhurji .... Scrambled eggs
Bhutta .... Corn
Bidi .... Cheap cigarette
Biji .... Mother
Bikul Angrez lagda eh .... Looks English
Bindi .... A red dot that married women in India put on their foreheads
Biradari .... Community
Biwi .... Wife
Brahm .... Absolute God
Brahmin .... Priest class
British raj .... Occupation of India
Brindavan .... Garden
Bua .... Father's sister
Buddi .... Old woman
Budhi .... Mind
Budhu .... Silly
Budhu Kahin Ke .... Silly
Burfi .... A dessert

Chachaji .... Uncle
Chachas and Mamas .... Uncles
Chai .... Tea
Chalo .... Go
Chalo Kan Pakro .... A gesture of apology
Chalo under .... Go in
Chalo utho .... Get up
Chamar .... Untouchable
Channa puri .... Chickpeas and fried bread
Charpoy .... Woven bed
Chaukidar .... Gatekeeper
Chikna .... Smooth

Chit .... Mind
Chitar.......... Slipper
Chitta.......... White
Chokras .... Young lads
Chokris .... Young girls
Chote Mama.......... Mother's younger brother
Chote Chacha.......... Father's younger brother
Chuddu.......... Useless
Chutti.......... Freedom
Cowherder.......... A reference to Shri Krishna

Da.......... Brother or friend
Dada.......... Brother or friend
Dadi .... Paternal grandmother
Dadaji.......... Paternal grandfather
Dalai Lama .... Tibet's Buddhist spiritual leader
Dalia.......... Porridge
Dandas.......... Long sticks
Darban.......... Guard
Darbar.......... Emperor's court
Daris.......... Woven throws
Deen Iman.......... Morality
Deeva .... A small earthen cup with oil and a wick of cotton, lighted at the end
Devdasis.......... God's female servants
Devtas .... Demi Gods
Dewan .... A seating place with many cushions
Dewanji.......... Prime minister
Dhaba.......... Tented food outlet
Dharma.......... Duty
Dharmic.......... Righteous
Dharvi.......... A huge slum in Bombay
Dhoti.......... Cloth tied at the waist, falls to ankles
Di.......... Sister or friend

Didi .... Sister or friend
Diwali .... Festival of Lights
Do Karak .... Two strong tea cups
Dol .... Big metallic container
Doli .... When the bride is brought to bridegroom's house
Dongas .... Casseroles
D.S.P. .... District Superintendent of Police
Dupatta .... Veil
Durga Ma .... Demi Godess Durga

Ekdum .... Immediately
Ekdum nikkama .... Absolutely useless

F.O.B. .... Fresh off the boat

Ganeshai namah .... Salutations to Demi God Ganesh
Garib .... Poor
Garibee hatao .... Remove poverty
Garib ko paisa do .... Give money to the poor
Gavtakia .... Round pillow
Gayatri mantra .... A verse from Hindu scripture
Ghee .... Heated butter
Gita .... Hindu's Bible
Gora .... White male
Gori .... White female
Govind Gopal .... Another name for Shri Krishna
Graha .... Astrological planets
Gundas .... Rogues
Guru .... Spiritual teacher
Gurudev .... Spiritual teacher
Gurukul .... Guru's abode

Hakim.. Naturopath
Haldi.. Turmeric
Halwa... A dessert
Halwai.. Sweet's maker
Hangama....................................... Noise
Hanh.. Yes
Haramzada..................................... A swear word
Havan Kund .... A hollow structure made with bricks, to light fire
Haveli... Mansion
Hune Lo .... Right away
Hukkah... Smoking pipe

Insha-Allah..................................... God willing in Urdu

Jaimala... Garland
Jagat... Universal
Jajna .... A ritual using fire
Jalianwala Bag ....Jalianwala garden
Jalsa .... Procession
Jamandar .... Sweeper
Jameendar .... Landlord
Janams .... Births
Janana... Where women reside in a house
Jao maf kiya ....You are forgiven
Jeevan Mukt................................... Free while alive
Jhola... Cloth bag to receive alms
Jinnah .... The first Prime minister of Pakistan
Jora... Wedding costume
Joota... Shoe
Jugnu.. Fire fly

Kabab... A beef dish
Kaise ho kaka .... How are you?
Kal.. Infinite time

Kala dhanda.................................... Black trade
Kaleen.. Carpet
Kali... Black
Kali kaluti....................................... Dark complexioned
Kaliyug... An immoral epoch
Kameena... Lowly
Kameez... Shirt
Kamzorilal kahin ka....................... Weakling
Kanyadan.. Giving away daughter in marriage
Karak.. Strong
Karak chai...................................... Strong tea
Karma... Deed
Karamphal...................................... Fruit of deed
Kasam... Swear
Kathopnishad................................. A Hindu scripture
Keshav.. Another name for Shri Krishna
Kewra.. Rose
Khaba.. Left
Khadi Kurta.................................... Handwoven shirt
Khaki... Brown
Khalis.. Unadulterated
Khalistom movement...................... Sikhs wanted their own nation, called Khalistan
Khana.. Food
Khichri.. Lentil and rice dish
Kholi... Windowless room
Kirtan.. Devotional songs
Kismet... Destiny
Kotha... Prostitutes place
Koyal... Song bird
Kshatriya.. The fighter class
Kuli.. Baggage handler
Kumkum... A red powder married women in India put on their foreheads
Kundan... Jewellery with mirrors
Kurta... Long shirt
Kumari kuan.................................. Maiden's well

Kurukshetra .... An intense historical war
Kya hal hai apka .... How are you?

Lafda .... Complication
Langar .... Food
Lassi .... Buttermilk
Lathi .... Long stick
Lehnga choli .... Long skirt and blouse
Loji garam garam .... Take it hot
Loji phata phat .... Take it quickly
Lord Agni .... Demi God of fire

Madhyamic .... A branch of Buddhism
Mahal .... Palace
Maharani .... Queen
Maha Sanyasi .... The greatest ascetic
Mai .... Mother
Main nahi manta .... I don't believe
Maletch .... Low caste
Maletch ko mere so door nakho .... Keep the low cast away from me
Mali .... Gardener
Malik .... Master, Reverend
Malmal .... Muslin
Mamaji .... Mother's brother
Mandap .... Canopy where marriage ceremony takes place
Manhoos .... Inauspicious
Mansarovar .... A lake in Kashmir
Mantras .... Verses from Hindu scriptures
Manu's Vidhan .... A scripture, guide of conduct written by Rishi Manu
Masala .... Spice
Masiji .... Mother's sister
Masis .... Mother's sisters
Mast .... Carefree
Mataji .... Mother

Maya.. Illusion
Meera Bai .... A Hindu saint
Mem Saheb....................................... Madam
Mere Bhai .... My brother
Mere Pitaji .... My father
Mithai .... Sweets
Mogra .... Jasmine
Moh.. Attachment
Moksha .... Ultimate freedom
Motia.. Jasmine
Mrityulok... World of the dead
Mukt... Free
Mukti.. Freedom
Mukut... Crown
Muyur mukut .... Crown with peacock feathers

Na Hanyate Hanyamane Shrire..... Soul does not die when body perishes
Nai dulhan .... New bride
Nai ji... No
Nakhra.. Pretension
Namaste Bahenji .... Greetings sister
Nanaji... Maternal grandfather
Nani .... Maternal grandmother
Narad Muni...................................... A sage who never stops travelling
Nargis and Madhubala.................... Film actresses
Nathuram halwai .... Sweetsmaker
Nirvana... Ultimate bliss

Oy chai la sale .... Bring tea
Om Namo Bhagwate Vasudev........ A verse of devotion to God

Pagal ladki.. Mad girl
Pahari .... Mountain people
Paisa .... Penny

Pakhandi .... Pretender
Paki .... Pakistanis and Indians
Pakoras .... Deep fried snack
Palloo .... Edge part of a saree
Pan .... Betel leaves
Panch Bhautik .... Made of five elements: air, earth, water, fire and sky
Pandit .... Priest
Parantha .... Fried homemade bread
Parlok .... Life after death
Partition .... At the time of India's independence, it was divided into two nations; India and Pakistan
Patel .... Mostly business people
Peetamber .... Yellow robe
Phataphat chalo .... Go fast
Pheras .... During wedding ceremony, the bride and groom walk around fire
Pitaji .... Father
Pitashri .... Father
Prabhu .... Reverernd
Praja .... Humanity
Pralay .... Doom's day
Prana .... Life force
Pranam .... Greetings
Presswalla .... The man who irons clothes
Puja .... Worship
Punya .... Righteous deed
Puppy .... Kiss

Rabinder Sangeet .... Lyrics and music composed by Nobel Laureate Rabinder Nath Thakur
Raga .... Music composition

Rai Saheb Tayaji.............................. Owner of the house Meera's family lived in
Raita.. Spiced yogurt
Raj .... British occupation of India
Rakshsi... Femal demon
Rig veda .... An ancient Hindu scripture
Rishi.. Sage
Rishta.. Proposal
Roti .... Homemade bread

Sab .... Gentleman
Sadhana.. Persistent endeavor
Sadhu.. Ascetic
Saees .... Horse carriage driver
Sag... Spinach
Saheb .... Gentleman
Saheli .... Friend
Sajja... Right
Sale, bhar utha theek se .... Pick up the load properly
Salwar .... Indian style pant
Samadhi.. Meditation
Samosas .... Deep fried snack
Sanskar .... Predispositions
Samved... A Hindu scripture with all music compositions
Sanatan... Infinite Religion
Sanskrit... Language of Hindu scriptures
Sanyas Ashram .... Ascetic phase of life
Sardarji .... Sikh gentleman
Sarkari afsar .... Government official
Saraswati.. Demi Godess of knowledge
Sarod... A string, musical instrument
Sarpanch .... Head of five administrative people in each village council
Sati .... A woman who burns herself with her dead husband
Sati Savitri.. Devoted wife

Sat Janam.. Seven births
Sat Sri Akal...................................... Sikh greeting
Satya, Dwapar, Treta Kalyug .... Four cyclic epochs
Sepahi.. Sepoy
Sehra.. A head gear a groom wears with strings of flowers falling in front of his face
Shabakhair...................................... Goodnight in Urdu
Shabash.. Expression of pride
Shakangavi...................................... Lemon drink
Shakti.. Power
Shamianawalla................................ A man who erects a tent for wedding ceremony
Sharab.. Liquor
Shastrvidya..................................... Knowledge of weapons
Shingar ras...................................... Music of passion
Shishyas.. Disciples
Shivji... Demi God of death
Shrimad Bhagwat Gita................... Song of God, Hindu's bible
Shri Krishna.................................... Incarnation of God
Shudra.. Lowest caste
Sidh.. Fulfilled spiritualist
Sindoor... Red powder bridegroom places in the parting of bride's hair
Sitar.. A string, musical instrument
Sthitpragya..................................... Equanimous in pain and pleasure
Sudharo.. Improve
Suhag.. State of being married
Sufis.. A sect of Islam
Swami.. Ascetic

Taanpura.. A string, musical instrument
Tabla... Drums
Tamas.. Darkness
Tamasha.. Drama
Tandav.. Shiva's dance of death

Tapasya	Penance
Tattwa	Raw material
Tayaji	Father's older brother
Tayiji	Tayaji's wife
Tehkhana	Basement
Te Jijaji kithe ne	Where is your husband
Thana	Police station
Thanedar	Police inspector
Theek se	Properly
Tikka	A jewellery piece hung on the forehead
Topi	Cap
Trishul	A metallic rod with three pronged sharp edges at one end
Triyachritra	Pretensions
Upanishads	Ancient Hindu scriptures
Urdu	Language of Moslems in India and Pakistan
Vaishnav	Devotee of Shri Krishna
Valid	Father in Urdu language
Varn system	Caste system
Vedanta	Culmination of knowledge
Vedas	Ancient Hindu scriptures
Vedi	A decorated space where marriage rituals are performed
Venis	Strings of flowers
Verandah	Covered area in front of a house
Vichola	In between
Vikars	Pollutants of mind
Vilayat	England
Vilayati	English
Voh	Husband
Vritti	Attention

Wahe Guru .... God in Panjabi language

Yajman .... Client in religious rituals
Yajna... A ritual using fire
Yama... Demi God of death
Yar .... Friend
Yeh apka bacha hai?......................... Is he your child?
Yogi .... Someone united with God
Yog sutra .... The path to unite with God
Yug .... Epoch

Note: Demi Gods and Demi Goddesses are akin to angels of Christianity.

CPSIA information can be obtained
at www.ICGtesting.com
Printed in the USA
LVOW08*1757300617
539446LV00007B/3/P